ASHLEY MACK

Take to Heart

First published by Infinity Plus One 2023

CONTENT WARNINGS: physical assault and violence, child abuse, parent death (discussed, not in story), alcohol, gambling addiction, kidnapping, captivity, graphic sex and sexual situations

First edition

ISBN: 978-1-960161-09-3

This book was professionally typeset on Reedsy.
Find out more at reedsy.com

Peter. You will 100% never read this book,
but I can attribute my deep appreciation
for memes as 100% your doing.
Did you know that Viggo Mortensen
broke his toe in the Two Towers?!

Goodbye, my pride is gone, it left me
Dead on the floor, I'm sorry I'm yours...

– "Sorry I'm Yours" – Circa Waves

Contents

1 Neo 1
2 Perri 5
3 Neo 12
4 Neo 17
5 Perri 22
6 Perri 26
7 Neo 32
8 Perri 36
9 Perri 42
10 Neo 49
11 Neo 57
12 Perri 63
13 Neo 69
14 Perri 72
15 Perri 74
16 Neo 79
17 Perri 83
18 Neo 87
19 Neo 95
20 Perri 99
21 Neo 113
22 Perri 116
23 Neo 121
24 Perri 128
25 Neo 134
26 Perri 141

27 Neo 148
28 Perri 151
29 Neo 155
30 Perri 160
31 Perri 167
32 Neo 181
33 Perri 190
34 Perri 197
35 Neo 202
36 Perri 206
37 Neo 212
38 Perri 219
39 Neo 225
40 Perri 230
41 Neo 239
42 Perri 243
43 Neo 250
44 Perri 254
45 Neo 262
46 Perri 268
47 Perri 271
48 Neo 278
49 Neo 281
50 Epilogue - Perri 284
Playlist 289
Acknowledgments 290
Also by Ashley Mack 291
About the Author 292

1

Neo

Technically, I wasn't working tonight, but since I was at a club "celebrating" my boss's wife's birthday, I might as well have been.

It doesn't matter that said wife, Nicolette Maines-Zastrow, otherwise known as Nim, has been one of my best friends since elementary school. It doesn't matter that more than enough of our most trusted guards, the ones trained specifically for keeping an eye on Nim, are on duty tonight. The piece of me that's always on alert when I'm with a Zastrow can't be turned off. I was born into this.

Nim wanted to go to Delta to celebrate her golden birthday. She's the last of us to turn 26 this year. Somehow Harrison, the third leg of our triad and technically her stepson, got out of this event. Her husband, my boss, wouldn't be caught dead here. At least Delta is full of other people in our world so I can do a little reconnaissance, keep an ear out for gossip, or eye up who doesn't seem to be doing too well. I never know when a piece of information will become important.

In the other corner of the VIP area is the other large booth, and I was intrigued to see Cassandra Warren was there with her usual crew. She was one of the heirs of Warren Media, and her father had just signed the preliminary documents in a massive deal with Zastrow Ventures. If the deal came to fruition, someday it might be hers to maintain. It was my job to think about the big picture, to see long term threats.

This was a chance to observe Ms. Warren in her natural, albeit drunken, habitat.

Her table seemed to be celebrating something, as they all kept toasting the dark blonde woman in the green dress. Even from this far away I could see how red she was, blushing every time they talked about her. The blonde woman did not like being the center of attention, but it was clear she was tight with Cassandra from how close they sat together and that Cassandra kept reaching over to pat her with reassurance.

It appeared that Cassandra was a good friend who didn't need to be the center of attention. I focused back on Nim and her birthday. Once and awhile, I needed to be a good friend too.

Nim was beautiful. It was hard for me to see it sometimes because we grew up together, and it was even weirder to think it when she was not only married to your boss, but that boss also happened to be your other best friend's dad. But I needed to be aware of it because she was the kind of beautiful and had the type of personality that led people to get fixated on her.

Before marrying her, Andre Zastrow's personal life had only been in the news when his first wife passed away. Three years later, he married Nim as part of a business deal, and suddenly they were everywhere. Paparazzi followed her wherever she went, she got letters and gifts, and then there was all sorts of wild speculation about if she was really sleeping with Andre or if they were cheating on each other.

The truth of that was complicated.

It was why the guards assigned to Nim had to be trained and trusted beyond a shadow of a doubt. Their integrity was essential to everyone in the Zastrow family being able to live their lives the way they wanted.

Nim was tall and thin, but solid. She had auburn hair that give her a hint of mischief, dark brown eyes, and teeth that reminded me of a wolf. That was what gave her a hint of danger and intrigued people. She was also unbelievably kind, enthusiastic about everything, and too open-minded. To a fault. To her detriment.

I could tell that she was getting bored. Delta had been the choice tonight because it was obvious. They'd be seen, photographed, and the sharks would be fed their bait so that she could celebrate her birthday the way she truly wanted. The modified party bus was waiting outside for her and the trusted few that got to join her after party. Not long now.

Nim met my eyes, asking a question. I shook my head. We needed a little bit longer or they would speculate that something was wrong. There was a lot of math involved in appeasing the paps. How long did she need to stay out to avoid speculation that something was wrong, but not long enough that she could be labeled an irresponsible party girl.

In my experience, it was a fifteen minute window between 12:45 A.M. and 1:00 A.M. We had 20 minutes to go.

Nim looked away from me and her gaze landed on Marco. He was pretending to listen to the guys that were talking to him, asking him questions about racing, or trying to convince him to let them drive his car. It was a miracle he had even been able to get here tonight, but I'd never known him to let her down.

I set the timer on my phone and start people watching again. Noting who is interacting with who, who is sitting and talking versus dancing, who is out without their partner or appears to have a new one. It's interesting to see how much people communicate with their bodies. Bodies are far more honest than the words people speak.

The next time my gaze sweeps to Cassandra Warren's booth, it's empty. Interesting.

I made a note in my phone to have someone do a deep dive on her since we'd only really looked into her father and her older brother. Even though we were around the same age, Cassandra had gone off to boarding school while Nim, Harrison, and I stayed in New York. We knew her older siblings Seth and Calliope from school and business, but Cassandra had been a mystery.

Finally, the alarm buzzes and I signal Nim. She starts shoulder tapping the few friends she trusts who all signed non-disclosure agreements to go with us for the rest of the night. I trail them through the bar, trying not to overstep the guards that are actually on duty, and try to remember what it was like to just hang out with my friend. We don't really do that anymore, and a pang of sadness hits me for that. I wouldn't have survived without Nim and Harrison, and I've gotten to keep him. I need to make time to catch up with her for real.

My phone buzzes and I check the text.

Harrison: *Surviving?*

Me: *You're an asshole.*

Harrison: *No, I can afford better presents than you so I don't get forced into this stuff.*

Me: *see: asshole*

We get outside the club and I lean against the bus, waiting for the last of the group to trail inside. One of her friends is really drunk and stumbles before going up the stairs. I catch her before she can fall and when she looks up, I'm caught in a golden green gaze like I've never seen before. This woman is crazy drunk and crazy beautiful. My arm is wrapped around her and with every breath she takes her breasts press into my chest. Her hands are hot where they rest on me, and I can feel that touch burning into my skin like a brand. Fucking hell.

It's imperative that I break eye contact, so I quickly look away, step back, and help her up the steps. I don't know all of Nim's friends, it would get too complicated, but I wish I knew who that woman was. It's rare that I react to someone like that. It'll needle into my brain for weeks and then I'll crack and ask Nim and then she'll get obsessive and play matchmaker, then the woman and I won't really work because my life is Zastrow, and then she'll get her heartbroken when I inevitably end it by telling her it's not her, it's me.

Rinse and repeat. It's why I took myself off the market a year ago and went celibate. No emotions, no fucking, I keep things clean, my heart safe, and my mind focused. I don't have the energy for distractions like that.

When no one else seems to be coming, I follow onto the bus, and the guards on Nim's detail close ranks and close the doors. Time to get this shit show on the road.

2

Perri

If they toast me one more time, I am going to pour my glass of champagne on Cassandra's head. I know she's proud of me. I know they all are because these are my best friends who earned all of my truths, the good and the bad, but they live in a different world than me. It's why I haven't told them about the impending doom coming for me soon.

They are rich. So rich that they could spend money on every whim every day for the rest of their lives and still have money for multiple generations. They can act without thinking or planning and they will always be able to land on their feet.

I was a kid who strategically used her parent's life insurance payout to go to boarding school, pay for college, and pay for my certification exams, while also applying for every scholarship that I could. Currently, I have just under two thousand dollars in my savings account and $21.57 in my checking. My lease ends in a week and I am planning on living in my car until I find a job and get my first paycheck.

It would horrify them to know that. I know they would bend over backwards to help me, but I'm never going to be that person. I'm not going to ask for help, at least not yet, because I haven't reached the point of desperation. Our lives are about to change and diverge, and I don't want them to feel like they have to hang on to me out of guilt.

Going out with my friends tonight was Cassandra's doing, because they are genuinely proud of me for not only passing my CPA exam but getting an astronomically good score (97. NINETY SEVEN.) For me, it's an internal last hurrah as I leave their privileged life behind me. It's not that we won't be friends anymore, or that I won't be there in a second if they need me, but I'm being reminded very forcefully that we are not the same.

They're going to move around at their family businesses until they figure out what they want to do. They have something to fall back on and cushion them if they don't start working right away now that we've graduated.

I have tons of applications submitted to companies all over the city, and I know that I'll be a heavily desired candidate with my exam score. It won't be long until I get on my feet. As soon as I get paid, I'll lease the tiniest, cheapest apartment I can find and figure out what I want the rest of my life to look like. After my parents died and my aunt met her minimum obligations to my existence, everything became about getting a degree and a job so that I was secure. I needed to survive to figure out what it meant to thrive.

Cassandra would give me everything she could in a second but I don't want to depend on anyone else. Sometimes I'm not even sure I can depend on myself. Sometimes I wonder what's the point of it all, and why I'm still here. It's not survivor's guilt. It's a real consideration. On my own, I'd spend tonight overthinking and stressing out.

So instead, I let my friends get me drunk.

I try to absorb their kind words and encouragement. I try to believe that they love me. That the second I'm truly out of their sight for the first time in 12 years they will still keep me in mind.

"One more to our baby, Perri," Scarlet crows. She's got pale hair, pale skin, and pale eyes, the opposite of her name, but still beautiful. Her twin brother, Shaw, also of pale hair, skin, and eyes, raises his glass too.

"To the smartest person I'll ever know," he adds. While Scarlet never gave a crap about school and did the minimum to pass, Shaw worked hard for good grades. We've spent hours together working on homework in our various school libraries, or over Zoom when he was in Connecticut and I was here in New York, tutoring each other. Shaw actually wants to take over Fischer Hotels, while Scarlet is considering working on the design aspect. I suspect

Shaw will work and Scarlet will exist.

Hela and Cassandra lift their glasses too, so we all drink.

And drink.

And drink.

Cassandra and Shaw are starting to send each other obvious horny looks across the table. I don't know why they're bothering to keep things a secret anymore. For one, we all know about them, but for two, I cannot think of a single reason their parents wouldn't be all for their relationship. Then again, maybe that's why. They'd be adhering to expectations and falling into the same traps as the people before them. Both of them have confessed to me that they're in love, and I don't understand why they keep it a secret.

I'm frowning at Shaw so he hands me another drink.

We drink more. Hela starts making tiny little braids in my hair while whispering in her soft, accented voice and it triggers my ASMR tingles, something she used to do when I'd panic over exams. They all know about my ASMR addiction.

Tingles plus drunkenness feels so good I almost forget my worries. Hela came here from Norway to get away from her family, but she'll be drawn back to their oil and energy company because she wants it to be better, and now she's got the education to make that happen. I lean into her and let her do what she wants while sipping from my endless glass of champagne.

I listen to them talk and absorb them and love them, missing them already when we're not even separated yet. But we will be. It's inevitable.

"You okay, bunny?" Cassandra asks. She uses my very ancient nickname, one I earned because I was always still and quiet, and ran at the first moment someone paid attention to me.

"I'm good."

I drink.

And I drink.

Then I need to pee.

I wobble my way to the bathroom, making Cassandra and the others promise not to leave without me because sometimes she gets an idea in her head and is a bad mother hen in terms of making sure everyone stays with the group.

"I promise."

"Promise?" My finger is in her face but I don't realize how close I am until it squishes into her cheek.

"Promise."

Of course, after going to the bathroom and coming back out, the booth is empty.

"God. Damn. It."

I huff and make my way through the VIP section and start down the stairs out of the bar. I'm supposed to be staying with Cassandra tonight and I'm counting on her to be my ride since her driver is working.

A flash of a silver dress in the crowd draws my eye and I speed up, pushing people out of my way to catch up to Cassandra. Thank god she always wears eye-catching glittery stuff like that so I can find her. My tongue feels tied in my mouth and I can't call her name, or when I try it doesn't come out sounding like her name. I chase the silver dress and the little group of people around her out the door.

There's a party bus parked on the curb and the flash of silver disappears onto it. I didn't realize this was the direction they were going in for the night, and it means Delta is not the only place we'll be partying at. Most likely we'll ride around the city for the next few hours until we blackout and find our way to Cassandra's apartment to pass out.

As I move to get onto the bus I trip, and a strong arm catches me and stops me from face planting onto the sidewalk. My mouth drops open when I look up at the man who saved me, and is still holding me close to him.

He's fucking beautiful.

I'm really proud of myself for not saying that out loud.

Dark, dark hair that's shaved close to the scalp, sharp gray eyes, an obvious scar that curves from the corner of his left eye and down over his cheek bone, like he got cut with part of a broken bottle, but it does nothing to take away from the straight lines of his nose and jaw, or the sensuousness of his lips.

I want to lick him. My drunk brain is certain he would taste good.

We stare at each other until he snaps out of it. He makes sure I'm steady before letting me go, and I climb onto the bus.

After a moment, he joins too and sits in the seat across from me. I lean to the side, blinking slowly and taking in the surroundings of the lush party bus. Big fluffy furniture, LED lights, drinks everywhere.

I turn my head toward the back, looking for the flash of silver and Cassandra so I can find out what the heck is going on.

I don't see Cassandra.

Anywhere on the bus.

Oh fuck.

I squint my eyes as I try and focus on what the hell is going on around me. About 10 people are scattered in various groupings around the bus. In the back in the center there's a couple that's making out, so voraciously that I can see their tongues moving against one another. He's got a hand up her silver dress, cupping her ass.

The same silver dress I thought belonged to Cassandra.

My eyes slide up to pale skin, and then deep red hair.

Definitely not Cassandra, who is a tan brunette.

The couple stops making out and I get a look at the two of them, and then I have to smother a sharp gasp.

Nicolette Maines-Zastrow was tongue-fucking with Marco Albion.

Nicolette is very, very married. Publicly married, and is being constantly harassed by the press trying to find a vulnerability in that marriage because everyone knows it was about business. It's already scandalous because his oldest son and heir was one of her best friends growing up, and they have a 28 year age gap. People want it to implode; they want to find something salacious or unseemly about the supposedly bland marriage.

I'm seeing proof right now that she is, in fact, cheating on her husband with a popular F1 driver. From the way they lean close and the comfortable way they're talking to each other, their body language says this isn't the first time. She touches him with open affection. So easily I almost feel jealous.

This is bad. I need to get the hell out of here and pretend I never saw any of this.

It's hard to move with all this alcohol floating around inside me. Like I'm stuck in the quicksand I worried about as a kid. Eventually, I get my face to turn toward the guy sitting across from me. He seemed like some sort of security person so I hope if I signal to him that I need to get off, he'll let me go.

Except when I finally swing my head his way with enough focus to see his face, I'm immediately scared.

That beautiful face is nothing but hardness and darkness, glaring at me.

"Who are you?" he snarls.

"Nobody," I answer softly and automatically, the truth spilling out of my lips. I shake my head and feel nauseous. "I'm nobody."

"Fuck," he swears, and it makes heat coil in my belly. Even frustrated, he's sexy.

I watch without saying a word as he makes a call on his phone, and some moments later the bus jerks to a stop. The other guests protest, but shut up when hot guy security man stands up and looms over all of them.

"Behave yourself. Happy Birthday, Nim." Then he turns that furious gaze on me. "Come on."

He doesn't wait for me to say anything, but hooks that big hand around my bicep and drags me off the bus. I nearly lose a shoe but somehow manage to hold onto it as I stumble out onto the sidewalk. Another big security dude all in black is waiting, and looks shocked.

"This is what you were worried about?"

I stand up straight, indignant. Hot Guy doesn't let go of me.

"I'm a person, not an object."

"Sure, baby doll." He gives me a surprisingly soft smirk, then focuses on Hot Guy. I wonder for a second if I could seduce my way out of this situation, but I am not built for that. Plus if these guys work for the Zastrows, they've seen women leagues more beautiful than me.

I lean on Hot Guy. "Take me wherever you're gonna take me please, I have to pee." I don't, but it's uncomfortable standing out here like this and I want to get whatever is going to happen to me over with.

Hot Guy grunts and starts walking. It takes three steps of mine for every one of his, and then I'm shoved in the back of an SUV. The windows are so deeply tinted that I can barely see anything.

"What-" I start to ask but get interrupted when an itchy black bag is thrown over my head. Well, fuck. I'm in for it now.

I take a deep breath and resign myself to everything as they also tie my wrists and ankles. It's tight but not painful. My brain slips into practical mode, and I accept everything that's happening to me. I was going to fade out of everyone's existence anyway, dying isn't that much different.

This is probably where my life was headed all along. I was supposed to be in the car with my parents when they were hit. I was supposed to be dead, too. After asking myself enough times why I'm here, the universe listened and conspired to take me out. The chances that I survive the night are low.

While the Zastrows aren't criminals, they're powerful, and they want to keep their secrets. I know a secret now. A secret that could disrupt their life and possibly fuck with their business. I don't know how shady they are, I've never heard anything bad about them, but when someone has that much money they can and will do anything they want to keep their secrets. The little people don't matter.

I focus on my breathing as the van starts to move and force my body to relax. There's a big warm body on either side of me, surprisingly cozy, and eventually the drunk wins over and I fall asleep.

3

Neo

She fell asleep.

Have we met the most fearless woman in the world? Where's her adrenaline?

If she had stayed that calm and not fallen asleep, I'd think she was a reporter and had been expecting this. Or orchestrated it. Her face is in the front of my thoughts as I try to place her. It takes a long time for me to recall her as the dark blonde at Cassandra Warren's table that they kept toasting.

I'm less convinced this is intentional, but I can't rule it out entirely.

Her covered head is resting on my shoulder and like the torturous pervert I am, I watch her breasts rise and fall where they're pressed inside her dress. This woman is sexy and I hate it. Compact, curvy, and cute. The three C's that fucking sink me every time. It makes her dangerous, even if she isn't up to anything meant to harm the Zastrows or spy on Nim. I promised I was done with women, even for casual fucking, for the rest of my life, and the only person I never break a promise to is myself.

Now that she's unconscious, I reach into the tiny improbable bag that's on a chain across her body. It has her phone, a small wallet, and a single key on a key chain with a bedazzled dollar sign. It seems very out of character.

I examine the wallet and look through her information, then open a call with Benji. While he can physically hold his own, where he excels is the technological side of things. He can find anything about anyone. I give him a brief rundown, ignore his swearing, and start giving him the information he'll need to pull together a file on this woman within the next hour.

"Perri Kane, 22." I read her driver's license number. She's not dumb enough to keep her social security card on her, and I respect that. He promises me he'll have something ready by the time we get back to the warehouse and get her secured.

It's a long drive from where we were, and she sleeps the whole damn time. She doesn't scream money like her friends so I'm guessing she's a normie who got pulled into their circle somehow, and works for a living. To be this exhausted in this kind of situation, there has to be something wearing her out.

The warehouse looms ahead, and as soon as we get through the secure fencing around my little compound, I feel better.

The warehouse is three buildings, technically - barracks where security staff can live, the gym where they train, and then the large central warehouse, a hold over from older days built of solid red brick. The bottom floor is a mix of rooms for interrogation, imprisonment, a nice open space for storage, as well as a computer area where we keep secure information and our backup operations center if something would happen at Zastrow. The upstairs loft is my personal residence.

My closest security staff are the ones that stay in the barracks since like me, they don't have much of a life outside the job. We're the best of my staff and we're always ready to go. The rest of the guys have lives and families and being security for Zastrow is their day job. Either the daytime guarding of a member of the family or staff, or working security at the building.

Wilder is driving the van and his usual partner Thomas is in the back with me. When Wilder pulls up to the main building, he presses a garage door opener that lets him go right inside.

I step out of the van when it parks and immediately turn to pick up our guest. Perri groans and shifts but doesn't wake up. I can tell even through the bag over her head that she's still asleep. It was a mistake to grab her though because her body is lush against the hardness of mine, and that's my goddamn weakness.

Wilder and Thomas follow me through the winding halls until we get to a room for questioning. I set Perri down and Thomas moves to alter her restraints so she's bound to the chair. My back goes up when he touches her, even though it's nothing inappropriate. I don't want anyone else to touch her.

When she's secure, I take off the bag, and signal for the others to leave the room. My one kindness, before closing the door, is that I leave the lights on.

Benji is waiting for us at the conference table outside the computer rooms. He hands me an iPad with everything he could find on short notice about Perri Kane. I read through it but he knows I want him to talk me through the highlights anyway.

"Perri Kane, 22, single, an Aries Sun, and has posted memes about being a Taurus Rising." I glare at him because I do not need his amusement with astrology right now. "You know Aries and Aquarius vibe, right?" His grin gets bigger. I think he's trying to decrease my stress about tonight but it's not working.

"Get back to business," I grit out.

"Originally from Maryland, parents died when she was 11, guardianship went to her aunt who I can tell on paper was a bitch. Got herself into St. Elizabeth's a year later until high school, then NYU where she just graduated with a degree in accounting and got a fucking scary score on her CPA exam. Social media indicates that she's one of Cassandra Warren's inner circle, maybe even her certified bestie, otherwise she's quiet. About to be broke and homeless unless her friends are picking up the tab."

"An accountant?" I check.

Benji shrugs. His hair is currently bleach blonde and contrasts harshly with his dark eyes. "An accountant. I think all of this was a series of unlucky circumstances."

"Never talk about luck to an Irishman," I snarl. "What the fuck do we do now?"

"Talk to her?" Wilder drawls. He was frustrated and confused when I brought her out of the bus, not understanding why any of this was a big deal. "Scare her into silence and let her go? She's got no family, no job, nothing to hold over her head. We can't exactly threaten her friends because they're all too fucking important. It's a payoff or the shove off."

"Can't do that, that's not who we are." I shake my head. "Now I know she needs money and she saw with her own damn eyes something she could get paid a lot for."

"What did she see?" Benji prompts. He knows the rules for Nim's nights out. He also knows as well as I do that she breaks them, especially the rule that her and Marco are supposed to behave on the bus. He reads my look. "How far?"

"His hand was up the skirt of her dress and they were swallowing each other's tongues."

"Fuck," he sighs. "Talk to her first. Maybe there's a way to keep her quiet."

I nod. That's really the only damn choice.

Without another word, I turn and walk to the room where I left her. Benji follows behind me, ready to be my backup and take notes during questioning if needed.

Perri is awake and alert when I open the door, and the look she gives me when our eyes meet is chagrined. Like this is all her fault and she's getting ready to apologize to me for something that was ultimately our error. It was our responsibility to keep anyone unauthorized off the bus. She opens her mouth but I start talking before she can say anything.

"Okay *mo dhuine ar bith*, how did you end up where you didn't belong?"

"I was with Cassandra Warren. She was wearing a silver dress, and when I lost her at the club I followed the first silver dress I saw. It just belonged to the wrong heiress. I'm so sorry. I know you can't take my word for it that I won't say anything, but I won't."

I step closer to her so that she has to tilt her head back to look at me. I watch her throat bob as she swallows heavily.

"Listen," Perri starts explaining to me where her car is parked. "Make it look like a car jacking gone wrong. Anything else and Cassandra will look into it, and you don't want that. As long as she thinks it was a tragic circumstance from living in a dangerous city, everyone's secrets will be protected. It's okay."

Benji and I exchange looks, and he's as bewildered as I am.

"Do I look like a killer to you?" I ask, curious about what her answer will be. This tiny little nobody who swims in a world with big fish, who is more perceptive and giving than anyone I've met and I barely know her at all, is offering herself up like her life has no value.

Perri Kane stares into my eyes, and straight into my fucking soul for almost a minute before shaking her head in the negative.

"No. You're not a killer, you're a protector. That's all you're doing." She breaks eye contact with me and takes a deep breath to steel herself before looking again. "It's okay," she says again. "Sometimes bad things just happen."

I can't look away from her calm resignation. This sad woman who has lost so much - her parents, any protection since her family didn't step up, and she was about to lose her place to live. A little nobody with nothing, and yet she was showing more integrity than even the poorest rich man I'd ever met.

I take a few steps back because I still don't know what the hell to do. Before I leave the room, I stop and look at Benji.

"Untie her, but keep her locked up in here. I'm going to talk to the boss."

"Neo," he starts in question, but I shake my head and cut him off.

4

Neo

The door slams behind me and I walk quickly through the warehouse, ignoring the calls of the others until I get in my car. My Aston Martin Vantage is a bland black and I bought it secondhand from Harrison even though he tried to give it to me. It's nice enough that I fit in but not so flashy that I get noticed, especially since it's a subdued color. It's also fast, and helps me weave through traffic until I get to the Zastrow penthouse.

It's not as secure, and I hate it when they stay here versus the house out in Long Island. The house that has millions of dollars worth of cameras, sensors, dogs, and staff, versus the penthouse that has cameras, sensors, and staff that we have minimal control over or access to, and Andre still refuses to just buy the whole damn building. He says it's gauche, as if I care about shit like that.

I park in the underground garage and type in the code that gives me access to their floor. The second the doors open, the furious click of high heels on marble greets me.

"If you killed her, I'm going to take your balls!" Nim has an angry finger pointed at me and I take the threat about as seriously as if she was a toddler. Even if I had done it, she wouldn't last 30 seconds engaging in violence. She faints at the sight of blood.

"Calm down, sweet girl," Andre says as he steps into the foyer after her, and he rests a hand on her lower back. I flinch slightly and hope they don't notice. Even years later it's still kind of weird to see my best friend's dad treat our other best friend like a woman and his wife.

Nothing gives Nim more disgusting satisfaction than reminding Harrison and I that they fuck. From the beginning, they've had an open marriage on her side. Neither of them wanted to get married to each other, and it took some time for her to see him as a man and not her friend's dad. He'd always been an important positive male figure in her life, but the dynamic had to shift. He also felt guilty that she was having to leave behind the man she was in love with, and told her that as long as she was discreet and didn't get pregnant, Nim and Marco could continue their relationship.

It seems to work for all three of them.

It's also how this entire fucking situation happened. Because Andre was a mature man who'd been cornered into marrying a young woman and because he wasn't a monster, he wanted to keep her happy. Andre had his heir in Harrison so they didn't need to have children; marrying Nim had been about business, and in the end, saving her.

"We aren't killers." Andre kisses her temple and she deflates. He focuses his gaze on me. "Let's talk."

I follow them both through the foyer and into the large living room with the insane but also slightly terrifying view. I don't like heights.

Neither of them says anything when I move so that I'm standing with my back to the window. They both stare me down until I give in and sit in the leather armchair across from the couch where they've perched themselves.

"Tell me about her."

I do what my boss asks. I lay out the entire sad story of a young woman who ended up at the wrong place at the wrong time, and saw something she shouldn't have. Nim makes soft noises of sympathy and her hands flex where they rest on Andre's knee.

"There's nothing to blackmail her with or hold over her head, and we both know that if it's about money to keep her quiet, it will be easy to give her money to make her talk."

Andre stares at me. He wants me to give him an answer to the situation and I don't have one. For the first time ever, I have no idea what to do to fix a problem for him. I've engaged in plenty of threats and blackmail, I've taken hostages, I've demanded ransoms for people to protect Zastrow secrets. To protect Zastrow lives.

It's the least that I owe him. He's been more my father than my actual father, and we both know it.

"We aren't killers, Neo," Andre says slowly. "We aren't criminals."

"I know."

Before we can break it down further, the elevator pings announcing another arrival, and Harrison strolls in. His light hair is a mess like he rolled out of bed and came over here, except he's also wearing a suit but it's a light color which means in his mind, it's casual. I think he's been wearing suits as his normal clothes since we were 16. Like he got his first Brioni and decided he was never wearing anything else.

Nerd.

"Well, you're really fucked now." He steps up to the couch and hands Nim his phone. Andre leans over to look, and they both raise their eyebrows.

"What?" I push. I stand up and take the phone.

Instagram is open, and I'm looking at a picture of myself. And Perri Kane. Looking like a couple in a heated embrace. Her back is to the camera so my hand on her lower back is visible. I'm looking down at her, and it's the expression on my face that's gotten us in trouble. The heat, the need, that I failed to disguise.

My association with Nim and Harrison means that every once and awhile the media likes to get up in my business too. The caption implies that I've gotten into a relationship with Cassandra Warren's best friend - and Perri's social media handle is tagged. The woman I've currently got held captive in my warehouse is my girlfriend, according to the public.

Now there's a trail connecting us.

"Fuck." I pinch the bridge of my nose. "Now what?"

"Did you know she has an application in at Zastrow?"

"Really." Andre leans forward, his frown deepening. "What area? Did we pass her?"

Harrison unlocks his tablet. "Venture financial analysis. We flagged her for interview. She's an excellent candidate."

"So you're telling me that this poor girl is about to be homeless, broke, is looking for a job, and the media already thinks she's with us?" Nim looks between Harrison and me. I nod. "This is fate, babies. She's meant for us."

Nim has too soft of a heart. It's surprising, considering what her upbringing was like, but it's also why we were the perfect trio. Harrison was the brains, I was the brawn, and she was the heart, directing our talents toward the right causes. She was our moral compass until we figured out our own.

Andre sits up, a glint in his eye. "I think you're right."

He turns to look at Harrison. "Hire her. Push it through."

Harrison nods and starts working. Andre swings his attention back to me.

"If she has nothing to leverage, we become her leverage. Bring her into the family. A job, a purpose, a place to belong." His voice is hard and his jaw flexing, imparting to me how important this is. "Make her love us."

My head snaps back automatically. "I can't make her love me."

Andre and Nim share a look and it takes me a second to realize my error. I made it about me. About Perri loving me. Visually, she's my weakness, the type of woman I have to fight wanting now that I've decided I want to be alone. Pair that with her attitude, the way she was forgiving me for something she viewed as inevitable, and Perri has already sunk her fingers into me without knowing it. Without even trying.

I'm vulnerable to her and I don't like it.

Andre stands up and I follow automatically, mirroring his stance.

"This is your responsibility."

Even though I want to call him out on that, I don't. I wasn't even working, technically. If anyone should be responsible it's Wilder.

The thought of anyone else being with Perri fills me with a molten fury I've never experienced before. She is mine. She's my responsibility, my problem, and until I think we can trust her, she's my captive.

"Not to mention, if it gets out that this random woman got past our security, we'll look weak. We have to put on the show, and make her association with us unquestionable. Until further notice and as far as anyone outside this room and your immediate staff is aware, Perri Kane is your live-in girlfriend. It's best if she's at the warehouse."

I blanch.

Nim barely contains a devious grin and out of habit I give her the finger. Andre grunts but doesn't say anything.

"She can start Monday, we've got an orientation session scheduled anyway," Harrison adds to the conversation. "Can't wait to meet her." I narrow my eyes at him and he just grins. Of course he'd think a fake girlfriend being forced onto me was hilarious. Someday he's going to want a woman and I'm going to make it hell for him.

"Make Perri part of the family, Neo. The job at Zastrow is the start, but you do the rest. Make her love us. Make her loyal. No one is better for that than you." Andre glowers at me and he's in full boss mode. "Do your job. Have our back."

"Yes, sir."

With a nod, I dismiss myself and leave the penthouse.

This time, I don't rush on the drive and I don't mind any delays from traffic. My brain needs time to process what's going to happen when I get back to the warehouse. Perri Kane is the biggest inconvenience I've ever encountered, and that's saying a lot considering the pile of bullshit that is my father.

Not only does she know a secret that could make life extremely difficult for people I love, and could potentially render the business deal between the Maines and Zastrow families void, but I want her. I wanted her the second we were face to face when she drunkenly tripped getting onto the bus. Then seeing how good and self-sacrificing she was? Fucking forget about it. This is going to be the longest captive situation of my life.

Time is already moving slower and she doesn't even know about any of it yet.

Make her love us. Make her a Zastrow.

It sounds simple.

5

Perri

The guy with the badly bleached hair told me his name was Benji, untied my arms and legs, and then locked me in the little room. At least he left the light on, and it didn't bother me at all when I crawled onto the cot in the corner to try and get some more sleep. There was no blanket but the mattress was deceptively soft.

Even if I was going to die, I was going to do it as well-rested as possible. Plus, my ability to sleep seemed to make them all unnerved and that gave me some satisfaction. These big bad boys didn't scare me. Not when they seemed so openly upset about this situation.

I wake up to the sound of the metal door groaning open.

Hot security guy, who they called Neo, stands framed in the door. He's imposing, and there's a dark look on his face that immediately makes my stomach clench. I'm going to brace myself for this. Wrong place, wrong time, and this is what happens. Sometimes life is just like that.

I slide off the bed and walk over to him, stopping when I'm a few feet away. His expression is tortured, almost nervous. There's no way someone as confident and competent as him has never killed anyone before, and it gives me a weird sense of solace that at least the man who is going to take my life has a conscience. It gives me hope that he'll remember me. That the man who took my life will keep it with him.

"Please don't drag this out," I say quietly, keeping it between us because I don't know who else is out in the hall. "I get it."

Neo stares me down, and it makes me shiver in an unexpected way. A sexy way. Have I had a weird death or danger kink this whole time and been unaware of it? Or is it just that I don't think anything comes after this life and toiling the way that I have been has finally exhausted me?

Why the hell do I feel relieved that I'm about to die?

"Don't you have anything worth living for?" he asks, voice raspy.

I shrug, not giving him anything. "I guess not."

He takes a step forward, invading my space, and his finger hooks my chin before I can move away, tilting my head up so I can't look away from him.

"That's going to change *mo dhuine ar bith,*" he says, and I'm mesmerized by the way his tongue moves around the unfamiliar words. "You're mine now."

I blink a few times but can't seem to compute the words. "What?"

He leans closer and I can feel his breath on my lips as he speaks. The scent of his mouth is oddly erotic, enticing even. I've never thought about someone's breath before unless the scent was unpleasant. With him, my mouth waters at the hint of his taste.

"You're right, I'm a protector, not a killer, so until I can trust you, I'm going to keep you. A photo of us hit social media, calling you my girlfriend. Me and you? We're tied together now. Publicly. We're going to use that."

I open and close my mouth, struggling to process what he's saying and what it means.

"From now on, you're going to stay with me so I can keep an eye on you. As far as anyone outside of this building is concerned, you're my live-in girlfriend." I scoff at him but he gives me a semi-cruel smirk and keeps going. "You, Perri Kane, are obsessed with me. Love at first fucking sight. You worship the ground I walk on and I own you, heart, soul, and body." The way he says body has my nipples tightening and I mentally berate myself again.

I was attracted to him before all of this happened and it makes it so much harder to be controlled and rational. My brain had already started wiring that pattern, laying the groundwork of want, and I don't know how to undo it. The idea of being owned by him sounds great, even though I know that it won't be. Even though I know I'll have something to prove with every move I make and my life will hang in the balance.

"You don't do or say anything without my permission. Got it?"

"Got it." I swallow heavily. I went from being resolved to my own demise, to trying to figure out how to live under surveillance and keep my real attraction within fake boundaries. My stomach is pooling with anxiety and dread.

Neo holds my gaze for a few more moments before dropping his hand and his eyes, and turning away from me. My body sags in relief. I'm more afraid of his attention than I am of a gun, and that's probably not a normal response to the situation that I am in. I want him as much as I'm afraid of him.

Still, I'm alive, so I'm going to take the chance and do the work to keep it that way. I didn't lie when I told Neo I had nothing worth living for - maybe the truer statement is that I have nothing worth fighting to live for. Sad but true. Neo's challenge gave me another fight, when I felt like the war I'd been waging against my circumstances was finally coming to an end. Neo is the new battle.

There are worse people to be bound to, I guess.

I will keep reminding myself that this is not sexy. Being his captive and hostage girlfriend is not hot in any way whatsoever.

Neo gestures for me to follow him, and I try to pay attention as we wind through hallways until we're back out in a more open area. It's clearly a warehouse that's been converted into various purposes, including a tiny little prison that I got to visit. Most of it is clean, open storage space, as well as a garage, but one side is a walled off area with a very intense security door, and outside of it is a conference table where various bulky dudes are sitting and talking. Silence falls when we walk toward them.

Neo opens his arms. "This is the warehouse compound. It's got enough security to keep you in and everyone else out. I'm Neo Ryan," he gives me a grin that feels fake. He's putting on a show for his men. "Head of security for Zastrow Ventures." That makes sense.

"These are my regular staff - you met Benji," bleach blonde guy waves, "and there's Leander, Wilder, and Thomas. If you can't get me, you get them. Don't trust anyone else." Leander has a shaved head and dark, dark eyes that are kind of creepy. Wilder has soft brown hair and a face that still has baby fat in his cheeks. He almost looks sweet if he wasn't wearing a holster around his shoulders with two shiny silver guns in them. Thomas is blonde and buff, and has mastered the neutral face. So this is what I'm up against. Got it.

"Come on, Perri, let me show you your new home." That sounded ominous.

6

Perri

I give a small smile and a wave to the guys, unsure if there's anything else to do, and then I have no choice except to follow my new forced boyfriend. Neo heads across the warehouse to a staircase along one wall that leads up to a loft. I'm nearly running to keep up with him, and I'm out of breath when I get to the top of the stairs.

He types in a code and the door unlocks.

"I'll get you setup with your own code."

"Why?" I ask as I step inside the apartment and flinch when the heavy door slams and locks behind me. "I'm trapped here, right?"

Neo turns around and eyes me from my toes up to my eyes. "No. You've got a job at Zastrow starting Monday. I hear you're a pretty smart accountant."

The jolt of pleasure I feel is uncontrollable and I step closer to him in my excitement. "I do? What department? What will I be doing?"

A hint of a real smile appears on his face. "You'll be doing some kind of analysis - everything will be explained to you. It's how you can be useful while still under my eye."

I gulp and step back. "Okay."

"Just assume I'm always watching you. Here," he says and gestures around the apartment that I haven't really looked at yet, "and at the office. The only space not covered by a camera in this place is the bathroom."

That's when I finally look around at my new home. It's a huge open loft that's divided by shelving units and curtains. The kitchen to my right is large and chrome, with a huge metal island like you'd find at a restaurant. It's industrial but nice. To the left is a living area that's unexpectedly cozy, with a large area rug, a huge, squishy sectional, and a large TV with various gaming consoles. In the far corner is a desk with a laptop resting on it, where he probably works from home.

Straight ahead is a curtained off area that I assume leads to his bedroom. I can see a huge king-sized bed with a black comforter from here. Just inside the curtained area is the single door which I assume leads to the bathroom. The apartment is shaped like a giant L, and there's basically no privacy.

It's oddly charming, probably because it feels lived-in. There are plants, magazines, books, and the controllers for the consoles are haphazardly placed and clearly used. The nicks and dents in the chrome of the kitchen surfaces show he uses it, which is good because I like to cook.

I walk away from him, deeper into the apartment and through the curtain into the bedroom area. He's got a metal rack that functions as a wardrobe and a nice, solid dresser. There's matching side tables with matching lamps, and the bed itself has a cushioned black leather headboard. It's all very masculine, but in a rich, cozy sort of way.

"I'll have your car and the contents of your apartment delivered tomorrow, so you can make yourself at home."

Neo's voice close behind me makes me jump. I didn't realize he'd gotten close to me again. It makes me sway on my feet as the adrenaline continues to overwhelm my body and my back brushes his chest.

"Okay." I don't know what else to say at first. I'm overwhelmed at the turn my life has taken, and how narrow all of my choices have suddenly become. The thing is, I'm a survivor. Always have been. If the opportunity is there, I'm going to take it. That's what this is - an opportunity. An alternative to disappearing, to ceasing to exist. The fight that didn't exist in that tiny cell when I thought I was going to die roars to life inside me.

If anyone can get through this and make it work, it's me.

"Can I borrow some clothes? I'd like to get out of this dress." I step forward and put space between us before turning around to observe him again. Neo's eyes rake my body and I see heat there, but just as quickly he smothers it. The attraction is mutual, but so is the need for boundaries. Neo steps past me and toward the dresser. He removes a pair of boxers and a clean t-shirt.

The boxers are soft black cotton with Santa hats all over them.

We both stare at them.

"I've never worn them. They were a gift and I prefer briefs."

That makes me glance automatically down to his crotch, imagining the fitted material beneath his jeans, caressing his cock, and I blush furiously. I dart forward to take the shirt and boxers, avoiding his eyes and the vicinity of his groin, looking anywhere but him.

"I'm going to take a shower." I don't wait for him to answer, just dart through the door and close it before I even turn on the lights. I lean back against the wood in the dark and take a few deep breaths.

Taking a minute to think, this seems extreme. Are they really that concerned that I'll tell someone? And what's the big deal if I do? I won't, it's not in my nature to interfere with someone else's decisions like that, but at the end of the day isn't it just another society wife married to an old dude who's got a guy her age on the side? Her husband probably has a young mistress somewhere. If there's anything I've learned as an observer in the world of the mighty and wealthy it's that fidelity means very little to them.

I can't be mad about the job, though. Zastrow Ventures was one of the places I was most excited to hear back from. I'd applied to work in their financial analysis division - basically, the job is to assess ventures the company is considering investing in for financial soundness. It's going through the books and projections and checking if everything is accurate, and making a recommendation if the payoff seems worth it. It's very entry level because my analysis will go through 2-3 levels before they make a final decision on investing, but it's the kind of math I find fun.

And honestly, until all of this, I respected the company and the man who ran it.

Andre Zastrow lost his wife 8 years ago, and he'd very publicly mourned her. It had been a shock to most people when he married a 21 year old Nicolette Maines only 3 years later. His obviously real devastation, and their odd behavior around each other in the early years, is probably where the fixation on their marriage came from. It was a scandal, in as much as those exist in the world anymore. Plus, it's easy to be obsessed with other people's messes rather than cleaning up our own.

The stress is starting to tighten my throat, my breathing getting shallow, so I do what I always do: stuff it down. There's never been the time or the freedom for stress or a breakdown. It's always been me on my own, protecting myself, and this is no different. I'm pretty sure I only have one shot at this trust thing, and I'm not going to fake that. I'll show them all that I'm worth it, and I'll give as good as I get.

I flip on the light and look around the large bathroom. It's got a long marble counter with double sinks and a huge mirror that goes along the entire length, a standing shower, and a separate, massive bathtub. The question of whether Neo chose the tub or if it was already here crosses my mind, and then I'm imagining his ruthlessly muscled body in the tub, with a hint of bubbles. The contrast of his masculinity and the soft bubbles is appealing.

Without dwelling on that, I step toward the shower and get it started, turning the water to a temperature just past comfortable before I strip out of my dress. I'm wearing a strapless bra and a thong, both items of torture in the name of fashion, and I toss the thong straight into the trash. I'm done with that, and the reaction to Neo that it gives away.

I step under the shower head and douse myself in hot water, turning my pale skin red, soaking the day and the fear and stress out of my muscles. When I feel like I've relaxed as much as I'm going to, I steal Neo's soap with it's very masculine mountain-themed smell and wash my body.

When I'm done and dressed in the comfy boxers and giant t-shirt, I step out of the bathroom.

Neo is sitting on the end of the bed, scrolling through his phone. He looks up when the door opens and that heat is back in his eyes. I can't look away from his mouth when he licks his lips. It's fantastically annoying that we find each other attractive and are bound by this situation where boundaries are more necessary than ever.

I'm his girlfriend in appearances and as far as the outside world knows, but it's all so they can keep control over me.

"Where am I going to sleep?" I ask softly, feeling the wall of alcohol and exhaustion hit me as soon as I say it.

"Here," he gestures to the bed and stands up. "It's a big bed, and honestly, I don't sleep much. I won't touch you, princess. I'm not that guy."

I don't ask what he means by that and I don't react to anything he said other than a nod. "Do you have a side?"

He indicates the side nearest the door, which makes sense. Even unconsciously, even for me, he'd be in protective mode. I have a feeling when he sleeps at all, it's spread out diagonal across the bed, and his choice was made without thinking.

I move around to the other side of the bed. Neo tosses his phone down in front of me, but then I realize that it's my phone.

"Text Cassandra, she's been freaking out. We added our tracking app and backdoor to it, so assume that I can look at it whenever I want."

I don't know what he expects me to say to that.

"I added my number, and Benji's too. If you can't get me, he's your first call."

I open up the phone and see a new addition to my favorites: MY MAN with the green heart emoji after it. I roll my eyes at it and see that he's added Benji to my favorites as well.

Neo comes up behind me and watches as I open my text thread with Cassandra. She's messaged me multiple times, first telling me where to meet them, then where they went after leaving Delta, and then a series of increasingly panicked and drunken messages. I love her but she's not reliable when it comes to taking care of someone on a night out. Tonight wouldn't be the first time she left me or lost me.

Cassandra loves me, but she's only as dependable as what she can do when I'm in front of her. After that, it's like goldfish brain - once I'm out of sight I'm out of mind. It's why I know I'll be able to fade away from her easily. If it's not big drama, it's not stuck in her head. It's why she's an oddly solid reporter; she gets obsessive.

With Neo watching, I send her a text that I'm fine, I went home with someone, and that she she could call me when she's sober and I'll explain everything.

"Good." Neo smacks my ass in a weirdly friendly kind of way and I jolt. "Now get some sleep."

He walks off, leaving me stunned, and pulls the ties that close off the bedroom to the rest of the apartment. I have no choice but to crawl beneath the comforter and the very surprising top sheet. It takes moments before I feel myself being pulled into sleep, done with fighting the inescapable.

If I'm going to make this work, I'm going to need all the rest I can get.

7

Neo

I lied to Perri about the cameras.

They are all over the apartment, and that includes the bathroom. I don't trust anyone, even the few people I've given access to this space. If there hadn't already been one, I would've added it so I could watch her.

I'm the only one with access to these cameras, although I can give it to someone else in a pinch.

So when she flees into the bathroom, I pull up the camera feeds and watch her.

It's invasive, sure, but I need to observe her when she thinks no one is watching. When she thinks she can let her guard down. I watch her look around the bathroom and take everything in.

I watch her strip out of her clothes and try to focus on her face instead of looking at her tempting, delicious body. I laugh when she throws her panties in the trash and I already know that I'll be pulling them out later.

Perri is all business and goes straight for the shower. Once inside it, I can't see her clearly. Between the steam and the frosted glass of the doors, all I get is a vague sense of her shape. It's an apt metaphor for what I know of her now. She's a vague shape, and I'm going to learn everything until she's crystal clear. Until I know her well enough that I can determine her thoughts as she thinks them.

So well that I'd be able to feel her impending betrayal inside my own body and be able to cut it off before it happens.

Life loves to fucking test me, but I didn't expect this. A woman built for me in looks and personality, but one I can't trust. The perfect woman sent to me after a year of celibacy, where I hadn't struggled for a single day, and now I was going to be doing nothing but managing my hard, aching cock every time I looked at her. I'd be living in close proximity to my biggest temptation, knowing that she wanted me too.

But I really didn't want to be that guy. I don't want to take advantage of her because she's as stuck in this situation as I am.

Well, I won't entirely take advantage of her.

Because I definitely don't stop myself from watching her get out of the shower and towel off. I watch as she pushes up her generous breasts to dry the underside. I watch her bend over and dry her legs, appreciating the lush curve of her round ass.

I lock my phone as she comes out of the bathroom and pull out hers, seeing more messages from Cassandra. I pretend like the primal animal inside of me that wants to fuck her until we both pass out isn't delighted to see her in my clothes. Delighted that she's already bearing a sign of my ownership.

This is going to be hell.

We go through the last few details, and I leave her to sleep it off. Based on her previous behavior tonight I'm sure she'll pass out in a few minutes. I sit on the couch and watch her on the camera until I think she's asleep. Except I don't stop watching.

I get lost in the rhythm of her breathing. My mind keeps circling the fact that she's wearing my clothes and used my soap, and that if I would press myself against her and inhale she'd smell like me. Like mine.

Part of me wants to throw all my morals and vows out the window, go rip the covers off the bed, and pound her into oblivion. Own her body with my cock so I can work on owning her heart and soul, until she exists for me. Until betraying me would be like betraying herself.

Except I can't do that.

While I think I'm capable of love and loyalty like that, the rest of the world has shown me I'm the odd man out. One who believes is fidelity, family, and trust. The women in my life have always betrayed me, or wanted something from me, and their care was never really about wanting me, but what I represented. It's why I gave up, and dedicated my life to the job even further than I already had. My family would have to be enough.

We'll win over her heart and her mind. To Zastrow, not to me. I will show her they are worth loving and being loyal to, and that she can have a place there if she's willing to work for it. If she falls for me, I'll navigate that problem as it comes. The hard line I know I'll never cross is falling in return.

I step back from watching her sleep and go into the bathroom. I grab her panties from the trash. They're damp, soaked almost, and when I raise them to my face I can smell her. Not just the sweat from a night out or the smell of her skin, but the sweet musk of her cunt. Perri struggled with her arousal as much as I did.

Her panties fit perfectly in my pocket, and I step out to watch her again.

There's nothing on under my boxers that she borrowed. Perri makes a soft cry in her sleep that brings me back to the moment, and not the depraved fantasies in my head.

Snapping out of my creeper watching, I leave the apartment.

The guys are gone, in their places in the barracks or on duty. Except Benji, who's never far from the computers. It makes him feel safe to be there, and when he can't sleep the hum of the technology is like a lullaby. I know he's not okay, but he won't let us help, and it doesn't get in the way of him doing his job. At this point, I want him to sleep more than I want the other things to be fixed.

"You good, boss?" he asks. He's working on a laptop at the conference table.

"I'm fine."

"More photos showed up." I'd given them all the short version of what happened and how we got here. Wilder kept apologizing until I told him he was asking for a black eye if he didn't shut up. This wasn't only his fault.

Benji turns his laptop, and it shows a series of pictures of me and Perri. Before she falls, my arm was already out, reaching for her. I hadn't realized that. Watching the sequences of photos, it doesn't look like she fell. It looks like she came to me and I pulled her in. I wish I could see it from the other side, to get a chance to analyze the way that she's looking at me.

Embarrassment burns through me that my obvious desire for her is caught in the photo. That they've all seen it and recognized it.

"At least she's hot?" Benji hedges.

"She's part of the job, Benji, don't talk about her like that," I snap, both irritated and oddly jealous.

He looks up, surprised, then shrugs.

"I need her set up with her own code, and I need physical trackers to place on her when I get her stuff here."

I wasn't going to sleep, so that gave me an idea. "I'm going to her apartment. Have it ready when I get back."

Benji shakes his head but starts working. "Whatever you want, boss."

8

Perri

The next morning, I wake up alone, and I can't tell if Neo slept in the bed at all. I stay in the t-shirt and boxers because I don't have anything else and wander out into the living area. No one is there, and it's just past 8:00 A.M.

My eyes snag on a white piece of paper on the island.

Your things are downstairs. Your code is 2197. No leaving the compound today. Help yourself.

Brief but not unkind, I can roll with that. I open the door out of the apartment and see a pile of boxes and a small line of furniture surrounding the bottom of the stairs. The furniture I won't be able to move on my own but I could start hauling up the boxes and the clothes.

I lived in a tiny studio and have spent my life convincing myself that I don't need material possessions. Besides my clothes, there isn't too much. It takes 15 minutes and three trips to haul everything up and I take it straight into the bedroom. It takes another 15 minutes for me to locate clothes that I feel like wearing and it also makes me realize that one of these guys probably packed up my delicates and definitely found my vibrators.

Which I realize I haven't found after going through the boxes.

It makes me wonder if Neo gave the order to get rid of them.

To be fair, awkward; but also to be fair: what an asshole. I'm already unintentionally trapped so it's rude not to at least leave me the ability to masturbate to my own satisfaction. Especially when I know that I won't be getting that satisfaction from him or anyone else.

I'm still pissed when I stomp into the kitchen and look around, eventually making myself a bowl of cereal and eating it like it personally offended me.

After that I'm lost. Even if I could unpack, there's nowhere to put things. My kindle is dead, so I plug that in to charge, and then stare around the apartment.

I dig around in the fridge again and decide that I'm going to make dinner, but I need a few ingredients. Skipping the urge to contact Neo for help, I go right to Benji.

Me: *Are you here?*

Benji: *Yeah.*

Me: *Can you come up?*

He doesn't reply but 10 minutes later there's a knock on the door. I open it, and he's looking flustered.

"Uh, I have a code?" he says, stressed.

"Are you expected to use it when you come in here?" Benji nods. "Even when I'm here?" He nods again.

"I didn't want to be rude and come in without your permission."

I frown, then shut the door in his face and walk back to the kitchen island where I've written out my list of ingredients. It started with dinner for tonight but then expanded into dinner for the rest of the week, and prepping for my lunches at work. I don't know if I'll be expected to pay Neo back for any of this, but I figure if I'm feeding him, too, we can split some of those costs.

Eventually, Benji figures things out and I hear the beep of the keypad and the clink of the door unlocking. He steps inside and closes the door. I'm assuming that Neo will want a record of anyone who comes in or out, so Benji using his code is an awkward necessity.

"What did you need? Did Neo not answer?" he asks as he walks over to me.

"No, but I figured you'd be here, and I've been told not to leave." I wave Neo's note in his face. "I need someone to go grocery shopping. I made a list."

I slide it across the island. Benji grabs it and looks it over, his eyebrows raising as they scan it from top to bottom. Then he looks over at me, frowning.

"You need all this?"

"I do."

Benji takes a picture of the list and then sends a text. "Should have it in an hour or so. Uh, anything else?"

"If someone could help me get my furniture up here?" I'm not asking them to do it for me, I'm asking them to help me, but it still feels like I'm taking advantage of the situation. Benji nods and starts heading toward the door.

"We got this," he reassures me, and uses a cinder block I didn't see before to prop open the door. Together we trod down the stairs and after a lot of careful coordination we get my two dressers, my mirror, and my big fuzzy chair up into the loft. The chair is the easy part, and fits nicely with the rest of the furniture in the living room.

It's my favorite place to read and nap, and I'm relieved I have something comfortable and familiar here. It's not surprising that I'm on edge, jumping and flinching at every little noise, and constantly bracing myself to be hurt or yelled at, even if neither of those things has happened since I got here.

It's all ingrained in me from the few months I lived with my aunt before my first school year at St. Elizabeth's. That left scars I'll never recover from.

Benji and I slide the dressers into the bedroom, and I can tell he's never been back here before because he gets even more awkward, refusing to look around at all. I get my mirror propped in the corner and decide to worry about hanging it up another day. It's good enough that I can judge my reflection for now.

"You're good, Benji, I can handle the rest of my unpacking."

He nods, swallowing heavily. "I'll be back with the groceries."

"Okay. When you knock, when I'm ready for you to come in, I'll knock back."

Benji's shoulders drop a little in relief. "That would be helpful, thank you."

I get lost in the job of unpacking and a fresh chance to organize my clothes. I steal some hangers from Neo's rack for my best dresses and a few pairs of trousers that I'll be wearing at work, but otherwise I have more than enough room for everything. I'm not the type to pay for dry cleaning, so most things can be folded and tucked away.

Time escapes me and I jump and let out a little scream when there's a loud knock on the loft door. I put my hands over my face, blacking out the light, and take a few deep breaths. This vigilance is keeping me safe, but it's also exhausting me. I might not even make it to dinner tonight before I need to go to sleep.

I walk to the door and knock twice. Benji lets himself in, followed by Wilder, and they pile the bags of groceries I requested onto the island. It's more than I realized.

"Do you guys want to come to dinner tonight? I'm making chicken piccata and there will be plenty for all of us."

They look between each other, then Wilder shrugs. "Sure. When?"

"Around 6:00 P.M.? Will Neo be back by then?"

Wilder snorts, but it's Benji who speaks. "We'll let him know."

I'm miffed by their responses but don't push it.

When they leave, exhaustion overtakes me and I barely have the power to set an alarm before laying down on the sofa to sleep. It's comfortable and smells more strongly of Neo. He must sleep here more than in his bed. The scent is oddly comforting and that sense of peace and safety follows me into sleep.

The klaxon sound of my alarm scares me from sleep to waking, and I spring up from the couch, confused about my surroundings for a long moment. When I remember where I am and why I'm here, I slide back onto the cushion and put my face in my hands.

I've always made lemonade out of lemons.

I had benignly oblivious parents for most of my life. They did everything required to keep me alive and didn't deny me the reasonable things that I wanted, but they were bewildered by parenthood. Like they never accessed the part of themselves for the emotions and energy of parenting. They had me but they wanted to keep devoting the majority of their time to their lives, hobbies, and each other. The best thing I can say about my parents was that they were clearly in love with each other.

In some ways, that's the solace to the fact that they died together. They were driving back from an anniversary trip when their car hit black ice and slid off the road and into a tree. They died instantly, together, and left me behind.

My only living relative was my aunt, Cindy, and she was bitter that they left me to her but felt like she couldn't give me up to the system either. She and my mother barely spoke, and Cindy loved to tell me how much my mother knew that she never wanted kids, and saddling her with me was my mother's punishment from beyond the grave.

Apparently, that was also her excuse to hurt me. Cindy told me they raised me to be soft and she needed to toughen me up. When the insurance money came through she relaxed a little because quite a bit went to her and the money for me was managed by a lawyer. The second I wanted it for education, Cindy and the lawyer signed off, and she disappeared.

Other than a check-in call on my birthday, I haven't heard from her since the day I turned 18. It was freedom for both of us. In a weird way, I think once she realized I didn't want or need anything from her, she had a grudging respect for me. I would do it all by myself, like I always had.

Part of my drive to be successful on my own was absolutely to spite her. To show her that she was wrong about me, and that I was never as soft as she thought. Being soft spoken didn't make me any less vicious, smart, or determined. It meant I used people's tendency to underestimate me to my own advantage.

No one thinks the quiet girl will stand up for herself.

I think that's why Cassandra liked me. I'd heard some other girls talking about a prank they were going to play on her that would've involved Cassandra being exposed to the whole lunch room. Even though I didn't know her, I walked straight up to her and asked to speak with her.

She trusted me after that, and we eventually became friends. I was accepted by her friend group because she vouched for me, and when any of them tried to crap on me for being a scholarship kid or an orphan among the rich, she never let them. Cassandra has been my defender for a long time, even when I didn't want or need it.

This is a situation she can't save me from.

I start working on the chicken piccata. It takes me awhile to find all the items I need, but Neo's kitchen is decently stocked and the pans are high quality.

I'm almost done cooking when there's a double knock on the door.

"Come in!" I call out.

Benji enters the loft and sits at a stool on the island. Awkward silence falls for a bit.

"Uh, tell me about you?" I finally ask. I don't like to talk but I don't like the quiet either. Mostly I enjoy absorbing other people.

Even though he stumbles over his words with nerves, Benji tells me about himself. He's the computer guy on the security team, originally from California, kicked out of school for coding a program that wrote his English papers for him, and eventually discovered by Neo when he came to New York and applied to work at the technology service desk at Zastrow.

He speaks about Neo like he's a hero. Someone who saw all the potential in Benji even without a completed degree and put his skills to work.

I also find out that behind the big metal door downstairs are Zastrow's backup servers, and the hub for all of the security at Zastrow properties. Someone is always in that room, or Benji is on the premises with a tablet that will alert him to anything that happens on the system. I get the feeling he doesn't leave here a lot.

"Can I ask you a question?"

Benji shifts nervously. "Sure?"

"What's with the hair?"

He laughs, relieved, and before he can answer me we both hear the beeps of the keypad and the thunk of the door unlocking. Neo is home.

9

Perri

We all freeze and stare at each other. Neo frowns, and it deepens as he looks between me and Benji. His nostrils flair and he seems to get back in control of himself.

"Smells good," he grumbles, and walks past us into the bedroom.

Benji and I exchange a look, and since Benji also looks confused I let it go. Instead, I focus on plating our food. In addition to the chicken piccata, I made mashed potatoes and green beans. There's no dining table but there are three stools at the island, so I assume we'll eat there.

I pull one stool around the corner and put my own plate there, and set Neo up to sit between me and Benji. I have a feeling that there should be space between us for Neo to be satisfied.

He comes back into the kitchen and I want to drool. Dressed down, relaxed Neo is tantalizing. He's in black joggers and a white t-shirt, his feet bare. They're oddly attractive: smooth, pale, veined, and his toenails are clean and cut. I'd swear he gets pedicures to keep his feet that nice when he's on them all the time.

We eat in silence and Benji finishes before both of us.

"Thanks for dinner," he mumbles, already heading toward the door.

"Thanks for all your help today." He nods and moves so fast it's just short of running.

Then it's me and my captor again.

"You could've called me," Neo rumbles.

"I didn't want to bother you with something trivial."

"I won't mind," he moves so that he can look at me and keep eating. "It'll be a nice break." I notice then the bags under his eyes and the exhaustion in his body.

"Is there a problem?"

"Yes."

I wait.

"Do you want to talk about it?"

He sighs. "I can't."

I nod and wave my hand, brushing it away like I never asked. "That was stupid. Of course not. You don't trust me."

Neo looks slightly chagrined but shrugs in agreement. "This is good. Thank you."

"I actually really love to cook, so, I'll be doing that. Because I need to." For my sanity, for a sense of control, for feeling more like a guest or like it's my home instead of the captive truth.

He lasers his gaze on me, looking through me again, assessing me. A long moment later, he nods.

I'm surprised when he takes our dishes and cleans up, putting them right into the dishwasher. He leans against the counter and I want to drool looking at the picture he paints, even when he's trying to look deceptively relaxed.

"I need you to call Cassandra and tell her about us, and your new job."

"What's the rush?"

"We're in the middle of negotiating a deal with Warren Media. We don't want any distractions." His use of the royal we when talking about Zastrow is fascinating. I hope he'll eventually let me in enough to tell me how he ended up working for Andre Zastrow, and all the way up to being in charge of security at such a young age. He can't even be 30 yet.

I shrug, and grab my phone from the counter. Neo gestures for me to put the call on speaker. Cassandra answers in two rings.

"Where are you? What's going on?" I push down my irritation because *she* was the one that was supposed to call *me* today, but whatever. Her voice sounds more curious than concerned.

"Well, I haven't told you because it was pretty new, but I've been seeing someone. He asked me to move in with him since my lease was ending soon." It's easier to lie than I expected. Then again, I was already preparing myself to lie to her about a "new apartment" anyway. At least I really am in an apartment and not living in my car.

"WHAT!" I hear a slamming sound from her end of the phone, and then what sounds like Shaw's voice. "Not only do you have a boyfriend but you're also living with him and we've never even heard a word? That's ridiculous. You don't even know this dude. Come live with me, it'll be fine."

It would not be fine. I'd be living in a guest room with her and her parents, and as polite as I am, I need somewhere to decompress. After a few weeks of being treated like a well-behaved puppy by them, I'd lose my mind.

"Plus, I was going to talk to dad about getting you a job when we have lunch on Monday." I can almost hear her pouting. Again, her heart is in the right place, but if she was going to ask her dad to help me it would've been nice to do that a month ago. When I could've planned things differently because the future wouldn't have been full of so many questions.

"I got a job, too."

"What the fuck, P. We were together yesterday night to celebrate YOU, and you didn't think to tell us any of this?" Okay now I'm putting together how suspicious this all sounds. I scramble to come up with either a solid explanation or a way to redirect the conversation.

"Where's the job?"

"Zastrow Ventures."

"That's going to take over your whole life!"

I almost laugh because she has no idea, but Cassandra is just getting started.

"I can still talk to my dad. There will be a lot less pressure in accounting at Warren. You know he won't say no to me, even if they don't have an opening."

"That's not what I want, Cass," I sigh, feeling like we're having this conversation for the hundredth time.

"It's not charity when you can actually do the job. It's not like I'm getting you a job you aren't qualified for."

"But if the job doesn't exist, you're taking something away from someone else by forcing me in. The money that's paying me could be a raise for someone else. Or a job for someone else in a different department that will make their workload better. Money does not grow on trees. Jobs don't grow on jobbies."

"I swear to god, if you do that *It's Always Sunny* joke to me right now I will strangle you through the phone."

"Only if you admit you like it."

There's a long silence. "Fine. Okay? I like it."

We laugh together, some of the tension broken. Cassandra likes to use her money to solve the problems of the people that she cares about, and she donates a lot of it. She also uses her rich girl down time to do charity work and fundraise, but it's hard sometimes to draw a line between being her friend and being another project. I am not the orphan she teaches to be a princess.

"I'm really excited about this job. I'm excited about this guy," I lie, meeting Neo's eyes. The smirk on his face when I say it doesn't help either. In some unknown amount of time I will also have to be heartbroken when our "relationship" ends and I actually move into my own apartment. Better start making it believable now.

"That's all that matters. When can I meet him?"

Neo is listening to our conversation so I lift a brow at him in question. He mouths back: *soon.*

"Soon. Let me enjoy the honeymoon phase right now."

"Hot. I need more details - is he good with his tongue? I know how much you love oral." In a panic I slap the speaker button off and put the phone to my ear.

"We can catch up on all that in person. I gotta go, bye!" I blurt it out quickly and end the call as Neo steps closer, reaching for the phone to stop me. His big hand wraps around my wrist when I try and pull the phone behind me. We're stuck there, my arm slightly behind my back, trapped in his grip, my back slightly arched and my chest thrusting into his.

Neo looks down at me, amusement and heat in his eyes.

"For the record, I'm very good with my tongue."

He lets my wrist go and steps back, staring a little longer before he turns around and resumes doing the dishes. I'm mesmerized for way too long and then snap out of it.

Neo keeps doing the dishes, entirely unfazed. It's soothing to watch him work, the rhythm he falls into rinsing the dishes I used to cook and putting some in the dishwasher while he leaves others to soak. I sit at the island, chin in my hand, and get some great ASMR tingles as he starts hand-washing the bigger items and the pans. The sloshing of the water, the crinkle of the bubbles, the sound of the sponge on metal, it's all lulling me into a hypnotic state.

It takes me a few minutes to realize that not only has Neo stopped washing the dishes, but he's also said my name a few times. I must look like an idiot staring at the sink like it fascinates me.

"What just happened there?"

"Do you know what ASMR is?"

"No." He sounds like it personally offends him.

I open YouTube on my phone and go into my playlists, pulling up my favorite video. It's just a cute girl with nice nails scratching a microphone, but even looking at the little moving thumbnail sets off tingles.

"Here." I show him. "Focus on their hands. It's better with headphones, but the visual trigger is still pretty good."

He watches the video and I watch him, and I see the goosebumps raise on his neck and the jolt of his body as the feeling moves through him. Neo exits the app and hands the phone back to me.

"I get the appeal, but that's a little bit creepy."

I laugh, and a flash of a smile appears on his face. It makes the skin around his eyes crinkle and reveals that he gets those sexy smile indents around his mouth, like his lips are framed by parentheses.

"So, you're saying I can't have inaudible whispers playing when I try to fall asleep?"

"Only if you want me to think there's a fucking ghost in here." While the smile is gone, the teasing tone in his voice is still there.

It makes me wonder what we'd be like under different circumstances. If I had met him that night at Delta in a normal way, would he have even looked at me? Would we have had a chance with each other?

Instead, the attraction is present but it's alongside the world's most enormous barrier. At the end of the day, I still know something that I'm not supposed to and it's his job to keep that secret. I'm supposed to be convincing him he can trust me and I don't think ASMR videos and cooking dinner is the way to do it.

I don't think anything but time will prove it to him, and even then it might not be enough. I don't know what he's looking for, or what will finally deem me worth trusting.

The overachiever in me wants to earn it, and that bitch will do whatever it takes. There's never been a challenge or setback I couldn't overcome, and this won't be any different. Neo Ryan will trust me. End of story.

Neo's expression goes stiff, turning on a dime, pulling back. Recognizing that for a second he got comfortable with me.

"You should get ready for tomorrow."

"Right." My first day at my new job.

"I'll be back later."

"Okay." I stand in the kitchen and watch him leave.

He wasn't wrong that I'd want a lot of time to plan for the next day. I go through multiple outfits before settling on a nice black dress and my favorite flats, and I get together a work bag and any of the items that I think I might need. Everything is in place for me to get the maximum amount of sleep and take the minimum amount of time getting ready.

I return to the kitchen to meal prep and pack lunches for the week for both me and Neo. I even label them, which makes me feel dumb, but I also doubled the protein in his so I don't want him taking one of mine and ending up hungry. If he takes it at all.

By the time I'm done and starting to get sleepy, he still isn't back. I want to text him and ask what he's doing or if he'll be back at all, but I don't want to bother him. Despite the fact that we get along, I know I'm an inconvenience, and I want to reduce my level of inconvenience however I can.

I'm choosing to suck-up to my captor. Mostly because he's not so bad.

Without sending a text, I get ready for bed and fall asleep pretty quickly.

At some point, some noise wakes me up. Neo isn't in bed, but the lights are out, including the ones that I left on for him.

I move quietly from the bedroom toward the living room, where the TV is flickering with a show, the only thing illuminating a sleeping Neo, crashed on the couch. I kneel down in front of him and use the moment to my advantage - I reach out and stroke his cheek. It's got a little stubble on it from the day, but his skin is soft and warm.

"Neo," I say quietly, and it takes a few times before he stirs. "Come to bed."

"Okay." He doesn't really open his eyes but he sits up and he stumbles with me toward the bedroom. He doesn't fight me when I push him down on his side of the bed and cover him up.

Before I can move away to get back to my side, his hand reaches out for me and just barely catches the tips of my fingers. I don't move.

"Thank you," he murmurs. Then his hand drifts away, landing on the bed. I stare down at him in the dim light for a little longer, worried about both my heart and my sanity, before I go back to bed myself.

Stop being attracted to the man keeping you prisoner, idiot. Those stories never work out.

10

Neo

Perri fidgets in the passenger seat as we leave the warehouse compound. I type in my code and the gate opens, then closes, behind me.

"Your code works for the gate too," I tell her, "but you still can't leave without permission. I'll get an alert every time your code is used and if I didn't give you permission to leave, I swear to god I'll chain you in here. Indefinitely."

Perri swallows heavily. "I won't leave." There's a long silence before she adds, "I have nowhere to go."

I disagree with her but don't say it out loud. Any of her friends would take her in; I've seen enough rich kids like them to know they wouldn't even bat an eye at another freeloader hanging out at their place. They'd be lucky to have a guest like Perri who would try to pull her weight and not rely on them for anything other than a roof over her head.

It's like she *wants* to disappear from their lives and I don't get why. Cassandra has texted her multiple times already this morning trying to be supportive, asking for a picture of Perri's first day of work outfit and wishing her luck. It's almost a shock to me how kind Cassandra is considering the brutal shark that is her father, and the limp, oblivious noodle of her mother. I've literally never seen the woman say a word, she just downs martini after martini, and I'm not sure why she's been present at any of the Warren Media/Zastrow Ventures meetings.

Still, Norman Warren has nothing on Roger Maines. Nim's father is truly a monster, and I'm counting down the days until he dies. Harrison and I have hatched plenty of murder plots over the years but none of them that were clean enough to guarantee we'd get away with it, and despite everything, it would hurt Nim. He's what she has left of her family, and he's already caused her enough pain.

We ride to the Zastrow building quietly, but it's not a tense quiet. While Perri is definitely nervous, it's more about the job than it is about me. It bothers me that I don't make her nervous. I make everyone nervous, it's basically the job description.

I definitely make Perri feel something, but outside of her unwanted attraction, I don't know what it is. I'll own that we both like looking at each other, but it seems clear that neither of us has any interest in doing something about it. We know the boundaries of this fake relationship without ever having to say a word.

Not that it stopped me from shoving her panties in my face and jacking off in the bathroom before I went to sleep last night. A year of celibacy, of rarely feeling any sexual impulses or physical need to get off, and she undoes me in less than 24 hours. Perri Kane is a menace and I can't even hold it against her.

"I'll check you in with security and drop you off at your floor. I'll pick you up there at 5 to head back to the warehouse."

"Okay."

We pull into the underground parking garage and even though I turn the car off, I don't make a move to get out.

"If anyone asks, yes, we're dating. I'm going to touch you, and you need to act as if you want it." I know she wants it, and the asshole inside me loves that I'll get to toy with her in this way. That I can touch her, tease her, and then leave her hanging. It'll also be torturing myself, but I can handle that. Pushing Perri to the edges will show me who she really is.

"Anything you want to know?" I prompt.

"No," she shakes her head. "But, um, I made you lunch." I watch with confusion as she dips her hand into her nice black bag and pulls out a plastic container. Through the clear cover I can see chicken, rice, and green beans. "Yours has twice the protein of mine."

"Why did you do this?" My voice comes out harsher than I mean it to, and she snatches her hand back, leaving the container to rest on my thigh.

"I was making my lunches for myself and I...thought it would be nice."

"For the whole week?"

Perri shrugs then looks up to meet my eyes, finally. Something like annoyance and determination in her gaze. "It's what I'd do for my boyfriend, if I had one."

For some reason that makes me laugh and she frowns at me, then shakes her head. This girl has a sweet streak that makes my teeth hurt. I won't mind the lunch though. I'm not a morning person so I don't pack one for myself, and I usually get so caught up in things that I forget to eat altogether, or eat it late enough to spoil my dinner. Not a good thing when part of my job is being present and aware, and being able to count on my mind and body to perform. Being well nourished is part of that.

I swallow down my own discomfort at someone taking care of me to try and communicate honestly with her.

"I appreciate it and I will definitely take advantage of it, so please don't feel like you have to do this."

"It's not that hard."

"Okay." I tuck my car keys into my pocket and pick up my lunch. "Let's go."

We get out and walk through the garage, and I use my key card to get us to the lobby. Perri jumps when I take her hand, but this feels like allowable PDA that will make the story that she's my sudden, live-in girlfriend believable.

Our longest-standing security staffer is working the desk this morning. Aaron Monson has been manning and organizing the front desk of Zastrow Ventures since before we even had our own building, since I was a kid. He's two years away from retirement and even though we both agreed on the replacement he'd train, there's no way I'll ever trust the guy the way I trust Monson.

Monson gives me a nod and his neutral expression falls into a frown when he sees Perri's hand trapped in mine. Her cheeks are pink, and for some reason I want to brush my thumbs over them and feel the heat of her bashfulness. I want to feel the way this makes her react.

"Monson, this is Perri Kane. New hire on 7."

"For venture analysis," he nods, recalling her name because he would've prepared for it as soon as he got in this morning, knowing that we had several new hires starting today. He'll know each one and where they're headed.

"I'll take her through security registration."

Monson nods slowly as he makes a note in the computer and notifies the appropriate areas that she'll be arriving so they can be ready. His eyes drop to our joined hands again.

"Perri, this is Aaron Monson, my best employee." Monson snorts. "Perri is also my girlfriend."

"It's nice to meet you," she replies automatically.

Monson can't even school his expression, his eyes blowing wide and mouth gaping a little bit. After a long second he collects himself and gives her a tight smile, which is more than most people have ever gotten from him. Outside of work, he's kind, smiling, beloved by his children and grandchildren, but once he walks onto these premises he's locked down.

"Good luck," he finally says, and I know he doesn't mean about her first day. He means me. Seeing as he's known me since I was a kid, knows all about my daddy issues, and had to get involved in the end of my worst relationship, he's not wrong in thinking that she needs it.

What he probably doesn't realize is that I need it, too. I have to make Perri Kane love us, feel so loyal to us, that she'll never want to leave. That nothing and no one could ever tempt her to reveal what she knows. She doesn't realize how much trust she's already been granted, considering the access she now has to the warehouse, but there are so many fail safes for the information there that she couldn't do much damage and neither could anyone else.

What she knows about Nim is far more damaging.

Part of the deal with Maines Manufacturing is that there can be no infidelity on the part of Nim or Andre; it won't just end their marriage, it will end the entire contract. It means we'd have to find new production and manufacturing relationships insanely fast, and at much higher prices. Right now, Roger Maines thinks someone has his daughter under their thumb with the side benefit of making him a fuck ton of money.

If anything ever threatened the deal, especially if it was an action of Nim's, her father would kill her in a heartbeat. She doesn't believe that, but we all know it. She doesn't believe us that he's killed men before, and for less. Few people know the specifics of the marriage contract because it isn't public record, and they have no idea what's being put at risk.

It's up to Nim to tell Perri anything, if at all.

Perri's hand automatically flexes in mine as we walk around the desk. I let her go and let her walk through the metal detector, going around it myself because it would absolutely be set off by the various knives and firearms on my person. I hold out my hand on the other side and wait for her to take it.

She does, and I lead her back past the elevators to the security suite. This is the hub of most of the security operations for the Zastrow building and for any internal staff safety issues. The hub doesn't have access to any of the other property security, it's only about this building. My office used to be here but with the other issues we've run into, it made more sense for me to be up on 10 with Andre and Harrison.

When we walk in, one of our administrative security staff is there. They do double duty working for me and for HR. To my chagrin, it's Tabby, who probably dibsed the job when me working as the new hire escort was noted. She's been trying to get in my pants since a week after she started 3 years ago.

Like John, her eyes drop to where Perri's hand rests in mine. Rather than frowning, she pastes on an even bigger smile.

"Oh my god, Neo, hi." She comes toward us and runs a hand down my arm. I step back, taking Perri with me. Tabby and her terrifying smile turn toward Perri. "You must be Perri Kane, welcome to Zastrow, I'll get you all set."

Tabby turns around and grabs a file off the counter and hands it to Perri.

"Here's your login, instructions for setting up your password, and a written copy of our computing security policy. You will have to take a brief quiz at the end of the week." Tabby puts her hand in between Perri and I and cups

Perri's elbow, pulling her away from me. Our hands let go, and Perri turns back to me, looking confused and frustrated.

"Let's get your employee ID badge done."

Perri stays quiet as Tabby directs her to the photo station, and even though Tabby tries to catch Perri off guard, my little nobody's controlled expression means she takes a good photo anyway. When they're done, Perri hustles back to me.

I offer her my hand but she doesn't take it, stepping in front of me, leaning her back against my stomach. I'm not sure what she's doing, but I go with it, and rest one of my hands on the curve of her neck. Automatically, my thumb works the tense muscles there, and I watch the goosebumps rise on her skin.

"It was so nice of you to bring her in, Neo," Tabby somehow says through all of that smiling. "I can take her up for you."

I don't smile back, which isn't unusual, but I know she can read something different in my glower when her smile dips a little bit.

"Oh, please, don't worry about it. Neo wants to drop me off on my first day," Perri chimes in before I can. "He's got that whole overprotective boyfriend thing on lock." Her voice is soft and polite, and I can hear the culture in her tone from all those years in a fancy boarding school. Perri turns and rests her little hand on my chest, and looks up at me with hearts in her eyes. I did not expect her to be such a good actress, but she is selling this. Tabby isn't smiling anymore.

"Boyfriend?" Tabby says through clenched teeth.

Perri looks back at Tabby. "Yeah. I moved in this weekend, just in time to start my new job. Another step in building our life together."

Holy fuck, I want to laugh, but I don't. This is going to spread like wildfire through the building. Tabby is a gossip, which comes in handy sometimes because she'll find out about things that security needs to know and bring them to our attention.

I adjust us so I'm holding Perri's hand again.

"I didn't know you had a girlfriend." Tabby's voice has a lot more accusation than it should, considering I've told her many times I'm not interested in being more than her employer. Zastrow is fine with employee relationships as long as it's noted with HR. Obviously, Harrison has handled that aspect of my "relationship" with Perri since it's part of a security issue. As far as HR knows, this is real.

"I don't mix business and my personal life, you know that," I respond, dismissive. "But Perri is such an asset I can't hold her or Zastrow back."

Perri's cheeks turn pink. Tabby hands over Perri's badge, which she puts on a lanyard and loops around her neck. Without another word, I tug her away from the security offices.

"Despite how we got here," I tell her, "you really are an asset. Your application was already marked as a priority interview."

All she says is, "Oh."

I wish I could make her tell me what she was thinking, but that seems like a step too far, even for me. Then again, Perri isn't the one making the rules. She wandered into my world and now I have her trapped until I can figure out what to do with her. If I told her she needs to answer any question I'll ask and that if she lies or I suspect she's lying, there will be a consequence, would she doubt it?

Then I'd have to think of ways to punish her. Bending her over my knee and spanking her round, jiggling ass is tempting, but dangerous. It's far too tempting to make every consequence sexual. To punish the both of us with our bodies. When my mind is set on something, I'm unstoppable. It's the idea of catching more flies with honey - I would get more truths out of her with orgasms.

But I'll save that as a last, desperate resort.

Because I fucking want my little nobody, and there would be nothing stupider than for us to cross those lines. At the end of the day, I'll make her one of us, part of the family, give her a place to love and to belong, but nothing but grief awaits us both if she makes the bad choice to fall in love with me. Perri's too sweet and too alone. I'd break her in a way that I don't want to, that she wouldn't deserve. It would be inevitable.

I drop her off at the 7th floor and hand her over to Zadie, head of analysis. She's one of Harrison's friends from college, and while she doesn't know everything about this situation, she knows enough. One of Zadie's dark eyebrows raises when I press a quick kiss to Perri's temple before I say goodbye.

The last I see of Perri as the elevator doors close, she's still blushing because of it.

11

Neo

My lips tingle on the ride to the executive floor. We'd never touched like that. We'd never talked about it either. I'm already planning an apology for something I don't even know if I have to be sorry for. Somehow, I'm going to get back at Andre for this. Some way that's subtle and stupid.

I never disobey, and this was an order. But he also did it to annoy me, and I deserve to return that in kind.

I wave at Ryan and Kayla, the two admins on the exec floor, and head toward the small break room.

Harrison comes in behind me as I'm putting the lunch Perri made me in the fridge, and I hope that I'll remember to eat it today.

"Whoa, lunch?"

I rub the back of my neck. "Perri made it for me."

Harrison stands up straight, shock, and then a hint of disgust on his face. "Did you fuck her?"

"No," I snap. "I'm not - it's not - she knows it's fake, I told her the plan. She's just...nice." I turn away from him, not wanting him to see how much she's gotten under my skin after less than two days. My jaw clenches and I know that he can see it.

"I can't wait to meet this girl." His laughter gets my back up.

My eyes flash to his eyes and I glare. I open my mouth to tell him to back off, that she's mine, but that's not true. Even if she's mine by proximity, by captivity, there's no reason to stop Harrison from interacting with her. No reason to respond with possession when he knows the truth. I grit my teeth and hold it in. If she likes Harrison, it's another tie to us. Another hold on her loyalty.

Everyone likes Harrison, despite how buttoned up he is. It's almost annoying.

He and I were friends by proximity at first, my dad working for his dad, so I was always around. We were each other's best friend by choice pretty easily after that. I had his back, and we would always be real with each other. Especially as kids we could pick up on how some people could be, hearing and sensing their lies.

When we started first grade, we met Nim. She was popular, even in a little kid sense, because she was loud and kind, and everyone knew her mom. Isabel Maines was a famous actress, not only beautiful but talented, too. She loved Nim, even if she wasn't around as much as they both wanted. When she died in a fire on set when we were 13, everything she wanted for Nim went out the window. It was supposed to be one of Isabel's last roles before she was going to take some time off to be there for Nim's teenage years.

Instead she was dead. Posthumously winning the Emmy that made her an EGOT.

The three of us were best friends before, but that year was the one that nearly broke us all. It was the year my dad started gambling, an addiction that would lead to my life falling apart and the reason I'm so loyal to Andre. It was the first time they found a tumor in Harrison's mom, even though it was taken care of quickly and with a positive prognosis. Then Nim lost her mom, and her dad became even more of a controlling monster.

Sometimes it felt like all we had was each other.

I wondered, when we got older, if Nim and Harrison would ever be more, but was relieved when nothing changed. They were the most important stable influences in my life. Our bond to each other was familiar and platonic, and we'd never crossed those lines.

When we leave the break room, Harrison follows me back to my office. We had a meeting on the calendar first thing, so he must be anxious to get going.

"I think we need a team on this thing with Nim." Harrison throws a newspaper down on my desk. The headline says: "WHO'S HER DADDY?" And it's about the age gap between Nim and Andre, using one of their wedding publicity photos. It makes my stomach roll.

"There's too many possibilities," I agree. "Business or personal, Maines or Zastrow? Because he's got as many enemies, if not more."

Harrison pinches the bridge of his nose. "Fuck."

"I almost wonder if it would be easier if they never got married."

Harrison grumbles. "Believe me, I tried that conversation the day of the wedding. With both of them. Nim wanted out, dad wanted the deal."

We both scoff in disgust at the same time. I've never had money at the level that they do so I don't care, and Harrison is trying to be a better kind of billionaire. He gives away every cent he can, is constantly giving employees raises, but because of the nature of Zastrow Ventures, business is always booming. He's making money faster than he can give it away, not for lack of trying.

I wave Harrison off and spend the next few hours putting together a team like he suggested. People who can dedicate all their time to figuring out who is going after Nim and Andre, and also have enough discretion not to talk about it with anyone else.

There are three levels of security staff - the admin sec on the first floor, the physical and tactical security staff that operate in subbasement 1 and stay within the law, and then there's high level discretionary staff, who don't care about the law. That's me and my guys, the ones at the compound and around Andre, and we only worry about making a scene that we can't control.

At 10 to 10, Harrison knocks on my door and asks me to accompany him. I'm still lost in my head and don't pay attention to where we are until we're standing in front of a room full of people. About 30 of them with Hannah from HR up front, introducing both of us.

It's new employee orientation.

Once I'm looking, my eyes immediately seek out Perri.

She's sitting at the end of a row, a notepad perched on her knees and it's full of notes, a few pages in. I almost smile at how diligent she is and wonder if I should've given her a notepad to take down all the rules when we took her, too. Part of me wants to buy her a special notepad and a fancy pen to make sure she knows every direction I have for her, and can refer back to them.

Keep our secret. No going anywhere without my permission. Do what I say and don't ask questions. As far as anyone outside the loft knows: you love me, worship me, are utterly obsessed with me, and must act accordingly. Tell me if anything feels off to you.

I need to talk to her about that last one.

Hannah introduces Harrison, who gives a brief speech about how happy he is to have them all onboard. Perri watches him with a rapt expression and I hate it. She's leaning forward, eager and attentive. Harrison dismisses them all for the social, where he'll hang around and let people annoy him while also snacking on decent pastries.

I stand by the door and let it happen, zoning out, checking on Perri occasionally, and then there's a sound.

A sound I know even though I've never heard it before - Perri's laugh. Maybe it's because her voice haunts me, soft but strong, smooth but direct, that my mind already imagined her laugh. It was pretty accurate.

When I find her again she's talking to Harrison, just the two of them, while eating a lemon bar. My favorite. There's powdered sugar in the corner of her mouth and she knows, and keeps trying to lick it off. I start walking over to them, and move faster when Harrison's hand starts to lift. As if he's going to touch her.

"Hey." I step up and put my arm around Perri, pulling her into my side. She looks up at me with a tight smile. "You've got something there, *mo dhuine ar bith.*" I reach up and brush the sugar away with my thumb, then bring it to my mouth.

Perri watches me, mouth slightly open, and I see her tongue chase the spot where the powder was. Like she's trying to find the taste my skin left behind on her mouth. My cock is getting hard paying too much attention to her mouth and tongue, and how they'd look licking me. She's so fucking perfect.

"Harrison, I see you've met my girl, Perri."

Harrison grins and it's full of mischief. "Indeed. Your application was very exciting. I think Zadie is going to love having you."

Perri blushes because she can hear the truth in his words. "Thank you. I've always wanted to work here."

"Welcome aboard." He offers her his hand and she takes it, and I sneer when his other hand comes up so they both wrap around hers. With a nod he lets her go and returns to mingling, but I can see him making his way toward the door. He'll leave quietly.

"You good?" I check.

Perri gives me a small smile. "Yes. These lemon bars are good."

She takes another bite, powdered sugar dusting her lips, and I can't look away as she licks them. The way her tongue slides along the dark pink flesh, leaving a little bit of a shine behind as the sugar disappears.

My thoughts are absolutely filthy, and I can't control the way my hand that still rests on her hip squeezes tightly. When my eyes finally make it back to hers I glare because she knew exactly what she was doing.

Game on, little nobody.

I wrap my hand around her wrist, and move it toward my mouth. I take a bite of the lemon square as I look into her eyes. We're so close that I can see her eyes dilate. I lick my lips, slow and lascivious. She drops her gaze to watch my mouth.

I let her wrist go with a small squeeze, and walk away.

Harrison pops out the door and I follow him.

Once we're back in the elevator, he bursts out laughing. "You are so fucked."

"I don't know what you're talking about."

"There isn't a woman who exists that's more your type, it's as if you made her yourself. I give you...3 weeks at best before your vow of celibacy and loneliness goes out the window."

"I'm her fucking captor, Harrison. Regardless of attraction she's not going to fuck me, she's never going to love me, and I'm never going to love her. That's not my life." Suddenly I feel hot and my skin is tight all over. It's hell.

"Stranger things have happened."

When we get to our floor, I leave him without another word.

12

Perri

We fall easily into a routine over the next month, and the domesticity makes me nervous. Neo is still distant and snarly as ever, but I know it's a front. I know because every night he gets into bed beside me. Every day he takes the lunch I made him with a thank you. He never gets less uncomfortable about it.

He doesn't know how to accept someone else taking care of him, and if that's how I get under his skin...so be it.

We get home, I make dinner, whoever is at the warehouse that night joins us. Benji has started calling me mom, even more often once he realized how much it bothered Neo. I take care of them. I can't help myself. I've never had the means to take care of anyone else before and it's kind of addictive.

They talk to me about the women and men in their lives, their families, funny stories about each other and Neo. I'm the arbiter of common sense as well like yes, Thomas, you need to go to the dentist when it's been two years, and no, Leander, surprising the woman you like by breaking in and hiding in the backseat of her car is not a good idea. They make me laugh. They make me feel like I belong out here.

Neo let me order more stools for the island and I'm thinking about convincing him to buy an actual table. There's room for it. But that feels too...settled. That's more than finding a place for my things while I stay here, that's moving in.

I make the mistake of telling Leander we should get a table when he ends up being exiled to the couch one night when we run out of seats. Lasagna night is popular.

Three days later, there's a table and chairs waiting when I get back to the loft.

I have to hold back tears when my eyes meet Neo's. He gives me that one-sided lift of his mouth that means he wants to smile but he won't.

We stand side by side at the head of the table and watch our men eat. Wilder, Leander, Benji, and Thomas feel like mine to watch out for, the same way Neo watches out for them. We're friends in a way I've never had friends before, and it's because despite my inability to leave, we're on even ground somehow.

I'm content here in a way that I didn't expect. There's so many decisions I don't have to make or think about because they're being made for me. Everything in me should be rebelling at the idea of control being taken away, but it's kind of a relief. After doing it all by myself for so long it's nice to be looked after, even in this odd, dark way.

Cassandra calls to check in but I avoid seeing her because I don't think I'll be able to lie. About anything about Neo. Am I here by choice? Nope. Do I still want to hump his leg? Yeah. He gets more handsome to me every day and I hate it. I'm constantly walking around with a pit in my stomach, trying to brace myself against the next time I see him. Every single time it's like a shock to my system. A jolt of awareness of him.

It doesn't help that I barely get any chances to get myself off. I've never been a fan of getting off in the shower because I overheat, so even when I try I never quite get there. The bedroom is monitored by two cameras and I'm not sure how well they see in the dark. Not to mention Neo got rid of my vibrators when he packed my stuff.

Yeah, Benji let that detail slip. That Neo himself packed up my apartment. The excuse was that he wanted to search through my stuff to make sure I was who I said I was and didn't have anything dangerous. Sometimes when I'm extra frustrated I want to snap at him and ask how exactly my vibrators were dangerous - to his ego? To my peace?

Neo leaves after dinner, every night, after all of them do the dishes. I don't know what he's doing when he leaves like that, or if he even leaves the warehouse. But he definitely leaves the loft.

Sometime in the night, I feel him come to bed.

And that's how nearly every day goes.

Until it doesn't.

First, because Neo tells me he's going to be late because he has to go to an event with Andre and Nim. I've seen Andre around the building a few times but I haven't seen Nim since the night everything went down. Neo's also very guarded about me being around Harrison, and it almost feels like jealousy.

After dinner, Neo leaves. He's dressed in a black suit with a black dress shirt, no tie, and a nice watch. It makes him look delicious, but still unobtrusive. He won't stand out wherever he's going with them.

I follow my usual evening routine.

I'm scared out of my sleep by the front door slamming loudly. I leap out of bed and grab the nearest thing that feels like a weapon, which ends up being one of Neo's shoes. He's got huge ass feet so his boots are heavy as hell. I step out into the living room, boot raised over my shoulder, ready to swing.

Neo's on his knees on the floor, one hand holding himself up and the other holding onto his stomach. When I drop the boot with a loud thunk and run toward him, he looks up and I can't stop myself from crying out.

"What happened?" There are small scratches across his face, some deeper than others, some dripping blood. There's a larger wound on his stomach if the blood stain on the undershirt he's still wearing is any indication.

I slide over to him and put the arm of his uninjured side over my shoulder. We lift up together and start walking toward the bathroom.

Neo looks down at his lone boot sitting on the floor. "Really?"

"What else was I supposed to use?"

He laughs and then groans.

"What happened, Neo?" I ask softly.

"Bomb in Nim's car. Blew up when I was going to get it, probably early. This is mostly from shrapnel."

"Your face sure, but what about your side?"

"Just help me clean up and I'll take care of it tomorrow. Right now, I want to sleep."

"Okay." He's been around all this his whole life so I'm not going to fight him. I get us into the bathroom and help him slide up onto the bathroom counter. He directs me to the first aid supplies, which is an absolutely giant plastic briefcase under his side of the sink. Apparently I haven't been nosy enough if I didn't know this was there.

I take the scissors from the kit and move toward Neo.

"Whoa, what are you doing?"

"Cutting off your shirt."

"I can take it off," he scoffs, but when he goes to lift his left arm he groans, ineffectively smothering the sound.

"That's what I thought." I step between his knees and cut the shirt at the sleeves. My hands trail over his arms, the curves of his biceps and triceps, my fingers tingling from the texture of his warm, silken skin. I catch myself and move to cut up the front of his shirt.

This exposes even more of him, and even bruised and bleeding my mouth waters. His smooth, defined pectoral and abdominal muscles, the soft, dark dusting of hair on his chest and stomach, and I don't even stop myself from dragging my hands over him as I push the shirt away.

There's a long gash along the right side of his body, and it's already turning purple around the edges of the cut, bruising fiercely. I push him back so he's leaning against the mirror and focus on the wound.

I get a clean cloth and warm water, not looking at him as I start to wash it and clear away the dried blood and grit. I take an alcohol pad and don't give him a warning that he doesn't need that the pad is going to sting. He knows.

Neo hisses, but doesn't move. When I think I've disinfected the area well enough, three pads later, I grab a large bandage and place it over the wound. When I'm done taping it, that's when I finally look at Neo. He's looking down at me, eyes lowered. It's a penetrating, infuriating gaze. Like he's waiting for me to do something I shouldn't.

I shiver, my nipples getting hard and my pussy clenching around nothing.

"Who's doing this?" I ask, barely a whisper.

"We don't know. There's too many choices."

"I'm sorry. It must be hard having people you care about in danger like this."

He's silent a long time. "We've been through a lot together, Nim, Harrison, and me, and the only good parents in the bunch were Harrison's. Andre and Colleen were...dream parents. They took us in, they gave me opportunities, and Harrison and Nim never left me out. It would've been so easy for them to do that - at the end of the day, I'm the help."

I scoff before I can stop myself, and hear him let out a sharp snort.

"Badass help, but still the help. There were plenty of times when I'm sure to all of them I was more trouble than I'm worth."

"Don't talk to me about your worth," I grumble, trying to hold it in.

I use a fresh cloth to start cleaning the cuts on his face. My hand rests on his neck, thumb under his chin to gently direct him where I need him to go. His face isn't as bad as I first thought, a lot of it dirt rather than blood.

"I owe everything I am to them."

I start dabbing the alcohol pad across the scratches.

"No," I disagree softly. "This is who you are, they made sure you had the chance. It's not the same."

Neo reaches up and grabs my chin, tilting me down to focus on his eyes.

Both of my hands are on his face, and I suck in a breath when his other hand slides to my hip.

"And who would you be if given the chance, *mo dhuine ar bith?*"

"I got my chance. I'm an accountant," I say with sass, breath hitching because he's still holding me. "What language is that?"

"Gaelic. My mother was an immigrant, sent to America to get married and have a better life, taught me enough until she died." Silence passes as our eyes search each other, as I find myself swaying closer to him. Close enough that I can feel his breath on me, once again smelling bizarrely good. "Aren't you going to ask me what it means?"

"No." I shake my head and his hand slides from my chin to cupping my cheek. "But don't stop saying it either."

I gasp when he runs his thumb over my lips and my eyes fall closed, my head swaying as I give in to the way that he makes me feel.

My head drops forward and I open my eyes. At first I can't look away from his heaving chest, but then I notice the press of his erection against his dress pants. Damn. I seem to affect him as much as he affects me, and the blatant evidence of it is so dangerous.

I cannot want this man.

I will need to be able to walk away from him someday.

I've never been in love. Love got in the way of my goal of survival and success. There was never the time or the energy for another person. I hooked up to scratch an itch and fulfill an urge, sometimes with the same person on a regular basis. It was self-care, like keeping my gym schedule or not having caffeine after 2:00 P.M.

Now, I have all the time in the world to be in love and be successful. I have all of the vulnerability inside of me that could so easily be exploited. The sense of belonging I get from being with him, as part of this little family within Zastrow, is unlike anything I ever knew existed, let alone that I wanted to feel it. Even with my own friends, who I love and love me, there was always something that kept it from being family. I feel...safe and wanted here. Leaving them is already going to break my heart irreparably.

Losing Neo? Especially if I really got the chance to have him? Unsurvivable. We are so alike it's like fate, and I hate that this is the position we are in. This temporary, fake, fucked up situation where our real attraction is getting in the way of the boundaries we've both set.

I know that if I tried to kiss him right now, he wouldn't stop me. He'd kiss me back, and I'd get to know if he tastes as good as I think he will, until one of us comes to our senses and pushes the other away, or until I'm dripping come on his bathroom floor, a piece of me forever left behind with him.

Giving myself an inch, I move my hand so my thumb can trail over a line of unblemished cheek.

"I'm glad you're okay," I whisper, then squeeze my eyes shut and take a step back. Neo's arms drop and so do mine. "Let's get you into bed."

13

Neo

Perri maneuvers me into bed, and I don't fight her. Thomas is in charge of investigating the explosion because he's got the background in it, and I'm no use to anyone when I'm in this much pain.

In the past, I would've eventually made my way to the bathroom and cleaned up my wounds. It went much faster with Perri here to help. I wish she wasn't so fucking kind in addition to being beautiful. I wish I didn't have to watch my closest men fall a little bit in love with her with every dinner full of laughter and jokes. I wish it didn't feel like a complete family when she was at the table.

The room is spinning around me and my head and ears are still ringing from the blast.

I didn't even suspect it.

Nim and Andre had done their mingling, and she was going to leave a little earlier than him. He had a late night deal to work out, and she wasn't that fond of this group of people. While they'd arrived in the same car, I'd arranged for a second car to arrive and wait. The driver hadn't responded to my initial text but I knew that sometimes the signal wasn't good enough down in the garage.

I left them with their usual detail and headed out of the party and downstairs.

My thoughts were distracted, more than they should have been. Norman

Warren was still being difficult in contract negotiation and challenging some of our conditions regarding environmental standards improving in the first five years. It only made him look good in the end, and would also open up new avenues for revenue.

Not for the first time, or the tenth, I wished Seth Warren was around to work with us on this. He was in charge of almost everything already, and I had no idea why Norman was keeping him out of it.

He kept talking about taking the deal further, making it stronger, but when pressed, wouldn't explain what he meant by that. Everything about Warren Media's stability and growth checked out - he didn't need us in the same way that we needed him. It was confusing and frustrating to be going around in circles for a deal that should've been easy.

Cassandra Warren checked out, too, which had me loosening up on checking her and Perri's communication. It was amusing to see what Perri would say about me in their texts though, even if it was a lie.

I should've known something was wrong when I stepped out of the stairway and didn't immediately see the driver sitting in the car.

Two steps, and I was hit by a wave of heat that knocked me on my ass and had me slamming into the wall. Car alarms were blaring but the sound was dimmed by the ringing in my ears. I felt the blood coming from the wound in my side before I felt the pain of the injury.

My first priority was getting out before anyone arrived.

Luckily, my phone was cracked but not broken. I stumbled out onto the street and called Wilder, who was upstairs. I told him what happened, that I was getting the hell out of dodge, and to get Andre and Nim out ASAP. With our safety plan activated, and having taken myself out of it, I could focus on my own body.

I made it to my own car and left, probably unsafe to drive, and the next thing I remembered were Perri's hands on me.

It cleared my head and made me focus.

I almost kissed her in the bathroom. With my guard lowered like this, I couldn't fight the way I felt about her. The way she made my life feel more whole and complete.

The deep well of hatred I felt for myself and my feelings for her took over, and the darkness followed me into sleep.

I woke up shouting, the last moment of my nightmare was the wave of the explosion slamming into my body. Pain shoots through my abdomen and I groan.

"Neo," Perri's soft voice comes out of the dark, and I feel her hand on my chest. "It was a dream. Go back to sleep. Do you need pain meds?"

"No," I rasp. "No, no, I'm sorry."

"It's okay." Her hand pushes me back down onto the bed. "It's okay."

We both fade away into sleep, her hand over my heart.

14

Perri

Despite the attack, Nim is unstoppable.

She walks up to my cubicle at Zastrow on a Friday morning. Her long auburn hair is streaming behind her and she's wearing a neon pink jumpsuit that is perfect for the summer heat but not so much for the icy cold of an office building. Our eyes all get pulled to her even though she doesn't make a sound. It's like a ripple goes through the floor and then I'm turning to look at her.

When her eyes meet mine she grins, and I'm surprised to see she's coming for me. Nim slides to a stop at the opening to my little office space which is covered in organized piles of different ventures I've been assigned to assess.

So far I've stayed ahead of the deadlines on everything handed my way, but not so early that I can't give myself some flexibility in the future. I'm managing expectations to keep control.

Her smile is big, but not a creepy one like that security woman downstairs. Anytime I've seen her since she's given me the eye and I've given her my best sweet shy smile. The one that makes people backpedal when they want to be mean to me.

"Hi. We're going out tonight."

"Oh," I scramble for a response. "I have to ask Neo."

Nim waves that away. "I'm his boss, I'm going to tell him that you're both coming out. Since my last outings both got interrupted, not your fault, babe,

I am in need of another one. Plus, it'll get the idea out that you're inner circle and not to mess with you."

"I'm not," I start but she waves that away too, effectively silencing me.

"I'll let Neo know what time to meet us at the club." Nim leans in close to me and whispers, "Let's put on a good show."

She pinches my cheek but it doesn't feel at all condescending, and then walks away. Word must've gotten to the offices that she was here because both my boss Adam and his boss Zadie are near the elevators. Nim waves Adam off but chats with Zadie for a moment before getting in the elevator.

That was quite the second first impression.

For the first time, I text Neo. I've done a great job not needing him, not getting in to trouble, denying any impulse I have to find out where he is or how he is, or when he's coming back to the loft. I've worked very hard not to need him, and not to impose. Earning his trust is about being reliable, and showing that I keep my word.

Me: *Nim said we're going out tonight.*

Neo: *You don't have to go.*

Me: *She meant me and you, and said she's your boss so you have to.*

Neo: *Shit. We don't have to stay long.*

Me: *Okay.*

Looks like I don't have a choice.

15

Perri

Neo is waiting for me in the kitchen, leaning against the island, when I come through the curtain from the bedroom. He looks sinfully delicious in black pants and a gray shirt, and his biceps are nearly busting open the sleeves.

When he hears me coming he looks my way and then immediately stands at attention. His eyes are stuck on me, roving up and down my body in a way that makes me clench everywhere. I decided to wear a pale pink dress with a strapless top and a swing skirt. It makes me look curvy as heck but I think that's what Neo likes about me.

It also has pockets.

So I have my ID, card, and phone tucked in them, and don't have to worry about carrying around a purse.

"Let's get going." His voice is a low rasp and he holds out his hand for me. I'm wearing flats but appreciate the gesture all the same.

For some reason I feel the need to fill the silence on the drive, which never happens to me, but I think I'm scared of what tonight is going to be like. Neo hears all about my job and my coworkers, a little bit about some of the ventures that I'm analyzing, and how I have far too much fun with running the numbers.

"So it's a good fit?" Neo asks, pulling into a parking garage.

"It is."

He nods at that, and then gets out of the car. Its still odd to wait for him to open my door and help me out, and then he doesn't let go of my hand. Even holding me softly and definitely not on duty tonight, his head is on a swivel, he's on edge, and ready to step into action at any moment.

We're about to walk around the corner to the club when he grabs me, his big hand pressed against my stomach and yanking my body back into his. I feel his breath on my ear and my eyes close as he speaks.

"You're mine tonight, *mo dhuine ar bith,* and you need to convince anyone watching that it's true. That you're obsessed with me. Head over heels in love. Willing to do anything for me. Devoted to me."

"What about you?" I somehow manage to say even though it feels like every nerve in my body is awake in a way it never has been before.

"What about me?"

"Will they think you feel the same?"

"Do you want them to?" There's genuine curiosity in his voice.

"I want it to look like I would never betray you because you'd never give me a reason to, Neo. Because you give me back everything I give to you."

"Done, princess." Neo presses a quick kiss to my neck, and then pulls me under his arm to walk toward the door of the club. I've never been here before. There's a symbol above the door but I don't know what it means. Neo greets the bouncer.

"They inside?"

"Straight on in, my friend."

Neo and the bouncer shake hands and I'm fairly certain Neo gives him cash. We head into the throbbing noise and heat of the club, and he doesn't let me go. Instead, he holds me closer and pulls me into him so he can speak and be heard.

"I know all the bouncers and I'm nice to them so they'll be nice to me. But that guy, goes by Echo, I've been trying to steal him for Zastrow for years."

"You aren't asking nice enough," I tease, and run a hand across his chest. Time to be as possessive as I want to be. Nim told me to put on a show, and I intend to follow through.

We get through the crowd and past the staff to a slightly raised VIP seating area and bar. Neo signals to the bartender and then heads to the left where

Nim is basically her own source of light in the corner, surrounded by other glittering people. When she sees Neo and I, she waves excitedly and calls our names.

Neo takes a seat on the edge of the area and pulls me down to perch on his lap. She introduces us around and I barely take in anything because Neo has put his hand under my dress to grip my thigh. I shift, stupidly turned on from such a small touch, but I'm also insanely pent up and I already know tonight is going to make me combust.

Neo is talking to the guy next to us, looking bored but polite, and his thumb works back and forth on my skin. It takes everything in me not to jump when he leans forward and places a lingering kiss to my shoulder. If he's going to give then I'm going to take, and maybe drive him a little crazy in return.

I turn so that my arm is around his shoulders and I start stroking his nape, teasing his short cut hair and tickling the back of his neck. I pretend to be very interested in the conversation he's having with this finance bro about security systems. From the tone of his voice, the guy should know that Neo is humoring him, but he doesn't pick up on it at all.

Nim laughs loudly and I look over to where she's having fun with her friends. I do feel bad that I ruined her night. She's the kind of person I don't understand and I don't know how to be, but I can also tell from the way Neo talks about her and why she got married that things in her life weren't great. I remember seeing a younger version of her on the news during the coverage of her mom's funeral.

I get caught up in my own head, still teasing Neo with my hands, the press of my breasts against his chest, and every once and awhile I slide my ass along his crotch. I'm so shameless right now it's tempting to grind on him until I orgasm in front of all these people. I'm going to get all worked up with no outlet, but it might be worth it to make him feel half of the sexual frustration that I do.

Nim stands up and her girl friends follow. She reaches a hand out to me and I go, leaving Neo without a glance back as we move toward the dance floor. Dancing isn't normally for me but the group of women around me are so extra that I don't have to do much. I swing my hips and lift my hands and

I give Nim the smile she demands of me when she dances over and holds my hands.

We swing together, smiling, and she leans close. "He likes you."

"That's not what this is."

"Doesn't matter," she shakes her head and woos, and the group follows suit. "He swore off women. No relationships, totally celibate, and then BAM, you." I can smell the alcohol on her breath, and I wonder if she would tell me this if she was sober.

"Harrison was so excited after he met you. Like you were made for him."

It makes all of this more confusing. My heart clenches in my chest and I feel lightheaded and sweaty. Apparently it's not just our dynamic that's keeping distance between me and Neo, at some point he was hurt enough, and tired enough of hurting, that he decided to isolate himself.

It makes me feel guilty for wanting him. For teasing or pushing him. Even if I was being unintentionally disrespectful...if he wants to be celibate, then I should try and respect it.

I open my mouth to ask her something but feel hands on my hips. For a second I think it's Neo, but then I see the look on Nim's face and feel a sweaty body pushed against my bare back. Nim looks both disgusted and entertained.

With all my strength I push the hands off me and step away toward my group. Nim grabs my hand and tugs me to her. Just as I'm turning around to give grabby hands a piece of my mind, Neo is there.

I step to his back and wrap both my arms around one of his.

He's leaning over saying something to the guy that I can't hear, but even in the flickering lights I can see grabby hands get pale. He holds up his hands in surrender and backs away, then straight up runs for it.

Neo turns to me and takes my face in his hands, then slides them down my neck and back until he's got a hold on my hips. Holding the same place as the guy did, replacing the touch with his own. He leans over me, forehead pressed to mine, our eyes locked. In any other situation, I'd be tilting my head to kiss him. To devour him in gratitude.

I have to sell it, right?

I slide my hands from Neo's biceps up to his jaw, and pull his head down as I raise up onto my toes. Our lips crash together and I inhale, letting my mouth drop open. Neo takes the opportunity and slides his tongue inside to meet mine.

There's no way he misses the moan tasting him causes to slide out of me. He tastes so good. Something about his mouth tastes fresh without being minty, and I wrap my arms around his neck. I'm not expecting it when he pulls back, lifting me up and wrapping his arms around me in return. Our bodies are pressed together and I want to do exactly this, but naked.

We snap out of it when Nim and her friends start whooping.

Neo slowly lets me drop to the floor and puts space between us, although he doesn't let go of my hips.

When I meet his eyes, they're guarded again. He's not letting me see him, but at least now I understand why.

"Do you want to go?"

I nod. I've had enough of people and noise, and more than enough of putting on a show even if I enjoyed it. Neo looks over my shoulder at Nim, and I'm assuming we get permission because he tucks me under his arm and guides me out of the club.

16

Neo

Being able to casually touch Perri was a special kind of torture. My arm around her. My hand on her thigh, the small of her back, her neck, her cheek. Tasting her, even the little bit I allowed, before we went to the doors of the club. She smelled amazing, and when I licked my lips there was a hint of her there that will haunt me. It was almost enough to distract me.

But the second we stepped up to Echo, I felt the eyes on us. I saw the cameras. They'd probably already photographed Nim and her friends, and I was sure a photo of Perri and I would join the cycle of speculation about tonight.

The first year after Nim and Andre got married, I was her personal security guard. Even though I acted professionally while on duty, she was still my friend, and we still hung out when I wasn't working. That set off a fire storm of allegations that her and I were having an affair. It put a strain on Nim, and it interfered with any relationship that I tried to have.

There was always a little seed of doubt in their minds that I was fucking Nim, or dealing with media allegations that any relationship I had was a cover for being with my boss's wife.

It didn't matter that there was also nearly two decades worth of a paper trail of our entirely friendly friendship.

Any time I'm out with her, even casually, even if we barely acknowledge each other, somehow the idea that I'm her on and off, or previous, affair partner comes up. It's why I'm being overly touchy with Perri. When I'd bring my real girlfriends out in the past I wouldn't lay on the PDA like this. It's not my style. There'd be hand holding. Letting her sit on my lap, sure, but mostly it would be together but distant.

The twist of it all is that I like being this way with Perri. I let myself fall into the illusion and I know without a doubt that I'd want to have a possessive hand on her all the time. My hand wrapped around her thigh is the bare minimum of what I'd be doing if she was really mine.

In addition to touching her, I'd have my mouth on her whenever I could. Kissing her shoulder, her neck, her knuckles when she leaves me to dance with Nim and her friends. I'd want to mark her, so that any man that would dare to look would immediately see Perri was owned and protected.

The need to bite into her skin and leave the imprint of my teeth on her neck is harder to fight than it should be.

When they leave to dance, I watch.

I watch her relax and have fun, and I see the show drop a little bit. Nim genuinely likes Perri, and I like seeing Nim with a quality person. I don't think Perri would ever hurt her on purpose. Under normal circumstances, I do believe we can trust Perri and I don't believe she'd betray the secrets that she knows.

What I need to do is find a way to test her under abnormal circumstances. I'll have to think on that.

"Makes you glad to be a man," a voice interrupts my thoughts. I look over at the guy who was talking to me, and see him staring at the group of women we came with as they dance.

"To witness that level of beauty," he continues. "To know that they did that for you."

"They didn't do shit for you, or me, my man. They did that for them, and the fact that you don't see it is why you'll be going home alone tonight." I finish my drink, which has barely any alcohol in it, just like I wanted. The bartenders here know they give me drinks for show with barely a hit. "By the way, you're completely wrong about motion sensors being superior to sound, and I could rob your place undetected in less than 15 minutes. Hire a professional because you aren't one."

I leave him with his mouth hanging open and head toward my woman.

Mine for right now. For tonight.

Before I can get to her, another guy steps up behind her and grabs her waist, yanking her back into him. Perri's body language screams discomfort and she yanks herself away from the guy.

I'm there before she needs to do more and I step in between them.

I lean over the man, who already looks apprehensive.

"It takes so little energy for you to ask a woman to dance. To get permission to touch her. If I ever find out you grabbed a woman like that again, I don't care how drunk you are, I will find you and I will cut off your fucking hands, and then make you eat them. Get the fuck out of here."

Even under the flickering lights, the guy's face pales because he can see and hear how serious I am. I would absolutely do what I threatened, especially if he tries to touch any of the women under my protection. I'd let them watch if they wanted. If they could handle it.

Perri wouldn't want to, and she couldn't handle it.

I turn to her and don't like the rattled look on her face.

I want it to look like I would never betray you because you'd never give me a reason to, Neo. Because you give me back everything I give to you.

It's not a conscious thought when I reach out and try to reassure her with my touch. There's a need inside me to check on her, comfort her, and when I remember what she asked of me it's too damn easy to lean into it. To indulge in the feel of her skin, to grab her hips and overpower another man's unwanted touch. To get a hint of what it would be like to sink my fingers into her thick hips, bury all of myself inside her, and hold onto her after.

My head falls forward until it meets hers. Perri is staring up at me with a look I wish was real.

I'm not expecting it when her head tilts and she pulls my mouth to hers.

I'm not expecting the way she lets me in without hesitation, and I can't hold back from tasting her. All that is Perri explodes on my tongue, burning into me and fundamentally altering my DNA. I would happily stand here and kiss her until we died. Until the world crumbled around us.

When the kiss breaks, I know it's time to go.

Over her shoulder, I make eye contact with Nim.

In this moment, I wish she didn't know me so well. I wish she didn't know my history and my heartbreaks, the dreams I've given up on, and the hurts that are barely healed. I wish she couldn't see immediately that this was real, and that we didn't consider that when I was told to make Perri love us, we were running the risk of loving her back.

Nim nods, giving me permission to leave.

The ride back is quiet, but not tense. Perri leans back against the seat and closes her eyes. She seems relaxed. I, on the other hand, am struggling to ignore my throbbing erection now that I'm alone with her and can still taste her tongue in my mouth.

The harder I fight the desire to pull the car over and fuck her, the more worked up I get. By the time we pull up to the compound and I get us to the warehouse, I'm breathing hard. I need to get away from her or I'm going to cross a line that we'll both regret.

Perri gets out without a word and I wait until she's inside before driving off.

I don't go far.

The second I put the car in park I pull up the cameras on the apartment and watch her. Her clothes are a trail from the curtained entry to the bed, and I watch as her panties drop and she crawls up and moves onto her back before spreading her legs open.

I've never caught Perri masturbating on camera.

Without taking my eyes entirely off the screen, I drive back to the warehouse. I walk inside, quick and quiet, and enter the loft.

If I thought she'd hear the beep of the door, I was wrong, or she's choosing to ignore it. Perri's breathy sounds reach me immediately. With care, I walk closer to the bedroom area.

I lose all rational power over myself when I hear her moan my name.

17

Perri

Neo drops me off at the warehouse, waits for me to get inside the building, and then I hear the squeal of his tires as he drives off. He hasn't done that since the early days when he'd leave and only come back for dinner when one of the guys texted him.

Damn it. I've really upset him. I shouldn't have kissed him. The drive here was so intense.

My skin is tight and itchy.

I'm so worked up, so miserable, and so confused. I should not want this man. The fact that Neo makes me play the part, that he can be such a doting and possessive fake boyfriend, all while holding me hostage outside of business hours is beyond complicated. He's not a bad man. He's a man who does bad things for what he believes to be the right reasons.

Which is part of the most important truth that I need to beat into my own head: he doesn't want me here.

He might *want* me, physically, but it's not like I'm here by choice or even by his idea. Andre told him to keep me here - I've gotten that much out of the guys when they tease him about this. Neo is following orders, period.

At the end of the day, I will never be more than a job to him.

Knowing what I know now, that will never be enough for me. If I experience another side of him I'll want to keep it. I will want to keep everything that he gives me. I know that it's beyond fucked up to want him, but I'm honestly not sure I can care. My life hasn't been normal. I was benignly neglected, orphaned, then openly hurt and hated.

I've spent my entire life running toward the next thing that meant survival and marked success. This situation with Neo has taken so many of my little day to day worries off my shoulders that for the first time in my life I think I'm standing still. I'm in stasis, waiting for the blade to fall or to be given my reprieve. Either he trusts me and lets me go, or something goes horribly wrong and I'm dead.

I want him so badly.

I want him so much that my skin feels like it's on fire.

I stumble into the bedroom and leave my shoes as I go. My dress goes next, dropping to the floor to pool at my feet. I can't stop. If I don't relieve this need I'm not going to be able to function anymore.

My panties drop down, and I crawl onto the bed and roll over onto my back. Touching my clit makes me hiss and my hips rise, and I'm already soaked. I grasp my own breast through my bra, squeezing and massaging as I work myself up to the edge. Even masturbating I make myself work for it, taunting my clit with light touches and rolling my hips.

In my mind, it's Neo that's touching me. His big rough fingers teasing me, his raspy voice telling me to beg for it, to tell him what I want and admit that I'm this messed up over him. That I dream about him and wake up wet, right by his side, his presence all the aphrodisiac I need.

"Neo," I moan, and slide two fingers inside myself. The noise is loud in the quiet and it makes me cry out, imagining the mess I'm making and wishing he was here to clean it up with his mouth. I want to feel that short buzzed hair beneath my hands as I press him into my pussy. I want the heat of his wet tongue. I want to kiss him and taste myself on that utterly delicious mouth.

There's a noise in the room and my eyes snap open.

Automatically, I jolt and my fingers curl, pressing into my g-spot. I cry out and can't stop when I register a second later that it's Neo.

I'm mesmerized as I watch him kneel at the end of the bed. He slides his hands up until they're cupped around my ass, and I cry out and then gasp when he yanks me to the end.

"We're going to pretend this was a dream, okay princess?"

"Neo, please," is all I can say. I can't get anything else out as I feel his shoulders press my thighs apart. You couldn't pay me enough to close my eyes as I watch his head lower to my aching, desperate pussy. He doesn't look at me. He's focused on my core like it's the best thing he's ever seen.

I feel his breath and then ecstasy when he takes a long lap of my slit with the flat of his tongue. He groans and presses more firmly against me, diving his tongue between my lower lips and lapping up the pleasure he unknowingly caused.

Neo eats my pussy like he's been starving, and he uses his hands to tilt my hips up slightly so he can fuck me with his tongue. I do what I wanted and skate my fingers across his hair, my nails dragging along his scalp.

"Keep doing that," he tells me, finally looking up and meeting my eyes. "Don't stop."

One of Neo's hands moves down and I let out a sound I've never heard from myself before when he slides his fingers inside me. His tongue moves quickly on my clit but his fingers press deep and slow inside me. The contrast works me up even more and I flex my hands, doing what he wanted while he breaks me apart.

In this moment, I would rather die than be told to leave. I would give up my freedom and be locked like a princess in a tower, guarded by my growly dragon, than ever see the sky again if this is what he would do to me. If I could belong to him wholly.

I've always been protective of myself. I don't let people in.

Neo never gave me the choice. There was no letting. There was only ever going to be conquering.

He's conquering me right now, and tomorrow I'm going to have to pretend like it never happened.

"I'm coming," I cry out, pressing tight to the back of his head, squeezing his fingers as they press deep. Neo sucks on my clit and I scream, the orgasm rippling through my entire body. The vibration of his groan against my core adds to the intensity of it. All of the air leaves me, I'm gasping, clinging to consciousness, it's so pent up and it's been so long since I've come. Not that

I've ever come like this in my life.

"Neo," I gasp and chant a few more times before I collapse back onto the bed.

He licks softly, then places gentle, tickling kisses to the inside of each of my thighs.

I force myself into a sitting position and stop him from standing because even if he would hate it, I know him. He's going to shut down and step away and I'm not going to let him. If this is the moment, I want us both to get pleasure from it.

My fingers wrap around his shirt collar and I pull his mouth to mine. Even on his knees he's still taller than me. He tastes like me, but still like him too. I moan into his mouth, and when he doesn't fight back I slide my hands up so I can wrap myself around his neck. I squeeze his torso with my thighs and draw him closer.

He lets me have him, only stopping when I slide a hand down to touch him.

"No, Perri." His voice is serious but strained. "There's no need."

"What?" I ask between desperate kisses.

"I came when you did," he mumbles against my mouth. I gasp, insanely aroused by that revelation, and the confirmation that at least our bodies are equally as untamed about each other. Saying it seems to break something in Neo, because his hands slide from resting on my thighs to squeeze my hips, then up, cupping my breasts where I think he'll stop, but he doesn't. Neo moves until he's cradling my face, angling me to take the kiss deeper, and I feel him inhale deeply as if he's trying to absorb me.

Neo breaks the kiss, breathing hard, and holds me to him.

"Get ready for bed, princess." He presses his lips to my forehead. "Sweet dreams."

I feel loss and disappointment when he stands and leaves me, but not rejection.

He wants me.

I can live on that validation, and the power of this orgasm, for a long, long time. Even if I know I can never have him again.

18

Neo

Perri does what I ask, and doesn't bring up when I crossed the line with her. She's careful not to touch me, and sometimes she looks at me with something like pity in her eyes.

I'm on duty tonight with Andre and Nim. They're having dinner at a restaurant that charges astronomical amounts of money for tiny bits of food.

The two of them are talking softly, and I've picked up on their pattern for showing how happy their marriage is - how many minutes pass between him taking her hand and stroking her knuckles. When she reaches out to cup his face across their tiny table. Even Nim running her foot along Andre's calf, implying arousal. It's all a show because I know tonight after dinner she's going to the Long Island estate for the weekend and he'll be in the penthouse for a morning meeting with an international investor. But no one will know that until we make our next stop, when they get into separate cars.

Although Nim loves to tease us about her love life with Andre, we know she exaggerates to gross us out. They don't often spend the night in the same residence unless it's a special occasion or if Nim's dad starts sniffing around their relationship. Andre is protective of her and he loves her as a woman, but he'll never love anyone else like he loved Colleen.

It irritates me that when contemplating a love like that I think of Perri. Someday she'll love someone that way, and she'll find someone who can return that level of adoration. My gut wants to say that it's me and she's mine, but my mind and heart know better. I'm not worthy or capable of being what she needs. What she deserves, once I feel it's time to let her go.

It's been six weeks but there's part of me that still doesn't trust her, no matter how she makes me feel. Feelings aren't facts and the way she makes me feel makes me trust her less.

She makes me breathe. She makes me rest. When I'm with her, everything inside me slows down. I take better care of myself. I eat lunch and dinner, I sleep in my bed, I listen to my men and sometimes I laugh. I've even been known to smile with her sometimes.

On the flip side, she also makes my blood run hot and my heart feel like it's going to pound of out of my chest. I've had to get myself off almost every day she's lived with me to make sure I could control the draw I feel for her. It didn't surprise me one bit when feeling and tasting her come on my mouth made me explode. I was still hard as fuck despite that, and had to jerk myself off one more time before crawling into bed with her.

I want her and I shouldn't. She wants me and she shouldn't.

How is this fucking happening?

Nim's hand slams down on the table and it draws my attention. At first I think she's being emphatic like usual, but Andre's face has me moving from my spot on the wall over to them. Nim's face is getting red and she's wheezing for air.

"Call 911," I shout, knowing that if the restaurant doesn't, my second will.

"Feels...like...allergies..." Nim wheezes out, still holding her throat like it's going to make a difference. I look at her dinner and start pulling it apart - its some kind of layered thing and I feel them before I see them - pine nuts.

I pull Nim out of her chair and lay her down on the floor. She's gasping for breath and starting to claw at her throat.

"Andre, come hold her hands."

He does what I say, kneeling on her other side and holding her hands down as I reach inside my jacket for her epi-pen. I raise her skirt a little but make sure that nothing is visible, and stab the thick needle into her thigh and hit the plunger.

After a few seconds, her body relaxes, and Andre's hold gentles but he doesn't let her go. I can see a rash spreading over her body, even if the epi-pen is going to make sure she can breathe until an EMT gets here. Andre lets one of her hands go and strokes her forehead.

"Slow breaths, in and out," he tells her as he strokes her sweaty forehead. "Slow breaths."

Hayes, the secondary guard tonight at the restaurant comes to me, phone still up to his ear. He looks as worried as I feel.

"A minute out. The manager is waiting at the front to guide them."

"Take that plate. Tell the manager we want to speak to the staff. This wasn't an accident."

Hayes nods and steps away. Nim is exceptionally careful about her allergy. She would have reviewed the menu at the restaurant and had her assistant call to confirm the ingredients so she would have her entire order for the evening planned ahead of time, and could also ask for accommodations if necessary. She's also an excellent tipper, and had relationships with most of their common restaurants so the restaurants didn't mind helping her be careful of her nut allergies.

This was one of their favorite places, and they come here often.

Something like this happening here is...concerning.

But it just hit home for me that people will do anything for money, even the people you think you can trust.

Before getting into the ambulance with Nim, I send Perri a text that Nim was attacked and I won't be home tonight. I call it home, and know even though I want to deny it that it's her home too. I know that if I didn't let her know something was going on, she would worry.

In the past I've let her know through one of the guys, but it feels different now. Her response is quick and makes my stomach flutter, which is stupid.

Perri: *Let me know if you need anything.*

I need the only thing I should never have: her.

Nim is released from the hospital and sent home around 2:00 A.M. and she goes with Andre to the Long Island compound. I activated extra security around them, and head back to the warehouse where our perpetrator is contained. My men began questioning people within minutes and apparently one of the line chefs folded immediately.

The manager and the chef didn't even protest when they dragged him away, and even helped keep staff out of the way when he was loaded into the trunk of Leander's car.

We'll be going back there to dine. The restaurant saw the betrayal as personally as we did, and I know they'll be extra careful with Nim in the future to make up for it.

I look up the stairs toward the loft as I enter the warehouse, thinking of crawling into bed beside Perri. We sleep platonically, even if tension is there, and yet it's still comforting. If you removed how we met, why she's here, it would look like we were a happy couple. Domestic fucking bliss.

She makes me happy and I want to hate it.

By all appearances, she's content with the strange life we lead together.

I walk into the interrogation room. It's nothing like the one where I first kept Perri.

It's a bleak light and a drain in the floor. Zip ties and a metal chair.

The man is crying his eyes out and has already pissed himself; he thought he was bad helping them poison a woman and take their money, but couldn't stand up to the consequences of his choices.

Andre said we aren't killers and he's right, but this man is going to hurt and give me answers. We made a police report at the hospital, and one of my men will drop this son of a bitch off at the station where he'll confess what he did. The police are giving us time to do our own work, and then they'll make sure he finds some kind of justice.

I roll up my sleeves and Wilder locks the door behind him as he steps in with me.

It takes barely an hour to get him to spill everything he knows, which isn't much.

It's especially insulting that Nim could've died for $10k.

It's been almost 48 hours since I've seen Perri. She's been trapped in the loft for the entire weekend and other than a text asking if I needed anything, and feeding the guys dinner, she hasn't bothered me.

For some reason that irritates me. Even though she's being considerate, and helping me prioritize my job, I want her to miss me. I want her to reach out. During my down time, I've watched her on the cameras. Moving around the apartment, cleaning, doing chores, watching TV. Her entire night time skin care routine and the sadness on her face when she looked at the bed she'd sleep in alone for another night.

When I get in on Sunday night, Leander and Benji are sitting at the island talking to her. She's smiling but it looks like a mask, I can see the lines in her forehead. I think I put them there and it's oddly gratifying.

They all look up as I enter.

"Find your own dinner tonight," I grumble, and they both hop up to go without any push back, not even in jest. They know what the last few days have been like. I know that Nim has been texting with Perri, so she's up to date on why I've been gone for days even if she's not going to know what I've been up to during that time. She might notice the bruises on my knuckles but I don't want her thinking about the physical violence that I'm capable of and going back to being afraid of me.

Not right now, anyway. The time to test her will come.

Perri gives me a tight smile and puts the glass baking dish she's holding onto the table. I watch her as she prepares the table, and even scoops some of whatever is in the dish out onto a plate for me. I go to the fridge and grab a beer before collapsing into the seat.

"Thank you," I tell her and I mean it for more than making the food and making my plate. I hope she hears it, because I won't be able to explain it. The words wouldn't come out even if I tried.

"You're welcome." Perri's body relaxes, and she serves herself and starts eating.

"If I would let you go," Perri stills at my words, her fork halfway to her mouth. "Where would you go?"

She starts moving again and takes her bite, chewing thoughtfully.

"Anywhere. I know how to fight to stand on my own two feet."

If there's anything I've learned from this it's that she's stronger than she looks, and more adaptable than any person should have to be. Never once did she fight these circumstances because she knew it was pointless. She went with the current instead of fighting it, and she is finding a place with us. Andre's strategy was right, and Nim's view of her was correct: she wanted a place to belong. We gave it to her, but how can I tell that she feels it? How can I tell that it's enough to choose us over money, and the freedom that would provide her?

"I would want to keep my job at Zastrow. I really do love it."

"Even without this, chances are high you would've earned it."

Perri laughs and it shocks me. "I could've bombed my interview."

I roll my eyes and it makes her laugh again. "Tell me when you've bombed an interview. Ever."

She takes a sip of her water, thinking, then relents. "Fine."

"Why do you like it?" I ask her, genuinely curious.

"I like the creativity. It's not even about the product or the venture, but how they get creative with the funding they want and how to use it, how to be responsible with it, how they expect to turn it into more. Sometimes I can find where they went wrong, but it's even more exciting when I figure out a revenue opportunity they missed. When I can recommend for more instead of less. It keeps my mind going and it's been a long time since something could keep me occupied that way. The day just...flies away. I feel like I've barely said goodbye to you when my alarm goes off to meet you."

"You have to set an alarm?"

"Just in case. I don't like being late."

I shake my head at her and we eat in silence, but it's the usual comfortable one. The bubble that we have when we drive in the car together, the few nights when we sit side by side on the couch and watch something, even the quiet when we're in bed with a solid foot of space between us and waiting for sleep to claim us. It would be so easy to slide those moments into something more.

"I get why people love it there. Why they stay." Perri's voice is quiet and reflective. She's saying it to me as much as she's saying it to herself.

"Andre built his company to reflect who he is; it's hard not to be loyal to him."

She hesitates but then asks, "Why are you?"

"It's a long story."

"I'm not going anywhere." The simple, common response douses me in internal ice water. She's not going anywhere because I won't let her. I need to make sure she understands why it's a choice I took away from her.

"My father worked for Andre. He was head of security at the Long Island estate, that's how I grew up with Harrison. My mom died when I was 8, and my dad slowly fell apart. Andre and Colleen acted more like my parents with every passing day. When I was 13 he started gambling. Couldn't stop. I lost him. Lost my home, my sense of safety, because he was betting but he wasn't winning. Eventually, Andre had to fire him. He had no choice."

"What happened to you?" Perri reaches out like she's going to take my hand and then pulls it back, catching herself.

"Andre let me stay with them, at least during the school year. In the summer I had to go back to my dad. When I was 17, I got jumped by some guys who worked for the guy he owed money to. Ended up in the hospital, and got saddled with this beauty." I point to the scar on my face. "Got stabbed with a broken bottle like I was in a fucking bar fight." I scratch it reflexively. "Andre paid the debt, and they took me in. As soon as I graduated high school I started working for him. I knew all the people and the players, the properties, better than anyone else. He put me in charge of security when he made Harrison CPO."

"He's a good man."

"No wealthy man is ever good, but there are worse."

She stares at me with her eyebrows raised, my statement unexpected. This is what being Harrison's best friend taught me. He is the world's most reluctant billionaire. Since he got a dual degree in economics and human resources, his whole thought process is about making the world better for the people that work for us. It's why most of Zastrow Ventures is focused on climate projects now.

"I started boarding school braced for impact. Sure that I'd get out with a great education and still be on my own. Cassandra wouldn't let me. I did one nice thing and she never let me forget it. She had plenty of reasons not to trust people either, so when I got pulled into her circle, the real one, I got good people too. I don't let them make me their pet and I think that's why they like me. Scarlet and Shaw and most of the time Hela. Our lives are different but they never let me get bullied or pushed around. They made me have fun sometimes."

"Only sometimes?"

"I don't know if you know this, but I'm pretty serious."

It's my turn to laugh, but I mostly hold it in.

"I don't owe them anything, but I am grateful."

"You can go see her, them, you know. You just have to ask."

Perri's lips twist but eventually she smooths out her expression and nods. I said the wrong thing and I know it. This time she's the one that got the harsh reminder of our arrangement and what this really is, even when we wish it wasn't.

If she leaves to visit her friends, someone will be watching her. I'll expect to be told about every move she makes. When she gets back, I'll demand to know everything she did and said and I'll expect her to tell me. I'll want to know every interaction she had even if it was just smiling at a stranger walking down the street.

She'll get a temporary leave and return to her prison.

Where I am her jailer.

Things won't ever be any different.

"It's been a long weekend," she sighs out as she stands and starts clearing the table. "I'll take care of the dishes tonight."

19

Neo

Harrison is at the warehouse meeting with all my men. We're sitting down to talk through the threat against Nim, because it's clear now it's not about Zastrow or Andre, it's very much about her. Every attack that's been made, even the ones in the media, have been focused on hurting her.

"I still think it's her father. The deal hasn't been as lucrative on his side as it has been on ours, even if he's still making millions. Especially considering the environmental constraints he agreed to that are tying his hands." Harrison taps nervously on the glass table, his anger translating to anxiety.

"He loses everything in a divorce. He's mean but he's not stupid," Wilder counters. "Not to mention, Roger is far too wrapped up in his latest affair to maneuver this kind of thing. He gains nothing."

"Are we sure there's no one in Andre's past? Or his wife's?" Benji asks the question softly, knowing that he's talking about Harrison's mother. We never refer to Nim as his wife, because in truth that will always be Colleen.

Wilder met her by chance, just before she passed, doing some moonlighting as a guard at a party. He was a bouncer I poached who could charm information out of anyone, and it came in handy. He's our pulse on the gossip in the club scene, from dance clubs to strip clubs. The bouncers basically have their own information network.

"Colleen's family is clean." That way I say it makes it clear that's final.

"They aren't the type to hold grudges, and they know what it really is between Andre and Nim. They're too far removed from what we are to care in that way." To be honest, they're who I looked at first. None of us were comfortable with Andre remarrying so soon, but her closest remaining relative, her sister Shannon, understood what was really happening.

"What about Perri?" Harrison asks. "Timing is awfully convenient."

"She's got no connections other than Cassandra Warren, and the Warren media deal has been solid," Leander chimes in. "But they could have any motive for increasing their negotiating power. Part of the deal is that we'll control some of what's being published about Zastrow. That's got to be a ding to their journalistic integrity or whatever."

"And dad's plan, regarding Perri?" Harrison pushes. "Did it work? Is she loyal?"

"She's doing what I ask and she's happy at her job." It's all I give him, and it's all I'm willing to give him in front of my men. Harrison gives me a nod that he understands. The men are too close to her. I know that under orders they'll do what I say, but they won't like it.

"She loves us," Benji adds. "Fits in like she's always been here."

"That only makes her more dangerous," Harrison counters. It echoes a thought I've had myself.

"It's been nearly 2 months," Benji tries again.

"And a sleeper agent could be embedded for years. Don't let her make you soft." I command my men and they put their heads down, acknowledging what I'm saying. "Be nice, fine, but she hasn't earned trust yet, and you can't give that to her without my permission. The best you can do is trust that she's not poisoning your dinner."

The guys laugh but I know it's forced. It's why I'm in charge and they're not. Because I can recognize my weaknesses and guard against them. It's why I knew the second I locked eyes with her outside that damn bus that I had to arm myself against Perri Kane. I can feel what I feel, acknowledge that I want her, and still be in control. My awareness is how I prevent the trap of making an emotional decision.

The time will come when I put Perri to the test, and then I'll know.

"Leander, I'm having you dig into the Warren deal and anything that might have to do with Nim. We've already done background on them, but look at it as a whole and see if it ties to her."

"Why me?"

"I trust you."

"You're not going to do it yourself?" He seems genuinely perplexed by my decision.

"Do you want the responsibility or not?"

Leander nods.

"I've got my hands full. I need you on this one."

"Perri making you soft, boss?" Thomas teases.

I whip my pen at his head and he catches it before it hits. One of the reasons I keep him around at all.

"I've got my hands full," I repeat. "Get your shit together."

We hammer out some more surveillance details, and assign more jobs for digging into the possible source of the threat. While our attacker doesn't seem to want anything except Nim dead or doubted, it's hard to figure out why they're doing it. But that's my job, so I'm going to make sure we leave no stone unturned.

I dismiss them, and Harrison hangs back to talk to me.

"Listen, I know she's cute and she's your little fantasy come to life, but it's still suspicious, Neo. You have to test her."

"I will. I have. I know how to do my job, Harrison."

"We all have our blind spots," he says softly.

"It's not like that." Despite the other night, it isn't.

"Even if she's innocent, and has nothing to do with what's happening, you won't know until you force the issue."

We glare at each other until he backs down. Harrison is principled and protective but when it comes to a fight, I will always beat him. He's never survived the things that I have, and knowing about them secondhand isn't enough. Harrison didn't feel the bruises forming beneath his skin or hear the crack of his own face and bones breaking. Harrison was never betrayed by the people that brought him into this world.

Harrison has never been truly, utterly alone.

He's got a point though.

"I like Perri, you know that, and she's doing great at Zastrow. Knows her stuff. But you've been keeping her prisoner without pushing anything. That has to end."

"I'm doing what I'm told."

Harrison stares me down. "Okay." He sighs and puts his hands in his pockets. "We dig into Roger Maines, and the Warrens. They're the only directions that make any sense."

I nod in agreement.

Harrison leaves but I stay still, thinking about everything that we talked about tonight. Even if I feel like I'm keeping the lines clear between Perri and me, I'm starting to worry about the men. Despite their training, they've lived hard lives. Having someone with such nurturing energy around is dangerous. What most don't realize is that rather than seduction, the appearance of unconditional motherly love is significantly more effective.

Most men who do the things we do for a living have mommy issues, if they even knew their mothers at all. Someone so soft and desperate for people to take care of, who wants a family to belong to like Perri...that's hard to guard against.

Her sweetness is a tsunami. A force that wipes out everything in it's path until she is all that remains.

Perri Kane is going to devastate me. I know it. I see that trap and I'm going to step into it, while already having a plan to survive it. That's all that matters. My burgeoning feelings for her won't stop me from doing what needs to be done to test her. To make her prove she's with us.

20

Perri

I'm preparing for a quiet, lonely Saturday when there's a pounding on the door of the apartment. For a second, I'm so surprised at the unexpected arrival that I don't move. I just stare at the door.

"Open up, Perri!" Nim's voice calls through the door. "Neo refuses to give me my own code."

To be fair, I don't blame him. Nim would absolutely bust into his safe, quiet space whenever she wanted and drive him crazy. After a deep breath and a brief internal argument about whether or not Neo would give me permission to let her in, I open the door.

She breezes inside and then stops, turning around to take in the apartment. I realize she probably hasn't been here since I started living here, and try to see what she sees. The kitchen table that's always set, more decorations than before - little pops of color I added to the kitchen and living room. A new rack on the wall for coats and a stand for our shoes. It looks slightly more feminine than it did when I first got here.

"Wow. I've heard about the dinners but I didn't think he'd break down and get a whole table. It's downright homey in here."

"Thank you?"

She turns and focuses her x-ray gaze on me. "You're welcome. We're going out."

"We are?"

"I need to do some shopping and I need someone who has no reason to kiss my ass."

"Well that's not true," I reply without thinking, and I'm amazed at how much my barriers have come down since living here. It's hard to keep them up and enforce my silence when the guys are so damn chatty, and won't let anything go. If they see it on your face they make you say it.

Nim raises her eyebrows at me.

"I'm your family's hostage. I have every reason to kiss your ass."

She shrugs. "Okay, maybe, but it won't be coated in so much sugar it makes my teeth hurt, right? Get dressed, let's go."

I don't say anything but walk to the bedroom and slide the curtain closed. Immediately, I send a text to Neo that Nim showed up and wants to go out. He replies telling me that it's easier to just give in, and that we'll be safe with her security staff. That is not what I was hoping he would say.

So instead of settling down in my pajamas with a baking show, I'm putting on a sundress and some bike shorts to avoid chub rub, and checking that I have everything I need in my purse.

I make sure that the apartment door closes securely behind me, and give the camera hovering above it an eye roll because I know that Neo will check it even though I told him where we were going. He told me to assume he was watching at all times and after our pretend it was a dream moment, I believe it's likely true. Neo is watching me all the time.

It makes me kind of sick with myself that I like the idea of that. I should be fighting to get out from under his thumb but all I want is to get under his body.

Nim gets into her car, and there's a security guy I recognize but don't know in the car parked behind it. She has a flashy Maserati convertible with doors that open like wings. It's also an obnoxiously violent color of blue, and it becomes clear to me again that subtle is not her game.

Honestly, I'm impressed that she can drive a manual car.

The way she drives it just might kill me.

We fly through the streets and she never uses her signal. I can't believe the sedate sedan of her security guard can remotely keep up, but he does. She pulls into a parking garage near a boutique shopping area, and we jerk to a stop.

I put my hand to my chest and feel my rapidly beating heart, and take a second to catch my breath. The funny part is, Nim is breathing hard too. Like the drive was work for her and took something out of her.

It's hard not to want to ask her if she's okay. If there's something going on, because she's still got one hand on the wheel, her gaze lost in the middle distance, no smile on her face as she stares down whatever thought is taking over her mind. Despite appearances, and I am sure she's a very convincing actress, Nim is not okay. To be caught up in all these secrets has to be even more isolating for her than it is for me.

I don't know what her relationship is like with Andre, Neo is always in protection mode and not great with emotions, and I have no idea what she's like with Harrison. I have no idea what anyone is like with the real Harrison, as I've yet to meet him. I've met Harrison Zastrow, the next CEO, but I haven't met Harrison Zastrow, Neo Ryan's lifelong best friend. He's always in a mask when we meet, and I know it's because he doesn't trust me.

Nim shouldn't trust me, but I don't think she has anyone else. No one real, anyway.

"Are you okay?"

She takes a deep breath and then her standard smile appears. Her eyebrows and her nose scrunch, like I'm being silly. "Of course I am."

We get out of the car, and the security guy is already waiting. I follow a step behind Nim and he's a step behind me, probably tasked with keeping an eye on both of us. She steps into the first store she comes across and I have no choice except to follow.

"How's things with Neo?" she asks, super casually, while looking at mannequins wearing the newest arrivals, and then indicating to the assistant whether she wants it to try on or not.

"Fine," I answer, unsure what else I could say.

"Harrison says everyone likes you. Do you like them?" Interesting that her and Harrison were talking about me. About the situation.

"I do. It's not so bad, and I love my job...I wanted to work for Zastrow."

"I know. The night of my birthday we found your application. You would've gotten the job on your own, you know, we just sped things up. Andre is like that."

"Are things...I mean, I kind of screwed things up that night. Is everything between you two...?" I trail off, entirely out of my element about how to continue. Nim laughs, and waves at me to follow her to the dressing room. She pulls me inside when I linger, awkward, and the guard takes up his place outside the door.

Without a shred of hesitation or insecurity, Nim takes off her clothes and starts going through the items on the hanger in the room.

"Andre and I have an open relationship - on my side. Our marriage is a business arrangement and he will never truly be a husband again, not like he was." There's a hint of sadness in her voice but I don't think it's for herself, I think it's in memory of his wife. Nim would have known her too. As well as the boys did, and it was obvious how much Neo loved Colleen Zastrow.

"I've been with Marco since I was a teenager. I've loved him since before I knew my dad would marry me off to whoever he thought would make him the most money. Andre didn't want to take that away from me, and Marco and I...he's on the circuit. He has his fun with no commitment, I have Andre, and when Marco is home, we're together as much as we can be. It's definitely not traditional, but it works for us."

Nim shrug and shimmies into a purple dress.

"No," I say, used to shopping with Cassandra and giving my opinion. I shrink back, apologetic.

Nim waves me off. "Are you sure?"

"The shade isn't right with your hair, and it makes your skin look washed out. No."

"See? This is why I needed you." Nim takes the dress off and hangs it back up. I wander over and start skimming through her choices.

"So...you and Andre never..." I blush, the delicacy of the question embarrassing me.

Of course, Nim laughs. "Oh, we definitely have. Have you seen him? Silver fox. Total daddy." My blush deepens and she pokes me. "But it's not often -

special occasions, if he's feeling it. We don't even sleep in the same room, but I'm there if he needs me."

"Neo told me he thought you and Harrison might become a thing someday -"

"What?!" She spits out, and the security guard knocks on the door to check on us. "We're fine, Steve!"

Nim crowds closer, a sleek black dress in her hands. "Me and Harrison? Hell no, ew. We're all too close. Despite my open mind I still get the ick once and awhile that I've not only fucked Andre, but come all over his face. The man has a tongue, let me tell you. But Harrison is like my brother. My completely non-sexual life partner."

I have got to be purple from bashfulness and embarrassment with how hot my cheeks feel right now.

"Is Neo?"

Nim pulls the dress she was putting on down around her body and turns to look at me, gaze shrewd and knowing.

"Yes, Neo is like my brother. Nothing has ever happened between us. Not even a kiss."

"Right, of course," I try to cover that I asked out of semi-jealous curiosity. Nim is a force of nature. She's beautiful, powerful, and an extrovert. It's hard for me to imagine anyone not wanting her, let alone resisting her if given the opportunity. Spending most of her life being close to two undeniably attractive men leads to the logical conclusion that at some point something must have happened.

"What about you, Perri? Anything happen between you and Neo?"

"No," I answer to quickly, and she tilts her head, silently calling out the lie. "He's too principled for that." Other than our show at the club, she doesn't need to know about anything that happened after. I bet Neo's tongue could give anyone's a run for their money. I can't even come anymore without thinking of his head between my legs.

Nim frowns, because she can't disagree that Neo would keep to the boundaries he set when it comes to me. She knows what kind of guy he is, even better than I do. He would feel bad because to him it would appear like he's taking advantage of me.

She turns away from me and silence falls between us as she tries on a few more dresses, and I give a very basic yes or no when she asks. Most things look good on her, but it's clear she's looking for a wow factor.

"I think we're done here." Nim goes through her discarded items and grabs a soft green dress that made her look like a fairy. "On to the next."

We leave the dressing room and are trailed by Steve to the counter. Nim pays for the dress without even thinking about the price, something I could never do, but am once again used to from enough time with Cassandra.

It makes me feel guilty for being out with Nim when I've turned Cassandra down every time she asks to hang out or get together. It's not that I don't want to, but I don't think I can lie to her. What's happening is big and scary, and it's safe being with Nim because I don't have to explain anything to her. She already knows, which takes a lot of the pressure off. Other than my own feelings, I don't have to be dishonest.

I've never lied to Cassandra before, not in any big way, and I try not to tell little lies either. One of the reasons our friendship works so well despite our differences is because she knows I'm almost brutally honest with her, and she'll be the same with me. Cassandra is protective and generous when it comes to me, but she'll also call me out when I get up on my lone wolf high horse, or start to put distance where it doesn't need to be. I would've drifted away from our friendship out of self-preservation but she didn't let me.

I miss her, but I can't go to her unless I know I can keep the truth of everything to myself and make her believe it. We talk almost every day, but I know it's not enough for either of us. She wants to meet Neo and know more about us, she wants to talk about my job, and I know she'll ask invasive questions about our sex life since my biggest excuse for not coming out is that I'm with him and it's our honeymoon phase where we can't get enough of each other.

I wouldn't even mind if that was true. I've never had a huge libido, or so I thought, but the idea of a week long fuck fest with my captor sounds totally awesome. I want him to fuck me so hard I can't walk. I want his hand prints on my ass and my scratches down his back. I want my thighs chafed red from his scruff. I want to leave a bite mark on his delectable ass. I want to kiss every scar he has but especially the one on his cheek, the one that makes him feel the most unloved, I could hear it in his voice. I want to fuck him and love on him all at once, and that combination is the red flag I should be paying attention to.

I don't just want his body, I want him. Every piece of him that he reveals clicks inside me, matching up with a piece of my own. Like he was made for me.

When in reality, all he's made to do is break me.

I follow Nim into the next store without paying attention because I'm not buying anything, and I'm suddenly surrounded by lace. It's a lingerie store.

Nim clicks her fingers. "Earth to Perri, whatcha thinking about?" She has a knowing look on her face.

"Scars," I tell her, because it's the only safe thing in my thought process. The ones we can see, and the ones he's going to leave behind inside me that will ruin me forever. Why him? Why does he have to be the one that I want, and why did I have to meet him like this?

Her face falls, and I see a hint of the real her again. "We all have those."

We share a look, a flicker of kinship blossoming between us. There's a chance I could make a real friend out of this, and I want to take it. Even when Neo decides they can trust me and he lets me go, I'll still be in the Zastrow orbit. I'll still know something I shouldn't. I'll never truly be done with them, and I need to hang on to what allies I can. Nim could be one of them.

"How's the job?" she asks.

I notice that Steve waited outside, and I think that's a bad move, but who am I to say anything? Nim flits around the store and picks things up, leaving them in a pile on the counter where the staff member smiles. Places like this have commission so the more Nim spends, the better it is for the staffer.

"I love it. It's everything I wanted it to be - it's never boring."

"I'll take your word on that," Nim laughs.

"Did you ever want to do anything?" I realize how that sounded and try to backtrack. "I mean, you went to college."

"I did. But my dad was very clear that it was not so I could work. It's even part of the marriage agreement - I can't have a job. He doesn't want there to be any way for me to make my own money." Her face falls and she grabs more things off more racks. This is retail therapy if I ever saw it, and I hope that it does bring her some measure of happiness or relief.

"Why would Mr. Zastrow agree to that?"

"He wanted to get me out, and there were certain hills my asshole dad would be willing to die on, and that particular detail was one of them. I might be married to Andre Zastrow but my life is still beholden to Roger Maines."

"I'm sorry."

"It's okay. It could be worse," she says to me but I can tell she's saying it more to herself. "I'll do whatever I want when he's dead."

"I'm surprised he's still breathing," I mutter as I pretend to look at something on a rack, not really seeing it. I know as well as she does that family can be our biggest enemy. The ones who tear us down when they should be shielding us or building us up.

"They wouldn't do anything without my permission," she whispers back, and then gives me a teasing nudge. I smile at her. "I need real people in my life, Peep."

I'm not sure about the nickname but I don't think I'll win an argument with her so I don't protest.

"I want to be friends with you. Don't abandon me, okay?" While the pout on her face is exaggerated, the vulnerability in her voice is real. "Give me your phone."

I hand it over unlocked and she sends herself a text message. Before this, I was intensely protective of my phone even though it's not like I had anything secretive or salacious on it. But it was private, and has access to a lot of things about my life. Now that Neo can get into it whenever he wants, and realizing that I have nothing to hide, I oddly don't care about anyone being on my phone. Nim could keep it and look through it now if she wanted.

Instead, Nim gives me my phone back. I wait by the door while she makes her purchases. Looking out, it takes me a minute before I realize what's wrong.

Steve isn't there.

Before Nim gets to me, I step out the door and look around for him.

"Where's Steve?" Nim asks, and she starts to step out but I block her. She looks surprised but doesn't try to move again. There are cars parked on the street and people walking, but it's not overly busy even for a weekend. No one seems to be looking at us.

"Come on," I tell her, and we walk down the street. I pretend to be fixing the skirt on my sundress and look behind us. Two men are staring right at us, about 20 feet back, and gaining. They're built, and wearing jackets when it's a hot day.

I've learned from the guys that's usually an indicator they're concealing weapons.

I push Nim toward the door of the next store and she goes inside.

"Go to the back."

We move through the displays and I realize we've walked into a baby boutique. Everything is tiny and adorable. A smiling sales person approaches us, but pauses when she sees my face.

"Please, my ex - can we go out the back to get to our car?" I let my fear into my voice.

"Of course, sweetheart." The woman signals to someone else and then guides us to the employees only door, and through the storage areas in the back. Even stressed I recognize how ruthlessly organized it is and it soothes me a little.

She leads us to the back exit and it opens into an alley. If we turn left and move quick we'll get back to the parking garage and Nim's car before the guys following us can catch up, or realize that we're backtracking.

I think about the bomb that blew up her previous car. Or that they might have someone watching it, waiting for us to come back.

This might be dumb, but I don't know what else we can do.

"Thank you so much," I tell the woman, and Nim echoes me. I take her hand and basically drag her down the alley. Eventually, nerves get the best of us and we're running, only slowing down when we reach the door to the parking garage.

I make Nim stay behind me as we slowly walk up the small flight of stairs to the level we parked on. There's too many cars for me to be able to tell if any of them are occupied, and I can't see anything obviously suspicious.

"Give me your keys."

She hands them over, and it occurs to me then how much she trusts me to keep her safe in this moment. The guys at the warehouse talk and strategize a lot, and I've picked up more than I realized. It's instinctive to try and protect her right now. Here's Neo thinking that I might be a risk to them, and yet Nim trusts me to keep her alive. For all she knows I could be leading her to danger and capture.

I walk toward the car, unlocking it. We both stop and wait.

Nothing happens.

"Get in."

Nim gets in the passenger seat, and I look around the car, even getting down on the ground to look under it. I don't actually know what I'm looking for but maybe a bomb is like porn, you know it when you see it.

Except I don't see anything.

Risking it, I get in the car. The engine rumbles underneath me and I wish that I was driving it under more enjoyable circumstances. Nothing happens when I pull out, or when I exit the garage.

"Call Neo," I instruct Nim.

As soon as I make the first turn, I'm fairly certain someone is following us. Traffic isn't heavy, but there's an SUV that seems to be weaving in between everyone to get closer to us. I follow my instincts and head for the nearest highway, even if it's going to be a roundabout way of getting back to the warehouse. I need to be able to go fast without putting anyone in danger, and get some distance between us and the people following.

"I'm busy, what?" He sounds frustrated and a little bored, so I guess we're about to wake up his day.

"Neo?" I speak before she can. "Someone is following us."

"Perri? Shit." I hear him talking in a muted voice to whoever is with him, and then the sound changes and I think we're on speaker. "I have your location. Harrison is with me - do what he says. Come to the Zastrow building."

"Okay."

"Are you driving?"

"Yes."

"The Maserati?" Harrison's voice chimes in.

"Yes."

"Thank god. Nim would crash," he snarks.

"Fuck off," she replies, but I can hear how much her voice is wavering. She's scared.

Harrison starts telling me where to go - I'm turning and trying to be quick about it, following Nim's example and not using my signals, but these guys know who Nim is. They know that she'd try to get somewhere safe if she realized she was being followed, and the closest location is Zastrow.

It's not long before I recognize where we are, and the confidence I feel in knowing where I am and where I need to go helps. I've tuned out Harrison and Neo, not even answering them let alone understanding anything they're saying as my heartbeat pounds in my ears.

I can see the Zastrow building but it's still blocks away. The SUV is right behind us. Close enough that I can see the driver, and I know that he was one of the guys following us on the street. Whoever wants Nim is really determined.

The Zastrow parking garage is approaching and I push harder on the accelerator, willing this beast of a machine to go that much faster and get us to safety. Except we're back in the city with too many cars and too many people. Anxiety swells in my chest but I shove it down, focusing on the moment. I will get us out of this, period.

Farther down the block, I see Neo step out onto the sidewalk and wave. It's not exactly hard to miss the violent blue Cielo in a road full of blacks and grays. I pull to the left to pull over, thankful it's a one way street. The SUV whips to the right and the driver guns the engine.

The SUV swipes us, sending us right into the curb. We smash against it and then bounce off, the noise loud and grating, almost painful considering we're in the open air in the convertible.

The SUV drives away and I watch for the license plate, ignoring Neo and

Harrison as they run over to us.

"Are you okay?" Neo is ripping open the door, and I see the dent at the bottom where the curb ripped it up. Harrison went around to the other side and got Nim out, and he's already pulling her to the sidewalk and into the building while I'm sitting in the driver's seat, dazed.

"It wasn't a New York license plate. It was white, but there was blue and yellow. HDA-7714."

"You got the license plate?"

I nod. Neo reaches into the car and picks me up. I think I'm in shock because I was chased and hit and then they drove off. I'm shaking. There's all this adrenaline running through me and it has nowhere to go. My hands hurt from how hard I was clenching the wheel and the gear shift.

He's carrying me in his arms and I can't even pay attention to it, because I keep looking over my shoulder and waiting for the SUV to come back. For them to attack us. Do more than sideswipe the car. They were armed.

I know they were armed. They could've shot us on the street if they wanted. They could've killed us, but they didn't.

I squeeze my eyes shut as we walk into the lobby. Neo doesn't acknowledge anyone as he carries me past the metal detector, and no one tries to say anything to him either. At least it's empty because it's a Saturday, but I hide my face in his neck, embarrassed to be seen like this at work. Yet no matter how I try to force myself to move or relax, I am unable to snap myself out of it.

It's as if I'm made of ice. Frozen and still.

I was in danger when Neo and the others took me after being on the party bus, and I had stared them down and told them to take my life. I hadn't been afraid. Maybe because there was no obvious malice in their actions. It all felt like horror and sadness, and for some reason that had kept me calm.

This was malicious. Violent. It terrified me even if I managed to keep my shit together and protect Nim in the moment.

I close my eyes and try to take deep breaths.

"That's it, breathe *mo dhuine ar bith.* You're safe now, I've got you. You did it. It's done. You did so good," he keeps up a steady stream of encouragement as he moves.

"I want to go home."

"I'll take you home. Thomas is almost here and then I'll take you home."

We sit down on a bench in the lobby with me in his lap, and he rocks gently like I'm a child in need of soothing. It's so oddly nurturing and I didn't expect it of him. His big, warm hand rubs up and down my back, and after awhile I realize I'm breathing normally again. My heart has slowed.

"Where's Nim?"

"Harrison took her up to Andre."

I nod.

There's a commotion as Thomas, Leander, and Wilder all burst into the lobby and look around for us. They run through the metal detector, their guns setting it off and the loud beeping echoes in the mostly empty lobby. I sit up and shift, uncomfortable with them seeing the oddly intimate moment between Neo and I.

I move so I'm sitting beside him, but my legs are draped over his thigh.

Wilder gets to us first, dropping onto his knees next to us.

"You good?"

"I'm good," I manage to get out a weak smile.

"Nim?" Leander asks.

"Fine, she's upstairs," Neo tells him. "Thomas, you're on duty. Wilder, find Steve."

Shit. I'd completely forgotten about Steve.

"He disappeared."

Neo looks over at me, his jaw clenched. I don't say anything else.

"You drive?" he asks Leander.

"Yeah. I've got the Denali."

"Good. Get us to the warehouse."

Even though I try to protest, Neo picks me up again and carries me back out. The large vehicle is pulled up onto the sidewalk, the guys clearly not giving a fuck in their rush to get here. Neo manages to open the door while still holding me, and he sets me inside. Leander gets in the driver's seat.

I watch Neo round the front and assume he'll get in the passenger seat, but he surprises me by getting in the back next to me.

"I'm never leaving the warehouse again." I'm joking, but part of me wishes it was true.

"Not without me," Neo answers, and sounds completely serious.

21

Neo

About halfway back to the warehouse, Perri started talking.

She told me everything that happened, described the men (one short, brown hair, big nose, black jacket, workboots; the other, the driver, tall, bald, thin lips, no neck.)

Part of it was her telling us what she thought we needed to know, and part of it was her needing to get it out. To expel what had happened, to allow her brain to start to process what she experienced.

Neither Leander or I said anything as she exorcised the events from her psyche.

We were almost home when she fell asleep, her chin hanging down onto her chest before her head lolled to the side. Leander pulls the Denali right into the warehouse, and Benji is waiting, pacing the floor.

He approaches as soon as the car turns off but I don't acknowledge him. Leander can handle that while I get my captive back to her prison. I wasn't kidding that I wasn't going to let her leave without me. Not for a while, at least.

The way I felt when she called, when I heard the fear in her voice, is something I never want to experience again. My heart stuttered in my chest and knowing that she was so far away, unprotected, made me feel more powerless than when I got jumped all those years ago. Then, I could've fought back, the enemy was right in front of me, but this? She was miles away. Unprepared.

When they pulled up I made Harrison get Nim because I was genuinely afraid I'd yell at one of my oldest and dearest friends for putting Perri in danger. It wasn't a rational, or responsible way to feel when I'm one of the people that's supposed to prioritize Nim's safety over everything else.

I didn't *want* to prioritize her over Perri, and that's just fucking stupid. It's dangerous for everyone. The crazy thing is that Perri prioritized Nim over herself, and made decisions that probably saved them both.

I get Perri out of the SUV and walk upstairs to the loft, letting the door slam behind me because I'm not letting go of her to catch it. It's also a definitive message to the guys not to come up here.

Perri's wearing this cute as fuck yellow sundress, and it makes her tits look amazing. I want to take a bite out of her. I want to bury myself inside her so I can feel that she's real, warm, and alive. That she's whole and safe. That might be true of her body, but something cracked in her mind today.

Despite how she came to be here, the danger became real this time.

Associating with us and our secrets has consequences, and today she felt them.

Now, we're more at risk than ever for her to betray us. Things are more volatile, and I need to show her that things can be steady. That we'll keep her safe, and she has no reason to be afraid. Because she's one of us, part of us, and we protect what's ours.

That I protect what is mine.

I lay Perri down on our bed and take off her shoes, then the dress.

Technically, I don't have to, but it's what I want.

I peel the straps down, showing me the innocent white bra she's wearing, and the completely unsurprising matching white panties after skimming it over her stomach, and then getting the dress over her hips. It's tempting to take off her bra too, because she never sleeps in one.

I stare down at her, and decide fuck it, I'll be the villain, but at least she'll be comfortable.

My hand slides up her back until I reach the clasp, and I undo it with a twist of my fingers. I pull the bra away from her body and her tits fall, moving with her deep breathing. With zero guilt I admire her dark pink nipples and the luscious curve of her breasts, big enough that it would be more than even my big hands could hold.

If I was a worse monster, I'd have her any way that I want. Wake her up with my mouth, my fingers, my tongue, my cock, distract her from the stress and fear with orgasms. Even if she was awake, I don't think she'd stop me. I know she wants me. I've watched her get herself off multiple times since I ate her pussy, and I've heard her say my name into the dark.

I can never tell if she knows I'm watching and does it to torture me, or if she thinks she's getting away with it.

Shaking my head to clear it, I tuck her under the blankets.

Then I go jack off in the shower before crawling in beside her. For the first time since she started sleeping in my bed, I hold her. Perri is here, safe and sound, and I'm going to make sure she stays that way, unless I say otherwise. My captive, my little nobody, is only mine to make decisions about.

I don't care what Harrison says, I don't even care what Andre wants at this point, this is a test playing out between her and I, and no one is going to interfere.

22

Perri

There's no words to describe the gratitude I feel for the distraction my job provides, even if it's my association with Zastrow that caused the disastrous events of last weekend. Neo drives me to and from work every day like usual, but I can see his vigilance has changed. We don't talk anymore during the drives, and he's been taking the Denali instead of his Aston Martin.

Oddly, it does make me feel safer even if the Denali isn't as fast as his sports car. We're the collateral damage if they want Nim, and we know it. I'd rather have more metal and airbags around me to protect me from impact.

He drops me off on my floor, then takes his broody mood elsewhere.

I'm kind of lost and staring at the computer when a voice snaps me out of it.

"Earth to Perri," my boss, Adam drawls. "You okay?"

Not really. I'm getting a headache and my body feels weird, but I think I'm just tired. It's been a weird couple of days of sleep and I don't do well without sleep.

Instead of saying that I don't feel well, I force a smile. "Sorry, got caught up doing math in my head."

Adam smiles. He's decent looking and dresses well, and I appreciate him for not being gross. Everything about him screams finance bro but he's been completely professional with me, and with any of the other women he's interacted with. No one has a bad word to say about him, and that respect really helped me settle into my place here.

Then again, I don't think Zadie would tolerate that from anyone.

She's a force, and I am both intimidated by and drawn to it. When we have staff meetings, everyone sits with rapt attention as she speaks. Not only is she a great accountant, her understanding of Zastrow and the economic landscape teaches me more than I could learn in a class in college. She's so grounded in what we do, and feels really passionate about curating the projects that we're assessing.

Basically, we run the numbers and if they work, we pass it off to Adam for a review. If Adam passes it, Zadie takes one last look and then initiates the process of Zastrow investing in a venture and she's the one who gets to see the successes and failures. Our pass to payout rate is pretty good, and it's because Zadie is discerning.

She shares the decision to invest with a market coordinator, but I know Zadie's word carries a lot of weight.

In short, I want to be Zadie when I grow up. She went to college with Harrison but is older than him because she had to take years after high school to save up money to go on to higher education. I had a leg up that she didn't with my parent's insurance money, but I've always felt a kinship with Zadie in being women who had a path we wanted to follow and fought to do it.

"Listen, I need you to finish this analysis by the end of the day. You up for that? You look...off." Adam looks genuinely concerned. I guess I can appreciate that he didn't say I look like crap or I look tired.

"I got it. It'll be done." And it will, because I'm on the last set of projections for this project anyway. I think I can hold it together long enough to finish and then zone out.

"Good. Drink some water." I'd take that personally except it's basically Adam's sign off. He says it to everyone, all the time.

This time I listen, and fill up my Zastrow branded water bottle and try to take sips as I run through this last page of numbers. The thing I really like about my brain is that when I see numbers, I remember them, and remember what they're tied to. They linger in my mind. Like sometimes when I close my eyes right now the license plate of the SUV floats through my brain, pushing me to gather more information.

It was a Pennsylvania plate. Neo won't tell me anything more about what they found out or if it led to anything. We had a very silent and awkward dinner when he told me that. They attacked me too, and I felt like I had a right to know. Then again, I don't know this world and its enemies or bad guys, so they might have told me who the plate was registered to and the name would mean nothing to me.

If there was any chance the name was connected to me, I'm sure I'd be tied to a chair in my little interrogation suite and spilling my guts.

I'm working on autopilot, and then my eyes snag.

Familiar numbers.

I look through the spreadsheet again, and the numbers are the same...

I minimize the file and go through my backlog, pulling up another spreadsheet from a different analysis for a completely different project. Like I thought, the numbers are the same. Ultimately, that's not very weird because some projections of needs for things like the cost of rent, transport, or gas, are based on a market so they might be similar or the same.

This is a project for production cost and material sourcing.

That's going to be extremely specific, and usually a rate per item produced, not a general budget number. The rate per item is the same on both spreadsheets even though the items are different, and below that, the administrative costs are also the exact same.

It's like someone copied the last page of the spreadsheet and changed it to match the proposal, but the projections and the project itself aren't actually connected.

That's...odd. And potentially fraudulent.

The previous project was one that already made its way to Zadie and was passed on. We haven't started production yet but the company that submitted the older proposal has already received several hundreds of thousands of dollars from Zastrow.

I go back and finish the analysis that Adam wanted and send it to him.

Then I start at the beginning and compare each proposal. Every detail that

I have, side by side on my screen. I make notes and highlights, pointing out where things aren't right or where they are too similar. Looking at them in comparison, it's not only the numbers but the sources and data they reference that are exactly the same.

Zadie and Adam see even more proposals than I do, and it's completely possible neither of them noticed this. It's possible neither of them dug into it deep enough because they trust the analysts to catch if something looks weird on this basic of a level. There might not be a second set of eyes on this, and maybe not ones that remember things the way I do.

I make a note to look through previous analyses for any of these numbers together.

It'll be a hell of a search but I feel like it's important.

It's been hours and I feel weak, my headache is pounding despite water and ibuprofen, and I feel like I need to sleep for days. I'm so out of it that Neo gets all the way to my cubicle before I realize what time it is.

He gives me a concerned frown, but that's kind of his normal look these days.

On the car ride to the warehouse, I lean back and close my eyes, falling into that weird place between asleep and awake that makes it feel like I'm jumping through time. Every time I open my eyes we're miles from where we were before, and then suddenly we're slowing down so Neo can code open the compound gate.

He drops me off outside the main building like usual, and just walking up the stairs to the loft leaves me exhausted.

When I get inside, I don't even bother to turn on the lights. I let my bag fall wherever, step out of my shoes, and in the bedroom I strip down to my underwear. The only light I mess with is the bathroom because I need to find more ibuprofen. When I look in the mirror after swallowing the pills and taking a drink, I don't even look like myself.

I know that I'm looking at me but it doesn't feel like me.

I turn the light back off and nearly crawl to the big king bed. The sheets feel cool against my flushed skin and the room tilts around me, like I'm very drunk and have the spins. I curl up on my left side, face burrowed into the pillow, and fall asleep.

23

Neo

Even though I had things to do, I'm anxious to get back to Perri. She hasn't been sleeping well, and I know she's having nightmares even though she tries to be covert about waking up in the night. On the ride home, she seemed really out of it.

I get back to the loft earlier than normal, so I know I'll have beaten the rest of the guys to dinner. I want to check on her alone before they all barge in.

When I open the door it's dark. No lights are on and there's not even a hint of food in the air. We've definitely been taking it for granted, but she's also been clear that she loves it. Sunday nights she meal preps for both of us and I feel like I've never had more energy in my life. Perri is making me take care of myself because she's taking care of herself in the process.

The dark isn't a good sign. I let the door close and step into the apartment, almost tripping over her bag. I pick it up and put it on the little table by the door where it belongs.

The first thought to cross my mind is that she left. That Perri found a way around my security and she's gone, after months of lulling us into this sense of family, she's run away. It makes me furious and there's an actual, physical pain in my chest.

After a moment, I come back to rational thought and move deeper into the apartment, looking for signs of her or a sign that something is wrong. Maybe she didn't run, maybe she was taken...

When I walk into the bedroom, the shape of Perri is visible beneath the blankets. Relief floods my system, and the radical theories inside me quiet down. I look around the room. There's also clothes all over the floor which is unlike her, and from what I see on the floor she's in bed in only her panties.

I step over to her side of the bed and squat down to look at Perri through the dim light of the crystal lamp she keeps on her bedside table. Even in the shadowy light I can see the sweat beading on her forehead. Carefully, I brush her hair out of her face, then step away to the living room. I turn on a lamp on the lowest setting, and send a message to the group text that Perri is sick and there's no dinner tonight.

Immediately, they respond back asking if there's anything they can do. I let them know I'll let them know, and ask that everyone goes to the barracks. Except Benji, because he's on server duty.

Then I get some water, and fill a Ziploc bag with ice. It's what always helps me when I have a fever, and Perri definitely does.

Before going back in, I make an executive decision and text Zadie. I have the personal cell phone number of every department head, of any person that I think I might need to contact for any reason within Zastrow. My phone contacts are a complete disaster of names with labels reminding me who they are. I've had very few occasions that warranted texting Zadie.

The last time was when I gave her instructions about setting Perri up at work, and to let her know the lay of the land regarding her. Zadie knows there's more going on, and she knows it's not that Perri is my girlfriend and I'm being overprotective. She doesn't know the truth about Nim and Andre's relationship - she's not that far into the circle - but she knows sometimes we do weird things for the right reasons for Zastrow.

Me: *Perri is sick, fever, the works. She won't be in tomorrow.*

Zadie: *I'll handle it. No problem. Let me know if I can do anything.*

Another offer to help Perri. I don't think she realizes how easily she endears herself to people. She's already earned the loyalty of so many so easily, but I still don't quite believe that we've earned hers. Perri keeps her walls so damn high and she's been betrayed by people that were supposed to care before. We're caring about her by choice, not obligation.

Still, a lifetime of having to be protective of herself is hard to change. It's not easy to dig inside someone and set hooks, tethers, ties, that would override her need for self-preservation and self-protection. She loves us, but not enough. Not yet.

I go back to the bedroom and set the water and ice pack on the table.

"Perri," I call, not loud but not a whisper either. "Princess you need to wake up right now."

She grumbles and I can see her fighting to open her eyes. "Neo," she sighs, and it's almost a moan. "I don't feel good."

"I know. Did you take anything?"

Perri nods.

"Good girl. I want you to drink a little more water and I've got an ice pack for your forehead."

She struggles to bring herself all the way back to awake, and I perversely enjoy watching her lashes flutter as she fights to open her eyes. Then she's looking at me, and I can see her pain and exhaustion. Without thinking, I reach out and cup her cheek.

"It's okay," I assure her. "I got you."

Perri sits up but is aware enough to hold the sheet over her. It does nothing to stop my eyes from dropping to the swell of her cleavage, even when she's sick. I hand her the water and she drinks it long and slow, her pretty throat working as she swallows the water. I don't know why seeing her in a vulnerable state like this is turning me on, but maybe it's because she's letting me take care of her. Without question or fuss.

"What do you need?" I ask her after she hands me the empty water glass.

"A shower." She leans her head back and closes her eyes, groaning. "My head hurts and I feel sticky."

"How about a bath? I'll wash your hair."

Perri cracks one eye open skeptically. "Fine."

"Stay here." I get up and go to the bathroom to start filling the tub with lukewarm water. I find the peppermint bath salts that Nim gets me almost every year for Christmas because they're supposed to help sore muscles, and sprinkle that in the water as well. Then I get Perri's shampoo and conditioner from the shower and set them on the ledge of the bath.

When I go back into the bedroom, Perri is sitting up and leaning against the headboard with her eyes closed.

"Come on, princess." I step closer and move to pull away the sheet. Perri fights me at first but she hasn't got much strength in her to push me away. Once the blankets are out of the way, I lift her up in my arms. Perri doesn't waste energy trying to protest.

Holding her nearly naked, I can feel how hot and clammy she is, and the way she's nearly boneless in my arms. Despite how gorgeous she is, concern finally kills my boner.

Perri needs me, and I'm going to take care of her.

In the bathroom, I set her down and pull her panties down her legs with no fanfare and no peeking at her pussy. She sways on her feet and I have to catch her, but it makes it quick work to slide her into the water.

Perri moans and sinks in up to her neck, then after a second dips all the way under. Panic makes my heart beat faster every second she's under, but then she slides back up and rubs at her face.

"That feels better."

"Are you cooling off?"

"Yes. I'm good. You don't have to..." she trails off as she looks over her shoulder and meets my eye. Yes, I do have to, and I will. She can see that on my face.

Perri curls up into a little ball within the tub, and after a long pause I reach for her shampoo. With a decent-sized amount in my hand, I start working it through her hair. Once I loosen it up, I dig my fingers in down to her scalp, massaging it and releasing the tension. Perri tries to hold back her groans but she's unsuccessful.

"Let it go. Let it out. I'm taking care of you."

Eventually, she rests her weight in my hands, and after I massage her scalp I slide my hands down the length of her blonde hair. I pull Perri back, letting her head dip into the water and rinsing away the soap. When it's gone, I massage her scalp more, then her neck and shoulders, before I start applying the conditioner.

When Perri rinses it out, she's a little more herself. Her hair is silky and thick, and I can't stop running my hands through it. Under the water, Perri pulls the plug and the water starts to drain. We can't look away from one another as more and more of her is knowingly revealed to me.

I reach forward and grab her hair in my fist. She gasps when I pull it back, but then I gentle my touch and start squeezing to get the water out. Still holding her eyes, I reach out for a towel and wrap it around her, then grab the other towel that she uses for her hair.

When she seems steady, I stand up and help her out.

Perri is standing in nothing but a towel, naked and so ill she's overly aware and stimulated, and I just guide her to the mirror so I can brush her hair. We watch each other through our reflections.

I get a deep sense of satisfaction from taking care of her like this. There's never been a chance to take care of anyone else in my life this way, and it feels good that it's her. That Perri is the one I get to be soft with when she needs it, even if she's probably too sick to remember it.

That's probably for the best.

Perri shivers and her eyes close. I know from watching over her shoulder that one of the "triggers" she likes in her ASMR videos is hair brushing. The brush does make a satisfying sound as I move it through her wet hair, and I move nice and slow. After a bit I start following the brush with my hand, stroking her forehead, the sensitive skin at her temples, dragging the rough pads of my fingertips across the curve of her ear. Perri sways and eventually leans back against me, sleepy and relaxed.

Once again, I pick her up. When we get to the bed, I pull the towel off. She doesn't event protest.

Perri is tucked under the covers in my bed and I lay down beside her. Instead of drifting off immediately, she's fidgeting. Moving and shifting like she can't get comfortable. I roll onto my side and move so that I'm a wall of heat against her body, and steady her with a hand on her hip over the blankets.

"What do you need, princess?"

She lets out a high, needy huff, and grumbles something that I can't understand.

"What was that?" I lean over her, putting my face next to hers, aligning our bodies even further.

"I need to get off," she grumbles, but this time I can understand. "It helps my headache."

I'm hard immediately. The vision of whipping off the blankets, ripping off my pants, and sliding into her from behind goes through my mind so quickly and clearly it's violent. I can't help rolling my hips and pressing my erection into her ass, my fingers squeezing her hips.

To my surprise, she rolls back, her body pressing into mine.

I tease her earlobe with the tip of my tongue.

"You gonna let me take care of you?" I shift my body away and pull down the blanket, exposing her smooth back to me. "I want to take care of you." It does not escape me that when I say it, I mean more than just in this moment. I mean it about more than getting her off so she feels better. I mean that I want to take care of her all the time. Be the steady thing that she can rely on for anything, no matter what.

I can't be, but god do I want to be.

Two months ago and I was almost a year into a vow of celibacy, and I wasn't even struggling. I didn't miss sex, companionship, or the other benefits of anything even close to a relationship, situationship, or even a one night stand. I was fine on my own.

One wayward woman and now I know when she leaves me it's going to feel like losing a limb.

"Please," she begs, and pushes the blankets further down, exposing her sweet ass to me. I give it a squeeze and she moans, her back arching.

I slide that same hand around her hip to the front of her body and dive between her legs. When the tip of my finger parts her pussy lips to get to her clit, I can feel that she's already slick and ready.

It's a literal ache in my chest that I can't kiss her.

But between the intimacy of the act and the risk of getting whatever it is that's making her sick, I hold back. Instead I focus on playing with her clit, paying attention to her reactions and doing what she likes. It takes a second for us to find our rhythm together, but it's not long before Perri is grinding against my hand and panting.

I watch her cup her breast, note the way that she pinches and tugs at her nipple.

When I move my finger faster, she cries out. "Yes!"

Doing exactly the same thing, even when my wrist is starting to hurt, is completely worth it when her thighs clench around me and she comes. I don't stop, working that sensitive little bundle over and over as she writhes next to me, her ass pressing into my cock and her head thrown back so I can bury my face in her hair, inhaling the addictive scent of her.

When she comes down, I pull my hand back and suck on the tips of my fingers. They taste of her, a perfect blend of sweet and tart.

I can't help it, I press a kiss to her temple.

"Get some sleep."

I lay next to her in the dark until she's breathing slow, finally passed out.

In my life, there's never been anything that put the Zastrow family in second place, not even close. Everything I am, do, decide, has been centered around what they need. Even as a kid, they came before my own family. Protecting them, being there for Harrison, telling the truth about what was happening with dad...no loyalty was higher than the loyalty I had for Andre and Harrison.

Perri is becoming a problem.

She's a close second, only barely, and there have already been times in the last few weeks especially where I have chosen her over them. When I put my possession of her over what I would have done in the past. She matters, and that makes her a threat.

A different kind than I expected, but a threat nonetheless.

She's also strong, smart, and relentless. Nim would be dead without her, of that I have zero doubts. Nim wouldn't have noticed anyone was following them or been concerned about Steve disappearing. We still haven't found him. She would have gone along with her shopping trip until they'd kidnapped her.

Perri Kane is my weakness, and it's starting to scare me.

24

Perri

Neo turned off my alarms so by the time I woke up I would have been very late for work, and I started to panic until I saw the note he left telling me I had the day off.

Even though I was feeling better, it was like I was recovering from a marathon. My body was tired, although not nearly as achy. Part of me thought that maybe Neo getting me off so I could fall asleep was a fever dream, but even a fever dream couldn't have given me an orgasm that good. I don't know what to do about the tension between us anymore, and every day I care less and less about the power dynamic. I care less about the threat of him.

It's like he's making his way inside me, and I have no defenses. My walls don't work against him.

When Neo gets home, he actually smiles when he sees me in the kitchen. Those full smiles are so rare and I cherish every time I see those lines around his mouth.

"Better?"

"A lot. Sometimes stress does that to my body. Lingering effects of last weekend."

He steps up behind me, close but not touching. I'm wearing one of his t-shirts and a pair of his boxers. It was a gutsy move on my part but I wanted to see how he would react to me wearing his clothes.

"I'm sorry," he says quietly. When he steps closer, I automatically lean back into him. One of his hands touches my thigh, fingertips teasing, rising high enough to lift the leg of his boxers. It's an intimate touch. Neo kisses the crown of my head, and I swear I swoon, my eyes fluttering shut and a sigh escapes me. The last of the painful tension leaves my body and is replaced by a whole different, but more pleasurable kind.

"It's okay. I'm okay."

He says nothing, just inhales me, and then lets me go.

"I'm going to take a shower. No boys for dinner tonight."

I laugh. "I'm too tired to cook that much. This is just for us."

I look over my shoulder when he doesn't say anything and I don't hear him move. Neo is watching me, heat and sadness in his gaze, and I understand that look completely. I feel it inside myself, the thing that makes my heart hurt whenever I think of him. We're perfect for each other, and yet...I can't trust him, and he doesn't trust me.

Trust him with my body, sure, but my heart, even in my life? I don't think so. I will always be a question or a game piece, and that's not how I want to live my life. Part of me recognizes that when I walk away, I will miss him forever. No part of my heart or soul will ever be complete, ever again. But it's a piece of me I'll sacrifice to be safe.

Neo nods and turns away.

I'm dumping my pasta into the strainer when the keypad for the front door beeps and opens. The guys were all told in the group chat that there's no dinner tonight, so if one of them is coming in it must be an emergency.

I turn to greet whoever it is but it takes a second for me to process that I have never seen this man before, and I don't know who he is.

"H-hello," I greet him. He's older, probably in his 50s. The man's hair is still dark but the scruff on his face is a mix of black and gray. There's a bleary look in his eyes that tells me he drinks a lot, and might even be a bit drunk right now.

"Hi sweetheart," he leers at me. I feel sick at the way his gaze rakes me up and down, as if I'm not wearing any clothes at all. I'm regretting my clothing choices and the fact that I'm not wearing a bra. My body instantly curves in on itself. "Neo around?"

"He's in the shower," I answer. "I can go get him?" I don't wait for an answer and start moving toward the bedroom, but the man takes a step toward me that blocks my path to it. If I move again he'll intercept me, and every inch of me is screaming at the idea of this man touching me. I know he's going to try, so I'm putting off the inevitable.

There's no way he got all the way here without one of the guards seeing him, and he had his own code to the door. This is a known entity to them. I have to reassure myself of that. I take a deep breath and step back toward the sink to continue preparing dinner.

"Have a seat and wait for him," I suggest, feeling like an idiot for turning my back on him but also feeling like it's my only choice. If I act normal and like I'm not afraid, then he won't think he can play with me.

The man snorts. "Ordering me around like it's your place. Ain't that something."

I'm not sure what he means by that so I don't say anything. I prep my pasta and dump it into the pan with the sauce I made from scratch, finishing making dinner.

"So you're what tempted him away from his vow of celibacy? I knew he was full of shit when he said that."

"I don't know what you're talking about," I reply quietly.

"Sure you do. I bet he thinks you don't count because it's not real."

My hands freeze. This man knows about our deal? The harsh statement that what Neo and I are isn't real makes my heart slow to one heavy, painful thump. He's right. We're not real. We're trapped together and tension is inevitable. None of this is real. I repeat it to myself and half tune the guy out as that thought takes over my entire mind. Not real. It's entirely possible my own feelings are because of our proximity and not based on anything true. It could be the same for him.

I don't know Neo Ryan. Anything he reveals to me, anything he does to me, is all part of a test. There's no way for me to parse out truth from manipulation.

"You are a sweet little piece though. I can see why you tempt him."

My skin crawls, and I turn the burner down to low, bracing myself to confront whatever the hell is going on. I turn around and he's sitting at the island, eyes focused on where my ass just was.

"How much do you run for a full night?"

"Excuse me?"

He sneers at me. "Don't play with me. It won't help with negotiations."

"I don't know what you're talking about."

"If I wanted to fuck you, how much would it cost me, bitch?"

"I'm not going to fuck you," I bleat out, fear tightening up my body and making me shake. I don't have the energy for this after the beating my body took last night from the fever.

"You too good for my money, huh? Just because Neo makes it through that fucking company doesn't make it any better than mine. It's still green."

"I don't know who you think I am, but I'm not - I'm not a sex worker."

The man snorts again. "Sex worker. Even that shit is woke now. You're a whore and I'm going to pay you to suck my cock and then take it up your ass, isn't that good enough?" He slams his hand down on the island and I jump.

It triggers my adrenaline and I run from the kitchen and into the bedroom.

At first, I don't hear anything, then I hear the violent shriek of the stool skidding against the floor and the sound of feet coming after me. It's going to be okay, as long as Neo didn't lock the bathroom door.

My hand hits the handle and it turns, making me whimper as I fly inside and slam the door behind me. The lock clicks loudly, and I turn and press my back to the door, breathing hard.

I can't even enjoy seeing Neo naked in the steamy shower. He stares at me in shock for a second before moving quickly. The water snaps off and he's stepping out, naked as the day he was born, thick cock swinging in front of him as he moves to me.

"What's the matter? What's happening?" He cups my face and makes me look at him, what appears to be genuine concern in his eyes.

"A man came to the apartment. He - he thinks I'm a sex worker and wants me to fuck him." When I say that out loud it sounds kind of silly, and a hysterical giggle escapes.

"What's he look like?"

I describe the man to Neo and watch as a mask falls over his face, until nothing but hardened fury lives in his expression.

"Fuck. I am so sorry Perri. I didn't think..."

"Who is he?" I ask. Neo is still holding my face and I lean into one of his hands, letting myself rest there. Exhaustion is building up inside me. This took all I had recovered - getting to him. Even if this isn't real, I still looked for him to save me.

"My father." Neo's thumbs streak across my cheeks absentmindedly, and then he lets me go. He turns away to grab a towel and at least now I'm in a place to enjoy the view of his fantastically sculpted ass. The desire to sink my teeth into it is powerful, considering the circumstances.

Neo walks over and pulls me behind him before he opens the bathroom door. He looks around and there's no one in the bedroom. He takes my hand and guides me to the bed, sitting me down and gesturing for me to wait. I get to watch as Neo dries off and gets dressed, never once trying to hide himself from me. It's pure torture to get to see him this way and know that I'll never have him. Even if he offered, I don't think I could do that to myself.

He pulls on his briefs, a pair of gym shorts, and a black t-shirt. Then he takes my hand again, pulling me behind him, and we walk out of the bedroom.

His father is sitting at the island, eating our dinner. Somehow that makes me angrier than anything else that happened tonight. How fucking rude.

"What are you doing here?" Neo snaps.

"I can't visit my son? Although I guess I should've called first." His gaze shifts to me and the sneer returns. "Sorry I interrupted your tryst. You'll have to ask for pro-rating."

"You're such an asshole," Neo says, disgust and disappointment dripping from his voice. "Perri Kane, meet my father, Martin Ryan. Da, you've already met and terrified my girlfriend."

Martin sits up at that. "Girlfriend? Huh. And she lives with you?"

Neo pulls me under his arm and I cling to him, still freaked out by the creepy drunk, and even more uncomfortable now that I know who he is. He wanted to fuck the same woman as his son, and that was probably a plus to him. I also know what a piece of shit he is and how he let down the man in my arms right now. I can't stop myself from glaring a little.

Martin laughs when he looks at me. "Aw, your little kitten wants to pretend she has claws. What's he told you about me?"

"Enough," I spit in response. "Enough to know you're lucky he lets you be in his presence at all."

"Ah, well, Neo's always been a sucker for family."

Neo stiffens beneath my hands, and I automatically start rubbing his back, trying to soothe the anger out of him. I can't decide if I'm surprised when it works, and that I feel him lean on me in return.

He turns to look down at me, everything in his expression soft. "Can we have a minute?"

"Of course. I...eat when you're ready. I'm going to bed."

"Thank you for making it." Neo takes my chin and tilts my head up, then presses the softest, most decadent kiss to my lips. It's a thank you and an apology all in one. When he breaks it, I press my forehead to his, willing for him that this isn't an entirely unpleasant interaction.

I leave without looking at Martin again, and crawl into bed. I catch brief snatches of their conversation. Try as I might to stay awake, I fall asleep to the angry murmur of their voices.

25

Neo

Martin chuckles as Perri walks away. "Apologies for upsetting the missus."

"Not accepted. What the fuck do you want?"

He doesn't say anything, just eats the food that Perri made for the two of us, helping himself to whatever he wants, as usual. Martin Ryan got a taste for taking, and he's never stopped. I've gotten better at not letting him take from me, but for a long time I gave him anything he needed.

I know he loved my mother. I know losing her broke all that was good inside him, and that what filled that empty space was something dark and ugly. The person I am looking at right now is not the father that I was born to, and it took a long time to accept that.

I do the bare minimum of keeping him alive, but that is the extent of my feelings of obligation.

"Ran into some trouble."

"Meaning?"

"A few bad bets. I was up and then I crashed hard." Martin can't even muster up a look of false shame. It's been a few years since I had to bail him out - since things were bad enough that I had to bail him out. Usually whoever is dumb enough to take his bet has him work off his debt, so this time it must be significant. Fuck.

"Who and how much?" I sigh.

"O'Connor, about $150k."

My stomach drops to the floor. The O'Connors are the ones who beat the shit out of me to get him to pay up. The ones that permanently scarred my fucking face and put me in the hospital. The reason that I got taken away from him. He promised me he wouldn't mess with them anymore. I couldn't get him to say he'd stop gambling, but I thought he'd at least have boundaries somewhere.

"Fuck you." I snarl at him. "I should let them destroy you."

Martin grins at me. "It's not me they'll destroy if they don't get their money."

He's not wrong, and it makes me sick. They'd come after me, after Zastrow, and now that I made the mistake of declaring Perri as mine, he'd probably tell them about her. They'd come after her to get me to pay them. He's backed me into a corner and there's only one way out.

The O'Connor family is ruthless. They wouldn't hurt Perri, they'd kill her. They know I have the money that Martin doesn't.

I lose my temper.

I shove him off the stool where he's sitting, him and his food clattering to the ground. Without a hint of hesitation, I step over him, grab him by the collar of his shirt, and punch him in the face.

It feels so fucking good, and it takes everything I have not to leave him a bleeding mess on my floor.

He squirms underneath my hold, trying to get away, but the person I used to think was the strongest man in the world is weaker now. He couldn't take me anymore, even on his best day. I hold him closer and wait until he looks in my eyes. One of his is already swelling shut.

"I'll pay the debt, but if you ever get involved with the O'Connors again, I'll kill you myself. Anybody else, but not them. Got it?"

"Got it," he grumbles. I shake him, hard. "I swear, I got it."

I let him go and step away, then think again and kick him in the side for good measure.

"Get the fuck out. You're not welcome here."

He crawls away and gets to his feet. Martin waits and looks at me. "You'll pay it?"

"Get out." I stare him down and say nothing, and eventually he turns and leaves.

The second the door shuts I pull up the cameras and follow his progress until he's out of the compound, the fence closed behind him. I turn on my heels, ignoring the mess of food on the floor, and go to the bedroom.

Luckily, Perri has fallen asleep. As quietly as possible, I change my clothes to go out, and gather my weapons. This is getting taken care of tonight, and until I know it's done, she's not leaving the apartment. If I have to, I'll make Zadie set her up to work from home until I know the threat has passed.

In the kitchen, I turn off the burner and cover the pasta she made for us. It looks delicious and my stomach grumbles, but I don't have time. I clean up the mess from my father, and look around the apartment. Everything seems fine, and I know that he left.

Downstairs, I head straight for Benji in the server room.

He turns to me with a grin and then drops it immediately. "What happened?"

"My dad was here."

"Shit." He swallows. "Is Perri okay?"

A raging jealousy fills me that his first thought is for her, and that she wouldn't be safe around my father. Keeping her under control is part of his job, but worrying about her isn't. I let it go, for the moment.

"Yes. I need you to deactivate his code, any access he has to my place. He hasn't used it in years, I assumed he'd have forgotten it."

"No problem." Benji pulls up one of our security programs and starts working.

"He's not allowed on any Zastrow property, but especially here. Get the word out. Officially."

Benji turns to look at me. It's a big move, and not one I would normally make. Issuing this means that if Martin shows up on any Zastrow property, he'll be arrested for trespassing. I've always done my best to keep him out of jail, and have paid for a lot of his mistakes, but for some reason scaring Perri, putting her in danger, that's the line being crossed that I cannot abide.

When or if I test Perri, there will be danger, but I will be in control of the situation. No one gets to hurt her or scare her except me. No one gets to elicit that kind of emotion from her except me. She is mine to keep, to play with, to rule over her fate. No one else will put that at risk.

"I have to go handle something. She's sleeping."

"Got it."

"Don't bother her, Benji. She's fine," I warn him.

Benji looks at me, disgruntled. "I said got it, boss."

We stare each other down, then I nod and leave.

Even though I stay away from them, I've made sure that I know enough about the O'Connors to keep it that way. I know businesses they have a hand in or own, I know where to stay away from, but I also know where to find them for the exact same reason.

For as long as they've been doing business, they can always be found at the Green Hill. It's a bar that does good business, even without the shadier stuff that happens in the backrooms. It's filled now, presenting a false vision of benign indulgence. The lights glow golden through the windows, the dark wood of the bar and the tables gleaming, and people are sitting around chatting and smiling, most unaware that their money is funding criminal activity.

When I step inside the bar, the people who do know take notice. One large bartender, and the men at one of the tables in the corner. They're there for the fight, not to do business. It's a weasel in a red leather jacket who approaches me.

"Neo Ryan. Thought we might be seeing you."

"Then let's get this over with."

The weasel grins at me and flicks his head, beckoning me to follow. We walk through the pub, down the hallway with the bathrooms, and into the office. Eamon O'Connor sits behind the desk, and I'm a little bit surprised. Most things these days are run by his son, Declan, and Eamon is considered retired for all intents and purposes. If you want something, it's Declan you deal with.

Then again, my father dealt with Eamon back in the day, so maybe Eamon wants to close the circle himself.

"Mr. O'Connor," I greet him with respect he doesn't deserve.

"Naomhan, how nice of you to visit." He uses my full name, knowing full well that I don't, and smiles at me.

"I'm here to pay Martin Ryan's debt."

"I'm sure you are."

That answer does not bode well for this conversation.

"Tell me where to wire the money."

Eamon stares me down. "You have the kind of money that you can pay it off, just like that? Must be nice."

"You make more than what he owes in a week. Where should I wire the money?" I press.

"There are many ways for a debt to be paid."

God fucking damn it. I should've seen this coming. I should've calmed the hell down and brought Thomas or Wilder with me. I wasn't thinking, I was acting, on impulse, fury, and fear. Even without Perri in the equation, I would have still ended up here just like this. I'm not rational where my father is concerned.

"It's cash, or nothing."

Eamon eyes me. "You aren't like your father."

"Thank Christ for that."

To my surprise, he gives a small chuckle. "In another world, that stalwart loyalty of yours would be with me and mine." Eamon shakes his head. "*Mbaineann tú le do mhuintir.*" He's telling me I belong with my people. Implying that the O'Connor family, and the work I would've done for the Irish crime families, is where I should be. That couldn't be further from the truth.

"*Baineann mé le mo chroí.*" I honestly don't know anymore if I mean Zastrow, or if I mean Perri. If when I say I belong with my heart, I mean both of them. I'm in denial because when I said it, I was only thinking of her.

"Spoken like a true Irishman. Fine, pay the debt."

"Tell my father his money is no good." The room changes with that statement, the oddly light tone we'd had going snuffed out.

"Money is money, boy," Eamon grumbles.

"And you know he's not good for it, and you know I'll never give in. Let someone else ruin his life. You're better than this." I swing for a compliment, hoping it gets me where I want to be with this conversation.

"I'll try, but no guarantees."

I raise my hands in surrender. "That's enough. Thank you."

One of the men comes toward me and we make the exchange. Giving them $150k smarts at both my pride and my savings, but neither will break me. I make a lot of money working for Zastrow and I spend very little. Perri living with me nearly tripled my food budget, but I don't mind.

I'll have to tell Andre about this. He'll need to be on guard for Martin to get up to shit, or try and rope Zastrow into his problems. It wouldn't be the first time.

Part of me wishes I was soulless enough to kill my father, but I know his own decisions will take him out when he least expects it.

When the exchange is confirmed, I'm allowed to leave.

On the way back to the compound, I call Andre. It's not even late, but I wake him up, and I hear Nim's voice in the background. That grosses me out a little bit but I move past it, explaining to him what happened tonight. What I had to do to make Martin go away.

"You should've called me first," Andre admonishes.

"Yeah. I should've done a lot of things, but I wanted him gone. I wanted it done."

"You're sure it's done?"

"From the O'Connors, yes. From whatever the fuck else Martin might do, I have no idea. He threatened Perri."

Nim exclaims something in the background and Andre shushes her.

"Is it time to end the arrangement?"

"No," I answer way too damn quickly. "I don't know enough yet."

There's a long silence and I can perfectly visualize the look that Andre would be giving me if we were having this conversation in person.

"It's not time," I add.

"Fine. But sometimes we don't get time, and life has other plans. Don't fight fate, Neo."

"Yes, sir."

He hangs up the phone without another word.

The compound is quiet and dark when I get back, and I curse the beeping of the door to the apartment when I get back because I hear Perri call my name.

"Neo?" It's soft and sleepy and a little bit scared and I feel fury again that my father put that fear into her. I slide off my shoes and walk to the bedroom.

"It's me."

Perri sits up, her hair disheveled from sleep, her eyelids heavy. There's so much concern on her face it breaks my heart. One day and decision at a time, I am ruining this woman's life. She's been living on the edge of a knife for months and yet she remains kind, calm, and cautious. It's in every line of her expression that she cares about me, and I can't take it anymore.

"I don't want a dream," I rasp into the dim light of the bedroom.

Perri freezes and her gaze flies to mine. She's suddenly awake. She watches me as I throw off my shirt, then do the same to my jeans, until I'm standing before her in nothing but my briefs. My cock was hard and aching the second I heard her sleepy voice, the vulnerability in it arousing me every fucking time.

I'm supposed to make her love us, but what I'm accepting in this second is that I also want to make her love me. Even if it destroys us both.

26

Perri

Neo stands before me, almost naked, completely hard, and the look in his eyes makes me wet instantly. I'm worked up and clenching and I might explode out of my skin if this isn't going where I think it is. If we haven't finally reached our breaking point.

"I want you, Perri," Neo rumbles. "Do you want me?"

"I want you," I answer, quick and desperate. He gives that small twist of his lip, the small thing that counts as his normal smile. It's gone fast, and he climbs up the bed like a panther stalking prey. I lean back on the pillows and spread my legs open, inviting him to attack.

Neo pulls the blankets down, finding me still in his clothes. He grins now, but it's dark and feral.

"Were you trying to tease me with this?" He slides a palm under the shirt, sliding up until he cups my breast and then pinches my nipple.

"Yes," I cry out, arching into his hand for more. Neo pulls back but it's only so he can remove the shirt entirely. There's a hunger that mirrors mine when he looks at my body.

"Lay down."

I do what he says and gasp as his hand slides up my leg and beneath the boxers, his rough fingers teasing my soft lips. Neo leans over me, his eyes on me, watching me react to the way he touches me. As if my reactions confirm something for him, he nods to himself and then dips his head to suck one of my nipples into his mouth.

It's almost violent, the way he tugs and bites at it, but I feel every pulse of his mouth directly in my clit, my arousal growing with each drag. I feel devoured and he's not even inside me yet.

My hands fly up to his head, running over his shorn hair and stimulating another one of my senses as he takes me apart with his mouth on my breast and his fingers toying with my clit. He's not trying to make me come, he's trying to make me lose my mind, and I happily concede all control to him.

He feels it in the way my body relaxes. He feels the moment I give in to him entirely.

"Get on your knees for me." His voice is growly and desperate and I moan at the sound of it. Hearing the way he wants me too.

I stand up and shove off the boxers, flinging them to the side, and then drop to my knees on the floor. I look up at him, not hiding a shred of the want that I feel, and he groans and bites his lip. I can't look away when he shoves his briefs down, freeing his cock for me. Neo strokes it and watches me, then leans forward and presses his thumb to lips.

Naturally, I part them and suck his finger inside. I love the taste of him. I love the rasp of his harsh skin against the softness of my tongue. I swirl it around the tip of his finger, then suck, taking a piece of him inside me. Begging him for something more.

"Do you want to taste me, princess?"

I nod, not letting up on my oral assault of his thumb. Neo watches, dark delight on his face.

"I don't want to be nice to you, Perri," he says as he pulls his thumb out, then drags it down my chin. He holds me there so I can't look away. "I want to take you in every way until you're screaming."

"Yes," I agree.

"This isn't going to be sweet, or romantic. I'm going to bruise you, Perri. I'm going to make sure you feel me in all the softest parts of your body for days. Weeks. I'm punishing you as much as I'm punishing myself, do you understand?"

"Yes," I moan, squirming eagerly on the floor. If he keeps talking like that there's going to be a pool underneath me. I can already feel how wet I am on my thighs and ass, even on the heels of my feet from how I'm kneeling. I have never wanted anyone like this. While I like a firm hand in the bedroom, there's this intense desire for him to destroy me. If he told me he was going to slap me I'd probably say yes and come on command when he did it.

I want him to own my pain as much as my pleasure, and that's an entirely new experience for me. Whatever he wants, I want to give him. It's not in my nature to please, it's more like me to want to soothe. I don't want to please or soothe Neo. I want to set him off.

"Give it to me," I beg, and then open my mouth for him.

"Fuck," he hisses before grabbing a handful of my hair and pulling me forward. Neo holds his cock and aims it for my mouth, pushing me down until his cock is deep and pressing against the back of my throat. He holds me there and I breathe through my nose, spit sliding out of my mouth and down onto his balls. Neo presses harder, deeper, and I relax my throat.

His hand relaxes in my hair, and then he gathers it all in a ponytail at the top of my neck.

"Suck, princess."

I slide up his cock, dragging my tongue along the underside and teasing especially along the sensitive skin at the top. Neo groans but doesn't push me down again. His grip on my ponytail is tight, but he lets me set my own rhythm. He feels good in my mouth, long and thick, and the slide of his velvety skin against my sensitive tongue is arousing. Not to mention the noises he tries to stifle.

Each muffled groan has my body clenching and flexing, and the sharpness of his breathing as he tries to hold off gives me satisfaction.

Neo pushes down on my head, and I take him into the back of my throat again, swallowing reflexively. He groans again and slides me completely off of him.

"Did you like that?"

"Yes."

"If I made you suck me until I came, would you swallow me?"

"Yes." There's no sense in denying it, or acting like I don't want to taste him that way. "You wouldn't be making me do anything," I murmur. "I want to do it."

He lets go of my hair and leans back on the bed, resting on his elbows. Neo's eyes have dropped, gaze heavy, and he looks ominous but sexy in the dim light.

"Prove it."

I move closer, and run my hands up his strong, thick thighs as I kneel between them. One of my hands moves to his balls, and the other wraps around the base of his cock. I give him a smug smile before I lean over and take him back into my mouth.

I'm a champion multitasker. I pulse my hand slowly around his balls as I slide up and down on him, playing with his cock with my tongue, getting him worked up and overly sensitive. Every few strokes I go deep, then slide up slow and tight.

Beneath my forearms, I can feel his thighs tensing and relaxing as he tries to forcibly stay his own orgasm. That's unacceptable.

I slide all the way down on his cock and then stick my tongue out further, the tip of my tongue putting pressure on the base.

"Oh, fuck," he groans and falls back, his hands diving into my hair. He's on the edge now, all I have to do is finish him.

"Come in my mouth, Neo," I whisper. "I want it."

I can feel him thicken against my tongue, and the tension in his body as he braces to come makes him shake. He makes a sound, a rumbling groan, and I know I have him now. The first spurt of his come is across my tongue when I'm halfway down his shaft. I swallow and keep going, tasting each salty burst until his head is all the way back of my throat. I hold there as his hips jerk and pulse, swallowing slowly as I pump his balls for that extra pleasure.

I slide off him and wait for him to recover. He sits up and stares down at me.

"With a show like that, I might come in your mouth every morning."

I give my head a cocky tilt as I look up at him. "Promises, promises."

Lightning fast, Neo reaches for me and has me over his thighs, my ass up in his face. Before I know what's happening, his big hand slaps my ass cheek.

"Are you a brat, princess?"

"Maybe," I hedge. While I would never have categorized myself that way before, it's fun to push and taunt him. It feels good to pick at the edges of his control. I don't want a controlled Neo. I want the animal he keeps chained inside. I want the monster.

He slaps my ass again, over and over, teasing me with each pleasured cry I let out. When he slides his hand between my legs and feels how unreasonably wet I am, he lets out an evil chuckle.

"I thought I'd have a snack, but you're giving me a whole damn meal, aren't you?"

I'm half out of my mind so I can only nod.

Neo moves me around like I weigh nothing, and I find myself on my back with my legs spread open and my knees pushed to my chest. He doesn't give me a second to think or breathe before his tongue is plunging into my pussy, licking up the mess he caused. He shifts so one of his forearms is pressing my leg up and his thumb can reach my clit.

I shake from the feel of it all as he licks me and presses into me, relentless and unstoppable.

"If you want my cock in this desperate pussy, you're going to have to come for me."

Neo slides his fingers inside me and wraps his lips around my clit. His tongue pulses against me and my hips lift, wanting more and wanting to get away at the same time. It doesn't stop him, his hands and mouth move with me, and I scream as I grasp at his head to hold him closer.

My orgasm is a pulse of pleasure that matches my heartbeat, pushing through my body until I'm gasping and writhing, pressing so hard into his face it has to be preventing him from breathing. Neo slides his fingers out of me, but continues to lick and suck at my clit, sending intense little aftershocks through my body.

He stands up, hard as ever, and I gasp when he leans over and picks me up. Neo crawls over the bed, holding onto me, until we're both fully on it.

"I'm going to fuck you raw, princess." I feel the head of his cock notched at my entrance, sliding in the slick come pooled there.

"I'm on birth control," I manage to answer.

That feral grin is back as he looks down at me. "It wouldn't have mattered. I'm taking you however I want, remember?" With that hanging in the air between us, Neo slams inside me. I scream, arching my back at how good it feels, wanting him to get deeper even if it's not possible.

Neo takes that as an invitation and leans down to bite one of my nipples. It sets off an immediate orgasm, my hips pumping on his cock, the friction of it drawing everything out. He sucks me into his mouth and lets me have my way with his body, teasing every ounce of pleasure out of me.

When he lets go of my nipple, he bites the top curve of my breast. I can do nothing but lay there and cling to him as he marks his way across my skin, leaving pleasurable bruises behind. Neo starts to roll his hips, sliding in and out of me in smooth, shallow thrusts.

One of his hands slides under me and grips the back of my neck, while the other drifts to my hip. His fingers dig in and I know he's trying to mark me there too.

Part of me wants to tell him he doesn't have to do that. He's leaving marks inside me that will never heal, never fade, and never be forgotten. If there's anything I've learned about him, it's that he feels like he constantly has to prove his worth to the people he cares about. Neo is worth everything to me, but I'll never say it.

I can show it, though.

I take his face in my hands and drag his mouth to mine. He gives in to me when he doesn't have to, and we ravage each other's mouths as his hips start to move faster. Neo's thrusts are sharp, his hips snapping into my body, causing me to squeeze around him over and over, like my pussy is trying to trap him inside me and never let him go.

Our tongues play as we move against each other, bodies grinding and seeking more. My nails dig into his neck as I start to come again, and I try and break away from his mouth to catch my breath but he won't let me. His big hand holds my head firmly in place as he forcibly kisses me, stealing my air until I'm seeing spots. I don't stop, and I don't fight him.

Neo maneuvers one of my legs over his shoulder, spreading me impossibly wide. That's when he stops kissing me. So he can look down and watch as he makes me come apart.

We fuck each other like its attempted murder. I rock into him, he pounds into me, and we never look away from one another. It's both a battle of wills and a tie that we can't escape. A bond is forming that I don't want to break. His thrusts get jagged and rough as he reaches the edge and it sets me off one more time - I cry out but don't look away. I let the feeling take over my entire body and scream his name.

"Perri," he groans, and presses his forehead to mine as he comes inside me. Neo stills and stays like that, holding us together, until he can't hold himself up any longer. He's heavy when he collapses on me, but I wrap my arms around him and bury my face in his neck. I don't know if this is a one time thing, or a from now on thing, but it doesn't matter.

Once was enough to ruin me. I want to regret it, but I can't.

27

Neo

It's been too fucking quiet.

It's made it too easy for me to disappear into a little bubble of fucking Perri's brains out, and then eating dinner together in bed. Too easy for me to get obsessed with joining her in the shower and washing her hair. I've started watching TV with her, cuddled on the couch together, and rubbing her back until she inevitably falls asleep on top of me. I know about her day and she knows what I can tell her of mine.

We're perfectly domesticated and it's terrifying.

It tells me that the time is coming to let her go. She's loyal to us. We've given her a home and a purpose, as well as enough in her bank account to be independent. Everything that she said she wanted at the outset, and everything that Andre asked me to do. Perri is part of the family.

Soon, I'll test her, and she'll walk away.

The time is coming.

At Zastrow, things are going well. The final stages of the Warren media deal are starting, and it also means that as a show of good faith they've killed any of the bullshit stories about Nim and Andre. Norman Warren is kind of a strange guy but he's sticking to his end of the deal.

The quiet means a false sense of comfort, which means I'm with Harrison, Leander, and Wilder in a conference room at Zastrow planning security for Andre and Nim's wedding anniversary party.

Harrison and I were both against it, but Nim said we had to keep up appearances, and rich people needed very little reason to throw a party. It's bizarre to me that they've been married for 5 years already. I don't feel old enough to have a friend who has been married for that long.

I look at Harrison across the room, where he's sorting through the guest list, and wonder when he'll finally give in to the pressure. Andre has been poking him about it for the last 2 years. Not that he needs to get married, but that he needs to establish a timeline for doing it. Even if that means a strategically arranged marriage or if he's suddenly going to start dating and find someone himself. Harrison has been lukewarm about it all. I haven't asked too much.

Up until Perri, no one really questioned my vow of celibacy.

I turn back to the blueprint on the board.

"The entire venue is rented our for two days. No one goes in or out without our notice after the sweep," Wilder confirms. "I've got low level guys that can monitor it all until the day of the party, and then we upgrade."

"Who will be on sight the day before?"

"I think Thomas. He's the one least likely to enjoy the party, so we give him pre-party duty and he'll be back up at home if something happens."

I grunt. It feels like "when" something happens. Things have been going too well, everyone has been too happy, and so many of our problems disappeared without us solving them. It makes me suspicious and paranoid.

"Fine. Start pulling the staff assignments together - a month's notice should be enough," I flip through my planning list. "Have all the vendors been vetted?"

"Yes. And we're bringing in our own staff, so they've been cleared as well."

"This is annoying," Harrison grumbles. "What's the point of having convenience at your disposal if you have to do it all on your own anyway?"

"Poor little rich boy," I tease and he gives me a frown. "You're too powerful for basic now. How sad for you."

Harrison gives me the finger, and I give it back.

"Boys, I raised you to be gentleman."

Harrison and I both snap to attention, turning to watch his father walk in the door. Andre looks casual, no blazer, no tie, and one hand is in his pocket. While it looks casual, it usually means he's been thinking something over and gets more and more disheveled the harder he has to think about it. Andre gets his best thinking done swimming laps in the pool at the Long Island estate.

"Sorry, sir," I apologize. Andre waves it away.

He steps up to the board and looks at the security plan, nodding, but it's just him delaying what he came here to say. I can't tell if he needs to talk to me or to Harrison, so there's no option except to wait him out.

"I think you should come for dinner tonight."

When I look at him he's staring at me, which means he invited me to dinner.

"Sir?"

"And bring Perri. I want to meet her." He turns away from me. "You come too, Harrison."

"Sure," Harrison replies with a forced smile.

Andre gives us a firm nod and then leaves the room.

"What the hell?" I ask Harrison.

"No idea."

My stomach swoops but I ignore it, and go back to working on security with Wilder. This is another test for Perri, and I hope that she's ready for it.

28

Perri

After being sick, I had to catch up on work and it meant my investigative project fell to the side. Now that things are back under control, I pull up my spreadsheet.

Part of me is hoping that it will tell me something different this time, but it doesn't.

Someone has been defrauding Zastrow, and it's been pushed through by the people above me. My instinct tells me that it's not Zadie, which leaves Adam and the other second level managers. The numbers are exactly the same, and when I looked into it, all the proposals trace back to the same series of shell companies.

One name keeps coming up over and over the deeper I go: O'Connor. It took me awhile to remember why that name set off warning bells in my head, but I remember the little bit of the conversation I overheard between Neo and his father. Martin Ryan owed money to the O'Connor family. I would bet they're the same.

A crime family is ripping off Zastrow, and they have internal help to do it.

The reason we have so many layers of review is so something like this doesn't happen. My guess is that whoever is doing this tries to spread out the fraudulent ventures so that we don't recognize the similarities. Somehow, I got assigned two of them within a few weeks and caught on.

I'm wondering if other analysts have noticed before and they got paid off to let it go through. It makes me paranoid to tell anyone.

I could tell Neo, but I don't think he'd understand it.

So instead of saying anything, I pull together the spreadsheet I made that compares the numbers of the different ventures, and highlight the highly improbable similarities. I save it on a thumb drive because I'm afraid if I leave it on the system it will be found.

I wait for Adam and the others to leave for lunch before approaching Zadie's office.

She looks up and gives me a smile, and I hope that I'm doing the right thing.

"Do you have a minute?"

Her face falls and she nods, indicating for me to close the door.

I place the drive on her desk. "Someone is defrauding Zastrow."

Zadie flinches. "Are you sure?"

"It's all there."

She takes the drive and puts it in her laptop, then pulls up the spreadsheet. The frown on her face deepens with each line she reads.

"Fuck."

I don't move, I wait, and she moves to the system files, clicking through a bunch of information faster than I could read it. She's swearing again under her breath, and muttering things to herself that I can't quite understand. Zadie pales when she runs some report that I don't have access to, and she looks at me.

"Thank you for bringing this to my attention. Things might get...ugly for the next few hours. Given the recent situations you've been through, do you feel okay to stay here?"

"Yeah, I'm fine. Is there anything I can do to help?"

"Harrison or the CFO, Mandy, might want to talk to you."

"Okay."

"I should've caught this," Zadie shakes her head and presses a hand to her forehead, her thumb massaging her temple.

"No. Whoever did this had a very specific plan to dupe our system, and it's not a bad thing to trust your team."

Zadie sighs. "I know. I know." She pauses, hesitating. "It was Adam, Perri."

My stomach drops and I feel sick. "I was afraid of that. I'm the one who should've seen it earlier."

"Based on how long you've been here he probably didn't think it was possible, and he probably underestimated you."

"Most people do."

We share a smile, which is odd given the circumstances, but I have a feeling Zadie got underestimated a lot, too. She nods at me.

"Thank you, Perri."

"I can't really say you're welcome, but thank you for believing me."

We share another look and then I leave her to it, wandering to the break room to heat up my chicken and rice for lunch. Most of the people on my floor go out for lunch, and I kind of enjoy my quiet lunches by myself here. No one bugs me if I want to read a book or watch videos while I eat.

It's one of the few times I feel truly alone.

Even if what Neo and I have feels like a relationship, I know that it's not. I know he's watching me on the cameras in the apartment, I know he's waiting for me to make a wrong move, and I know that he's holding back because when he's done testing me he'll be done with me, period.

In the break room is my little slice of peace where I don't feel surveilled.

The fucked up truth of that hits me, and I put my head in my hands and try not to cry. I don't know how my life got here, this bizarre mix of good and bad, safe and unsafe, a constant threat that's wrapped in the most amazing comfort. I take a deep breath and finish my lunch.

The afternoon is ugly.

I'm already back in my cubicle when Harrison and Thomas come busting onto the floor and straight to Zadie's office. Both of them give me a nod in greeting on the way, which surprises me but is also nice. There's a lot of gesturing and I can hear how frustrated Harrison is - it's almost enough for me to text Neo to get me out of here, but he probably knows about the situation and has to stay here.

When everyone else gets back from lunch, I put on my headphones and pretend to focus. I'm not actually getting much work done and given my state of mind I should stay away from anything important. It surprises me how good I am at looking busy when I'm actually tense and waiting for the blow up to happen.

Zadie calls Adam into her office. He's smiling, and when he sees Harrison is there he looks pleased, of all things. Like Harrison's presence means something good for him. That's probably going to change quick. They shut the blinds in Zadie's office.

It doesn't take long before the shouting starts, and the whole floor stills. Waiting. I know Thomas, and Harrison for that matter, can hold their own and wouldn't let anything happen to Zadie if Adam loses it and tries to get physical. There's some more shouting, and we all watch the windows of the office as if the blinds will suddenly part and all will be revealed.

The elevator dings, announcing an arrival to the floor, and as one we all swivel to see who is interrupting the show. It's Neo, escorting two police officers. My eyes get wide, and my thighs clench seeing him in work mode. He's big, brooding, and a little scary. His eyes stay straight ahead, but when he walks past the entrance to my cubicle his hand moves, like a little greeting just for me.

That shouldn't be nice. That shouldn't make the tightness inside me over uncovering this mess release from my chest. I'm breathing normally by the time the officers step inside Zadie's office. They walk out with Adam's hands cuffed behind his back, still escorted by Neo.

He looks delicious like this. Dressed well but radiating strength and that ever present aura of fuck with me and you will find out. I am drawn to how steady and sturdy he is; right from the first. Neo looks unshakable and I want someone like that to be unshakable about me.

It's no use hoping or wishing. It's what would kill me in the end.

29

Neo

As much as I feel a sense of pride for Perri discovering what her boss was doing, it also made a fuck ton of work for me.

After seeing Adam Smith safely into the back of a cop car, I head to the security office and initiate the separation checklist. I still have a private office here as well as the one upstairs in case I'm needed for an issue like this, but it's empty except for a desk and chair. My laptop is waiting for me, and I get started. I don't even bother turning on the light, but prefer to sit in the increasing dark and avoid florescent lights.

Shutting off his access to the building is priority one, then to every account or database that he was on - which is a ton since he was a supervisor - shutting down his email, and then putting a preservation hold on his technology. Our in house IT guy, Dillon, makes quick work of that. I also have to contract with a forensic accountant to sort through everything he ever touched.

I know that in a few years Perri wants to do the certification for forensic accounting. Given her attention to detail out of habit, I don't think she'll do anything but amazing. Even though Harrison explained it to me, I didn't quite understand what she found or how she found it.

Harrison is taking care of alerting legal since they'll be making sure every possible charge is pressed against Adam, and immediately ending or pausing the contracts for the fraudulent projects.

The thing that makes me the most anxious is that the shell companies are traced back to the O'Connors. Adam Smith was working for them within our own walls, stealing our money for all of their shit. I bet Eamon O'Connor was laughing his ass off on the inside when I gave him even more money the other night.

What I want to know and will probably never learn is if Adam did this by choice, or if they had something on him like they tried to do to me. While he was a competent employee, the second the cops showed up he deflated and stopped fighting. He knew he'd been caught.

I set an alarm on my phone because I want to get Perri with enough time to get to the compound to change before we have to head to Long Island.

It's a lot of paperwork, and I hate it, but I need to do this by the book. If he's been backed by the O'Connors, it means they're in the mood to fuck with Zastrow. That also means they'll probably hire him an attorney to file a wrongful termination suit in addition to fighting the criminal charges. Every motherfucking duck needs to be in a row.

I finish what I can and send the rest to Harrison and HR to fill out. We'll do the internal investigation stuff over the next week, and we don't want to interfere with anything from the law enforcement side either. It might only be a white collar crime but to whatever extent he can be prosecuted, we want it.

That does not stop me from messaging Benji to get one of his minions digging into everything about Adam Smith that might have led him to do this. If he was hurting for money, if he had a gambling problem or addiction, we need to know how else we might be vulnerable.

There's a knock on my door and I look up expecting Harrison, but instead it's Tabby. It takes everything I have to hold in a groan. I do not feel like dealing with her today. If she crosses a line, I'm reporting her to HR again. They have a file because I wanted a record kept but I also don't want to be the asshole that gets her fired.

She leans against the door with her arms crossed under her breasts, pushing them up so her cleavage is visible in the unbuttoned V of her polo shirt.

"How's it going, boss?" It's even more cringe when she calls me boss with a tone that makes it seem like she's really calling me "daddy." There's so much she insinuates with the way she says that one word, and I have to wonder where she gets the audacity. I have repeatedly rejected her. She never stops.

"Busy day," I grunt in reply.

"I heard. It's gotten around pretty quickly."

"Anything I need to know about?"

"Nope." She pops the p and then licks her lips. I look away from her and back at my computer, except I don't have anything to do at the moment. I had just wrapped everything up and was going to drop my laptop back at my office before grabbing Perri to go home.

Tabby pushes off the door and comes over to the desk, not stopping in front of it like a subordinate should, but coming around it. She moves her body to block my view of the screen, putting a hand on each arm of my chair. I rear back, but she's got an iron grip.

"How's your girlfriend?"

"Brilliant," I snap. I feel cornered. Tabby is crossing a line but she's also a useful employee. There has to be a delicate way to extricate myself from this that doesn't involve shouting or violence, and lets her walk away with her pride intact. At this point, Tabby is on the line of becoming a liability, but it will be worse if I fire her. She's the kind that would want to get revenge, unless letting me go is her idea. Or if someone else steps in to make it stop.

"Now that I know you're willing to mix business with pleasure, I'm happy to offer pleasure," she purrs out, and one of her hands drifts to my thigh and starts to slide toward my cock. I'm so flaccid and embarrassed I'd swear it's trying to shrink away from her.

My hand lands heavily on top of hers, halting her movement.

"I believe in monogamy, Tabby. I'm a one woman man." Even though I'd say anything to get out of this, that statement is 100% true. It's part of what led to my vow. If it wasn't going to be the whole, big, real love, I didn't want it, and I had given up on ever finding it. Being alone was better than being disappointed and betrayed.

She snorts. "Given who we work for, I find that hard to believe." Tabby licks her lips, and focuses her eyes on mine. I'm so distracted by the comment she made and what it might mean that I almost fail at dodging her attempt to kiss me.

I grab her hands and use them as leverage to roll my chair back. Tabby stumbles and rights herself, hands on her hips.

"I am in love with Perri. I only see Perri. I only *want* to see Perri. Please leave me alone." I grit out, both angry at the situation and freaking out that I'm saying things about Perri that I'd never say to her face. Even if I think I might be starting to feel them. "I don't want this to cross a line that I have to take action on," I warn softly.

Tabby stiffens and takes a step back from me. "Message received."

"Apparently not," a voice says from the door and both our heads snap toward it. A pit sinks into my stomach when I see Perri standing there. She has her hands clasped in front of her, looking demure and entirely unthreatening. I want to scoop her up and squeeze her to me. The desire to touch her and reassure her is enough to make my heart race.

"I know that your powers of observation are astute, Tabby, I've heard wonderful things about your work, but clearly you're ignoring every signal that you are making Mr. Ryan uncomfortable. It's also clear that he values your work abilities more than his desire to be comfortable. I'd take that for the gift it is and walk away now."

She takes a step into the room to clear the doorway, and gestures toward it.

Tabby won't look at me or Perri.

She nods and walks out. "Ma'am," she mutters to Perri and basically runs over to the other side of the office suite. Perri is still, and won't meet my eyes.

I close my laptop and stand up, walking over to her. Her hands remain limp when I take them in mine.

"Thank you. I'm sorry."

Perri takes a deep breath and looks at where I hold her. "This isn't real. You don't owe me anything," her voice shakes, "but please don't...with someone at work."

I scoff, unable to help myself.

"Perri, I decided to be celibate. I didn't miss sex. What we're doing..." I don't know how much to admit to her or how much it's going to obscure what's going on. "That's about you. This isn't real, but it's not...not real, either."

It's the most complicated thing I've ever done in my life. Everything that I thought I knew about myself, every line and boundary that I set, every expectation I had for my relationships, is completely out the window because of her. I'm in exactly the kind of thing I dreaded with her because I can't actually call her mine. We cannot pursue a commitment with each other and that's all I've ever wanted. This is the universe's big fucking test of my entire being.

She finally looks up at me, her eyes glassy with emotion and restrained tears.

"I get that. I'm sorry she's been bothering you."

"I should have handled it more firmly when it started."

"Despite your ability to kick someone's ass, you are reluctant to hurt their feelings."

I laugh and pull her under my arm, guiding her out of the office so we can head to the car. Even if it's partially a show, it also feels good. Like I have her, even if I don't.

"It's less about them and more about me." We wave to Monson, who has the evening shift at the main desk. "We're going to the Long Island estate tonight. Andre wants to meet you."

Perri stumbles a step. "Is that...a good thing?"

"Yes."

Andre's perspective on her is going to matter. It's going to give her more freedom, but it's also going to get me one step closer to truly having to test her loyalty. I keep my arm around her all the way to the car, knowing that this is finite.

30

Perri

We're almost to the Long Island estate when I crack.

"How do I play this?"

Neo tries to smother a smirk but fails. "What do you mean?"

"Is this a casual, friendly dinner? Is this a business dinner and I need to be in professional mode? Are other people going to be there and we need to act together? Can I be friendly with you or do I need to keep my distance?"

He bites his lip, trying not to laugh, and I want to lean over and bite it myself in retaliation.

"It's friendly. You don't have to fake anything, and you can be as friendly with me as you want to be."

"What if I don't want to be friendly with you?" I tease him.

Neo glances over at me, an unreadable but undoubtedly dark look on his face. "Then I guess I'll have to remind you how much you like it when I'm nice. What it's like when I take care of you. And I'll teach you what happens when you act like a brat."

I shiver, my nipples hardening and my pussy flexing automatically, and the echo of him inside of me is still there. I've never been fucked like he fucked me, and every single time it's been that intense. I feel it every time I move.

"None of that motivates me to be friendly." I hear how breathy I sound, and I know that he knows he got to me.

"I wasn't trying to," he glowers in response.

I groan. "Do we have to do this?"

Neo laughs. "Yes."

We pull up the long driveway to the massive stone house in the center of the estate. It's lit up and gorgeous, somehow homey and imposing at the same time. That kind of describes my experience with the Zastrows though. Nim is a force and can be overwhelming in getting what she wants, to the point that it's intimidating. Harrison is all ice on the surface with a warm core that he lets people that know him see. I've gotten a few glimpses of it, and he's an intimidating but fair boss and employees respect him.

Andre is nothing but intimidating. Even before all of this, I was nervous to work for him because of how he came across. A relentless businessman known for his harsh ethics and dogged fight. Yet, the people that are in his good graces can't say enough good things. With all the weird media stories that popped up, for every time they tried to trash Zastrow someone else had something good to say, and got defensive on his behalf. Andre and Nim have never given a comment on the stories, but they've got so many defenders they don't have to.

Even without meeting Andre, I'd defend them, too. I know enough from Nim, from working at Zastrow, from being around Neo and the guys, to know good people. My instincts have rarely ever failed me. Enough people hurt you, you get good at finding the ones that do it by choice.

We park and by the time we get out, Nim and Andre are standing outside the front door. Andre has his hand on her lower back, and she's bouncing up and down with excitement. When we get close she steps away and takes my hand, pulling me from Neo.

"Babe, this is Perri Kane. My friend and savior."

I extricate myself from her and offer Andre my hand.

"Nice to meet you, sir."

He takes my hand in both of his, and the imposing businessman mask is not present when I look into his face. "Likewise. You seem to be a savior in many aspects of my life."

I blush and step back, leaning on Neo automatically.

"Saving my wife, catching someone stealing from me...we made a good decision the day we hired you."

"That was my idea," Harrison says from behind them. "Come on. Apps are out."

The inside of the house is warm wood, dark fabrics, and ornate metalwork. It's medieval with a modern spin here and there. I follow them as they talk, winding deeper into the house until we reach a room in the back that has an entire wall of windows. It looks back onto a rolling lawn that's already covered in a creeping fog.

The furniture here is more modern, clean lines and in shades of gray and charcoal. There's a fire going in the fireplace even though the day was warm. There's a chill in the air, and I'm shocked to realize it's almost September already. I've been in this situation for months. I've been working at Zastrow for months.

My life looks entirely different than it did the night I stepped into that club.

I haven't seen my friends although the groupchat is as active as ever, and we've been doing a good job of keeping up with each other. I have enough money that I can find an apartment with no problem when I'm allowed to leave. Life feels sturdier, like I'm on solid ground between work, my savings, and my feeling like I'm adding something to the lives of the people around me.

My freedom might be compromised but on one level, this all feels like a small miracle.

I'm tired of pretending I don't want this.

Nim invites us all to sit down on the couches arranged around a coffee table that's full of treats. I move to sit next to Neo, and I see him and Harrison exchange a surprised look. Nim, on the other hand, looks delighted.

She fills up a plate for me and hands it over, talking a mile a minute about the media story because we went into a baby store. They left alone the cheating stories to speculate non-stop that she's pregnant, and used the last month's worth of photos to figure out if she had a growing bump. Nim thinks their speculations on her food babies is hilarious.

I don't know how she stands up to that kind of scrutiny, but it's impressive.

"Now, of course, they've turned to saying the baby isn't Andre's. My poor speculative child has so many daddies." She pats her perfectly flat belly.

I laugh. "Better than no daddies?"

"Cheers," she laughs as she clinks her glass to mine.

I shift so I'm facing her more directly, but Neo is still pressed up against my side as he talks to Harrison. Andre is staring at all of us with a soft look on his face that makes me feel a pang of envy. Despite his now sexual and romantic relationship with Nim, he spent his life protecting them. Raising them up. I'd be proud if I was him too.

"How's it going?" she asks, soft enough that they'd hear but wouldn't understand her.

"Fine?" I answer it like a question because something in her tone gives me pause. Like she's concerned about me, that something might be wrong.

"I mean, living with the guys, isolated in the warehouse, sharing space with that dork?"

To my surprise, her judgment rankles. "I like it. I don't need much and the guys are good company. Neo is good company."

"He can be. He hasn't been in a long time." She looks past me to him, and we both listen to him laugh at something Harrison said. There's this version of Neo that I've gotten to know because of our proximity, and because of the shake up I've caused in his life and his world. A version of him that I think came into existence because of me. Alongside of me.

Nim's comment makes me wonder what he was like before me, and what the versions of him before that were like, too. I'm a big believer in the idea that people can and do change. Maybe not in the ways we'd like them to, but humans morph and evolve all the time based on how we are affected by experiences.

There was the me I was growing up with my parents, the person I became after, the person I became after my aunt's abuse. Boarding school and college changed me, so did being pulled in by Cassandra and her friends. The job at Zastrow would've changed me too because I would finally have felt like there was an external entity worth dedicating my time and energy toward. I'd worked so hard for survival that now I have the space to think about what living successfully looks like to me. So many of my changes from all of this have been positive and have made me a better version of myself.

For Neo...life kept hitting him, and hitting hard. For every step he took forward he was smashed back with a wrecking ball. His mom dying, his dad's addiction, his assault, and the debt he must feel to Andre Zastrow for taking care of him. It wouldn't surprise me if he doesn't feel successful, or like he earned any of the things he has. It kind of breaks my heart to think about.

"I like you, Perri Kane. It was totally worth you crashing my party."

Neo hears and turns to us. "What was worth that?"

"Perri." Nim puts a hand on my knee and squeezes. "Maybe I should keep her instead."

Flattered as I am by that, I'm relieved when Neo wraps a possessive arm around me, his hand splaying across my waist.

"No." He tugs me closer and Nim's hand falls away. She laughs and then gets up to leave the room, whispering something saucy to Andre before she does. He shakes his head, like her antics don't even get to him anymore.

While I realize she was trying to get a reaction out of me, I hope I didn't show too much. It's hard enough to acknowledge anything I'm thinking or feeling to Neo, let alone the emotional invasion that would come from talking to Nim about anything.

I wish I could talk to Cassandra right now. Since she has to believe that it's all real, I'd be able to gush about him and brag about his bedroom skills without feeling embarrassed. With her I could pretend like things were real and had a future and I could let the dreams I don't let myself dream out of me. Exorcise my emotions.

When we get back tonight, I'm asking Neo if I can leave to hang out with her. I don't want her in the loft. I need to know that he's not watching.

Neo's hand flexes on my waist. "You good?"

"Sorry, lost in thought."

He surprises me when he leans over and presses a kiss to my shoulder. I'm not the only one who's surprised; Harrison looks like someone flicked him in the forehead.

"Dinner is ready!" Nim dances into the room and we all stand automatically. Neo keeps his hand on my back, guiding me through the house to the dining room. I'm apparently seated in a place of honor to the right of Andre. Nim is across from me to his left.

The food is served by plate, and everyone starts eating right away. It's funny how Neo, Harrison, and Nim fall back on old habits. I can so easily picture them as teenagers just like this, teasing each other and talking.

"Do you believe in fate, Perri?" Andre's voice interrupts my thoughts.

"I don't think so," because I honestly don't know. "I don't think I've ever had time to think about it. I've had to work for everything. There was never time for me to wonder if there was a reason."

He smiles at me but it's sad. Everything about him seems a little sad, except when Nim pulls more out of him.

"I understand that, so I'll believe enough for the both of us. The people at this table weren't born a family, but they made one. Fate brought them together to be what was needed when we needed it most. Harrison and Neo needed friends, they found Nim. Nim needed a safe place, and she found us. I think there is a place in this family for you, too."

Andre stares at me, waiting for a response but I have nothing to say. They could've killed me. Either disappearing me or making it look like an accident. They could have paid me off or threatened me, they could have made my life miserable to keep their secret. Instead, they brought me inside the circle. Granted, I wandered in by myself on accident, but instead of rejection, they've shown me acceptance.

They looked at me and found value. Personally and professionally. Much as I love Cassandra, our bond took a lot longer to form and it was built on mutual benefit rather than valuing each other. It was over time that we found our way inside each other's hearts, and the only reason the others let me in was because she vouched for me. They love me now, but I know that our foundation isn't as firm.

With this...I was offered a chance to prove myself, even if I didn't know it at the time.

"I don't think I'm ready for that, but I want to be."

Andre nods and his expression tells me that was a good answer.

"Either way, this dinner is really in honor of you." He grins and calls everyone's attention to us. "To Perri, who caught a thief." Andre holds up his glass.

"And had the paper trail to prove it so we could get him arrested," Harrison adds.

"Without making it a problem for me," Neo chimes in.

"I dunno, I just think you're cool," Nim raises her glass and everyone laughs. After taking a deep breath I pick up my glass and join them. We toast and we drink, and I settle back into my mostly introverted state of being and observe them.

There's tension between Harrison and Andre. While he's spoken to me, Neo, and Nim, he hasn't said anything directly to his father at all. Barely even looked at him. It can't be any issue with Andre and Nim being together because he has no issue with her, so something else is happening.

I wonder if Neo knows. I wonder if he sees.

He sees enough because he can tell when I've met my limit for the evening. Between the stress of the day, of meeting my boss's boss's boss at his house for dinner, and having to be something vaguely recognizable as social, I'm more burnt out than I've been in a long time.

In the car, Neo wraps his big hand around my thigh, and at some point I fall asleep.

I start to rouse when he's carrying me upstairs to the loft, but don't try to wake up the rest of the way. I burrow into his chest and rest there.

31

Perri

Every time we get closer, we take a step back.

Neo was gone when I woke up the morning after the dinner in Long Island, and barely spoke to me for days. I don't know what went through his head on the drive back to the loft, but it caused him to step back and away from me.

We ate dinner with the guys like usual, but I don't know if any of them noticed he never spoke to me. The bed we're sharing felt cold and uncomfortable, and I'd slept like total crap as a result, even when I tried sleeping with my headphones on and playing ASMR all night.

It was hard enough to manage the stress of getting Adam fired, but to come home and feel like I couldn't take off the mask of everything being fine was more than I could handle. I needed somewhere that felt safe to turn off, to let things out, or to complain or be upset without everything being analyzed.

I needed Cassandra.

Neo is doing the dishes when I approach him. He won't stop because he likes to finish the task in front of him, so it seems like the best time to ask for something because his focus will be split. Right now, I don't want him focusing on me. I'm afraid he'll see how weak and hurt I feel, and he'll press until he figures out why. When he realizes it's because of him, I'm going to get a lecture that I don't want.

"Neo?"

"Hm?"

"I'd like permission to go to Cassandra's for dinner tomorrow."

He stills, nods, and keeps washing. "Where does she live?"

"With her parents. I'll be at their penthouse in the city."

"And you want me to drive you there and pick you up?"

"I can drive myself." This is the biggest sticking point. It's a lot of control and a lot of trust. For all he knows, I could run. Get in my car and ditch my phone and go somewhere none of them would find me. Where I could nurse my stupid heart and try to get over him.

Neo turns to me, that laser gaze pressing into me as if he can read my mind. "You sure you're comfortable with that?"

Not the question I was expecting. "Trust me, I can handle city driving."

"Fine. Can you be back by 10? I want you here before shift change."

Neo doesn't actually wait for me to agree to that, he turns his body further toward the sink as if he's putting me behind him. Closing me off with his body language. I was going to thank him, but forget that. If he's going to start an ice war he's going to learn what it feels like to burn from the cold.

It feels weird to drive myself to work in the morning. The entire time I've worked at Zastrow, I've been driven to work. And home from work, or to wherever I'm told that I'm going after. This is a lot stranger than I expected.

The route is familiar though, and before I know it I'm pulling into the parking garage. Neo let me leave early because I think he sensed that I was anxious about driving myself, and even if he's being kind of a jerk right now, I appreciated it.

That does not mean I said a word to him all morning other than asking for permission to go. He's lucky I'd already done meal prep for the week and we're almost to Friday or he'd be finding himself lunchless today. I was tempted to steal it just to mess with him.

When I walk through the atrium and wave at the guard on duty, he waves back but looks confused because I'm alone.

It didn't occur to me that our separate arrival could give people reason to believe that he and I are having issues or are broken up. Crap.

I'm sitting down at my desk when Cassandra calls me.

"Can we go to your place instead?" There's something in the sound of her voice that has me sitting up straight.

"What's wrong?"

Her voice cracks with a sob. "I told my dad about Shaw."

"Oh." I knew he'd be grumpy but for her to be reacting this way it must've gone really badly. Shaw Fischer is a wealthy man from a good family, he doesn't have a party boy reputation, and he's devoted to Cassandra, and has been since she finally gave him a chance junior year of high school. There is no one better for Cassandra than him, which is why I've always pushed for her to go public with their relationship.

"What happened, babe?" I ask softly.

"He said that I needed to end it, keep my legs closed, and he would find me a suitable partner. It's not like Shaw isn't amazing. I don't understand."

"I don't either. Let me give Neo a heads up. Can you meet me here at 5? I'll drive."

Cassandra sniffles. "Yeah. I'm going to Shaw's but then I'll come to you."

"I'm so sorry. We'll figure it out."

She sniffles again. "I don't want to talk about it tonight though, okay?"

"Yeah, of course. Love you," I reassure her.

"Love you. See you at 5."

We end the call and I start to inhale a deep breath to soothe myself, and clear my head before sending a message to Neo.

"Who was that?"

It's like I conjured him with my thoughts. Neo's voice is low and harsh, and I clear my expression before I turn around to face him. He looms over my cubicle entrance like a dark demon and my eyes automatically narrow slightly. The accusation in his tone has me throwing my shoulders back, trying to make myself look bigger without actually standing up to get in his face.

"Cassandra. Change of plans - she'll be coming to us for dinner."

Neo frowns. "Why?"

"She needs a break from her parents. Do you mind?" I ask the question but it doesn't matter what his answer is - Cassandra is coming over tonight.

If needs be, I will kick him out of his own damn loft to take care of my friend. Tonight was supposed to be me getting a chance to let go around her, but this takes priority. I can keep it together a little longer.

After a moment, he nods. "Of course I don't. Do you want me to pick up takeout, or do you want to cook?"

I hate when he's thoughtful like that. It weakens my resolve to be mad at him. I've never been a grudge holder. It was energy that I couldn't spare. Now that I want to hold one I don't know how.

"Get chicken wings. It's her guilty pleasure food."

One corner of his mouth kicks up for a second. "Done. See you at home."

"I'll see you at your loft," I reply, making the distinction clear. His entire body stiffens but I don't look at him. I turn my chair back to my screen and make a very convincing show of getting to work. I feel him walk away as much as I hear it, and when I'm sure he's gone I put my head in my hands and squeeze my eyes shut.

Living a lie is exhausting.

Cassandra is waiting for me in the lobby when I walk out at 5:00 P.M. on the dot. She's dressed down for her, which means flats instead of heels, and a sweater instead of a fancy blouse and a blazer. I can tell she's been crying from her puffy eyes even though she tried to cover it with makeup.

Right now, I don't care that I'm at work, I hug my friend. Cassandra sags against me, and lets out a big breath.

"I told Neo to pick up chicken wings."

"You're the best," she murmurs into my shoulder. Then I link arms with her and guide her out to the parking garage and my car. It takes her a bit into the drive before Cassandra arranges her thoughts to talk about them, which is usual, because she likes to have things organized in a logical way inside before letting them out. Even though she said she didn't want to talk about Shaw and her dad, I knew she would. Cassandra needs to process out loud eventually. She got her degree in journalism, and is a surprisingly good writer, if a little bit vicious. She's the kind of person who would be dogged going after corruption, even if it put her at risk.

Which is probably why her father refuses to let any of his media outlets hire her as a reporter. If he's not careful, she'll turn her powers on him instead.

"I think dad is up to something." Cassandra's voice shakes. I've never heard her like this, and it scares me a little.

"Like what?"

"I don't know, but he...it was so weird, bunny. Like a villain making a speech about how the hero disrupted his plans to take over the world. He was talking about like, our responsibility to the Warren name, and how I needed to be willing to sacrifice to keep our place in the world. It was weird enough that I called Seth."

Seth is Cassandra's older brother, and they do not get along. Most likely because not only is he the firstborn child, but male, and was therefore the golden child who could do no wrong. Personally, I've always found Seth to be a perfectly normal, albeit broody, guy, but then again, he's not my brother.

"Really?"

"Yeah. I was worried we were in financial trouble or something. Seth said we were fine and that dad was probably scheming while drunk."

"Wouldn't be the first time."

"I know, but he seemed pretty sober." She gives me a nervous glance. "I needed to get out. Every time I've talked about finding a place of my own they stop me, and I don't come into my trust without their control for another three years."

"I'd say you could stay with us but there's really no space."

"Seth gave me his keys."

I almost stomp on the breaks in shock. "What."

"Yeah. He's going to be in LA for a few more weeks and said if I was that freaked out, I could crash at his place. Is this that whole thing where they say we'll have a better relationship as adults? Because then they might be right."

I laugh. "I'll never know." I get off the highway and start driving toward the compound.

"Uh...where are we?" Cassandra is looking around and I try to see through her eyes. Yeah, it looks a little creepy. We're driving in a clearly commercial area with large warehouse after large warehouse, imposing windowless facades in various colors from gray to rust. It definitely looks like I'm trying to kidnap her.

"I live at the security compound - it's a much nicer warehouse than these. It's old and made of brick. I love it." That's not an exaggeration. The old red brick is weathered but strong. Like the three little pigs story, no big bad wolf is going to come along and blow it down. I feel safe in it, even without the guards and the intense security fence.

I pull up to the gate and wave to one of the lower level guards who is on duty. He stops me, and I roll down my window.

"I have to register your guest, Ms. Kane."

Cassandra leans over my lap and grins at him. He blushes immediately.

"Cassandra Warren. Do you need my number?"

The blush deepens as he types her name into the computer. "No, ma'am." The guard steps back from the car and flips the switch to open the fence.

"You're shameless." I shake my head at her and drive past the training gym and the barracks until my warehouse comes into view. I'd never admit it to Neo that when I hear the word home, this is where my mind goes. I haven't had a true home in a long time, even the house I grew up in only fits the loosest definition of the word. Home is where the heart is, where the cooking utensils are, where I want to lay my head down. Home is the loft in the warehouse.

The garage door opens before I can get out to open it myself, and I drive inside to where my car has been slowly rotting for the last few months. I don't know the next time I'll drive it, or that I'll want to because I'd rather antagonize Neo on the drive to work than have that little bit of independence.

Benji walks over after we get out, and I'm guessing he's the one that opened the door.

"I'm supposed to tell you Neo is here, dinner is waiting, and that Ms. Warren can stay tonight if she wants, and he'll take the couch."

It's a bit of a fight to keep my expression controlled this time. Now he's looking for excuses to not even be in the same bed? Chicken.

Cassandra follows me through the warehouse with her head on a swivel, taking in every little detail with something even more intense than her reporter's eye: the eye that belongs to a protective best friend. I get that it doesn't seem like a lot on the surface, but I think she knows me well enough that by the end of the night she'll see why I like it.

We head up the stairs and when I open the door, I'm greeted by the sight of Neo in black joggers and a white t-shirt, barefoot, setting the table. The center is already piled with dishes of wings.

He looks our way and smiles. It's almost his real one, but I can tell the difference. The deep lines aren't there, and it doesn't crinkle his eyes. It's just showing teeth.

"Hey, princess." Neo comes to me, taking my chin, and presses a soft, quick kiss to my lips. When he pulls back he looks into my eyes, but I give him nothing.

I step to his side to turn and introduce Cassandra.

"Neo, this is my best friend, Cassandra Warren."

"Neo Ryan." He offers his hand and they shake, Cassandra giving him a pleasant smile but reserving judgment. "Sit down, I'll get drinks."

We go to the table and take our spots.

"He's cuter in person," Cassandra mutters to me. I snort in response.

Neo comes to the table with bottles of beer. When he sits down, I flinch a little when his hand lands on my thigh. He gives me a warning squeeze, then soothes it with strokes of his thumb.

We all make up our plates, open our beers, and start eating.

"So how did this happen?" Cassandra waves between the two of us. I've been super vague with her about how we met, and I still haven't come up with a good story.

"At Zastrow. Perri had to come in and sign some paperwork at security to do her background check and I saw her - and that was it. I wasn't looking, but I found her." Neo reaches over and takes my hand, his thumb running over my knuckles. "The more I learned about her, the more impressed I was, and sure I was absolutely swinging above my weight class when it comes to her."

"She is special," Cassandra agrees. "Not that she knows it."

Neo looks at Cassandra and they smirk at each other. "Right?"

"I'm right here," I snarl.

This only makes them laugh harder, so I snatch my hand back and aggressively bite into a chicken wing.

"Any good stories about Perri at boarding school?"

"Other than her saving my ass, not really. Perri is a good girl, through and through." Cassandra sighs, then turns to Neo with a glare. "So if you hurt her, I'll make your life suck."

"Not kill me?"

"Killing you is the easy way." The grin she gives him is maniacal, and of course, Neo observes that with respect. It makes an unexpected flare of jealousy swoop through my stomach.

"No one is killing anyone! Least of all on my behalf. Got it?"

They share another look that tells me they heard, but aren't listening.

"You'd kill for her, wouldn't you?" Cassandra asks, a weird tone in her voice. It makes me wonder what Shaw said when she told him about her conversation with her dad.

"In a heartbeat," Neo answers, his voice softer than I'm expecting.

"Stop being creepy, you two."

Neo reaches over and physically picks me up out of my chair to set me in his lap. When he buries his face in my neck, the sound I let out is real and uncontrollable. Feeling him touch me so intimately after days of nothing is what shatters the ice wall I was trying to build. His lips press against my pulse point before he leans back slightly. I look down into his eyes and can't look away.

"Go have girl talk. I'll take care of this and then leave for a bit. Okay?"

"Okay." My voice is weak. I want to resist him, but instead I lean forward and kiss him. "Thank you."

With seeming reluctance, he lets me go, and I drag Cassandra over to the couch. Neo starts cleaning up dinner and I put on a TV show we watched repeatedly in college when we were stressed and couldn't sleep. She snuggles close to me.

"I completely understand now why you've ditched me since you moved in here."

"I'm sorry," I start but she waves me off.

"I mean, you live out in the middle of nowhere, so the inconvenience factor is high, but being able to come home to your man every day, one who looks at you like he doesn't understand how you're there? Yeah that would overrule my desire to do anything else."

Guilt clenches my stomach so I say nothing, and turn the conversation back to her.

"Would you live with Shaw?"

"Yes," she answers quickly. "But I also want my family's legacy. Dad would find a way to cut me off forever if I left, and I want to be part of the empire my grandfather and great-grandfather built. Even if dad doesn't do shit with it, he's not ruining it either. I don't want to be written out of our history."

"Does Shaw understand?"

"Yes. He's worried about me, and we're not breaking up, but we have to continue as we are. Probably until dad dies."

"I'll murder him for you," I say, only half-joking.

"Shaw said that too, but he might've meant it."

"I mean it," I insist.

We kind of laugh, and I try to imagine my fit but nerdy friend killing anyone. Then again, under the right motivation, I believe anyone is capable of murder. If Shaw really thought Cassandra was in danger, I know that he'd do whatever was necessary to protect her.

We drift away from the topic, and I let her talk, watching as more and more of her usual energy returns. By the time I start blinking for too long, she's back to talking with firmness and authority in her voice, and the slight twinkle is back in her eye.

"Thank you, for this," she says as she pokes my cheek, snapping me back to being more awake. "I needed a safe night away."

"Of course. Any time."

"Can somebody give me a ride to Seth's?"

"I'm sure that can be arranged." I stand up and stretch, every muscle in my body calling for me to sit back down and fall asleep. After cleaning up, Neo left, but I don't know where he went.

Feeling bratty, I open the front door and shout his name.

It only takes him a few minutes for him to walk to the bottom of the stairs. His eyelids are heavy and I think he was probably dozing wherever he was hiding.

"Can someone drive Cassandra to her brother's apartment?"

"She doesn't want to stay here? Is she okay to go?" His concern is so genuine it makes my heart flutter. It reminds me that despite the weirdness between us, the good guy at the core of him is what keeps pulling me in. If she wasn't okay, he would let Cassandra stay. He would help me make sure she was safe, simply because she deserves to feel safe, not because he wanted anything from her.

It's a weird thing to have in common - we've watched people close to us be used by others, leveraged by them, or hurt because someone wanted something from them - and it made us extra careful not to be that way. We don't do things expecting anything in return besides good will.

"Thomas has a few hours left on shift. Benji can take over the watch until he's back."

I nod and close the door before he can say anything else. He's softened me, but I'm still trying to ice him out for how he's been the last few days.

Cassandra is getting her stuff together and I walk her out of the loft and down the stairs. We hug, and I squeeze extra hard.

"I'm only a text away," I remind her.

"I know."

She punches Neo in the shoulder and then walks over to where Thomas waits, holding open the door. Even though I know she's faithful to Shaw, she's still a flirt, and waggles her eyebrows at me after she gets a look at him.

"Hey, Neo," she shouts, and he turns to look at her. "Is being pretty a requirement to work for you?"

"I ain't pretty," Thomas quips. "I'm rugged."

We all laugh, even him after a second, and they get in the car.

I don't wait for Neo, I go upstairs.

Except I can hear him stomping after me, and I know this is going to turn into more than I want to deal with when I'm tired. Like a total child, I move faster, and try to close the door on him so he'll have to put in his code. By then I could be ensconced in the bathroom and he'd have to leave me alone.

It doesn't work, and I hear his big hand slam against the metal door and push it open. I don't stop, and do everything short of running to get into the bedroom.

I should've run, pride be damned, because Neo grabs me. I'm hauled back into his body, one hand around my throat and the other around my waist and trapping my arms at my sides.

"I need you to take to heart what I'm about to say, *mo dhuine ar bith.*" Of course he whispers it, and it makes my skin explode with a shiver and goosebumps, my nipples tightening, my back arching as my muscles all flex in response.

"What?" I'm proud of myself when my voice comes out flat.

"It's so easy to care. To fall into the illusion we've created." His hand flexes on my throat and his lips drag along my earlobe, then down to my jaw. "But never forget you're my prisoner, Perri. My captive. Mine." Neo lets out a harsh breath like he didn't mean to say that. Everything he's saying is terrible but true, and yet my body is still leaning into his, craving him, begging for him.

The hand that isn't around my throat loosens from my waist and drops down until he's sliding it down the front of my pants, straight under everything until his fingers are pressing against my clit. He toys with me then, the calloused tip of his middle finger swirling and stroking. Neo groans and presses his erection into my back.

"Should I fuck you like you're my prisoner?"

Neo rips my pants down and my clothes get stuck around my knees so I can't move. I don't want to move. I don't know where this is going but I want it. I want him. He turns us and bends me over the couch. Automatically my hands fly up and I grip the cushions to stabilize myself.

There's barely a sound as Neo pulls down his joggers and then I feel the hot head of his cock pressing against me. It's going to be so tight in this position and I'm already eager to feel it. I want him to hurt me while he pleasures me.

Neo presses forward, splitting me open on his cock.

I scream, the sound echoing in the high-ceilinged space.

"Louder, princess."

With a groan he presses all the way inside me and his hips press into my ass.

"If you can speak when I'm done, we're doing it again."

That's all the warning I get before his fingers dig into the soft flesh of my hips, and he starts to fuck me. His hips move back and forth, fierce and violent, and I feel every single inch of him scraping against the softest part of me. When he thrusts forward my clit smacks into the couch, sending off more shocks through my body.

"I can't hear you," he grunts. "Do you need it harder princess?" Neo wraps his hand around the back of my neck, holding me in place as he moves even faster.

The sounds that come out of me are inhuman, and the mix of pleasure as he hits places inside me that I didn't know existed combined with the nearly overwhelming pressure of how full I feel are sending my brain to a place I've never been before.

My hands are scrambling at the material of the couch and I'm trying to hold onto anything, as if it will stop me from spinning out. As if finding something to hold onto will give me back control over my own body.

I don't have any power over myself right now. It's all Neo. I am his toy and he's playing with me to the point of destruction.

There is no part of me that wants to stay whole. I know that this orgasm is going to shatter me into irreparable pieces, and that I've reached my point of no return. I no longer belong to myself, and I can't stop it. This is over the cliff's edge, falling into a dark love I'll never recover from. I'm going to drown in want for Neo Ryan for the rest of my life. I tried to fight it but there's no use.

Somehow, that gives me peace. I'll never have to worry about finding someone because I'll never want to - this is it for me. This is the only person I'll ever love like this, and I wouldn't give it up for the world.

"Neo!" It goes from his name to unintelligible sounds and something like begging but I can't form words.

"That's right princess, break on my cock. Scream for it."

He presses his hand down on my lower back, changing the angle and somehow increasing the pressure even further.

"That's it, make me come with your pretty pussy."

Neo cracks a hand across my ass cheek, and that's it.

I shatter.

I scream so loud my throat hurts, the sound trapped and garbled as I lose all of the air in my lungs as my entire body tightens against the onslaught of my orgasm. He tugs my hair tighter, urging me, stretching it out, and I cannot stop. Wave after wave shoots through me and Neo never stops fucking me.

When he lets go of my hair, I collapse forward.

I gasp when he lifts my hips so my feet are no longer touching the ground. I'm being entirely held up by him right now, ass in the air.

"Oh princess, I'm going to fill you up with my come."

Instinctively, I tighten around him again, and he groans as he follows through on his threat and fills me up. Pulse after pulse rubs against the already sensitive places inside me and I whimper, my voice raspy but satisfied.

When he's done, he gently lets my feet drop back to the floor.

I cry out, my throat raw, when he slides out of me.

But he's not done.

Neo kneels behind me and pulls my ass cheeks apart.

"Show me princess."

Somehow I know he means that he wants me to push the come out, so I do. I feel it drip down my pussy lips, and even onto my thigh.

"Dirty little prisoner, dripping come." Neo groans and then I scream again as he bites into my ass cheek hard enough to leave a mark. Almost no sound comes out, and it makes him chuckle.

"Let's clean you up."

I can't move, and after adjusting himself Neo picks me up and carries me to the bathroom to clean me up. I can't open my eyes I'm so tired, so I can't see how he's looking at me or gauge how he feels about where we stand.

All I know is that a part of me is going to stay here when I leave, and I'll never get it back.

32

Neo

It's time for me to put things into action to let Perri go. To see how far she can be pushed before she breaks, if she breaks at all. Despite her sweetness, she's made of sturdier stuff than I think any of us expected. Part of me wants her to fail.

Wants an excuse to keep her.

A bigger part of me fears the truth: she'll be fine. She won't let us down.

"Rina's mic is live." Leander is with me for this. He's the one I feel has kept the most control and distance when it comes to Perri, and he won't get defensive about what we're going to need to do.

Perri's been eating her lunch outside the last few days, enjoying the end of the warm weather as we head into fall. She hasn't told me, but I always have eyes on her so I've noted it. It presented exactly the opportunity I needed.

"Perri's been there a few minutes. Tell Rina to approach."

Leander gives the directions over the mic, and I put on a set of headphones to listen in. The other reason I wanted Leander here is because I knew that I couldn't direct Rina myself. I did have some doubts about my ability to control the situation, and I knew that he could. I'm here to know, and to advise, but my involvement needs to be indirect.

Perri has been quiet the last few days. The way I attacked her after the night Cassandra was over was both satisfying and shameful. It didn't seem to stop her from climbing on top of me the next morning and waking me up with her tight pussy riding me to the end.

But there's distance there. A hurt in her eyes that I can't fix.

I know it because I feel it, even if I don't show it the same way. I'm better at hiding than she is.

It's what told me I had to set this all in motion. I can't keep Perri in stasis like this any longer. I have to start making moves to let her go.

Even if it'll kill a part of me that I thought was already dead.

"Can I sit here?" Rina's voice snaps me back to attention. She's an actual reporter with a finance magazine, but she's been on our payroll since she got the job. Not only does she get inside information that she's happy to give us, we give her exclusive access to some of our business in the form of "anonymous" sources.

"Oh, sure," Perri answers.

A few minutes of silence.

"It's been beautiful weather," Rina starts. "Do you work here?"

"I do."

"Do you like it? Your hear kind of crazy stuff about Andre Zastrow."

Perri laughs. "I like it. I love it, actually. Dream job, right out of college."

"Wow. What do you do?"

"I'm an accountant."

The two women make small talk, Perri being kind but her answers ultimately not giving away much. She edges around stating what department she works in or giving any details about any of the projects she's analyzed. Even though Rina brings up Andre, Nim, and Harrison, Perri doesn't even let on that she knows them personally, let alone has her own relationships with them.

"I heard one of their managers got arrested a few weeks ago."

This is the first test.

"I heard, but I don't know anything."

Silence. "I think you do know, Perri Kane."

"Who are you? What do you want?" Perri's voice is sharp, and I can hear her packing up her things to leave.

"Please, wait, I don't mean any harm."

"There's more than one way to hurt," Perri snaps, but she waits. "Who are you? What do you want?" This time her voice is flat, as if she's only entertaining Rina to be polite.

"My name is Rina Carpenter, I'm a reporter." Rina rattles off her bonafides. "Look me up."

There's a pause and I pull up my own phone, opening the app that has the mirror of Perri's. She looks up Rina's name and her paper, and the top result is a photo of Rina and her bylines.

"We have a media department."

"I know," Rina laughs. "But the media department is about spin, not the truth. That's what I'm looking for. Don't you think people deserve the truth?"

Perri snorts. "What do you want?"

"I know you're dating Neo, I know that you know about that manager, I know you know details of the way the Zastrows work that no one else does. Not only will I expose them, I can pay you. Extremely well." At this point we instructed Rina to give Perri her card, with a payment amount on the back. "There's people who want the truth about Andre Zastrow and his company to come out, and they don't skimp on compensation."

"Who wants that? Who would I be helping by doing this?" There's a tone in Perri's voice that almost makes me laugh. She's putting on that pitiful, innocent woman act for Rina. Instead of walking away, she's trying to get information. Even Leander looks surprised.

"The people. Don't they deserve to know who's making their products, who's shaping the things they use? Harrison Zastrow is all about environmentalism and responsibility, but is that really who he is? Is Andre and Nicolette's marriage real, or is he willing to buy a young woman for business?"

Perri scoffs and I can perfectly picture her bristling.

"Who wants to know? Who would be paying me?"

Rina pauses, assessing the situation. It's not going the way any of us expected.

"Not a competitor, necessarily, but someone who has a better perspective."

"I see. Well, I have your number, I'll think about your offer, but I need to be getting back to work." There's the sound of Perri pulling her things together. "You have a nice day," she practically snarls at Rina and leaves.

I can't help it, I start laughing.

Leander shakes his head, and tells Rina to come back to the surveillance setup we have in a van around the corner from the Zastrow building.

"She's unbelievable. Interrogates the interrogator. Jesus." He puts the headphones down on the small counter and I follow suit. "What comes next?"

"We see what she does with this. Does she keep it to herself, tell me, report it to someone...does she call Rina? In the moment she could get defensive but if she's not with us, giving her time to think might have her turning on us."

Leander nods.

Rina pulls open the van door and climbs inside, closing it behind her. She starts removing the mic and I look away to protect her modesty. Rina doesn't give a shit; she told me to my face that men can look all they want but they'll never touch. She's been with her wife since they were 14 years old.

"I like her," Rina fixes her blazer. "She's got...grit."

"I know."

"What's going on, Neo?"

While I wouldn't classify Rina and I as friends, she's an asset that I cultivated and we've gotten to know each other over the years. Well enough that I was invited to her wedding. She was the one who gave me the idea for being celibate after releasing an article on studies about the sexual habits of high-achieving men. Not that I consider myself one of them, not really, but more than one study brought up the benefits of it.

"She saw something she shouldn't have, I want to make sure we can trust her."

"I've got good instincts, and I say you can. She was ready to take my head off, full blown protective mode, the only person I've ever seen get more defensive of Zastrow is you. That girl is all in."

"We'll see," Leander responds. "Your opinion has been noted, Mrs.

Carpenter."

She flips Leander off, gives me a wave, and leaves the van.

"Upload the recording to the cloud, get this put away. We're already monitoring Perri's communications so we'll see if anything interesting comes up."

Now I leave the van, take a deep breath of fresh air, and walk back into the building to get the rest of my work day done.

Perri is pacing in the lobby and wringing her hands when I come down to meet her. She turns to me and grabs my arm.

"We have to talk."

"Okay." I put my arm around her and we walk together to the parking garage. I can practically feel her vibrating against me, and I'm a total dick for being amused by that. She's freaking out over a fake situation but it's also kind of a relief.

We're a few minutes into the drive, settled in, when she starts talking.

"A reporter approached me today and asked me for inside information about you and they offered me a lot of money and I looked her up and the paper she works for is owned by Warren Media and I think they're trying to wreck the deal."

Okay, that went a leap too far. I should've known she'd look into it further when she went back to work.

"What?" It all came out in a rush that I could only follow because I knew what was coming, until that perfectly logical explanation she came to all by herself.

Perri explains to me everything that happened on her lunch break from her perspective, and that she researched Rina Carpenter when she went back to her cubicle.

"I thought about going to media relations but it seemed more like a you thing. If someone is targeting Zastrow and willing to pay for it, I might not be the only person they approach. They approached me because of my association with you, but the fact that it's a Warren paper is suspicious."

If this was real, she's right, that would be suspicious as fuck and I'd be all over it.

"Do you have the card?"

Perri digs in her purse and hands it over. I look at the card, at the amount on the back, and let out a sound.

"You weren't tempted?"

I can feel Perri's glare without even looking at her. "No."

I can't keep the smug grin from my face. "Calm down, princess. I'll look into it. Thank you for telling me."

Perri huffs and crosses her arms. When we get back to the warehouse, I break out into a full on grin as she stomps up the stairs and away from me. I send the men a text that there's no dinner tonight. The cook is going to be too busy getting fucked to feed them.

Not that I say that part.

I follow Perri at a leisurely pace. She's in the bedroom, already nearly changed when I catch up with her. She shoots a dirty look over her shoulder and I groan, my cock hardening at her sass. At the challenge she's giving me right now, like it won't take minutes, maybe even seconds, to conquer her will and have her bending and breaking for me.

I want to keep my distance but seeing her get like this deserves a reward.

I step up behind her and wrap my hands around her hips, pulling her plump ass into me. She tries to get away but all it does is bend her over, and press her backside more firmly against my cock.

"That's it princess, tease me."

"I'm not trying to tease you," she growls and it's so damn cute. "Stop it."

"No." I pick her up and throw her down on the bed. She tries to crawl away but I grab her ankle and yank her down toward the end of the bed, turning her onto her back as I tug. Perri tries to slap at me but that just makes it easier for me to catch her wrists and pin them down against the bed.

I nip at her chin and she stills. She doesn't move when I let go of her wrists and drag my hands down her body. I take that as permission and kiss along her jaw and down her throat while my hands start pushing up the long t-shirt she's wearing. I'm delighted to find she hadn't had a chance to put on any bottoms.

I lift my chest away from her and remove the shirt entirely. Perri is naked underneath me, hesitant but horny. She moans and arches her back when I continue the journey my mouth is taking to suck on one of her nipples. It beads against my tongue, and I bite and suck until she's whimpering, then take the other one until I get the same response.

By the time I get to her pussy, she's glistening and ready for my mouth. I lick at her, teasing until she tugs on my head and presses me harder against her, lifting her legs up and spreading her thighs wide, opening up for me. Two of my fingers slide easily inside her, and I press against her front wall as I suck on her clit. I know what she likes and I want her to come.

Perri tastes so damn good. While I've always been down for eating pussy, it's never been as good as it is with her. Not only because I love her flavor, but I love the way she responds. I love that she demands what makes her feel good and isn't afraid to communicate it, even if that means her nails are digging into my scalp holding me where she wants, or the way she arches her back or shifts her hips.

I pulse my tongue against her clit and Perri screams, back lifting off the bed as she comes. I lick her through it, sucking gently as she moans and writhes. Perri collapses and I let her go, crawling back up until I can look down at her.

"How do you want it, princess?"

Slowly she opens her eyes and I grin again, loving that fucked into a daze look on her face. I lean in and give her a filthy kiss, tasting her tongue with my own. Working her up until she's rubbing her bare pussy on me, needing another release.

I stand up and remove my clothes. Perri moves herself further up the bed, never taking her eyes off my body.

Finally naked, I crawl up to her, leaving bite marks and hickeys as I go.

Perri giggles, and it's a sound I've never caused from her before. I stop and look into her eyes.

"It tickles."

I move quick and press my cock against her entrance, pressing deep inside. Perri moans and her eyes close.

"Does that tickle?"

"No," she rasps, then pulls my mouth to hers. I press into her to the hilt and hold, letting her grind on me as we kiss. Even though being inside her feels like fucking heaven, I don't feel the need to rush anything. It feels amazing to stay on the edge like this, teasing us both.

I break the kiss to catch my breath and brush the tip of my nose over hers.

Perri's eyes open, and up close they're such a wild mix of gold, brown, and green. One of her hands comes up and the tips of her fingers gently trace across my scar. Even though it doesn't feel any different than her touching my unscarred skin, a shiver rushes through me and I throb inside her.

I can't move, I'm frozen balls deep inside this woman.

When she lifts her head and presses her lips against the places that her fingers touched, I feel like I'm outside myself. I'm looking at Perri and I, at the way she's looking at me and the way that I'm unabashedly looking at her. It's a raw, deep connection that we're both trying so hard to ignore.

I roll us and sit up, wrapping my arms tight around her so she can't move away from me. Her arms wrap around my neck, and even though we've barely moved, both of us are panting against one another. I know she feels this as intensely as I do.

I let my hands drop to her ass and start grinding her against me, sliding her up and down and forcing her clit to drag against my pelvis. We keep eye contact, and I don't think we could break it if we tried. It's slow and intense but the pleasure...I feel every grind of her pussy along my cock, every time she squeezes her inner muscles around me I feel it down my legs to the tips of my toes.

She's taking something from me right now and I'm willingly giving it. Unable to stop or control it, only knowing that it's hers to take and I'm responding to her demand to have it. Perri pulls her arms back, and takes my face in her hands. She's gentle as she touches me, and her gaze is full of worship I don't deserve.

Her mouth drops open like she's going to say something, then she swallows thickly and stops herself. Instead of speaking, she drops her forehead to mine, still holding my face like it's the most precious thing she's ever held, and closes her eyes.

I watch her as the orgasm builds inside her, each minute change of expression on her face as it spirals over and over, then collapses as she explodes with pleasure. Perri throws her head back and cries out, grinding on me wildly until she starts to come down. I wait until she tilts her head down, wait to see her eyes.

"Perri," I groan, and thrust deep to come inside her.

She's all I see, and all I want to see. I was celibate before because I thought I'd never find what I was looking for. That the emotions and connection that I wanted with a woman were a bar that was set to high, and could never be met. Then Perri stumbled into my life, and I know when I lose her that I'll never be with anyone else because they will never compare to her.

33

Perri

Something is changing. Maybe it's me, maybe it's that Neo and I are finally reaching some kind of understanding that we won't verbalize, and I know that I feel more confident every day I step onto the 7th floor. I also feel like we're picking up speed and heading toward the end.

We've returned to our version of normal - work, dinner with the guys, sometimes Neo and I hang out and sometimes he has to work, and we go to bed together but we don't touch. We sleep comfortably, separate but together. The last time we had sex was...a lot. I don't know how it happened, or how it happened like that, but it altered something inside both of us that we can't ignore. It's best we don't cross that line again. It's going to hurt enough as it is.

Cassandra has been a disaster. When her dad found out that she was staying at Seth's apartment he flipped out, yelled at the both of them, and demanded that she come back to their penthouse. She did, and she won't tell me what he said that freaked her out, but it must've been big.

Whatever it was, she's been on edge since. She begged me to come over and have dinner with her parents, and after a very stilted and awkward conversation with Neo, he agreed. They're letting Benji out of the cave to drive me to the penthouse and wait there, just in case.

It's been quiet, but it's more like the calm before the storm. The media coverage on Nim and Andre has picked up again, although this time they're trying to connect Zastrow to organized crime and accuse Nim of being a madame. Which would be kind of hilarious given her complete lack of discretion if it wasn't also demeaning to women and sex work.

Benji is driving me over, and he's more jittery than usual.

"Are you okay?" we ask at the same time, and laugh. I think of him like a little brother, and I wonder why he thinks I wouldn't be. He's the one showing anxiety.

"Why do you think I'm not?" I ask.

"I don't know. Vibes." Benji sighs. "If I tell you something, can you like, keep it to yourself?"

"Sure..." I hedge.

"Do you know why Neo decided to be celibate?"

"I made some assumptions but no, I don't know specifically."

Benji nods, then seems to make a decision within himself. "He was with someone. He took it seriously because he's built that way."

I feel sick to my stomach because even though he and I both have pasts, and we have no future, I hate the idea of him with anyone else. I hate him being serious and committed when we can't have that.

"Serious as in he brought her to Long Island, let her meet Nim and Andre, invited her out to the things they did together, tested the waters if she would fit long term."

"And did she?"

Benji shakes his head, and his frown deepens.

"What happened?"

"She was using him to get to Harrison. They all went on a trip to the Hamptons and she went to Harrison's room during the night, tried to seduce him. When Harrison basically flipped the fuck out, she tried to accuse Harrison of making a move and inviting her to his room."

"Harrison would never do that."

Benji flips a glance at me and nods. "He would not. He did not. Neo broke up with her immediately, had a staff member drive her back to the city. It crushed him, to be used like that. And then she went crazy and wouldn't let it go, started showing up at the office trying to talk to them. It got weird."

"What happened?"

"She sold some lies to the papers. Luckily, she never knew anything big or important, she never even came to the loft so she didn't know about the warehouse. It kind of set off this whole thing that's happening because a source tied to Neo claimed that Nim was cheating. Even though the real situation is more complicated, it was a runaway train."

"That's awful. What...where is she now?"

"Prison. She tried to start Neo's car on fire."

I laugh and then cover my mouth. But I can't stop it and it bursts out of me. "That's so stupid."

"No one would accuse her of being a bright bulb."

Silence falls. "Why are you telling me this?"

"Because he's like family, and has made a lot of decisions because he was hurt, and wanted to stop himself from being hurt again."

"Okay..."

"All I'm saying is that this is going to end with hurt, and I want you to keep that in mind when you decide whether or not you're going to forgive him when all is said and done."

That sobers me. I think about what Benji said for the rest of the ride, and we don't talk any further. I give him a wave and head toward the front door of the building. The guard at the desk recognizes me and waves me through.

When Cassandra opens the door, my concern flares. She's pale, with bags under her eyes, and she's wearing joggers and a t-shirt. Other than gym class, I have never seen her willingly wear athleisure. It kind of freaks me out to see her looking this rundown.

She puts a finger to her lips and we stay quiet until we get to her bedroom. She turns on music, just loud enough to be too loud. Cass pulls me down onto her bed and leans close.

"I need to get out of here."

"How can I help?"

She shakes her head. "I don't know. I don't know."

"What did he say to you?"

Cassandra looks away, opening and closing her mouth. Tears well in her eyes and then drip down her cheeks. She sniffles and then wipes them away.

"I'm not allowed to leave the penthouse. It's been almost two weeks. He's started checking my phone to see if I'm talking to Shaw. I'm basically under house arrest."

"Have you told Seth?" Cassandra shakes her head no. "Why not? What about your mom?"

"She won't do anything. He's got her so doped up and drunk most of the time, he's drunk most of the time. He...I don't know if he even realizes what he's saying."

"Cassandra, what did he say?"

"He said," her voice is thick and she swallows, clearing her throat. "That he'd sell me to the highest bidder and let them do what they wanted with me. That if I didn't keep my mouth shut and my head down he'd make sure I ended up getting what I deserved for being," her voice cracks, "a whore."

"Oh my god. Okay. Let me call Neo. Let me get you out of here."

"No!" Cassandra grabs my hands and stops me from getting my phone. "Let's eat dinner, I'll put on a good show, and try to get Seth to step in. I am not letting him cut me off from what's mine. I have to figure out what he's up to, Perri. I have to make sure no one else gets hurt."

"At what cost, babe?" I pull her to me and hug her, soothing her because I don't know what else to do. This is too far, but I also can't force her to do anything. I don't know what it's like to be tied to a legacy the way she is, or what it feels like to want it. I'll do what I can to reassure her that I'm here for whatever she needs.

There's a sharp, violent knock on the door. "Girls, dinner!" Mr. Warren's voice booms through the wood and into the room, invasive and unwanted.

Cassandra gives me a begging look, and I nod.

The table in the dining area is set, and I take a seat next to Cassandra. Her mother is across from us but doesn't say a word, or even acknowledge our arrival. She stares at her plate and into her meal like they are having the most interesting conversation.

Norman Warren sits at the head of the table. I know how these things work, so I wait. I wait as a staffer fills our glasses and then asks him if everything is alright before they leave the room. I wait as he glares around the table at all of us.

He's not actually angry, that's his normal expression.

Norman doesn't start eating because he likes this stupid power play. I will never understand where Cassandra and her siblings came from when I look at her parents. Seth is steady and focused, ambitious. Cassandra is smart, friendly, and committed. Calliope is a bit of an outlier, but she's creative and open-minded. None of them seem to get any of these traits from their parents.

Finally, Norman picks up his fork and starts to cut into his chicken.

The rest of us have been given permission to start eating.

"We haven't seen you in awhile. What have you been up to?" Alma slurs, her blurry gaze on mine. "You used to be here all the time."

I give her a tight smile. "Work keeps me busy."

"And your boyfriend," she laughs but it sounds...weird. "I've seen the pictures of you two."

The blush staining my cheeks is genuine. It's embarrassing.

"Things are going well at Zastrow, then?" Norman speaks and it's like a hammer falls. Like no other sounds are allowed in the room except his voice.

"Yes. I like it there."

"I would've gotten you a job at Warren," he chastises.

"Thank you, sir, but I wanted to do it on my own."

Norman scoffs. "Understandable, but sometimes," he continues talking to me but his gaze moves to his daughter, "people should take what's being handed to them."

I don't say anything to that. I go through the motions of eating food I'm not tasting. Cassandra wanted me to get through this dinner with her and I will, but it's uncomfortable. It's hostile. I can't figure out why.

"Do you see Andre and his wife often?"

"Sometimes." I take a drink of water to give myself a moment. "Since Neo is security he's usually working if he's with them. They're very nice."

Norman snorts. "Nice."

Cassandra reaches over under the table and squeezes my hand, then withdraws. She's trying to warn me, but I don't know why. I look over at her but she doesn't look back, her eyes stuck to her plate.

"So what do they have you doing then?"

I try and give limited and vague answers, but Norman won't stop pushing. He tries to ask how much many projects ask for, how much money we're investing, if the projects are held to the same environmental standards as other partners, if I think Andre is heading toward retirement (that one I answer with a no and a forced laugh,) and if I think Harrison is qualified to take over for his father. Mostly I dance around answers, but it's like an interrogation.

When he asks me about Adam's firing, and the arraignment that happened recently, I finally have to shut him down.

"I'm not allowed to talk about that."

"I won't publish anything."

"Okay," I respond and shrug. "I'm still not allowed to talk about it."

"Hmm," he sips his wine. "Zastrow does breed loyal employees. How interesting."

We continue to eating.

"Have you been to the Long Island estate? Do you socialize with Nicolette? She's supposedly one of your beau's best friends."

I swallow and take a deep breath through my nose. This is weird. When he asked the question, Cassandra stiffened, as if she was bracing for my answers to the question.

"I've been there, and I do spend time with her."

"No concerns about her...behavior?"

I'm done. I look Norman dead in the eye as I put down my fork and wipe my mouth with my napkin. I set it on my plate, indicating that I'm done.

"None whatsoever. I think I should be going."

"No, wait," Norman stands but I'm already heading toward the door. Neither Cassandra or her mother have moved from their chairs. I'm worried about Cass but if I don't get out of here, then there's nothing that I can do to help her either. Norman Warren is making every red flag and warning sign raise.

He was trying to use me for insider information, that much is true, but his focus on the personal more than the professional feels extremely weird. As far as I've heard, the deal is done. The details of the contracts between Zastrow and Warren are finalized, now it's just lawyers wordsmithing back and forth to make sure no one has any loopholes. Getting more information won't change that.

Norman stops chasing me when I reach the door. I look back and see him standing there, an expression on his face that makes my blood cold.

I tell Neo about dinner as soon as I get to the loft, and he calms my suspicions by promising to look into it. He leaves and doesn't come back until the early hours of the morning. The pit in my stomach is still there when I wake up the next morning.

34

Perri

Another week goes by and Cassandra has stopped answering my calls or texts. I know she's alive because I checked with Shaw and Scarlet. Hela is back in Norway for a few months and her answers to anything are sporadic. Shaw seems down, and Scarlet's being cagey, even for her.

I have no choice but to keep moving.

There's some sort of fall festival thing happening this weekend, not my scene, but since most of Nim's other friends are night owls I've been commandeered. Thomas and Wilder are on duty with us. Neo and the Zastrows are not taking any chances this time.

I pushed him before going out this time if there's been anything else, or if they know anything about who's doing this. After he realized he couldn't break my glare, Neo finally shared some of what they knew.

"Whoever is doing this has finally decided that Andre has no idea about Nim and Marco, so they're trying him directly now. There have been letters to the house, blurry pictures that we're trying to source...they want him to leave her."

"Which sounds like her father."

Neo nodded. "But I have that guy tagged and wired everywhere except his own asshole - I'd know. We'd know."

"I don't understand why."

To my surprise, Neo had pulled me against him. The hold he had on me was comforting to both of us, and I realized he needed it. Not being able to solve this problem was eating at him, and he needed comfort. I reminded myself to do it more, even if he wasn't asking for it.

"What happens if they get divorced, or if she's cheating on him?"

"The entire deal with Maines Manufacturing falls apart, and she's essentially penniless. We'd never let that happen, but the business side of it would be a huge fucking problem for Zastrow."

That's all swirling around in my mind as Nim loops her hand through mine and we stroll through the busy market. She's looking at everything but not buying, smiling and chatting with different vendors.

Finally she indulges in some apple cinnamon donuts and a cup of cider. I get one of each for myself and follow when she drags us over to an open spot on a concrete planter. Thomas and Wilder make a point of giving us some space, dressed casually but still standing out as two dudes at a fall festival that are clearly not talking to anyone or engaging with the activities.

"I want to ask you something, and I promise the answer stays between us - okay?"

"Okay." While I'll take her word on that, it doesn't mean I'm going to answer her.

"Do you have feelings for Neo?"

I sigh. I never got a chance to talk to Cassandra about any of the things that were happening between Neo and I, and that was without even touching our true dynamic. There's never been anything like this in my life - the extent of our physical relationship, the big feelings - and I need to talk about it. I'm not sure Nim is the best choice though. At the end of the day, she's his friend first.

"Yes."

"He's definitely got them for you."

My mouth drops open in surprise but I pull myself together. "It doesn't matter."

Nim shakes her head. "How it started is what doesn't matter. Why can't he keep you? Why can't you keep him? Why does there have to be an end date?"

Valid questions that don't have easy answers.

"It's what he wants."

She frowns but doesn't disagree with me. "What do you want?"

I laugh but there's no humor. "It doesn't matter. I'll take what I can get right now and hope it's enough to survive on when he's gone."

"That's...dark, Peep. You'd really let him go?"

"If it's what he wants, after everything he's been through, I'm not going to be another person who overrules him for my own selfish reasons."

"Ow," she jokes, but doesn't disagree with me. "On the other hand...I don't know that anyone's ever fought for him either."

That hits me right in the chest and I have to look away from her to take it in. It's true. It's true that he's always been the one fighting for himself and that the people in his life who should have tried to hold on let him go. I know that even if he wouldn't acknowledge it, feeling like he's worthy of anything he has is something that challenges him. Even though I know he wanted to find love, I believe part of the reason he never did is because he always believed he wasn't good enough for anyone.

Definitely not because we're meant to be.

I brush that thought aside. Who in his life ever stuck around and loved him other than the Zastrows? But it's not the same kind of love.

Maybe I will fight for him, and for us, when the time comes.

Nim smirks at me, knowing that she got her message through.

"So is he still being all chivalrous or have you too banged it out?"

The things that come out of her mouth when she doesn't even know me render me mute. However, the blush on my cheeks answers for me.

"Oh, damn. I thought he'd hold out longer. I owe Harrison $50 bucks."

I splutter. "You bet - on if we'd have sex?"

Nim laughs. "It was impossible not to, one, because Harrison loves a good bet, and two, you don't know this, but you are exactly Neo's type, down to your big ass." Nim slaps my side but because my ass is in fact big, she gets a piece of it. "I think it's his Irish - a strong, fertile looking woman who could carry his big ass babies."

"That's kind of gross."

"Probably. Sorry. The meds only work so well on the brain-mouth filter. But seriously. It's not just how you look, but who you are too. All that soft outside with a core of steel. Even when this drove him crazy it was so obvious he respected you. It takes a lot to earn his true respect and not just the respect that goes along with his manners."

"What would you do?"

Nim looks off and narrows her eyes. Her own situation is complicated. While Nim has a lot of energy and enthusiasm, I don't know that I would describe her as happy, or even content. The best I can say is that she's no longer hiding, even though I'm not sure what I mean by that. I think she worked hard for a lot of her life to make herself small and unnoticeable - as a fellow woman I've been there - and now that she is no longer required to do that, there's a lot of healing going on.

"Love looks different to everyone - I know a lot of people wouldn't understand that what exists between me and Marco is love, or me and Andre - but the love I have and the love I get from both of them is essential to my survival. It sustains me when I am too tired to sustain myself. Neo needs that kind of love, and I think you can give it to him." She finally turns to look at me, her expression more serious than I've ever seen it. "You need it just as badly. If given the chance Neo could be the kind of love that sustains you for a lifetime and beyond."

"Well try telling him that," I joke to snap us both out of the melancholy turn this conversation has taken.

She doesn't take the bait, but does smile slightly. "Don't think I won't, but I'm not the one he listens to these days."

We finish our donuts and cider and resume our wander through the festival. Nim does end up buying a bunch of random things and arranges for them to be shipped to the Long Island estate.

"I've been walking around in the shadow of Colleen, never letting myself see it as my house too. She'd hate that it came to this, but she'd want me to feel like it was mine, too."

"So you're filling it with pumpkins?" I tease.

"Kind of. I'm going all out to decorate for fall. The housekeeper nearly fainted when I told her what I wanted. I've kind of let her keep on making decisions because I didn't want to step on any toes."

"Well put on your best fall boots and we'll go stomping."

"You are so weird."

I raise an eyebrow at her. "Takes one."

She laughs, and we go to the next stall. Nim spends her money, and I get lost in thoughts about Neo.

35

Neo

When the door beeps and announces Perri's arrival, I don't expect her to do much other than say hello. I'm reading through the forensic accountant's report on Adam Smith, the words and numbers blurring together, astoundingly boring, all telling me that we'd already caught and flagged the project accounts that he'd defrauded us with.

Perri steps in front of me, grabs the report, and throws it over her shoulder.

When I look up into her eyes, there's something blazing there I've never seen before.

"Perri," I start but she leans over and puts a finger to my lips, straddles my lap, and slams her mouth to mine. When her tongue sweeps along my bottom lip I open for her, and groan as the flavor of cinnamon and her floods me. She grips my shirt and keeps me close as her hips slide along mine.

She lets the kiss go and wiggles away from me and dives her hands between us to undo my belt and free my cock. I'm already hard for her, taken off guard at her direct need. I'm more shocked when she reaches between her own legs and rips her nylons open at the crotch with one rough tug.

"Fuck, princess," I start but she shushes me again. There's nothing I can do but watch in worship as she rises up, moves her thong to the side, and impales herself on me. Perri is soaked and slides down my cock.

We stare into each other's eyes, something passing between us that we haven't named, and then she moves.

I can't look away from her as she grinds slowly, teasing me as much as she's chasing her own pleasure.

My hands fly to her hips and I help her move, lifting her and pressing her down, shifting my hips so I can grind her on me and stimulate her clit.

Perri leans over and kisses me, desperate, messy, and deep. She doesn't stop as her cunt squeezes my cock as she starts to come. Her movements are tight and short and her cries echo in my mouth, vibrating into my chest.

While she's distracted, I take back control.

I lift her up and move her onto her back on the couch, lifting her outside leg over my shoulder so I can pound into her even deeper. I look down at her, watching the flush of pleasure across her face as I move faster and faster, desperate to explode inside her.

"Neo," she moans and her back arches, changing the angle that we're fucking each other.

"Let me have it, Perri. Let me take you and fill up your cunt."

"Yes!" she screams and her hands dig into my shoulders, the pain giving me a fissure of pleasure. "Fill me."

Of all the things she's said before while we were having sex, she's never said that, and I swear it makes my brain short out in a way that makes me orgasm immediately.

I grunt as my hips jerk violently, come shooting from me and deep into her. I still and Perri moans and grinds on me, as if knowing how deep I am inside her turns her on even more. Watching Perri writhe beneath me keeps me hard and I start moving, fucking her with sharp, shallow strokes.

Perri whimpers with each thrust. Her hand slides up my neck until she's cupping my face and holding me, keeping my eyes on hers. I move a little faster and her body bows up toward me, her eyes shutting as she comes again, squeezing my cock so hard I see black spots in front of my eyes.

I sigh as I come back to myself, and I don't want to pull out of her. So I don't.

I decide we're going to make a fucking mess of this couch. Her ass fits perfectly in my hands as I reach down to grab it and yank her closer, before moving us back to the position where she's straddling me. It lets me be balls deep inside her, where it's hot and tight. If we sit like this long enough I'll get hard again, and make her come again.

Perri's head is resting on my shoulder as she catches her breath. She swings it up to look at me, shaking her hips to adjust herself and making me hiss from the sensitivity.

"I care about you."

I stiffen under her and don't say anything.

"I want to be honest in whatever time we have left." She cups my face in that way she's been doing lately, touching me with aching softness. Like every brush of her fingers is memorizing me to say goodbye. "I want you to know that I care about you, that I want us to do this and end this like adults because I think you care about me too."

Of course I do.

"So what are you saying? What do you want?"

"Be with me. Really with me. No games, no threats. Let me have you until you tell me it's time to walk away."

I stare into her eyes and try to decide if this is the worst idea anyone has ever had. It won't be her having me, it'll be us having each other. It'll be us letting one another in for a brief slice of time, until we cut ourselves open and walk away bleeding.

Fuck, if that's not worth it.

I lean forward and kiss her softly.

"*Mo dhuine ar bith, tá mé agat. Is leatsa mé.*" I kiss her again. "Until it's time to walk away."

She smiles but it's sad, and our mouths meet. The kiss is deep and intimate, our tongues speaking in a different way, communicating what we won't allow ourselves to voice.

I stand up, keeping her in my arms and my dick in her pussy, and walk us to the bedroom. We stay there, wrapped up in each other for the rest of the night. I'm giving this to myself because I know the end is coming sooner than she thinks, but god help me - I love her.

I love her and I'm going to have to hurt her more than she's ever been hurt before. I know everything Perri has been through and survived and yet it's not going to stop me from doing what needs to be done. The only way I can justify it to myself is that in the end, it's keeping her safe too. She's in the storm now, and all I want is for her to find safe harbor. Being by my side isn't it.

Maybe she'll forgive me, and maybe there's a chance, but I learned the hard way that some things can't be let go.

With my body, I let her know how I feel.

36

Perri

I'm eating lunch outside on what feels like one of the last truly nice days this fall. Neo and I haven't been able to keep our hands off each other since I cam back from my outing with Nim. It's like he's trying to tell me something but won't say the words.

He's giving me so much to remember him by.

I've started looking at apartment listings and making a budget for myself. Zastrow pays their accountants well, so I might be able to afford a loft or efficiency and not have to deal with a roommate. I've thought of asking Cassandra to get an apartment with me, thinking maybe if her dad knows she's with me he'll let her go. She's started answering me but it's sparing. I'm still worried but I don't know anything for sure. Shaw promises me that she's fine.

Fine being a relative term.

"Perri?" a soft female voice interrupts my fretting. I turn to see Rina Carpenter standing behind me, wringing her hands, clearly nervous.

"What do you want?" I ask as gently as I can.

"Please, I need to speak with you - somewhere private."

I stare at her. There are bags under her eyes and her lovely hair is pulled up in a messy bun despite the professional cleanliness of her clothes. The way she's darting glances everywhere as if she's afraid someone is out to get her raises all my red flags.

"Fine." I pack up my lunch and follow her, sending a text to Neo as I go. He has my location so I'm not too worried. Plus, we're going around a corner of the Zastrow building. This is my turf.

I follow Rina into a shadowed corner and she turns to face me. There are tears in her eyes and I immediately reach out on instinct to comfort her.

"I'm sorry."

There's a sharp pain in my neck and then every muscle in my body goes tight and tense, my teeth clacking together as my jaw slams shut. The pain is immense and overwhelming, and when it stops I collapse, twitching on the ground. A man looms over me, wearing a mask, and I see the needle in his hand before I feel the prick of it in my neck.

The world fades with each blink of my eyes until I'm consumed by the darkness.

Cold water snaps me out of unconsciousness. I'm bound to a chair, the bindings on my wrist just the other side of painful. My muscles ache, especially my back and my jaw, and it takes me a few tries to lift my head and look around.

In flashes, everything that happened to get me here comes back to me. Following Rina, texting Neo, the masked man and the needle. If I didn't come back from lunch, someone would have noticed. Whoever has me has no chance of hiding me from Neo and the guys. I'm sure they have me tagged in places I'm unaware of, just so they can keep tabs on me.

The man standing in front of me is big, pale, and bald. He looks more annoyed than angry or threatening.

"You're awake, good."

He walks over and opens a bottle of water in front of me, I hear the crack of the seal, and then holds it to my mouth. I drink as much as he'll let me have. If they're doing it to prepare me for whatever comes next, I'll take all the sustenance I can get.

"Tell me who Nicolette is having an affair with."

"I don't know what you're talking about!" I yell, hoping that high emotions make it believable.

The man backhands me. I don't taste any blood so I know he's holding back, even if my cheek stings and will definitely bear a mark.

"Tell me the code to the warehouse fence."

"If they know I was taken they've probably deactivated my code by now. It won't do you any good."

"What's Neo's code?"

I swallow because I know, I've seen him type it in enough times. "He'll get an alert. There's always someone there. It won't help you."

"Tell me anyway."

"No."

He hits me harder this time, and I feel the inside of my cheek shred against my teeth. The taste of copper floods my mouth, and I turn my head to spit. It lands on the ground, bright red.

"Then tell me about Nicolette's affair."

"There is no affair." It rings with truth because it is true - what is happening in her marriage and relationship is not an affair. She isn't cheating on anyone.

"It will do you no good to be loyal to her. Do you think she'll tell them to save you over keeping her secrets? Do you think she'd do the same in your place?"

I glare at him. He waits, the silence building, and he bends at the waist so our faces are even. "Do you think they give a fuck about you?"

"It's not about them," I burst out before I can stop myself. "It's about me. My integrity. I'm not telling you anything."

"We'll see." He takes something out of his pocket. "Tell me about Nicolette's affair."

I spit in his face.

Lightning fast, he thrusts his arm out. That same violent tensing of my muscles spreads through my body, and I twitch against the bindings as the taser sends electricity through me. He moves it away and looks at me.

"Tell me."

"Fuck you."

I try to brace against the bolts of electricity but I have no control over myself. He does this over and over. Different questions about the Zastrows, both the family and the business, and I say nothing. The burn of the taser doesn't register anymore, even if the shock still makes everything tense up. I get more and more worn down with every pulse, but it makes it easier to stay quiet.

He holds the taser against me for the longest amount of time so far, and when the tension releases I feel my pants get wet as I lose control of my bladder. The man stops the taser and steps back, looking down at my lap. He chuckles to himself.

"If you tell me the name of her lover, I'll let you change your clothes."

"No. There is no affair." I shift uncomfortably. It takes everything I have not to pass out. My eyes keep closing for longer and longer.

The man grunts and shakes the chair, waking me up and getting my attention. We engage in a stare down. It breaks when he slaps me again, blood and spit dribbling out of my mouth.

"They don't care about you. They're going to let you die here. No one is going to rescue you, Perri Kane. If you tell me nothing, I'm taking care of their problem. You might as well tell me what you know."

"I'm nobody. I don't know anything." I try another tactic, shaking with exhaustion.

"A nobody who fucks Neo Ryan and frolics in the park with Nicolette Zastrow? Nice try. Tell me, and I'll make you disappear. Let you go, get you out, they'll never find you."

"You must really think I'm an idiot. I'm dead either way, and I'd rather die than betray them."

The man gives me a look and then leaves the room. I let my chin fall to my chest, and then try to roll my shoulders and get them to relax. No matter how I move, nothing loosens up or moves. I'm very, very well tied to this chair.

I'm not getting out of here.

I'm not betraying my friends.

So, I'm back where I started in the first place. Tied to a chair, life threatened, and facing certain death.

Except this time I feel entirely different about it. I'm not giving up, I'm going down with a fight. Months ago when this all began, I was willing to die for circumstances I couldn't control because it felt like there was no reason to inconvenience anyone. I saw myself as in the way, without anything to live for. I was in a constant state of survival, without letting myself get a life or flourish.

Now, it breaks my heart to know that things were finally more. I finally felt like I belonged. Like life was a thing to enjoy. I've done and experienced more in these last months in my supposed captivity than the last 22 years of my life.

But it's okay.

The man comes back into the room and I stiffen when I see the gun in his hand.

"Finally," I bluff bravado. "Either kill me or let me go because you're not getting anything from me. Stop wasting our time."

He cocks the gun and brings it up, staring down the barrel at me.

"Don't you have anything to live for?"

I clench my jaw and it hurts like a bitch, but it doesn't stop the echo of that question from resonating through my head. Neo asked me the same thing and back then the answer was no. I close my eyes and think of them all, all these people that I've come to love, but especially Neo.

When I open my eyes, the man's expression hardens, seeing my resolve.

I lean forward until my forehead is pressed to the muzzle.

"Do it," I demand, wanting to get this over with.

I close my eyes and a single tear drops down my cheek. That's all he's going to get from me.

If these are the last moments of my life, I want it to end with only one thought.

"Neo," I whisper.

There's a long silence, and nothing happens.

"Fuck," the man swears and the muzzle is removed from my forehead.

I don't open my eyes, bracing for whatever comes next.

What I don't expect is for him to walk behind me and cut the ropes tying my wrists. A new buzz of fear floods through me, that he plans to do something else to me before killing me. I open my eyes, and see him walking away from me and out of the room.

I move my arms into my lap, my shoulders and wrists in agony.

I'm reaching down to work on the knots keeping my legs in place when the door opens again and I open my mouth, ready to sass this guy, but it's not him.

It's Neo.

"Neo," I say his name with complete relief.

Except he doesn't come to me, doesn't rush to help me, and there's no concern on his face. He stands just inside the door with his hands in his pockets, looking at me. My cheek is still bleeding, and that's only part of the reason a sick feeling is pooling in my stomach.

I spit the blood pooling in my mouth onto the floor.

"I didn't mean for that to happen," he says quietly. "I told him to hold back."

The confirmation that Neo set all of this up is enough to disconnect me from myself. I stare at him, the chasm between us wider than I ever could have imagined.

37

Neo

I'm furious and I have no right to be.

I watch every emotion fade from Perri. She retreats behind the mask she used to wear around me, the walls I hadn't seen in a long time. After a second of looking me over, she drops her gaze and resumes untying her legs. When they're free, she runs her hands up and down her calves. It's impressive when she leans back in the chair, back straight, and crosses one leg over the other.

She's still in her soiled skirt and blouse from work, and despite being a little tattered and the marks beginning to show on her face, she looks as cool and controlled as ever.

"I had to test you."

"I understand." The ice in her voice is subtle but powerful.

Perri stares at me, blinking in a way I can only describe as hostile. This went exactly the way I expected, and was also a complete surprise. I never doubted that Perri's integrity would hold. She's had it from the first night I met her. Even if she didn't love working for Zastrow, love Nim, love *me*, she's not built to betray anyone. Not even to save her own life.

I never expected her to be so reckless with it though. To offer her life up so easily. She leaned against that gun like she wanted it, and it broke something inside me. When she said my name, whispered it with such adoration and reverence, I wanted to burn the whole fucking world down.

Because I knew in that moment how deep her feelings for me ran, and because I hated that no matter how happy she seemed she was willing to let it all go.

I never wanted to find her. I never wanted to fall in love, let alone with someone worthy of that love. I didn't want her in my space, I didn't want this whole thing to bring her in and make her love us. It was dangerous when from look one I wanted her, and wanted to feel what it was like when she wanted me.

This was always supposed to end, but before it does, I have to know one thing.

"You still think there's nothing worth living for?" When I say it my voice is a rasp, weak and angry at the same time.

Perri stares at me, a flash of disbelief in her eyes. Then she wipes off her skirt and stands up, adjusting herself until she's collected again. Right now she's injured, disheveled, and stained with her own urine, and yet she has more poise and power than I've ever seen. I can't look away when she steps up to me, her heels clicking on the concrete floor.

Her eyes are glassy when they lift to stare into mine, and I see her ruthless control as she holds in her tears.

"No, Neo," she whispers. "I thought I'd finally found something worth dying for."

Without waiting for my response she moves past me and opens the door.

The only person besides Rina and my fake kidnapper Andrew who knew about this was Leander. He was manning the recording devices, making sure we had a clear copy to show Andre so we would have the evidence to let Perri go. I didn't tell any of the other guys that I was testing Perri. I didn't want them to get involved or talk me out of it.

Because they could have.

As she steps up to him he stands and swallows thickly. I've never seen him look nervous before, but he can't keep the guilt off his face as he looks at her. At the bruises forming on her cheek and the burn marks from the taser. A woman who fed him, gave him advise about women, taught him how to get a wine stain out of a dress shirt, and laughed with him nearly every night for months.

"Get me out of here."

"Yes, ma'am."

Perri walks toward the next door without looking back, and Leander gives me one apologetic glance before following her out into the bright light. It's late afternoon, and this feels like the longest day of my life.

Andrew is leaning against the wall, watching me. He's my undercover guy, someone who isn't quite inner circle but I've known for a few years. Andre bailed him out of some trouble with his ex-wife's new boyfriend, and he's been loyal ever since.

"You sure this was the move, boss?"

"No fucking clue," I answer him honestly.

I give her some time to get out. I have no delusions about what's going to happen next.

That doesn't make it hurt any less when I finally come back to the loft a few hours later and see that most of her things are gone, even the chair she moved in with her. I walk to the bedroom. Her dresser is still there but it's empty, and all her clothes are gone from the rack. As is the crystal lamp from her bedside table.

I wander into the bathroom and flip on the light. All her skin care is gone. The shower shelves are empty of her multiple products.

For some reason I feel compelled to look in the fridge, and she even took her half of the lunches for the rest of the week, and her coffee creamer that I stole dashes of every morning.

Perri is gone.

It doesn't take long before they descend on me.

I had to send proof of the outcome of the test to Andre, and decided to include Harrison. He's always been suspicious of her and I hoped that this would assuage that.

Whoever is trying to get into the apartment first has to hit the code multiple times before they get it right, and the door flies open with so much power that it hits the inside wall with a slam.

"WHAT THE FUCK DID YOU DO?" Nim roars like I've never heard her before. She must've used Harrison's code, or hell, my own, to get in. When I look over the back of the couch, I'm surprised to see Benji trail in behind her. He closes the door.

"What the hell man, she's got a huge bruise on half her face," he sounds appalled. Benji is pretty unflappable so it must look pretty bad. Guilt swirls in my stomach.

"Is she safe?" I've basically been ignoring Nim, who is standing next to the couch seething at me, so angry she can't speak yet.

"She's fine."

The door beeps again. I look back and Harrison comes in, his face stormy.

"The fuck." He pinches the bridge of his nose and lets the door slam shut. He looks over at Nim and raises an eyebrow. She shakes both of her fisted hands in the air, her face red with the exertion of trying to speak.

"I knew you wanted to test her, I know I said to test her, but this..."

"It was necessary," I defend. "We had to know. Now we do."

"You already knew, you idiot!" Nim finally finds her voice. "Just because it wasn't something you could prove doesn't mean you didn't know. WE ALL KNEW. She was one of us, she is one of us, and you hurt her. You let someone hit her. SHE WAS TASED." Nim screeches and turns away from me, burying her hands in her hair.

"God, you're that afraid of something real, aren't you? That you'd rather hurt her than own up to your feelings."

That one hits too close to the truth. I stand up and turn to her, unable to stop my fury from pouring through. The dam has broken and we're all fucked now.

"This wouldn't be happening if you would have listened to me for once in your fucking life!" I stand up and roar before trying to put myself back on lockdown. "This is your fault," I continue, on the razor's edge of calm. "We wouldn't be in this situation if you could've kept it in your pants on the party bus like you're supposed to," I growl low. If they'd kept their hands off each other, there would've been nothing for Perri to see. No secret for her to keep.

"Too far," Harrison grumbles.

"Is it?" I turn to him. "You're just as bad, asshole. How often have you left the fucking country without notice or taking a security staff member? Remember when your hotel room got broken into in Barcelona? The only reason your ass wasn't kidnapped for ransom was because I had a contact in country looking out for you. You're as bad as her.

"I make the rules to keep all of you safe, and how often do you disregard them? How often do you look at me and see your friend instead of your head of security, and it makes you think that it's a suggestion instead of a directive?" I move from the couch and pace in front of the TV. "Is it that fucking hard to respect me?

"I get that you two have been through shit, but you have no idea what it feels like to earn where you are. I'm not saying you don't work hard," I wave at Harrison, "but you could tell the job to fuck off and be fine. You have other options. This it for me," I hold out my arms, referencing my tiny warehouse kingdom where I try to keep these assholes safe. "If I fuck this up, I'm done. I'm not Andre's son or his wife, I'm the kid he took in because he knew he could mold me into what he needed. I'm grateful, but I'm not stupid."

"It's not like that," Nim tries to interrupt but Harrison shakes his head at her. He doesn't disagree with me. I know that I'm deflecting talking about Perri, but some of this has been a long time coming. I turn back to Nim, fighting to bury everything that I'm feeling. Yeah, I made some choices that weren't great, but I wouldn't have had to make them if she hadn't put me in this position.

"If you'd done what I asked, maybe things would be different." My voice is toneless, flat, and cold. A perfect cover for the fury and pain inside, and the visceral desire to rip myself to pieces.

Nim takes a few deep breaths and stares at me, trying to read past the mask. The fury leeches out of her at whatever it is she manages to see.

"You're right. What got us here is my fault because I didn't listen to you. I don't take the things you tell me as seriously as I should. I'll own that." She holds up her hands like she could press the next thought into me. "But this wasn't necessary. I knew without putting a gun to her head that she would never betray us, and would rather die than betray *you*. I know you know it, too. Own your shit, Neo."

Harrison agrees. "I don't like that we did this, and I say we because I'm to blame, too. I never gave you the chance to trust her. For the record, dad confirmed she's in the clear."

"Anything else?" I ask him, referring to his conversation with Andre.

"He said he's disappointed but he understands why you did it."

"Fuck," I snap out. Andre and Nim are the reason all of this happened. Their secrets, their contracts, and I'm their employee who did the best he fucking could to draw a line around the woman he fell in love with. What the fuck right does he have to be disappointed in me? This is what the job demands of me.

"We should go," he tells Nim, and she walks toward the door with him. She looks back at me once before they go, shaking her head.

I did the right thing. I know I did. But I also know something broke inside me that I won't be able to forgive myself for, and honestly, I'm not sure I'll ever be able to forgive Nim for either. I wish I could blame that on Perri, but I don't want to blame her for a god damn thing. She did everything I asked of her. None of this was her intention.

There was no real future for Perri and I, no matter how I feel about her. No matter how she feels about me. There was always going to be my responsibility to keeping Zastrow secrets and safety between us.

Benji stands after they leave. I'd kind of forgotten he was there, and don't exactly like that he heard my outburst. It was more insight into me than I want anyone to have.

"She asked me to tell you not to contact her, and that if there's anything to say or that she left here, you can let me know."

Jealousy burns in my chest that she's turning to Benji for comfort, but I've seen their relationship and how close they are. If I had to choose any of the guys to take care of Perri, it would be Benji. He'd try the hardest to keep her safe.

"I understand."

He takes a step toward the door and then stops. "Why?"

"I needed to have no doubts."

Benji nods. "I hope it was worth it."

He leaves, and silence descends on the loft.

Of course it wasn't worth it.

38

Perri

I've got an ice bag on my cheek and I'm curled up on a strange bed.

Leander paid for me to be checked into a hotel because I didn't have any of my things aside from my phone. As soon as I got into the room I stripped down and showered. It was a nice hotel so I put on the cozy hotel bathrobe and threw out my clothes, went into the hall to get ice from the machine, and then sat and wondered what the hell to do next.

In the past, my first call would've been to Cassandra. I'd never been in a situation this big or this bad, and she would be the cool head to get me out. At this point, I don't even know if she would answer the phone, let alone help me. Shaw had enough problems, and Scarlet was out of the country visiting Hela.

Hela was kind of scary and could probably help even from across the world, but I didn't think I could get help from any of them without telling too much of the truth. A truth I'm still determined to keep a secret. Neo might have hurt me and let me down, but I refuse to let down myself.

A soft knock on the door snaps me out of it. Benji stands there with my purse and my travel bag.

"Zastrow has some employee housing available. I got you a place. He won't know."

Benji's bleach blonde hair has almost grown out in the time that I've known him, and now it's mostly a soft brown. He looks almost as sad as I feel, but there's disappointment there too. Knowing what Neo did changed the way they all thought about him. Hurt as I am, I wish that wasn't true.

I wave Benji into the room and he sets everything down on the bed.

"I'm sorry."

"Don't be. This isn't your fault. He did what he thought he had to do."

"No," Benji disagrees. "He didn't have to do -" he swallows thickly and gestures to my face. "That. There was no reason to do that. I mean fuck we've been monitoring your every move for three months. I know you two are sleeping together. We all know who you are. You're family, Perri."

I give Benji a watery smile. "Thank you. Let me get changed and then let's go. I need to keep ice on this before it gets worse."

I take the travel bag and step into the bathroom. Because he's usually the one at the warehouse, Benji and I have spent a lot of time together. The only person who might know me better than him is Neo, but I didn't realize how well Benji knew me until I open the bag. It's my softest yoga leggings, my favorite hoodie, and my moisturizer, in addition to underwear. I don't love the idea that he'd been in my underwear drawer but need wins out. The fact that Benji knew that of all my skincare products what I'd want was my moisturizer makes me let out a laughing sob.

They were my family. Maybe they still are, but it's going to take a lot of maneuvering to figure out how we fit together now. Neo wanted to test my loyalty to the family, and he got his answer. This is where I belong, but maybe it's not where I'm meant to stay.

I change quickly, and we leave with my hood up over my head to try and hide the increasingly darkening bruise on my cheek. It hurts to move my mouth and my body still aches from the taser. I'll be feeling this for days, if not weeks.

Why am I not mad at him? Sad, disappointed, heartbroken, yes - but not angry. In the first moments I was, but it faded the further I got from him.

I keep asking myself that question as Benji drives me across town to a residential building not too far from Zastrow. The guard nods at us, and I follow him up to a little apartment on the third floor. It's basic - a living room, galley kitchen, small bedroom with a nice closet, and a decent bathroom.

More than I could ask for, and probably right at the limit of what I could afford.

"Don't worry about the cost. Harrison's orders."

Interesting. While Harrison has always liked me as an employee, he's been cagey about the other side of things.

"Do you need anything?"

"Anything you can get from the loft. Don't organize it, just toss it in and get it here. I can't go back there. My comfy chair, if you can swing it, but I don't need the dresser."

Benji taps on his phone and it immediately starts buzzing with responses. "We'll be back with everything in about an hour. You good, being alone?"

I shrug. "Who knows where I am?"

"Harrison, and the guys, but we're not going to tell him."

"Harrison won't tell him?"

"Not unless he thinks he deserves to know, and that will be up to you."

I nod. "Okay. I'm going to ice my face."

Benji opens his mouth to speak and I hold up a finger to stop him. "No sorries. Not from you."

"Okay." He gives me a nod, fights saying it, and then leaves.

I'm not mad at Neo because I think I would've done the same thing in his shoes. If I had someone to protect like that, if I felt my whole existence revolved around getting it right, that I'd be cut off for a single fuck up, or if I cared about these people so much and was used to sacrificing myself for them, it would be second nature.

Not to mention his desire to sabotage what was growing between us, and how much it scared him. Neo destroying us this spectacularly isn't surprising, although this method was more than what would've been necessary. There were a million other ways for him to push me away that might have been harder to see through.

This whole thing is so damn transparent that despite what he ordered done to me, I fucking pity him. I pity a man who is so backed into a corner that all he can do is bite when he could easily have run instead. When our time was finally up, I would've let him walk away because I would never have been able to be sure of him. He wasn't capable of asking me to stay.

The fact that he had to hurt me so badly shows how much I mean to him. It's beyond twisted how that speaks to me, and almost makes me feel better. Neo's feelings for me were powerful enough that he couldn't walk away, he had to shove me off a cliff so that I would have no other desire except to leave.

I've been able to lose feelings fast in the past. One transgression, one moment of clarity, and the feelings are gone in a snap. It would seem logical if that was the case in this situation, but it's not. My feelings for him are as deep and intense as ever.

It's sick, but I would take him back if it meant he'd stop lying to himself and we could build the relationship we both deserve. If he would let me love him, and love me in return. I would make him grovel his ass off and he'd probably owe me until the day he died, but Neo has become so essential to my sense of self I don't think I can give him up. Not really.

When did I become so damn toxic?

I flinch when there's another knock on the door. I don't move to answer it.

"Perri? It's Nim."

I groan but go answer the door. I don't feel like dealing with her right now, but I think it will be worse if I don't. Literally the only people I would be okay with engaging with outside of Neo himself are Cassandra and Benji.

Nim gasps when I open the door and she sees my face.

"They wouldn't let me watch the video."

"Good," I have to work to soften my snarl. It's not something I want anyone to see.

She nods, and holds up a bag. "I brought you some things - for the bruises."

I step back from the door and let her inside. She steps in and heads to the kitchen, laying everything out from her bag. "I got vitamin K cream, witch hazel, and arnica. I tried to find a good mask but they all seemed like bullshit."

"Thanks." I don't know what else to say.

"He didn't tell anyone what he was going to do. We would've stopped him."

"Okay."

She stares at me, trying to get a read, but I'm more closed off than I've ever been. I'm not sure why Nim is one of the people I'm angry at, but I undoubtedly am. This happened for her - because Neo believed he had to do this for her and her husband and her relationship. There's no room for me to feel bad for her, when I feel like my entire body is a throbbing bruise.

"I was there when Andre and Harrison got the video. They were horrified, Perri. We knew he was going to test you, but none of us imagined..."

"He would have me kidnapped and interrogated to see if I would break and reveal your secrets?"

Nim winces. "Andre would have stopped him. If he'd known."

I don't know if I believe that. While I have no problems continuing to work for him, on a personal level he's ruthless when it comes to defending what he feels belongs to him. Maybe things wouldn't have gone on for as long as they did, but I don't think Andre would've pulled the plug on the whole thing. Andre Zastrow lives in a world with his own rules, and proving loyalty is a big part of it.

Even if they'd let me go that first night on Nim's birthday, I never would have told a soul. It's not who I am.

They didn't know that, but I was kind of hoping it was something they'd learned. Maybe they did, but maybe they're so used to betrayal they can't help but go too far to avoid the pain of it.

"We both know Neo has trust issues..."

She gives a sad laugh. "Shit dad, insane ex-girlfriends, backstabbing employees...I guess it's a wonder he didn't do worse."

"At least you know I'm team Zastrow."

"I already knew that. Is there anything else I can do for you? I mean literally anything - do I need to get you out of the country? Does he know you're here? Do you want another job? Because I will make that happen."

Despite everything, I do feel a rush of gratitude and a reminder why she was fun to spend time with. I have no doubt that Nim would do any of those things for me if I asked, right now, no question.

"I need a few days off."

"Done." Nim steps forward and takes my hand. "It probably won't help, but no one is going to punish him as well as he's punishing himself."

"I don't know yet if that's sad or satisfying."

"Why not both?" Nim forces a smile. "Text me if you need anything. ANYTHING."

I nod and wait for her to walk out the door before walking over to the kitchen counter to try the miracle cures waiting for me.

It's tempting to send him a picture of my face because whoa the swelling and coloration has really kicked in despite my icing. I want to send him my face and ask him if it was worth it. I want to hear him tell me he was wrong, and sorry. I want him to try and justify himself so I can spit in his face and then run into his arms.

I want to hear him tell me he's sorry every day for the rest of our lives because I know this is going to hurt us both for as long as we live. Someday I might move on, but a piece of me will always be missing.

I hope that piece lives in the loft and haunts him.

39

Neo

Two weeks pass and I can't remember any of it, which is a huge fucking risk in my line of work. Nothing happens so I get lucky because if I was asked what happened yesterday, three days ago, a week ago, the only thing I can say is that I worked hard not to miss or think about Perri.

I'm not speaking to Nim and I'm not talking to Harrison or Andre about anything other than work. Things are tense with the guys, but they are the only people I was honest with. The day after the false kidnapping, I sat them all down in the warehouse.

"I know you might be angry with me, or with Leander, for what happened with Perri. I told you from day one that we were going to test her, that it was going to be harsh. She was cleared, which doesn't surprise any of us. Perri's family, whether she lives with me or not. I hope you maintain your relationships with her." I swallowed against the emotions clogging my throat. "She needs you."

They all stared at me and eventually nodded or told me they understood, and things got less tense after that. I know they have a separate group chat with her because yeah, I fucking check her phone still, but the only one who has seen her is Benji. If she runs into the guys at the office, she asked them to ignore her. She's not alone, that's all I care about.

I'm staring at my computer pretending to work when Thomas bursts into my office without knocking.

"Perri?" I ask, immediately, because honestly she's my first thought all the time.

"No," his voice is sympathetic. "Someone folded. There's a story about Nim and Marco."

"Fuck."

I pull up the website he tells me, and it's right on the landing page of the tabloid. The good news: there's no actual evidence that they are physically involved. The bad news: they've been secretly together since they were 16, and have been connected socially ever since. It's actually kind of surprising the allegation of the two of them being a thing hasn't been made sooner, considering he was at every single one of her birthdays even when it was during racing season. He would move heaven and earth to get there for her.

I read the story, noting specific details that might help us narrow down who was present at the events referenced by the source. There are only 8 people cleared to be with her when she's with Marco, and they've all signed NDAs. A violation of them will strip whoever it is to pieces. They'll be wiped off the map.

What pisses me off more is that the tabloid is owned by Warren Media, and we didn't get a heads up. It's fair that they might not be able to stop a story, but it's in bad faith not to tell us about this considering the stipulations in the final contract that's being reviewed.

"Start going over the approved guest list, dig deep into each of them, see who's having a problem." I scroll again. "Check if any of them are getting money that traces to the O'Connors."

"You think your dad is helping them fuck around?" Thomas is quiet, but I can hear his irritation as clearly as I feel my own.

Before we can discuss it further, Wilder is stepping in. His expression is an odd mix of pissed and smug.

"I know who caved."

I wave for him to continue.

"Chelsea Landry. Daddy cut her off and she got approached to talk about her friendship with Nim."

"How'd you find out?"

"Sometimes she hooks up with a bouncer at Club Ginger and she told him what happened. She was only going to get a couple thousand for the initial interview but once she let it slip about Marco, they paid her $250k."

"That's not fucking around money, that's pay off money. The O'Connors wouldn't have that."

"No," Wilder shakes his head as he thinks. "That wouldn't be worth it just for them to mess with you."

"But it would be worth it for Warren," I lead us to the logical conclusion. "What the fuck does this get Norman Warren?"

Thomas cocks his head and I nod. "Get Chelsea Landry."

Thomas and Wilder leave, and I make the walk of shame to Andre's office. He's on the phone and he looks furious, so I step in to Harrison's office until he's done. Harrison is frowning at his computer but I can't tell if it's his usual work frown or about the story.

"You heard?"

"Yeah," he sighs.

"You talked to Nim?"

"Yeah. She's fine." He looks over at me. "Still not talking to her?"

"Not until I get over the urge to apologize. I don't regret what I said, but I know I'll cave."

"Fair. I think the message got through even if the delivery could've used a little work."

I don't reply to that. I want to ask him how many times he's ever heard me yell. How many times I have ever lost my temper like that. The answer would be incredibly small and I wish that it made them both understand how hard this was for me. I don't think I've ever yelled at Nim before in our lives. I was just...done.

My phone buzzes with a text.

Benji: *Landry $ traces to Warren*

"God damn it." I repeat the message to Harrison, and he stands up to follow me to his dad's office. Harrison goes in, even though Andre is still on the phone. He can do that, I can't.

"Once again, Roger," Andre emphasizes as he glares at us. "There's no impropriety. It was a parasite trying to make money. We'll fix it." He pinches the bridge of his nose as Roger gets too damn loud on the other end of the phone. "I assure you, Nicolette is staying within the bounds of the contract. Mmhm. Yes. Dinner Saturday."

Andre hangs up the phone. "Tell me that I didn't tell him a complete lie."

"You didn't," Harrison starts, but I interrupt because it's not his fucking job.

"It was Chelsea Landry, and she was paid by Warren Media."

"Fantastic." Andre stops and frowns at his phone. "Although that does explain his call before I spoke to Roger. He talked about "sweetening" their offer if I find myself in need of a change."

"So they're setting Nim up so you can...marry someone else?" Harrison guesses.

"Cassandra Warren," I realize. "Perri said her dad has been weird lately, and was furious when he found out she was in a relationship. He hasn't let her leave their penthouse in...weeks. Not without her father as escort."

"That's really fucked up," Harrison grumbles.

"But it could also work in our favor. Norman Warren likes Perri. He think she's a good influence on Cassandra."

"You're unbelievable," Harrison turns away to look out the window.

Andre stares me down. "You'd have her go in and get information?"

"In return, we'd help Cassandra. Something is wrong in that house, and if Perri can save her friend, she will."

"I'd say I don't want to start a war, but he started it first." He clears his throat until Harrison is looking at him too. "Make it happen."

We walk out of Andre's office and back into Harrison's. I know Perri is in the building because I still get alerts when she signs in and out. I've stayed off her floor, not that I had any reason to be there except to see her.

"Who should make the approach?" Harrison asks.

"You." No hesitation.

"You sure?" He looks surprised, but I know. She'll still do it, but I don't want to cause any extra distress because I'm doing the asking.

"Yeah. Do you want me to be here?"

"In your office. I'll call you if we need you."

I nod and leave, a whole new tension living inside me.

40

Perri

Zadie scares the shit out of me when she pokes me in the shoulder. I jump, take a breath, and then take off my headphones. I've been wearing them at work since I came back - once the swelling went down and I could cover the bruise. Nim's creams really did help. But I don't want to talk or connect with anybody. I'm done on some level, but I don't know what that means.

"Harrison wants to see you," she leans in and says softly so we aren't overheard. "You can go right up, it seems urgent."

My heart turns over, heavy and fearful, at the thought that he might be telling me something happened to Neo. I squeeze my eyes shut and brush the thought away.

"Is it okay if I go now?"

"Of course. Go on."

I think I blackout because I don't remember getting in the elevator but suddenly I'm standing on the executive floor in front of their admins.

"Harrison is waiting, you can go on back," Ryan says with a reassuring smile. I'm sure it's usually very effective, but I currently feel like I'm going to vomit on his desk.

I try and smile in return but I don't know what my face actually does. I walk down the hall toward his office, knowing that I'm going to have to walk past Neo's office to get there. I try to tell myself that Neo isn't even in his office. That he's off dealing with bullshit and that I'll be walking past an empty chair.

Try as I might, I can't stop myself from glancing to the side when I pass. Neo is there, and I flinch. It's the first time I've been this close to him since I walked away. His hair is getting a little long, he's due for a new cut. His chin is resting in his hand and he's frowning. I don't know how I know, but I can tell he's fighting the need to glance at the door. To see me.

I don't make it hard on him - I walk more quickly to Harrison's door.

"Come in, Perri. Close the door, please."

I do as he says and then take the seat he indicates in front of his desk. Harrison looks the most flustered I've ever seen. He's fidgeting with the items on his desk and glancing between me and his computer screen.

"What's going on, Harrison?"

"I want to go into this telling you I feel like an asshole, and you have permission to call me one without your job being on the line. Okay?"

"Okay?" My stomach swoops with anxiety.

"Someone outed Nim and Marco. They were paid by Warren Media"

"Oh my god."

"It's being handled..." he trail off.

"But?" I prompt, hating the delay.

"But we need you to go the Warren's apartment and get information. In return, we'll get Cassandra out."

That's a low blow. I never bothered to ask Neo for help, but he had to know. If they're willing to start this kind of fight, Andre must be hopping fucking mad. This will blow up the entire deal they've been working on for almost a year. But they have resources to help her that I don't, and I'll be helping Nim.

"Asshole," I grumble, because we both know they're counting on my better nature right now. "What do I need to do?"

I cheat the system to get myself invited to the Warren penthouse. Instead of trying to talk to Cassandra, I call their landline. Mr. Warren's longtime assistant, Wesley, answers. He's delighted to hear I want to visit and invites me for dinner. If Wesley is acting that way, it means I've already been a topic of conversation.

When I get up to the apartment, it takes every ounce of control I have to keep my expression neutral when I see Cassandra. She's lost weight, and she was fit to begin with. Her cheeks are sunken, bags hang under her eyes, and her lips are dry and chapped. At some point she got her hair cut, and it's the shortest I've ever seen, barely touching her shoulders. The ends are a little choppy and uneven and I worry that she cut it herself. Her father always preferred it long.

She's wearing jeans, which is a good sign, and a soft cashmere sweater in an army green color that she probably chose to try and bring out some color in her faded complexion. If I didn't know that she'd basically been a prisoner in her own home, I'd think she had a serious illness.

Norman Warren is all smiles when I walk in, giving my cheek an air kiss and asking me immediately about work. I give him the surface answers he's expecting, and expound again on how much I love it as we eat.

"That article was quite shocking," he throws out.

I chew slowly, staring at him, softly indicating that I know his paper published it.

"Tabloids will tabloid," I reply. "I know you know I spend time with Nicolette - she's quite obsessed with her husband. While I understand the temptation to believe the worst, I don't think there's merit to the story beyond a friendship that's existed since high school."

"Really?" Norman is intrigued that I'm answering so directly, and it's the perfect distraction for him to ponder.

"Excuse me, I need the powder room."

I leave him staring at his steak and rubbing his chin, thinking about what I've said and another possible way to spin it, I'm sure. The bathroom is the door before Norman's home office. That's where I need to hide the little camera and recording devices that Benji gave me before I left the office.

Needless to say, he was not a fan of this plan of action, but that didn't stop him from handing the stuff over and explaining what I needed to do, and adding a little microphone device to my jacket. Just in case I need help. In a moment they can send in the cavalry.

Norman's office is unlocked because he's secure in his little castle. It's a pretentious room, half library, half study. Two of the walls are floor to ceiling bookshelves, one wall is mostly windows, and the wall with the door has a trophy case of media awards that Warren Media won, or photos of their reporters winning the big stuff. The amount of times that's happened during Norman's tenure at the helm is small. I can almost understand why Cassandra is willing to sacrifice so much to stay part of it - she wants to save it if she can.

The first thing I do is place a little node near the window, hidden by the curtain. It will boost the signal of both recording devices to make sure that everything comes through clearly.

That's the easy part. After making sure it's sticking to the wall and hidden by the curtain, I approach Norman's desk.

The sound recorder is a round tab with a wire sticking out. It fits under this desk drawer, and I make sure the wire with the mic is stuck tight to the wood. I open and close the drawer a few times pretty aggressively to make sure it's going to stay in place.

The camera is a little harder. There are bookshelves behind the desk, but nowhere unobtrusive enough to hide the camera. I figure they'll want to use it to see his computer screen and his phone calls. Norman has a tendency to pace when he's on the phone, which means his body won't be blocking the view very often. After staring for a second, knowing that I'm running out of time, I sink to hip level.

Norman never looks at these books and there would be no reason for anyone to be down here to notice the camera. I wedge it on top of the shelf, noting to ask Benji about this sticky stuff because it's impressive. I'm adjusting the angle when a shuffling sounds in the room.

I jump up and look to the door.

"What are you doing?" Cassandra asks, pale from fear. "We need to get out of here, come on." She waves for me, her motions jerky and panicked. I leave the camera as is, hoping we got a good angle, and run quietly for the door. I'm surprised when she grabs my hand and drags me through the apartment until we get to her bedroom, and then into her en suite.

Cassandra turns on the shower, the noise thundering in the small, enclosed space.

"I told them you weren't feeling well. What do you know?" she whispers.

"What do *you* know?" I ask in return.

"I know he's trying to get Nicolette Maines out of the picture. I've heard him talking about her lately when I try to be sneaky by his office. He keeps saying she needs to be "gone."

"So he's trying to kill her?"

Cassandra's eyes blow wide. "What?"

I sigh and pinch the bridge of my nose. "I'm only telling you this because I have their word they're getting you away from your dad, deal be damned. Norman burned all the bridges, the deal is dead, okay?"

"What did you get yourself into, bunny?" She tugs the end of my hair. "You sound like a spy."

"Today I'm playing spy, and maybe knight in shining armor if I can save you."

She stares at me a long time, trying to read me.

"Okay, I'm listening."

"I wasn't dating Neo, I was...kept. By the Zastrows because I saw something. They needed to know they could trust me."

"You're literally the most trustworthy person in the world."

"Yeah, well, we'll get to that another time because stuff happened with Neo and then he fucked it up big time, but the whole time we were - together," I don't know how else to say it. "There were attempts on Nicolette's life. Multiple. Not only attempts to tarnish her reputation but straight up kill her. I think your dad was trying to make way for you to sweeten the deal with a marriage offer."

"He's fucking unhinged."

"Yes. And he went too far. Andre is done, everything can be traced back to Warren and your dad. They said if I went in and planted devices in the office, they'd get you out."

Cassandra nods, taking in everything I said. Her brow furrows more with every second, and her scheming face takes over.

"Let's go. I've been collecting some things too, and in combination with this...it might be enough for Seth and Calliope to get him removed, and for Seth to step in."

"He's committing crimes."

"I know but getting his grubby idiot hands off our family legacy might be possible if we can leverage possible prison time. How are you going to get me out of here?"

"Through the front door," I smile at her. "They think I'm the sweet poor girl - no one would expect me to take you. Get what you need, and I mean need, material girl," I joke. "We have an exit strategy."

Cassandra nods. She keeps the shower running, then moves into her bedroom. She takes her favorite giant purse and starts shoving things into it. I'm impressed when she pulls back a painting on the wall to reveal a safe. In all the years I've known her and been in this room, I've never seen it before.

She holds in a laugh at my surprise and types in the code. There's a few stacks of cash, a velvet box, and a brown folder. Cassandra slides all of it into her bag, then grabs her phone and charger.

"Let's go." The resolve on her face makes me feel better about all of this. I text Thomas that we're on our way down. Since he's the guy who's best with a gun, or so I was informed earlier today, he's the one waiting in the car to get us out of here and to my new apartment as quickly as possible.

Since I'm not on any kind of lease and only internal documents with Zastrow, no one should be able to find us. My back up plan is to send Shaw and Cassandra out of the country until we fix this. She's taking a risk running with me and turning on her family.

We hold hands as we walk quietly down the hallway.

If you'd told little 6th grade me, the lonely awkward scholarship kid, that I'd be risking my life to help Cassandra Warren, I would never have believed you. The thing is, I don't doubt in this moment that she'd do the same for me. That I might have been selling my friend short all this time. If I'd tried telling her the truth and asking for her help when the whole captive thing first went down, she would've done whatever she could to help me, or found someone who did know what to do.

I need to get her out of here.

No one sees us or stops us, and I turn the knob to the apartment door very, very slowly. I open the door as little as possible and let Cassandra slide out first, and she slides along the door, to the wall, and into the corner of the hallway. I do the same.

We've snuck out of this apartment enough when we were younger to know the camera blind spots, and the lack of attention paid by the security guards. We keep our backs to the wall and slide along it until we get to the door to the stairs.

Even though we don't have to, we run down them. By the time we burst out the back entrance, where no one will see us exit, we're both breathing hard and giggling with hysteria. Thomas screeches to a stop in front of us and I run to the SUV, whipping open the back door and shoving her inside before following.

Thomas starts driving away before we even get our seat belts on.

"All good?"

"All good." I lean back in the seat and work on catching my breath. The ride to my apartment is silent as Cassandra and I both come down from the adrenaline. She seems to come back to herself as Thomas slows down outside the apartment building.

"You aren't in the loft anymore?"

"No."

"Do I need to cut off his balls?"

"Yes," Thomas answers right as I say, "No."

Cassandra shakes her head, but grabs her bag and we slide out. I give Thomas a wave as we walk into the building. I stop at the front desk and let the doorman know that Cassandra is welcome to come in and out and that she'll have a key to my apartment. His warm gaze takes in her gaunt figure and all he does is add her information from her ID.

When we get up to my place, she looks around, throws out her arms, and lets out a heaving sigh.

"Freedom!"

"Freedom," I confirm.

Cassandra heads straight into the little kitchen, steals a bag of cheddar rice crisps, and sprawls out on the stiff couch that came with the apartment. She rips open the bag, grabs a chip, then indicates my comfy chair with it.

"Sit. Spill."

I do. From the second she left me at the club, I tell her about me and Neo, leaving out the things she doesn't need to know about Zastrow. The conversation about my feelings and Neo that's long overdue, that I've wanted to have with her for a month now, finally comes pouring out of me.

It feels good at first.

To relive the things that happened between us. To remember how good he could make my body feel. The way he made me laugh. The nights when we'd do dinner just the two of us. Or when he'd play video games while I read a book. Getting sleepy watching movies together before crawling into bed. Taking care of him when he got hurt, and how he let me see him be vulnerable. The night he called me his prisoner and I didn't care because that was when I realized I was in love with him.

"So what happened? Why are you here?"

I get through the whole story. Cassandra is a great audience, and I keep her in the dark until the very end. When I talk about being hurt she gets up and moves closer to me, inspecting my face. I laugh when she licks her thumb and wipes away my concealer to reveal what's left of the bruise on my cheek.

I push her away and she sits back down.

"Then Neo walked into the room."

"WHAT?"

I break when I start to tell her this part. How it felt when I realized he'd set it up to test me in such a harsh way. Tears are dripping down my face faster than I can wipe them away. She's stunned and still, watching me.

When I stop and take a breath, she walks over to me and scoots me over so she can wrap her arms around me. It's a tight fit but it's comfortable.

"But you still love him anyway, don't you?"

"Yes," I don't bother to lie.

"You know, some guys will always be about the job. I think he made his choice."

"But he doesn't seem to understand that I would choose it too - I would choose them if it meant I got to be with him." I groan and look up at the ceiling. "Why is this happening to me?"

"You pathetic wench," Cassandra says sadly. "You finally fall in love and it's to a guy who's as emotionally chaotic as you are."

"Meant to be," I sniffle.

"Let's fix this whole my dad trying to murder your boss's wife thing, and then we'll fix the rest. One problem at a time."

"Right."

We stay like that, snuggled together, until my breathing is normal and my eyes are no longer burning with tears.

"Okay, bunny. Step one, you need to call my brother." Cassandra slaps my thigh and stands up. It's time to fight, and I'm relieved that I have my best friend by my side.

41

Neo

Perri had forgotten that she was wearing a live recording device when she took Cassandra to her apartment. It probably never occurred to her that I would have been the person listening on the other end, ready to send someone in to rescue her.

At first, I thought I should stop listening. That she deserved privacy.

But I'd never given her that, and I wasn't going to start now.

I needed to hear this. To hear everything from her side and drag myself through the torture of hearing all the emotions in her voice as she told our story. I needed to hear her say she still loved me, so that I could hold firm to my resolve to let her go.

I never want her to be in a position to have to choose between Zastrow and herself, or Zastrow and me. That's not what she deserves. Perri deserves a man who will always choose her over everything, and I still have too many of my own damn hang ups to be that guy. I wish I was in a place to say fuck everything and take her away.

That's a closer possibility than I want to accept, especially knowing that she'd go with me. If I went to her, told her I loved her, begged for forgiveness, I know she'd take me back even though I don't deserve it. I know that we could walk out of this life together, but I also know we'd both be looking back over our shoulders. I don't know what it will take for all this to be done, but it isn't. Not yet. Maybe not ever.

I have to let her go.

"I love you, Perri Kane," I whisper into the dark before killing her mic.

Within an hour of me cutting Perri off, Andre got a call from Seth Warren.

It took us 48 hours to get all the evidence we needed of Norman Warren's misconduct. It was more than enough for Seth to take to the board.

Less than 72 hours after Perri walked Cassandra Warren out of her parent's apartment, Norman Warren was removed from any position of power within Warren Media, placed under censure and warned that he was being investigated by the company for ethical impropriety and the mismanagement that they felt occurred during his reign in the last 15 years since his own father passed.

While the deal between us and Warren Media isn't dead forever, Andre and Seth agreed to let it lie until the storm passed.

It was immensely satisfying to wait outside of the Warren offices, leaning against Andre's favored black sedan, and watch as security escorted Norman Warren out of the building. Seth was right behind him, looking absolutely disgusted with his father. It's not like Norman didn't still have plenty of money, but now he was disenfranchised from power.

"You!" He screamed, coming at me. "You set me up!"

"You did all of this yourself. I'm just the one that caught you," I reply and keep as steady as I can. This worm was near Perri for almost half her life, and underestimated her the entire time. The things he said about her when he realized she'd taken Cassandra away were unforgivable. He was lucky I wasn't slamming his face into the pavement right now. Even if he hadn't spoken poorly of Perri, the shit he said about his own daughter was enough to want to end him as a waste of oxygen.

"Don't think you got away with anything." Norman sneered at me and then moved over to look at the blacked out sedan window. Andre was inside and probably annoyed with this entire song and dance, but he'd wanted to see it with his own eyes that the person with the power to come after them no longer had it.

"You're new money, Zastrow. My family owns this city, we're a bedrock institution. I'll be around long after you and your ventures have burned to ashes, and I'll be one of the people starting the god damn fires. This isn't over!"

Norman backed away and yelled again, "THIS ISN'T OVER!"

He looked like a rabid man in an ugly beige suit, screaming at demons only he could see. Maybe he was. There was nothing about him that ever struck me as in his right mind, but he'd always had so much influence that no one would ever have dared suggest he get help. The man had basically starved and imprisoned his own daughter.

I didn't blame Seth, or the middle sister, Calliope, for running the fuck away. Even if it meant they left Cassandra behind when they should've done better by her. Then again, I'm an only child, so I might have no idea what the fuck I'm talking about.

Everything falls into place, the threat to Nim is gone, and we can move on with our lives.

I don't sleep anymore.

If I'd been as creepy of a motherfucker as I wanted to be, I'd have recorded her sleeping. I wish I had, because I'd be playing it like one of her ASMR videos to help myself get some rest. The bed is too big and too empty.

I get so desperate I try watching one of her videos, but it only makes it all hurt more. It only serves to make me feel more alone than ever. I knew I'd miss her but I didn't think it would be like this. In the past, when my relationships ended I settled back into the rhythms of my single life easily.

Now it's like I wake up every day in a nightmare filled with too much clarity. I'm jumpy, paranoid, and easily angered. There's a threat around every corner, someone else waiting to make a problem for me, and another mess for me to clean up.

Nim and I still aren't really speaking. My presence was required at another family dinner and even Andre picked up on the change in my usual silence. It's not fair to blame her, but it's easier to do that than try and talk to Andre about what I want. What I might need. How do I tell the person who forgave my father's betrayal that I'd like my life back?

He could've let me fight it out for myself on the streets. I could've joined the O'Connors and been an enforcer for the rest of my life, until a rival took me out or I died from a coronary. Probably alone, and with only the maggots left to eat my corpse.

Andre gave me a family, beyond my closeness with Nim and Harrison. The kind of family I didn't want to walk away from, but suddenly felt suffocated by.

Every night I hate myself for what I did, but I knew it was the only surefire way to make her walk away from me. It was the only thing I could think of that would make her down me, and now I have to learn to live with it.

42

Perri

I'm having a logical feeling of deja vu when Cassandra talks me into going to Delta. Hela and Scarlet are back from Norway, she wants to celebrate officially moving in with Shaw and debut their relationship, and she thinks I need an excuse to get drunk and let it out because I've been holding too much inside.

That last part doesn't appeal to me at all, but I do want to celebrate my friends. I want to see Cassandra be truly free now that her father is out of the picture. She hasn't spoken to him or her mother, although her mother was there when she went with Shaw and some security staff to get all her things from the apartment.

I want her to be happy, and for her to be happy I have to go out to club where it all started.

Once we're sitting in our booth, I do feel better. It's easy to fall back into old patterns. Hela tries to teach us swear words and insulting phrases but none of us have the tongue for it, not even when we're drunk. She glares down her nose at us and our pathetic American skills. It only makes us try harder and laugh harder, and I can't lie that it feels good.

Watching Cassandra sit close to Shaw with his arm around her, watching the way her cheeks get pink when he can openly lean over to kiss her cheek or temple - that feels good too. She's gained the weight she lost back and the glow she's always had is back.

We're toasting again.

"To Perri saving the day!" Scarlet laughs. Outside of Cassandra, the rest of them only know a truncated version of the truth. They think I was dating Neo and that things turned sour when they asked me to spy on the Warrens. It was the lie that was closest to the truth. So this is also about trying to alleviate my heartbreak.

"No shit," Hela agrees, raising her glass. "Seth will owe you for the rest of your life."

"That's true," Cassandra answers, but she looks pensive. "Maybe it's time you let us find you another job."

My stomach sinks. "I like my job."

"Well your job doesn't like you. Seth would make something happen for you. Whenever you want."

I want to change the subject. "What about you? Have you asked him about your job opportunities yet?"

Cassandra turns an even darker shade of red with excitement. "I start as a copy editor at the Review on Monday. Arts and Entertainment section."

"Yay!" Scarlet cheers and reaches for the bottle at the center of our table to refill everyone's shot glasses. We tap our glasses on the table and throw them back. The vodka burns for a second before sending a cooling feeling through my gut.

"So much has changed already," Scarlet says sadly, going from celebratory delight down to reality. "Perri being a badass with her dream job, Cassandra being allowed to work at a paper and no more secret rendezvous with my brother. No more having to hear you two bang," her face twists sourly. "I'm not doing anything."

"You're helping me," Hela defends, and a look passes between them. "I want to work *for* my family's company but not *with* my family. I would be in prison if you hadn't been with me to talk to them."

Scarlet looks at Hela for a long moment, and it's like the intensity of it stops the world. Then she nods. "To me keeping Hela out of prison!"

We cheers and take another drink.

They fall into conversation and let me zone out in my own little world like usual. I do need to find a new job. A new start, somewhere that's only about my accounting and finance skills. It's painful to walk into Zastrow now. I'm always afraid I'm going to see Neo because even a glimpse will send me into a tailspin. It makes me feel like I'm having a heart attack because my chest gets tight and I can't breathe.

The satisfaction I got from my job before feels dull now. I don't want to leave. This was the job I wanted when I graduated but it's always going to be tainted. It will always feel a little bit like I didn't earn it, that it was part of a manipulation tactic to control me. I'll always be watched that little bit more than everyone else. There will always be eyes on me and I'm done with that feeling.

Even though he made the choice he did, I know he has feelings for me too. I know how he feels about sex and relationships. None of what we did was taken lightly by him, and it meant something to both of us.

I can't live knowing that my proximity is probably torturing him too.

I want to stay, but I don't know how.

"Fuck," Cassandra hisses, and then they're all moving, shifting around the table until I'm facing into the booth.

"What?" I go to look over my shoulder but Hela grabs my arm.

"Don't, bunny." For Hela to call me that means it's really damn bad. I'm immediately sick to my stomach.

"He's here, isn't he?" I hate that tears spring to my eyes just saying a damn pronoun that I'm attributing to him. That I want to run to him and away from him, and the impulses have equal strength. I hate that there's a lump in my throat and it hurts to swallow it down.

"Did they see us?" Neo wouldn't be here without Nim. Not by choice.

"Yeah," Cassandra frowns. She's grateful to them for helping her, but that doesn't mean she's going to give Neo a pass for anything. Especially not for hurting me.

"Where is he, compared to Nicolette?"

They all look at me weird.

"He's sitting next to her." So she dragged him out on a night off. If he was working he would be in a position to see more, and keep an eye on everyone.

"Then we need to get out of here."

"Why? You don't need to go because he's here!" Scarlet says indignantly.

"I don't trust myself not to talk to him. If he was working, that would be different, but I'm too drunk to stay away." I turn to Cassandra. "Anywhere you want. I'll stay out as late as you want drink every drink, but please. I need to hold on to a little bit of my dignity."

Hela puts her arm around me and pulls me in. "Fuck dignity. Let's show him what he's missing. You are Perri fucking Kane, self-made woman, math genius, spectacular lover, and for the rest of his life, you will be the one that got away. Correct?"

"Correct." I take a deep inhale and pour myself another shot. Everyone else follows suit. I raise my glass and drink.

When that shot hits, that's when Cassandra and Scarlet know they've got me in the right mood to pull me out onto the dance floor in the VIP area. It's smaller, and it's on the other side of where Nim, Neo, and their group are sitting. We have to walk past them to get there.

I stand up and sway on my feet, and let Scarlet and Hela link arms with me as we head toward the smaller mass of grinding and swaying bodies.

As we walk past them I lift my chin, put on my best face, and turn to make eye contact with Nim. Feeling cheeky, I blow her a kiss. She smiles, relief evident, then pretends to catch the kiss out of the air and puts it on her cheek. I laugh but feel teary again, missing her in a way I didn't expect. She pulled me out of my shell when I needed it.

I don't look at Neo, but even avoiding him, he's so big that I can't help but take in details about him. He's tense, and the small glance I let myself have shows that his jaw is clenched and his body language is turned away from Nim. He was definitely there by force, and very obviously angry with her. The frustrated glare shouldn't be a turn on, but it makes me remember how he'd snap and take me when he looked like that.

Hela takes me under the chin and turns my face to her. She leans in close, our noses almost touching.

"Spectacular lover, the one that got away."

"Right," I agree.

Then I move us a little bit faster until we disappear into the crowd. The thump of the bass feels good and the beat is quick. I take Hela's advise to heart, and say fuck my dignity and start to move. Shaw didn't come out with us, it's just the girls.

We laugh and take turns dancing with each other. We block guys from dancing with us because that's not what we're looking for. I move until I'm sweaty. Until I can feel it dripping down my spine, under my breasts, soaking my hair line. They look equally disheveled. Cassandra has mascara smudges under her eyes, Hela is glowing with sweat and her thin, soft hair is soaked. Only Scarlet holds it together other than her hair falling down from the intricate series of braids and twists as part of her updo. I swear to god she did some kind of treatment so she doesn't sweat.

I'm desperately thirsty and the world is a blur.

I make a motion to them that I hope indicates my intentions as I bounce through the crowd until I'm out, and head toward the bar for a bottle of water. On Cassandra's tab, of course.

The bartender smiles at me, and gives a quick glance down to my chest. I didn't want to wear the low cut dress, but Cassandra insisted, and now I'm kind of glad. It's reassuring to feel attractive after such an epic rejection.

"Doing alright?" he asks.

"Fantastic. Can I get a water?"

He winks at me and turns around to get a bottle from the cooler. I push myself up onto the foot rail and lean onto the bar. It pushes the girls up a little more. Pre-Neo, this was my love life. Chasing a night. Chasing a good feeling. Maybe I needed that, too.

"What's your name?" I ask him when he turns around.

"Dorian."

"Perri. Parents a fan of the classics?"

"Gay dads obsessed with Oscar Wilde."

I laugh with a hoot and he gives me a genuine grin in return. "I love that. You are pretty enough."

"Your parents obsessed with detective novels?"

"Perry Mason, that's a new one," I laugh. "But no, it was my mother's maiden name."

"It's classy."

"Thank you." We stare at each other smiling, and then he clears his throat and pulls it back.

"Should this go on Ms. Warren's tab?"

"Yes, thank you. Are you working until close?" I do my classic lip bite, because people often mistake me for shy and it's a move I know I can do even when I'm kinda drunk.

"I get cut in an hour."

"Find me if you want to keep talking about...the classics." Other than knowing Dorian is objectively attractive and capable of banter, I feel nothing for him. No spark, no real attraction, not even the mild hum I felt in the time before. But part of me thinks the old adage that the best way to get over someone is to get under someone else might be true.

At least it will be a start in erasing every time Neo ever touched me.

It will maybe dim the need I have for him to touch me again.

Dorian gives me a smile but not an answer, and walks over to customers at the other end of the bar. I step off the foot rail and turn around with my bottle of water, and run smack into a hard, warm body.

Before I can say sorry, every instinct inside me goes on alert. Recognizing Neo. Like I'm primed to always be aware of him in a second. I would know his touch, his presence, even with my eyes closed.

I take a step back, and then try to move around him.

"Perri," he grumbles, and I nearly drop to my knees at the way hearing him say my name rockets through my body. My heart might nearly stop in pain, but my pussy clenches with need. I haven't even been able to masturbate. I spent over a hundred dollars on a top of the line vibrator, one of the good ones that suck your clit, and I couldn't even bring myself to do it.

Sexually, I am locked up so tight and he's the only real key.

Hooking up with Dorian would be an attempt at picking the lock that would likely end in disappointment for both of us, and all it takes for me to know that definitively is one word out of Neo's mouth. He could've said "hey" and

I'd probably have had the same reaction.

I hate him and love him so much in this moment. I want to punch him in the face and then kiss it better. Then never stop kissing him.

I can't do this, and try to move around him again, but he moves with me.

Finally, I look up at him, working hard to retreat behind my mask. It's harder when I'm tipsy.

I don't say anything.

Neo opens his mouth but doesn't say anything either.

Anger overwhelms me as I lose my patience.

"What, Neo? What do you want?"

He takes a step forward and I take a step back. Hurt flashes across his face for a second, and it makes me feel powerful. This time I take the step closer, looking up into his face, getting as close as I can.

"Unless you're about to beg for my forgiveness, tell me that you love me and you're going to make it up to me on your knees, there's nothing you have to say to me. You can't control anything I do. So if you're worried that I'm drunk and flirting with that bartender, too damn bad."

"Perri," he says again.

"I love you, Neo." I watch his eyes, taking in every minute reaction to what I have to say. "But unless you're going to let me love you, you have to let me go."

After a long moment looking at each other, Neo nods and steps back. I watch his own mask rest more heavily over him. I watch the distance grow between us as his expression fades to nothing.

As I walk over to my friends, I don't look back.

The next move is his, but I'm not going to stop moving on.

43

Neo

Outside of brief, terse work-related communication, no one is speaking to me. After Nim dragged me out to the club in the hopes that drinking would get me to talk and instead led to my disastrous encounter with Perri, she's backed off. I know that if I needed to, she would listen, but I don't want to talk to her. It will be longer than I'd like before I feel fully comfortable with her again. Our friendship has been damaged. It's not irreparable, but it will take time.

Nim and Andre are my job.

I need to start seeing them that way, or I'll never have a life. Losing Perri showed me that very clearly. While I'll never deserve her again, I can't make work all that I have. Maybe I can be the man she deserves, or maybe I'll be too late. Who knows if I'll ever be willing to try a relationship again, but there's more to life than that, and I need to find it.

I also can't deny how quietly proud I am of Benji. If you would have asked me who I thought would step up and take a leadership role with my core men, I would've thought Thomas or Leander, because I treated them as my second and third. Instead, it's been Benji, and I realized that despite my recognition of his talents, I failed to recognize who he was as a person.

He's a leader. A quiet, steady leader. The kind of leadership they need right now as we work through this rift and find a way back to each other. They are my friends as well as my employees, and I will find a way to show them that.

I'm miserable, but I'm hopeful, with absolutely no idea how to move forward with my life.

When Harrison finds me, I'm sitting in my office in the dark, staring out the window. It's well past the end of business hours but I'm not on shift tonight and the loft is the last place I want to be right now. I didn't even realize he was still in his office.

"Drink?" he asks.

"I don't really feel like going anywhere."

"Come on," he jerks his head. "I know where he keeps the good stuff."

It feels weird entering Andre's dark office. It makes me feel like we're kids again, sneaking around the house and snooping at his work. Reading pages left on his desk that we didn't understand. The adrenaline of getting caught giving us the giggles at a time when we needed to be quiet.

Harrison feels like my friend again in this moment, and I need a fucking friend.

He moves a book on the shelf and behind it is a little alcove. So that's where Andre keeps the good scotch; and who else knows what's squirreled away back there. Harrison pours us each two fingers, and we sit down on the expensive leather furniture that Andre never uses. It's all for show. He almost never meets with anyone in his office. My ass might be the first to ever grace this chair.

"What's going on in your head?" Harrison asks, then takes a sip of his drink.

I sip mine, letting the smooth burn of the alcohol roll across my tongue and down my throat, giving myself a moment to think before answering.

"I wish I'd never met you. Your family."

Harrison looks stricken but manages to cover it up. "I can't say the same, brother."

"I'm not your brother." It comes out far more forlorn than I intend. "I'm your father's employee. I always have been. No matter how close you and I are, and don't doubt that I would die for you, Harrison. Bullet to the heart. I will never be more than an employee to him. One that's been molded and bred to love your family before anything else, and I don't think I can be that anymore. I will do my job, I will go above and beyond, but I'm done being callous with my own life for you."

"Part of me thinks he'd be insulted to hear you say that, but another part thinks he'd be proud, and that makes me kind of sick." Harrison leans forward and rests his elbows on his knees. "Maybe someday you'll be my employee and I'll fire you because I'd rather have my friend, if you won't claim brotherhood."

I take a longer drink. "I love her."

"I know," he follows the change in subject, although it's really more of a sidestep. "I would have stopped you. I would have forced you to pick her over us. My father's wishes were met - she loved us. Loved you. Even now, even furious with you, I know she's on our side, without question. I saw it. Why couldn't you?"

"Because I'm a jackass who was too fucking scared to love something new. To trust it to be real. Every day I wish I could go back."

"It's not too late, not yet," Harrison finishes his drink and I flinch.

"What do you mean not yet?"

Harrison sighs, realizing that he let out more than he meant to. "She put in her two weeks. She's leaving Zastrow."

"And you're letting her?" I shoot up, annoyed with him.

He puts his hand up to stop me. "Believe me, I tried. I met with her directly. I offered her a raise, a different position, shit I even offered her a transfer out of the city so at least she'd still be with us, but she said she needed a fresh start without..." Harrison trails off and looks away from me. I wait him out. "Without anyone watching."

Perri has no idea that I'll never not be watching. There's nowhere she can go that I won't find her. Not unless every single thing she owns burns to the ground. I have that woman tracked within an inch of her exact location. Even when they moved her and assured her that I didn't know where she was, of course I knew.

While the guys placed trackers and took care of those, they don't know about the others. She could travel around the world and I could show up at her doorstep if I wanted. I might not be able to have her, and when I say I'm letting her go I mean I'm stepping back, but I will never not watch out for her. I will always be checking in. As long as she's living and breathing, I can survive the pain of being without her.

So she can try to go, but I'll still be watching.

I drain the rest of my drink.

"What do I do?" I ask him.

"I don't know, but I think you can start with telling her how you feel, and that you want things to change. You can't do that alone."

"I guess not." I think about what she said at the club, and it makes me feel like she might be open to me begging for her forgiveness. There will be no problem with her chosen method either. I'll suffocate myself on her pussy if that's what it takes. The other piece of it though - she called me out. Perri knows I love her; I don't have to say it for her to see it and feel it. It's that after being hurt so many times I struggle to let someone love me in return, and I have to find a way to be vulnerable enough to let her all the way in.

It's more than asking for her forgiveness. It's imploding all my walls. It's the complete destruction of the show I put on to the world, and finding a way to open a door only she is allowed to walk through.

Perri Kane deserves to be the center of my world, and I'm going to find a way to make that my reality.

44

Perri

I got an email from HR confirming the acceptance of my notice and a to-do list before I can leave. I got it done pretty quickly, they can't assign me any new analyses, so I said fuck it and used my accrued vacation.

I'm packing up things even though I have no idea where I'm going. I never really organized anything after it was all brought here from the loft, so I do it now. Everything is in it's appropriate boxes with a room label, and assigned a number. The number correlates to a spreadsheet entry where I've listed everything that should be in the box.

Seth helped me find an apartment, and we're meeting next week to talk about possible positions with Warren. He promised me that he wouldn't shoehorn me in anywhere, and that if nothing worked with them he'd help me find something else.

Scarlet was very accurate in her assessment that Seth is always going to feel like he owes me. There are worse people who could feel beholden to me. I've got enough savings after not needing to pay for pretty much anything for months, so I have time to find the right thing.

There's a twist in my gut that tells me I'm doing the wrong thing.

I guess I'll find out.

My phone buzzes with a text from Cassandra. We're going to meet up for lunch and then I'm going to stay over at Shaw's with her since he's traveling for work. The text is a pin drop with a location; it's a cute little pub not too far away from here, although in a lower end neighborhood than she usually likes to go.

It takes me a few minutes to decide what to wear, and then I don't procrastinate any further. I don't really want to leave the apartment. I don't want to have lunch or stay over with Cassandra.

I want to wallow, alone, and replay the same things in my head a million times trying to figure out if I could have made them turn out differently. I want to drown in thoughts of Neo, in fantasies that he comes to me and begs me to forgive him, then ravishes me until I don't think I can have any more orgasms, then tells me we're going to be together for the rest of our lives.

I'm so pathetic, but I also can't help how I feel. From another angle, I understand why he did it. The ruthless streak I have inside me even respects it, because I think I would do the same. If I had something worth protecting, my morals might get a little blacker than they are on an every day basis.

I've never killed anyone, but I have no doubts that under certain circumstances, I would be decisively capable of it. Not a second of hesitation.

But I don't wallow. I grab my bag and leave. I hail a cab, I tip him well, and I walk into the Green Hill ready to fake it so good Cassandra won't see through it to the empty black hole that occupies my mind. She's too happy right at this moment to notice it anyway, and I'm not going to be the one that dampens her happiness.

The pub is empty when I walk inside, and I don't see Cassandra anywhere. That's not unusual. I walk deeper into the place, toward the bar, but the emptiness itself feels...eerie. Wrong. Like it's not only that there are no customers, there's no one, period.

Fear creeps up my spine and I turn around and walk back out the door.

But now there are people. Three large men giving me smiles that are anything but friendly. It takes me a second, but I realize that the one in the center was the driver. The man that hit me with an SUV. My heart races so hard that I can't breathe.

"Ms. Kane. We're going to do this the hard way."

Two of the men grab me and I fight back immediately, squirming, kicking, pulling, and I don't give it up until a cloying scent fills my nose as a rag is pressed over my face. Then everything goes dark.

Seriously, what the fuck.

I wake up slowly, and try to take stock of the situation as I do. I'm laying down on cold, damp ground. Neither my legs or my wrists are tied. My mouth tastes terrible, and my head is throbbing slightly from whatever they knocked me out with. I hear dripping water, and another person sniffling. Muffled male voices.

I groan as I push myself up into a sitting position.

"Oh my god, Perri," the sniffling turns into groggy words, warped by tears, and I blearily turn my head to look at Cassandra. She's a mess. Her sweater is torn and dirty, and she's got a split lip that's already crusted over.

"Cassandra? What's going on?"

She opens her mouth but then starts to cry again, shaking her head.

I sit up further and lean against the wall. I blink hard, squeezing my eyes shut, clearing them. Then I take a few deep breaths to do the same to my head, before opening my eyes and looking around.

We're in a bathroom. In disrepair but not completely disgusting. The dripping is coming from the faucet. It's bright, almost painfully so. There's nothing that can be used as a weapon. Even the top of the toilet tank has been removed. Damn.

"Who took us?"

"I don't know. They're speaking another language."

"Have you been drinking water? Does the sink and toilet work? How long have you been here?"

"Since yesterday. I dropped Shaw at the airport and they grabbed me from the garage. Sink and toilet both work."

"Okay. Okay." I have no idea how to get us out of this. Especially since I don't know who took us. I have suspicions, since it involves Cassandra, but I'm hoping they aren't true.

We both tense when the lock on our door clicks, and it squeaks open. A group of men enter the room - the three who took me, and a fourth, much older man. He ignores Cassandra but stares down at me, an appraising look in his eye. It's not lecherous, but it's judgmental for sure. He's deciding if I'm good enough and I don't know what for.

But I'm good enough for anyone, so I lift my chin and look him in the eye. If nothing else, I've got grit.

After a long staring contest, he smiles, and there's something grandfatherly about it.

"My name is Eamon O'Connor."

My breath huffs before I can stop it.

"You know who I am?"

I nod.

"Do you know why I have you?"

I shake my head. I have guesses. I'm also certain whatever it is he thinks he's going to get by taking me, he's wrong.

"What do you want?" I ask instead.

"I want your man to work for me, as he always should have, if his father hadn't gotten grand ideas of rising above. The Ryans need to be put back in their place."

I don't say anything.

"And I owed a man a favor." He finally turns to look at Cassandra. "You are the leverage to make her behave," Eamon tells her. "If Perri does what I want, I'll let you live, even though your father wants you dead." She starts to cry at that, and I think it's the first time they've confirmed for her that he's in on this.

If I survive this, I'm going to kill Norman Warren with my bare hands.

"Get them," he orders his men.

I rush over to Cassandra and grab her, pulling her to her feet and hissing encouragement. She does what I ask, clinging to me. I don't want these men to touch either of us, so I keep her close to me.

"We'll go without a fight," I tell them. The one who spoke to me outside the Green Hill seems to be their lead, and he waves his men off. His gaze is shrewd, and I know he's trying to read my intentions. Right now the only intention I have is hands off, and no more injuries.

I follow him out of the bathroom, the other two men falling in behind us. We're in a rundown office suite. There's stray paper strewn across the floor, dead light bulbs in the ceiling, and an air of run down that I can't quite articulate. It's not dirty or broken, but clearly abandoned for some time. We're led from the bathroom into an open area. It's empty except for one desk with a phone, and a couple of office chairs.

"Sit," the lead guy tells me. I don't know where Eamon went, but I can't focus on that right now. The windows are all frosted over, so I can't see outside or where we are.

Cassandra and I sit in the desk chairs.

She screams when her chair is yanked away from mine and one of the men pulls out a gun. He presses it to her temple.

I look back at the one in charge, and see he has a gun now too, held loosely at his side.

"What's your name?"

"Robert."

"Okay, Robert. I'm Perri. What's that for?" I tilt my head toward Cassandra. I'm not willing to make any big movements right now.

"To get you to do what I want."

"It's not necessary. I'm not going to fight you."

"Are you sure about that?" A voice says from behind us, and I flinch. My skin crawls, and I look over my shoulder to see a decidedly manic looking Norman Warren walk into the open area.

"Dad," Cassandra gasps, then looks down into her lap, trying hard to fight her tears. It's fucking real now. Eamon follows a few steps later.

"I'm not telling you anything," I vow, glaring at the both of them.

"That's not what you're here for, dear," Eamon answers.

"You're here because you're an interfering little bitch." Norman rushes forward and gets in my face. "I never should've allowed Cassandra to hang around with trash like you. Now look at her - she's ruined. Fucking the Fischer boy, unmanageable, unmarriagable. I can't even sell her to a dirty old man who wants a young wife to fuck because she can't keep her dumb brat mouth shut."

He turns on Cassandra now, and leans over to make her look at him. "Did you really think you could be a reporter? That you had the brains to do anything other than decorate someone else's life? You couldn't just do what I said and shut the fuck up. You had to let your little bitch friend ruin our lives and help your brother."

Cassandra doesn't say anything, she only cries.

I look away from Norman to Eamon, who looks annoyed but is trying really hard not to let it show.

"This is the man you owe a favor?" The derision is clear in my voice. Eamon meets my eyes and cocks an eyebrow.

"We all get into bed with people we regret from time to time."

"What do you want?" I ask again, hoping this time I'll get an answer.

"You're going to make a video." Eamon explains what he wants and I get more and more incredulous with each word out of his mouth. They aren't going to do anything he's asking, not for me, and they certainly aren't going to help Norman Warren. I think Eamon knows that, though. I think he's indulging Norman so that when Norman doesn't get what he wants out of it, Eamon can at least say that he tried.

Between the two of them, Eamon has more direct power, even before Norman was ousted from Warren Media. Eamon O'Connor is a third generation crime lord. He's got more resources and weapons at his disposal than Norman is likely even aware of, and he likely has little idea about the complicated connections between Eamon, Neo, and the Zastrows. Neo made sure I knew about the O'Connors and why we needed to worry about them after I discovered the fraud. These guys are...a different kind of scary than any angry rich asshole.

Robert moves to stand in front of me with a phone held in front of him, camera aimed at me.

"You're not going to get what you want from this," I try to reason with Eamon.

"Maybe I will, maybe I won't. Are you important enough to him that they'll give me what I want?"

"No," I answer honestly. He chose them, and I understand why. "Neo will never give into you, not for me, and he shouldn't. I don't matter to them, and you'll get NOTHING." Something inside of me breaks, and I'm crying before I can stop it, everything I've been feeling for the last few weeks comes pouring out of me. To Eamon O'Connor, of all people. I can't look away from him as I yell and sob.

"I am NOTHING TO THEM. You did this FOR NOTHING. You might as well kill me Eamon, because Neo Ryan will never work for you. Just get it over with. You're going to kill me anyway, and I don't care. I don't care!" Now I'm laughing hysterically, nearly tipping my chair backward before one of the men catches it.

I look over at Norman. "No one is going to pay you shit you crazy, ugly, selfish moron. The only good thing you ever did in your life was your children, and they're amazing in spite of you."

Norman starts to storm toward me but Eamon stops him, and then waves at me like he wants me to continue, so I do. I turn and stare straight into the camera.

"Neo," I sigh, saying his name, as if I'm speaking right to him. "They want you to cut ties with Zastrow and work for O'Connor. If you do, along with giving them $10 million, they'll let me go and leave Zastrow alone. They'll let Cassandra go," I add, even though that's not what they told me to say, but if they do send this it might give them a hint who else is in on it. "I know you're not gonna do it," I smile for some reason and I know it's unhinged. "And I forgive you. Don't worry about me. I love you."

I stare into the camera, silently, until Robert gives up and stops recording.

"Kill her!" Norman demands, looking wild. He points at me but shouts in Eamon's face. "Kill her!"

I'm slightly amused when Eamon rolls his eyes, and tilts his head slightly. The guy with the gun to Cassandra's head drops it and walks over to pistol whip Norman. He collapses to the ground with a heavy thump.

"Tie him up, we'll figure out what to do with him when we get what we want." The guy who hit him drags Norman Warren's body out of the room.

I hear my own voice coming out of the phone. Since they're too busy sending the video, I roll my chair over to Cassandra. She leans her head on my shoulder, and I rest my head on top of hers. Now it's time to wait for the end.

45

Neo

I've been forced into a family lunch. Harrison is hoping that Nim and Andre can talk some sense into me about a plan to get Perri back. I don't have one; not yet. There's too many things in the way that I need to deal with before I can be who she needs me to be; before I can be the person she deserves.

My dad's been calling almost every day, and that had me slowing my roll because it meant things weren't done. The closer she is to me, the more she's pulled into all the bullshit that's attached to me. All the threats Zastrow will always face, the drama of a gambling addict father and ties to the O'Connors, and the near constant knowledge that I could leave for work and never come home.

I can't do that to her. Perri deserves stable. Someone who can be there for her. There are boundaries I need to set, and this lunch is part of that plan.

Simultaneously, our phones buzz with a message.

Nim gets to hers the fastest, and before I can open the video in my message, hers starts playing.

"You're not going to get what you want from this," Perri's voice filters into the room.

"Oh my god," Nim says before covering her mouth with her hand. The video starts for me, and we all watch, Perri's voice echoing around the room. Her tears and sobs hitting me in the chest, her fury, her hysteria. The wave of violence that overtakes me is like nothing I've ever felt before. I try to breathe through it but I swear I want to stand and flip this entire giant table right now.

Someone took her because I wasn't there to protect her.

"Don't worry about me," she says, looking into me even through a camera lens. "I love you." I stand up and my chair crashes to the ground. I need to do something.

"Neo, calm down," Harrison starts. "We can get her. It's fine." He stands up from the table and comes toward me. When he puts a hand on my shoulder, I jump.

"He has Cassandra Warren, too. Norman is probably part of this," Andre adds. "Call the men. We hunt them down."

"No," I say. "You do nothing. I'll get them. This is my fight."

"You won't pay it?" Nim's voice is small, interrupting my rage

"No. I won't ever work for O'Connor, and we're not going to throw $10 million to make Norman Warren go away."

"Why not?" Andre asks, eyes boring into me.

"Where am I going to get $10 million?"

"From me."

I can feel the incredulity rocket through my body. "I would never be able to pay you back."

"And I wouldn't ask you to. I'd give it to you, if you thought it meant there was a better chance of rescuing Perri."

Something burns in my chest and I look from him to Nim to Harrison, trying to understand what's happening right now.

"Why?"

Andre sighs. "Because you're family. I've done a terrible job of letting you know it, but you are. I don't think I could ever look you in the eye again if anything happened to Perri. The guilt would eat me alive. I let you make the wrong choice; I failed you by making you think you couldn't have her, and I'll regret that for the rest of my life. You deserve to have one, Neo. You deserve a life, and you deserve her. Figure out how to save her, but if it comes down to the money, you have it, no question."

For the first time since he offered me a sanctuary after my attack, I hug

Andre. He squeezes me, and claps me on the back.

Nim chokes out a little sob and Andre lets me go, taking her into his arms instead. She peeks out from his elbow. "Go get her or so help me god I'll kill you."

I nod. Harrison and I leave the dining room without another word to get to my car.

"Get the men. I'm calling Seth."

We get into Harrison's car, and he talks while he drives. I brace myself for the response I'm about to get.

Me: *Everyone to the warehouse. Perri was taken by Eamon O'Connor.*

I don't look at their responses, but I get non-stop notifications as I pull up the app that has all of Perri's trackers. Most of them are centered on her apartment, the only two that are active are at the Green Hill. They wouldn't be stupid enough to keep her there and the background of the video didn't look like any of the buildings in that area.

She was in a desk chair. The carpet was old but corporate looking, that rough pile that's only in office buildings. I call Benji.

"What the fuck."

"Later. I need you to run O'Connor property holdings - anything corporate or office-like. Even if it's an office inside another type of building." I take a deep breath, thinking. "Then I need you to track my dad."

"On it." He hangs up the phone. Definitely still angry with me.

Before we get to the warehouse I check the chat. It's mostly swearing and anger. Even though I know it's going to make things worse, I forward the video we were sent to the chat. It's going to make them angrier at me, but it's also going to give a shorthand for what's going on, and what we need to do.

We need to find Perri and Cassandra.

We need to kill Norman Warren. Maybe Eamon O'Connor.

The gate slides open before Harrison can put in his code; they were watching for our arrival. The guys are all at the conference table, tablets at the ready to go over everything Benji pulled together on the drive over.

"They own too much fucking property," Benji starts as Harrison and I stop at the head of the table. "Too much shit with any empty office. That could be an office suite in warehouse, or in an old high-rise. Those could be fake windows into a hallway. There's no way to tell."

"What about Martin?"

"He's at a pool hall, has been all day. I pulled his geo data for the last week and he was at the Green Hill nearly every day. I think he officially sold you out this time." Benji frowns.

"Then lets go get him and find out."

"You go," Harrison directs. "I think I have a call to make to Declan O'Connor."

I stare at him. "You sure that's the right move?"

"I think we've done well unseating fathers and replacing them with their sons."

Wilder snorts. "Don't let yours hear you say that."

Harrison gives a mirthless smile and then drops is gaze back to his phone.

"I'll stay too, keep digging," Benji adds. Our eyes meet, and we come to a truce right then. I wish I had the time to tell him that things have changed. But I don't. I have to save her first.

We drive silently to the pool hall.

I send Wilder in to get Martin.

Of course Martin runs the second he sees him, and we're waiting in the alley behind the hall. It's like my hand moves on it's own as I catch him by the throat and slam him to the ground. Martin's face gets red, bordering on purple, and he drools as he tries to cough and then take in a breath as I cut off his air supply.

Leander taps me on the back, and I loosen my grip. Martin gasps in a breath.

"What did you tell Eamon?"

"What are you talkin' about?" Martin gasps out. "I didn't say shit to anyone."

I squeeze again, counting down, watching his face change. When I have what I want, I might not let go. His death on my hands would be hard to live with, but I'd get over it eventually. He's not the man that raised me in the beginning, and he never will be ever again. The good that he instilled in me no longer belongs to him. It's only mine now. I keep that good man, those good morals, that loyalty, alive all on my own.

"What did you tell Eamon?" I growl out again.

Martin stares at me, and whatever he sees...he knows. He knows that I'm deciding whether or not to kill him anyway, and his only option is to do what I want.

"I told him about your girl. How you got all protective about her, what her name was, that she worked at Zastrow. I'd watched the two of you enough that I knew when she moved outta the loft."

Fuck.

"Where did he take her?" I pick him up by the throat and slam his head down, giving him a good rattle to make him understand he isn't out of the woods yet.

"Somewhere on the west side. He said he owed a guy. Heard Robbie and McCarron talking about it."

I squeeze his throat again and this time he fights harder, believing that this is it. This is the time that I kill him. It's tempting but I won't. Martin Ryan is going to end up dead by his own devices one of these days, and there will be no one to shed a tear. In this moment, bringing him to the edge of the end, my father is officially dead to me.

"You ever come near me or her ever again, and I will make you regret it. Got it?"

"Got it," he wheezes out, and I let him go.

We leave him in the alley and head for the SUV. I text Benji what we learned to see if that helps narrow down a possible location, and just in case, check any of Norman Warren's personal property holdings.

Before we even get back to the warehouse, Benji knows where they are. An old office building that they own legitimately, and used to run a contracting and construction company out of, before they had to get a little bit shady. It hasn't been used for anything since the late 90s.

It was one of the only locations on the west side, and he sourced that corporate carpet, of all things. Apparently, it was a very distinct pattern and was still available for sale these days.

It's time to go to war, and it's personal for all of us. We regroup at the warehouse to make a plan.

"Andre replied to the video with a request for a drop location for the money, and requested to meet with Eamon to negotiate for you," Benji updates us. "It's a delay tactic, and Eamon seems to be taking the bait."

"Declan was responsive," Harrison adds. "After Benji narrowed it down, he confirmed the location. He wants to be involved and offered to handle the outcome."

That's shocking. Declan has been amassing power from his father for years now. He must be extremely confident that he'll take over, and that he'll be able to sell the lie. It makes me think there's more going on there than we know, and that Declan was probably fully aware of their plans. And knew how stupid they were.

"Then gear up. We're going in quiet."

46

Perri

After Norman ranted for a bit longer, mostly trashing his other children, Eamon finally let Robert and the henchmen take us back to the bathroom to wait out the response to their message.

"I'm so sorry," Cassandra whispers to me. "I can't believe he'd do this."

"You have nothing to be sorry for," I promise her. "I think this would've happened to me anyway. Eventually."

"Do you think he'll do it?"

I contemplate that. The word vomit I spilled into that video was the worst, blackest, most pessimistic version of my feelings. It was the way I felt at my lowest. Unloved. Second place. An afterthought. It was me falling back into that place where I wondered if I had anything to live for, or any reason to fight to live at all.

"No, but I do think they'll try and rescue us."

"How? How will they know where we are?"

I don't answer her. "We should try and sleep. Just in case."

With some gentle prodding, I make Cassandra lay down on the floor and put her head in my lap. I run my fingers through her hair, comforting both of us at the same time. I lay my head back against the tiled wall and close my eyes against the light.

Neo is too principled to leave us to rot. He'll have told Andre at least, because that's who they're actually demanding the money from. Andre might not be willing to pay up, but he isn't the kind of person who could let us die either. I'm sure to the very core of me that they're trying to find us, despite everything I said on the video. I didn't want to give these jerks any hope that their plan would work.

I don't know what will happen when they do. I don't know if that will change anything between me and Neo, or if I want it to. Part of me hates the idea that me being actually kidnapped will be a wake up call for him. Another part of me wants him to contemplate what it will feel like to lose me in a way that is final. There's no loss more final than death, and I know he knows that. He's felt it before, but never like this. It's a different kind of love.

Even though Cassandra said she's sorry, I know that this is my fault.

While she pulled me into the world of the elite and the wealthy, ultimately I'm the one that pulled her into the darker side of it. Even if I did the right thing helping her escape her father, if it wasn't for Neo and Zastrow resources, the idea of bringing her father down never would have crossed our minds. Seth would have had to fight that battle on his own and left his sister out of it.

I'm the one that bridged the two. In the end, it's my fault Cassandra is here. Sure, her father would have tried to get her back, but he wouldn't be trying to get revenge. I don't know what Eamon promised him, or what he asked for, but it can't be good.

The weird thing is that I don't believe Eamon has any intention of giving Norman what he wants. Eamon wants Neo with the O'Connors. I don't think Eamon understands how deep Neo's hatred for them runs, for what they helped his father become, and what they did to him.

Neo isn't vain - the scar doesn't bother him because it disfigures his face - it bothers him because every time he looks at it, he's reminded that his father failed him, and it was a time when he wasn't strong enough to fight back. It's his biggest weakness visible for anyone to see. Even though I see a survivor, he still sees the boy who was beaten down to pay for another man's failings.

Part of me wishes I didn't love him. Didn't get the chance to see him the way I did. The real him. The softer part he pretends he doesn't need to nourish.

It would be so much easier if we'd kept it a shallow physical attraction. The second I saw beneath the bravado, I never had a chance.

There's a shuffling sound in the hallway, and I tense, straining to ignore every other sound except what's coming from the hallway.

When the lock outside the bathroom door turns slowly, my stomach swoops with fear. I slide a sleeping Cassandra's head off my lap and onto the floor, and slowly make my way toward the door. I stand behind it, bracing myself to jump on whoever walks through it. It swings open slowly, and a gun enters, followed by arms.

I clasp my hands together, swing up, and then smash them down. The person overbalances and falls into the bathroom. I raise my wrecking ball hands to hit them again, when I realize I recognize them.

"Wilder?" I hiss.

He turns to me with a grin. "Damn, P, nice job."

"Shut the fuck up. Get Cassandra, get her out of here."

Wilder frowns. "I'm getting you both out of here."

"No. I need to get to Norman. Give me your other gun."

For a second he thinks about protesting that he doesn't have another gun, but we both know I'm not an idiot. He pulls it from his ankle holster and hands it over.

"Do you even know how to use it?"

I cock the gun and then my eyebrow at him. "You'd be surprised what they teach you at fancy boarding schools." Use of firearms for recreational purposes was encouraged. I'm not a bad shot, but I never thought I'd be using what I learned to attack a person. Defend my own life or the life of someone else, sure, but that's not what I'm about to do.

"The only reason I'm letting you go right now is because they've probably got everyone sorted already." Wilder frowns at me. He crosses to Cassandra and gingerly picks her up. She grumbles slightly but doesn't wake up. Lucky for us all she sleeps deep regularly, but after an adrenaline crash like she had, I won't be surprised if she sleeps until tomorrow.

47

Perri

Wilder and I go opposite directions down the hallway. I follow the sound of voices through the building until we're back in the open space where we were before.

Eamon is sitting in one of the office chairs, looking unconcerned. Norman is hog tied on the floor, raging through his gag. I can't help but laugh, and everyone in the room looks toward me.

I'm most surprised to see Harrison here. He's always so slick and professional, and to see him in gear with a gun is like seeing the President in his pajamas. You know he wears them, you're just not used to seeing it. Neo is standing across from Eamon. He's the only one that didn't look at me.

Thomas and Leander give me a nod and then return their focus to the three men they have captive on the floor.

"Perri, get out of here," Neo grumbles.

"You're not the boss of me."

Eamon laughs and I can almost feel how hard Neo is clenching his teeth in my own mouth.

"I'm the one they took. I want to know what you're going to do with them."

"We're about to find out," Harrison speaks up. "They're here."

I walk further into the room and stare down at Norman. "They're going to kill you, and I'm not going to regret it. You'll disappear and no one will miss you."

Norman grunts behind the gag and I get down on my knees. I rip it out of his mouth. Right when he has the chance to say whatever he wants to me, his mouth opens but nothing comes out. He has nothing of substance to say or add to this conversation. I push the gag back into his mouth, careful to avoid his teeth.

"That's what I thought." When I stand back up, I kick him over onto his back. His hands are tied and trapped beneath him, pulling his shoulders in a way that has to be painful. Good. He has years worth of hurting and controlling Cassandra to pay for - honestly, the kidnapping is the least of it.

I move next to Neo. It hurts to be this close. I want to lean into him, I want to be beside him while he makes moves to finally close this chapter in his life. But he doesn't want that from me, and I understand.

"You good?" he asks.

"Now I am." Because he's here.

He looks over at me, something in his gaze I can't read. "I was always coming for you, Perri. Even before this, I was coming."

I nod, but I don't mean it. I want to. The way my heart races at his words - that loyal, hopeful bitch wants to believe it more than she wants to beat. My brain on the other hand, recognizes that we say and feel things in extreme situations that aren't always the truth. That feel real then but aren't when the adrenaline washes away.

There are footsteps behind us and we all turn. I raise my gun, but Neo taps my shoulder. I lower it, but keep my eyes on the entrance to the hallway.

You could knock me over with a feather when Seth Warren walks in, followed by a stupidly attractive man in his thirties with dark hair, dark scruff, and a gleam in his eye that shines with both humor and danger. I feel an impulse to lick his jaw.

He laughs when he sees me looking at them, and I quickly close my mouth that dropped open in surprise.

Seth walks right over to me and pulls me to him. "Are you okay? Did they hurt you?"

"No. Cassandra got banged up but they needed me to be pretty for my movie."

"I saw. I'm so sorry, Perri." Seth lets me go, and when he looks over my shoulder whatever he sees has him stepping back further. I turn around but it's only Neo.

"We haven't had the pleasure," the mischievous attractive man steps forward and takes my hand, kissing my knuckles. "Declan O'Connor."

"Oh," is all I can say before I retract my hand and step back, bumping up against Neo. I'm surprised when he puts a possessive hand on my hip and squeezes. This must be Eamon's son. I turn to the father in question and he looks pale and furious, silenced by his anger.

"What are you doing?" he hisses at Declan.

"Cleaning up your mess, like I've been doing for the last five years." The gleam is gone, nothing but disappointment lining his lovely face. "Neo owes us nothing. Getting pulled into petty shit like this gets in the way of our bigger ambitions, and puts our men at risk. This is not who we are anymore."

"I decide who we are you ungrateful bastard."

"I'm only a bastard because you're a fucking rapist," Declan roars, stepping up to the chair. "A monster in an expensive suit, pretending to be a gentleman criminal." He leans over his father, talking low even though we can all hear. "The next time I go visit ma, I can finally tell her I ended you." The two men stare each other down, but Eamon looks away first.

Declan straightens up and looks at Neo. "We good?"

"Good," Neo confirms.

"Almost," another voice enters the room. I turn and can't stop my grin as Calliope Warren joins the party. "As the attorney in the room, I think there's a few details to attend to before you do things I want plausible deniability for."

She crosses the room and shoots me a grin. "Hey, bunny."

"Hi, Cal."

Calliope places her briefcase on the lone desk and opens it, pulling out stacks of paper. I glance around the room and notice Harrison staring at her like he's seen a ghost. It also doesn't escape my notice that she's looked at everyone except him.

"Declan, this will dissolve the shared property agreement between the

O'Connors and Norman Warren. The buildings will be solely O'Connor property. Seth has signed as my father's designee."

Declan walks over to Calliope, gives her a look that would strip me naked and does absolutely nothing for her, and then signs the copies in triplicate. Whatever Eamon owed Norman, it was tied to these properties. More questions than answers, but I'm glad that tie is severed.

"I'll file this first thing in the morning."

"You can also wake up with me first thing in the morning," Declan flirts.

"Fuck off," Harrison snarls, stepping between Declan and his view of Calliope.

"Put your dick away, Harry, I can handle this."

The room falls oddly silent. I've never heard anyone call Harrison anything other than his full name, not even Nim. Neo looks between Harrison and Calliope, and then his brows raise like he finally understands something. Calliope ignores them all and moves on to the next set of documents.

"This is the preliminary agreement between Warren Media and Zastrow Ventures. Harrison, can you sign on your father's behalf?" She speaks to him but doesn't look at him.

"I can," he confirms, his tone reverent.

"Seth has already signed for Warren. The company lawyers can resume their maneuvering come Monday." She gestures for Harrison to come over and he does, only looking away from Calliope to sign the copies of the agreement.

We're all watching them, probably to our detriment. Harrison starts to say something but she shakes her head to cut him off. She turns away, puts her briefcase in order, and starts to leave.

"I'm getting out of here, and I'll take Cassandra. You coming with me, Perri?" Calliope asks as she passes.

"Nope."

"I didn't think so." She grins at me and leaves the room. After a second, Harrison turns and follows her. No one stops him. The worst of it is over, and we don't need him.

Declan steps up next to Neo. "Let's get it done. Don't worry about the bodies. I'll consider it a final favor for getting us here."

"The final favor is that you'll leave me the fuck alone or I'll shove a knife so far down your throat I'll get it back through your ass. My father's debts are his own. Don't come for me or mine." Neo glowers at Declan, who is entirely unaffected by that visceral image.

Declan looks past him to me. "She yours, too?"

"She's mine," Neo confirms. "So if you want to keep your vision, keep your eyes on the job."

Declan winks at me but focuses back on his father. "Deal. Neo Ryan, you're free of the life, and all your ties."

Then he raises his gun to his father's forehead and pulls the trigger. There's a smaller spatter of blood than I expect, and Eamon slumps down in the chair. He wasn't who he appeared to be, and hearing what Declan said to him, I'm glad he's dead. I'm glad Neo is free.

Neo steps over to Norman and looks down at him. He's pissed himself in fear, finally realizing that he's playing with monsters above his pay grade. Norman Warren thought he was one of the big boys. It's satisfying to see him brought low.

"Do what you want with him," Seth speaks up from behind us. "As long as he's never found."

I see Declan nod, even though he's still staring at his father's dead body.

"Are you with me, Robert?" he asks.

"Yes, sir." I turn and glare at Robert, who gives me a shrug in return. He was only following orders.

Neo waves Thomas and Leander off, and Robert and his goons get to their feet.

"Let's go," Neo says, putting his hand at the small of my back, trying to guide me out of the room. I ignore him, and turn back until I'm standing in front of Declan. The gleam is back as he looks down at me.

"Make it slow and make it hurt."

He smiles, and even though the love of my life is in the room it's so damn pretty I feel a little weak. Declan looks nothing like his father; his mother must be incredibly beautiful.

"Just for you, I promise I will, *a ghra*," he puts a hand over his heart.

I smile back because I can't help it, even though we're talking about something so dark and gruesome. I turn and walk out of the room on my own, trying to put distance between Neo and I.

He came for me like I knew he would, but it doesn't mean anything. It's who he is, it's not about me. I can't let him get close, or try to comfort me, because it will break me in new and terrible ways. I keep walking even though I have no idea how to get out of here. I'm taking turns at random and finally see an exit sign.

Neo grabs me before I can reach the door, and pulls me into an empty office.

I stare at the ground.

"Look at me, princess."

I flinch, and he steps closer. I step back. He crowds me until I'm pressed into a corner with nowhere to go. With no choice except to take a breath to steel myself and look at him.

"I was always coming for you," he says, repeating his words from minutes ago. "I was trying to figure some things out, but kidnapping or not, I was coming for you."

There's nothing I can say to that.

"I love you, Perri Kane. I love you so much it made me see how small my world had become, how small I'd let myself become. You opened me up, and even when it hurt it was worth it. I want to let you love me," he breathes, and leans his forehead against mine so he's all I can see. "But I'm going to need you to show me how."

"Okay," I nod, moving both our heads. "I can do that."

"Good." Neo smiles, the real smile I've only gotten once before, and despite Declan making me a little weak, it's got nothing on what this makes me feel. I feel this smile in my whole body, like a golden light shooting through me down to my marrow. He's in deep now.

"It was always real for me, Perri. I wanted you from the first look." Neo slides his hands down my body and then the rest of him follows, until he's on his knees. "I'm sorry. I can't undo the desperate, stupid choice that I made because I thought I couldn't choose you. In a better time, in a better place, I swear to god you can kill me with your pussy until you think I've apologized properly, but know right now, on my knees, that I will make it up to you for the rest of our lives."

I look down at him, the sincerity in his eyes. "I understand why you did it. You have to put them first."

He shakes his head vehemently. "No. I don't. Andre, Harrison, and Nim are my family, but Zastrow Ventures is a job. A job that I need to leave when my day is over. Andre reminded me that I have a life that I need to live. I want that life to be with you."

Tears blur my vision. "If you ever try to get me to leave again, I will end you."

Neo huffs a laugh. "The guys will kill me, don't worry."

I watch him, then reach up to take his face in my hands. My thumb traces his scar, and his eyes shut.

"I love you, Neo Ryan."

A smile flirts with his lips again, but he steadies himself. His eyes open and the intensity of his gaze is arresting as he asks, "Enough to live for?"

I lean over him. "Enough to fight for." Then I kiss him, and the world and my heart repair themselves.

48

Neo

With Declan O'Connor in control, everyone associated with the remaining Warrens and Zastrow gets the hell out of there. Calliope and Harrison are arguing in her car, and when I give the signal that we have to clear out, she drives away with him inside. I'm not worried, but maybe I should be.

The rest of the Zastrow crew climbs into the van we came in. We met up at a random location in case anyone was watching us. Wilder is there, and confirms that Cassandra was sleeping in Calliope's backseat.

Perri crawls into my lap, puts her head on my chest, and goes to sleep. I still marvel at her ability to do that. The guys talking, the loud noise and movement of the van, does nothing to disrupt her. The guys don't question the way we cling to each other, and I'm grateful for that.

The van stops and she lifts her head up, disoriented.

"Getting my car, princess," I whisper before kissing her cheek. Now that the danger has passed, her adrenaline is fading. As I carry her out of the van, she gives a bleary wave over my shoulder before I tuck her into the passenger seat of the Vantage. The light is fading into evening. I have to hold back a smile when she snuggles into the seat and closes her eyes again.

I have to hurry. I drive like I'm the only one on the road.

"Is everything okay?" she asks, a hint of fear in her voice.

I reach over and grasp her soft thigh. "Nothing will be okay until I can get you alone. Until I can show you how much I've missed you, and start working on that apology." Nothing will ever be enough, so I'll have to keep proving my love to her over and over. I will never give her another reason to doubt me, or wonder if she's the priority in my life.

Perri turns to watch me, and it drives me fucking insane. The desire to grab and devour her is making every muscle tense. My jaw clenches, and my throat is thick with need. I glance over out of the corner of my eye and her gaze is fixed on my lap, where my erection presses against my pants, determined to get to her.

"You like what you see?" She's never seen me in tactical gear like this before. I can feel where her eyes linger on my shoulders, the fit of my vest. Perri shifts and presses her thighs together. We need to get to her apartment right goddamn now.

I park haphazardly, and nearly drag her through her building. When the door slams behind us, we're on each other, tearing at clothes, kissing, biting, scratching.

"How did you know where I live?" she asks, breathless, ripping open my tactical belt and tearing my pants down. Between kisses I remove my vest, and groan when she dives her hand beneath my t-shirt and scores her nails down my stomach.

"I always knew where you were." The fact that even comes out of my mouth coherently is mildly impressive.

Perri pulls back to look at me. "What?"

"I always knew, I gave you space. I told you," I yank her pants and panties down to her ankles and she steps out of them. "I was always coming for you." I hook my arms under her knees and lift her up. She collapses back on her rough little couch, and I dive between her thighs, inhaling the scent of her.

"Now princess, I need to make you come for me."

Perri is so worked up that the moment my tongue touches her, she slams her thighs shut, effectively trapping me up against her. I delve deeper, tasting her already slick and wet for me. The tip of my tongue presses around her clit, and I keep teasing it with soft, long licks until she relaxes and her thighs drop to the side. She's so pretty spread open for me, vulnerable and begging with her body.

When I slide first one finger and then another inside her, Perri's back arches in need, and presses me harder against her. I've learned her so well that it's easy to get her to the edge quickly, pressing deep into her while I suck her reactive little bud.

"Neo," she whimpers out, seconds before moaning long and loud while coming for me. I lick up her juices and soothe her sensitive flesh until I feel her go boneless. Staying on my knees, I pull her down until her legs wrap around me and I'm positioned at the opening of her slick cunt.

"I'll never let you leave me again." I don't give her a chance to answer, I press inside her, sealing that vow with our bodies connecting. Perri grinds down on me, and when she presses her mouth to mine, I hold onto the back of her neck and keep her there. We kiss and fuck, share breath and saliva, until she cries out into my mouth.

"I love you," she whispers, and hearing it again, and knowing deep in my goddamn bones she loves me above all others in the same way that I love her...that has me rocketing to my own orgasm. I pump into her deep and rough, and fill her pretty pussy until it leaks out all over my lap.

Perri collapses against me, but her arms still grip me tight as if I'm going to disappear.

"Let's do that again," she says, voice muffled by my chest.

"Give me 15."

Perri laughs. "Shower."

"Fine. Then we're getting everything and moving you back to the loft. Back home."

She lifts her head to look at me. "Yeah. I want to go home."

49

Neo

6 Weeks Later

The negotiations between the Warren Media attorneys and Zastrow Ventures got heated, and took an interesting turn. Apparently, Norman had done a very thorough job of planting a marriage contract into their heads. Even when every other detail could be agreed upon, the sticking point was creating a lasting tie beyond business. An agreement for mutual prosperity that went beyond the people in that room at that moment.

I don't think anyone was as surprised as Harrison himself when in one particularly argumentative meeting, he snapped and said fine, he'd marry Calliope Warren.

The room was so silent I heard someone's stomach gurgle.

The second biggest surprise was a day later when we got a message that Calliope agreed.

That's how we ended up where we are today - at the exclusive, thrown together but still expensive and high-end celebration of the marriage of Calliope Warren and Harrison Zastrow.

Perri and Cassandra are standing up with Calliope, and Seth and I are standing with Harrison. Even though I've been both wheedling and threatening about it, he won't tell me about his history with Calliope.

I know it was something that happened when we were all in high school together. There was always tension between them, I remembered that clear enough, but senior year something took a turn and they stopped speaking.

The look he had on his face when she walked into that room was one I'd never seen before. As if the answers to questions he didn't even know he'd been asking suddenly appeared.

All I know is that his security detail has been reporting that he's spent a lot of nights at her place. He's already prepared to move out of the Long Island estate to move in with her when they get back from their honeymoon. Two weeks in Fiji, and then back to work as usual.

I look across the aisle at Perri. It's easy to imagine standing up there with her.

In the past, I'd never let myself imagine or plan that far into the future. I never trusted what I had or how they felt about me. I never thought I'd find someone as loyal and committed to the people they care about as I am. Then I found her.

It helps that I learned after her real kidnapping she's shockingly skilled with a weapon, even if she'd never used it in a tactical situation. We've been working on that. The idea that we could help someone we care about, fight for the people we love, and do it side by side is more appealing than I would have expected. The possessive part of me would want to lock her away and keep her safe, but the part of me that knows her best accepts that would hurt more than it would help.

I'm going to marry her. Sooner rather than later.

Things aren't perfect. We've had a lot of hard, emotional conversations that I was entirely unprepared for, and decided to get a therapist. We've met with Miranda multiple times already to help us form our expectations for communication with each other, and mostly to help me set boundaries between my life and my job, and where my family blurs the line between the two. It's taken our connection deeper, and even if it was scary as fuck I'm glad we did it.

We took a week off work and spent most of it in bed. Even when we tried to do other things, we ended up christening or re-christening every surface in the house. Now that I could let my obsessive love for her out, I was insatiable.

I still am. I think I will be for the rest of my life, and at least once a day I find myself stunned that Perri took me back. That she's mostly forgiven me, and is open to working on the rest. Part of me will take a long time to fully believe that she's choosing me over everything else.

It took a little longer for the guys to forgive me, and for family dinners to go to back to normal. Perri reminded them that she was the one that was hurt, and didn't find it cute that they would hold a grudge on her behalf. That had them rethinking their stances pretty quick.

I watch as Harrison looks into Calliope's eyes. She's tearing up, which I never expected from such a fearsome woman. When it's her turn, she repeats the vows and Harrison's hands flex around hers. He's nervous. They both are, but I don't understand why.

When the officiant declares them married, both their shoulders drop in relief, as if they expected the other to call it all off.

"You may now kiss the bride."

Harrison slides his hand around Calliope's waist and pulls her close. She gasps and like any smart man, he seizes that as the opportunity it is. He kisses the absolute hell out of her, and the assembled audience cheers and claps.

I glance over at Perri who looks amused, and her eyes catch mine.

When Harrison breaks the kiss, he doesn't let Calliope pull away. He keeps her close as they walk back down the aisle. I move to meet Perri for our own retreat, and lean over to kiss her before we do.

"Soon," I warn her.

She shakes her head but she's smiling. "You have some tests to pass first."

"Bring it on, *mo dhuine ar bith.*" My little nobody. The first time I met her and asked her who she was, she said she was nobody. Even then I knew it wasn't true. I knew she was special, and was meant to be somebody to me.

50

Epilogue - Perri

Five Years Later

The elevator doors open too slow and I bang my elbow on one side as I rush out and into the small lobby of Labor and Delivery.

"Nicolette Albion?" I ask the nurse at the desk. "I'm her birth coach."

That had been a terrifying but worthwhile commitment. Learning so much about the process of birth and how to help someone through it had been enlightening, and oddly reassuring. Neo had been afraid it would scare me off having our own, but he was wrong.

"Name?"

"Perri Ryan." The nurse checks the computer, and I'm assuming she finds my name because she tells me a room number and points me in the right direction. I can hear Nim's voice before I find the room, and my husband's grumbling tones in response. He was on baby watch today, and I've never heard him more panicked than when he called to let me know her water broke this morning.

After telling him what to do I had a good laugh, eager to see what he'll be like when our own baby arrives. I needed to wrap some things up at work so it took a few hours before I could get to the hospital.

I step into the room and both Neo and Nim have matching looks of relief.

"How's it going?" I ask. I set down my bag of stuff, not sure how long we'll be here. Marco is on his way from Spain, and we're holding out hope that he'll be here before the baby arrives. He's taken off the rest of the season, and has been seriously considering retiring.

After Nim's father died almost 5 years ago, everything changed. Firstly because it was a fantastic scandal. He had a heart attack while fucking his secretary at work on his desk. The news had run stories for weeks, and it made it easy for Nim and Andre to quietly file paperwork to dissolve their marriage. Per the marriage contract, she was free and clear, and inherited a significant portion of her father's money and shares in Maines Manufacturing.

It was barely a blip in the news.

Marco came home from the season, and they eloped in Mexico. He kept racing, but their marriage wasn't open the way hers with Andre had been. Now that they knew they had a future and could proudly declare it to the world, neither of them had any desire to share anymore.

Once Nim and Marco were settled down, and Neo no longer had to be her security, things improved between them a lot. My friendship with her grew deeper as well, and our friend groups have blended. We're quite an intimidating crew when we go out these days.

I walk over to Nim and brush Neo out of the way, although I pull him back for a kiss.

"How far?"

"Far," Nim groans. "4 centimeters. Still about 10 minutes apart."

"That's great. Neo, see if you can get a location on Marco."

He practically cries in relief as he leaves the room. Nim grips my hand as another contraction hits, and I talk her through it, getting her laughing by the end of it. As she takes a deep breath, my phone buzzes.

"Hi Harrison," I smile into the screen. "Is he allowed to see you?" I ask Nim. She laughs again.

"He's seen me worse. Where are my grandbabies?" While Nim and Andre are divorced, she likes to remind Harrison that she was once his stepmother and could have been grandma, even temporarily, to his children.

"Sasha is on the potty," he grumbles, and I lean over so Nim and I can share the screen. He takes us into their bathroom where his 3 year old is swinging her feet while sitting on the toilet.

"Hi sweetheart!" Nim says, and Sasha grins.

"Is the baby here yet?"

"Soon," I reassure her. "Maybe by tomorrow."

"Yay!" Sasha then turns to look at Harrison. "Daddy, I peed."

"Good job." He puts the phone down and we hear him helping Sasha. The phone gets scooped up and Calliope and Hero fill the screen. Hero is a few months past his first birthday and looks so much like Calliope it's disconcerting.

"How's it going? Need anything?" Cal asks.

"Marco," Nim says, her voice breaking.

"He'll get there. He's so excited to be a dad, Nim. It's going to be great."

We both reassure Nim some more and end the call. Neo steps back into the room and we look at him expectantly.

"He'll be here in a few hours. Andre sent the jet."

Of course he did. Because marriage or not, Nim is family, and he always takes care of family. Watching Andre become a grandfather was an interesting experience. It had been a long time since he'd been around babies, but it was impossible not to warm up to Sasha. I had a feeling he'd happily be Papa to all of our kids.

Nim goes through another contraction, and I hold her hand as Neo steps closer rub my back. I'm supporting her and he's supporting me. The day goes on with more phone calls and well wishes, more friends checking in to see if they can help. Neo calms down as Nim's labor continues, and keeps her distracted by bringing up old childhood arguments that were never settled.

"Harrison's absolutely tasted better than yours," Neo shakes his head. "You mixed up the salt and the sugar. Colleen was being nice."

"It was better a little bit salty."

Neo looks at me as if I'm going to settle an argument about cookies that I never ate.

"She always liked salty and savory more than sweet, and you know it. Her bias worked in my favor."

Another contraction hits. They're closer together now. We're almost to the end, and Marco isn't here yet. It's going to be right up to the finish line, and I'm afraid the stress of that will hurt Nim.

Just as I'm about to ask Neo to give him a call, Marco walks through the door.

He only has eyes for his wife. Nim lets go of my hand and reaches for him. Even all wired up and uncomfortable, they manage to embrace. He gives her a kiss so passionate I have to look away in embarrassment.

"You look beautiful," he tells her. "Are you ready to meet our girl?"

"Are you?" A few moments later another contraction hits. Marco and I each hold one of Nim's hands.

A nurse comes in and Neo is allowed to go. I kiss him, long and steady, reassuring him.

"I love you." I squish my face into his chest. "Don't go far."

The nurse gets the doctor. It's just before midnight, and it's time. Marco and I do exactly as we planned. We each hold one of her legs, we focus on talking to her, reassuring her, never for a second letting her feel alone in this. Time passes but I barely feel it. We're all sweaty and strained, but all completely taken up in this moment.

"One big push," the doctor encourages.

Nim yells as she bears down, and I remind her to keep breathing.

"That's the head! One more - now!" Nim pushes on the next contraction and the baby is here, and then she's crying. The nurse maneuvers the little purple bundle until she's resting on Nim's chest. The nurse confirms that everything is okay. I slide my friend's gown down so her infant girl is right on her skin. I give Nim a kiss on her head, check that Marco is okay, and leave the room.

I'm dazed. When I get into the waiting room, it's just Neo. I'm glad, because when you get our family together we're a little out of hand.

He stands and I smile, "She's here." Then I burst into tears as the emotions and adrenaline crash over me in a wave. Neo rushes over and picks me up, then holds me in a hospital chair until I come down.

"You ready to do that?" I ask him.

"With you? Of course," he scoffs, playing more confident than he is, and he gives me a squeeze.

"How about doing it about...7 months from now?"

I feel him freeze around me, not even breathing. It's hard to keep the grin off my face so I don't even bother trying when I lift up my head from his shoulder to meet his eyes.

"Are you sure?"

"Yeah. I had to take the tests at work so you wouldn't find them, in case I was wrong."

"How many did you take?"

"Eight."

Neo laughs, and it's filled with wonder. "We're having a baby."

"We are." More tears fill my eyes, but these are different. The expression on his face imprints inside me - excitement, joy, and a pure love that I've never seen before. The expression of a man ready to become a father.

Neo picks up one of my hands and places it over his heart. "You are everything. I wouldn't have a life without you. I love you." He lifts his own hand to rest on my soft stomach. "I love us."

"I love us, too."

Playlist

Nobody's Baby - COIN

Dangerous Hands - Austin Giorgio

Sorry I'm Yours - Circa Waves

Teeth - 5 Seconds of Summer

Too Much to Ask - Niall Horan

Love is a... - PVRIS

October Passed Me By - girl in red

Winter Soldier - Young Medicine

Touch - Little Mix

Somebody to You - the Vamps

Take to Heart - On Spotify

Acknowledgments

As someone obsessed with pens and office supplies, I did not know that following @otrio.stationery on Instagram would bring me a meme that inspired this story. I highly recommend following them although guard your wallet because that store is addicting.

Husband. For being entirely unable to follow this plot when I verbally explained it to you, for sitting next to me on the couch watching *Hell's Kitchen* while I wrote this, and generally putting up with my neediness, self-doubt, and constant desire for Caribou coffee. I don't believe in soulmates, but I believe in you.

Annie, you are the bestest friend in the entire world. I will never have the words for how grateful I am for you. Come over to my house so we can sit next to each other and read in silence and eat rotel.

Thank you to the friends who listen, read, and make me feel like this is not a hollow venture: Cati, Viktoriah, Jenn S, Jenn M, Sylvia, Kim, and Brittany. Thank you to my various family members who support me even if they won't read because they don't want to know about the spicy parts.

Thank you to Valerie and Turning Pages Designs for my cover. It's lovely and you were amazing to work with!

Also by Ashley Mack

The Senses

The Sight of You (Alina and Derick)

The Taste of You (Aster and Freelancer)

The Sound of You (Aro and Harp)

The Feel of You (Anora and Owen)

The Scent of You (Aspen and Gailen)

Companion Novellas

Look at Me (Kade and Cara)

Savor Me (Dominic and Cleo)

Silence Me (Rebecca, Shane, and Connor)

Elmwood College Tales

Offerings (Colin and Elise)

Preservation (Rome and Cyn)

Transfigured (Tate and Halle)

Beguiled (Maeve and Bennett)

Constraint (Mathias and Willow)

Obscured (August 2023)

About the Author

Ash lives in the Midwest with her husband, two girls, a dog, and a cat. She reads during every spare moment. She hopes that her characters go in new directions with terrifying, strong women who go feral for their men, and that sometimes the men are the damsels in distress who need saving. Connect on Instagram and Tiktok at @totalsassreads

You can connect with me on:

http://www.ashleymackauthor.com

Subscribe to my newsletter:

http://www.ashleymackauthor.com/contact

www.ingramcontent.com/pod-product-compliance
Lightning Source LLC
LaVergne TN
LVHW010642110826
845149LV00014B/2927

9781960161093